A

THE
WONDER
TEST

THE WONDER TEST

A NOVEL

MICHELLE RICHMOND

Atlantic Monthly Press
New York

Two lines of "Legacy" from *In Mad Love and War* © 1990 by Joy Harjo. Published by Wesleyan University Press and reprinted with permission.

Epigraph from *An Astronaut's Guide to Life on Earth* by Chris Hadfield, copyright © 2013. Reprinted by permission of Little, Brown, an imprint of Hachette Book Group, Inc.

FIRST EDITION

Published simultaneously in Canada
Printed in the United States of America

This book is set in 11.5-pt. Scala LF
by Alpha Design & Composition of Pittsfield, NH.

First Grove Atlantic hardcover edition: July 2021

Library of Congress Cataloging-in-Publication data is available for this title.

ISBN 978-0-8021-5850-5
eISBN 978-0-8021-5851-2

Atlantic Monthly Press
an imprint of Grove Atlantic
154 West 14th Street
New York, NY 10011

Distributed by Publishers Group West

groveatlantic.com

21 22 23 24 25   10 9 8 7 6 5 4 3 2 1

for Oscar

When you're 200 feet above the ground, going 240 knots, you want to know where you are at all times, but it's easy to get lost on the prairie.

—Chris Hadfield, *An Astronaut's Guide to Life on Earth*

THE
WONDER
TEST

Prologue

We ride the elevator in silence, emerging on the third floor. The company has revamped an old warehouse, making stylish use of exposed beams and concrete floors. There are no offices, no cubicles, just a series of cafeterias and conference rooms enclosed in glass walls. We step into a café, quiet save for the clicking of laptop keyboards. Nicole leads us to a dimly lit booth, and Kyle and I slide in side by side.

Nicole returns moments later with three coffees in black cups bearing the company logo. She's stirring cream into her coffee, avoiding our eyes, when two young men in nearly identical tech uniforms—slim jeans, slimmer shirts, loud socks—pass our table. Nicole covers her face with one hand, but it's no use. "Missed you at the scrum," the younger guy says.

Nicole acknowledges him with a nod. I don't blame her for not wanting to be seen with us.

Kyle takes a red notebook out of his messenger bag and places it on the table. Uncapping his pen, he looks more like an eager college freshman than a police detective.

"I was wondering if you might tell us about that day on the beach," I begin.

Nicole glances nervously at the notebook, so I slide it off the table into my bag. Her shoulders relax. "All of it?"

"Yes."

She fidgets with a red string tied around her wrist. "It was a cold, wet morning. I went out to Half Moon Bay to meet someone—"

"Who?"

She pauses, searching for the right words. "A new friend. We parked at the beach." Nicole's eyes scan the room. "We ate sandwiches in his car, and then he left. Before heading back into the office, I decided to go for a walk."

"The day was cold and wet, yet you went for a walk?"

Nicole frowns. "I needed to clear my head. The sandwiches in the car were a bad idea. It didn't go quite the way I was expecting."

"Do you often eat sandwiches in the car?" Kyle asks.

Nicole glances at Kyle, annoyed. "It wasn't my first, but I haven't had one since." She turns her focus to me. "I suppose women our age shouldn't be eating sandwiches in cars."

"Sometimes one needs a sandwich. Not for me to judge."

"True." She almost smiles. "After a few minutes I sat down on a piece of driftwood to take a call from my assistant. There was no one else on the beach."

Kyle taps his pen on the table. "What did she want, your assistant?"

"*He* said I needed to get back to the office right away." Nicole picks at her cuticles, reluctant to say more. I sip my coffee, waiting. Two beats, three. She has green eyes, a few freckles emerging from underneath the makeup. I glimpse the Catholic schoolgirl she once was beneath the trappings of her tech exec exterior.

"My assistant was describing the latest fire I needed to put out when I looked up and saw a shape far down the beach. The figure was moving in an unusual way, slow but jerking, like an injured animal. It was disturbing and mesmerizing at the same time. My first thought was that a space alien had landed in the Pacific and drifted ashore. You know, creature from the black lagoon."

"Your second thought?" I prod.

"'How am I going to explain this in the office? How do I justify being on the beach in Half Moon Bay at ten o'clock on a Tuesday morning?' I wanted to hurry back to my car, but I couldn't move. I was hypnotized by this thing moving toward me. Shuffle, two, three, four. I'd never seen anyone or anything move that way, not so much a walk as a strange, gyrating groove. The figure was ashen white, glowing. The voice in my head told me to run."

"Why didn't you?" Kyle asks.

"It looked so"—she shakes her head—"so helpless. I stood up and walked toward it. My eyesight isn't great. Until I was about twenty feet away, it still looked like an amorphous blob."

I wait for her to look up at me. Her eyes are sunken, her face pale. At first, I thought her ravaged expression had come from working insane tech hours, staring at the screen, drowning in coffee, forgetting to eat. Now I understand it's something else. All these months, she has been haunted by her discovery on the beach.

She finally meets my eyes. I lean forward and ask, "When did you realize it was a boy?"

1

Assuming the universe is always expanding, at what point does it become less likely that you will find your lost keys by continuing to look for them? Diagram and discuss.

In the garage of my father's house, I find the bike wrapped up on the outer edge of a pallet, the smell of New York City still clinging to it. My son, Rory, is asleep upstairs. Since we moved to Northern California, I've been waking earlier and earlier, and Rory has been sleeping later and later. He is growing taller, his voice losing its adolescent scratchiness and settling into a baritone that reminds me of his father.

I cut through the plastic with scissors, nudging the bike free. Cruising down the long driveway and out onto the street, I turn my face up to the cold, wet wind. Down the hill, right on Santa Inez, left on El Camino. The momentum carries me, and I lean into the free-falling sensation—rolling effortlessly, barely slowing down at the intersections. The streets are empty, lit by the half moon and the omnipresent glow of the airport five miles south. I pedal faster and faster, into Burlingame, along California Drive, flying through the red lights.

The insomnia struck in adolescence. Even back then, my mind was prone to racing. Insomnia can drive you crazy, or it can just drive you. If not for Rory, asleep there in his warm bed in my father's house, I would just keep pedaling, race away, somehow escape this awful year, annus horribilis, the Queen would say. I would ride west, up over 92, left along the coast, all the way down Highway 1, pedaling through Southern California, into Mexico, South America, the miles melting away. Maybe I could even go faster than the speed of light, somehow turn back the clock, set things right.

Down Oak Grove, past McKinley School. Only when I turn the corner onto Broadway do I realize where I'm headed. The neon letters of the Royal Donut Shop reflect off the wet street, just as they did so many years ago. I'm surprised to find the sign is still standing, the shop still open. I'm even more surprised to find myself here. The Royal Donut Shop. Again.

In 1989, I was eleven years old, and I had a paper route. I delivered the *San Francisco Chronicle* to thirty-six homes throughout the Laguna addition. It paid fifty-four dollars per month plus tips. I woke each morning at five, folded papers on our cold doorstep, and rode my bike across the railroad tracks to launch newspapers onto porches before the fine citizens of Burlingame stepped outside in their slippers and bathrobes. Sundays were the toughest. The paper was thick, the bags heavy. After I'd delivered every paper, my load lightened, my arm sore, I would stop at the Royal Donut Shop. It was my favorite moment of the week, sitting alone on the green bench outside with a warm doughnut and a carton of milk, the sun just beginning to rise.

Eventually, I got to know the owner, Mr. Melfoy, and the kid who worked the counter, Vince LaRue. Vince was five or six years my senior, and his younger brother went to my school. I wouldn't say Vince and I became friends. It wasn't like that. I rarely talked, and he was busy setting up for the morning rush. But after months of my arriving at the same time Sunday after Sunday, always ordering the same thing, we became familiar. He usually seemed happy to see me, and I was more than happy to see him. He had a way about him, a strange light, a magnetic pull—charisma, I realize now.

One morning, as I walked through the door, Vince took a white paper bag from under the counter. As I made my regular order, I noticed his hands moving rapidly, as if he was doing some sort of magic trick. Then he rang up my glazed old-fashioned and milk—eighty-nine cents. I handed him my money, counted out to the penny, and he handed me the bag, filled to the brim.

"Enjoy," he said, winking.

Outside, on the bench, I opened the bag and discovered a treasure trove of doughnuts—fancies and plains, raised and cake, even a chocolate French cruller.

The next Sunday and every Sunday thereafter, the same thing happened. To this day, I can still conjure the joy of riding my bike across the railroad tracks, along the freeway sound wall, smiling giddily, leaving a trail of crumbs in my wake. It went on like that for nearly two years. And then one Sunday—by the time I was old enough to have developed a crush on Vince, to wear my hair in a ponytail instead of pigtails, to put on lip gloss—something happened: Vince wasn't there.

I didn't say anything to Mr. Melfoy that morning as he bagged my single doughnut and carton of milk. I went outside and sat on the bench, disappointed. Alone, I ate my doughnut, wondering why

Vince hadn't told me he'd be gone. The following Sunday, he was still missing. The third week, I gathered the courage to ask Mr. Melfoy.

"You didn't hear?"

"No."

Mr. Melfoy shook his head. "Rafting accident up north. Terribly sad." Then he handed me my doughnut and returned to the grill.

I didn't know what to say. I had never known anyone who had died. Until this year, this horrible year, when I lost both my father and my husband in the span of three months, I lived a fairly charmed life. In the past, death always made me think of Vince LaRue—the finality of his absence. Whenever I dealt with it in my work, I would think of him—the sad, sinking feeling I had in the weeks after receiving the news, how I rode my bike past the Royal Donut Shop every Sunday, haunted by the same thought: "Vince LaRue won't be working at the Royal Donut Shop today." And it haunts me again this morning, after all these years.

The green bench, now weather-beaten, is still bolted to the patio. I prop up my bike and open the door, the bell jangling a familiar tune. Inside, the aroma of fresh doughnuts hits me. The counter has moved a couple of feet to make way for a Lotto machine, but otherwise, everything is the same.

The young guy behind the counter smiles. "Morning, what can I get you?"

"One raised, one chocolate old-fashioned, and a coffee, please."

He pours the coffee and rings up the order. I pull three dollars out of my pocket, pleasantly surprised by the bargain.

As he's handing me the bag, he notices the writing on my sweatshirt. I forgot I was wearing it. Since the move, I've had trouble

4

finding clothes in our disorganized piles. "FBI New York," he reads aloud. "You really FBI?"

"Sixteen years. Taking a little break, though." It's awkward saying it out loud. I don't like the weight of failure that attaches itself to those words.

"Hold on." As his hands move quickly behind the counter, it all comes back in a rush—the sleight of hand, the friendliness, the unspoken gift. He passes a full bag across the counter. I wonder if I'm dreaming.

"But—"

"It's all good. The owner loves law enforcement. FBI saved his ass twenty years ago."

"Mr. Melfoy?"

"No, no, Mr. Yiu. Maybe one day you can get him to tell you the story."

Outside, I take my place on the green bench, leaning against the crooked boards. The heft of the bag, the fog over California Drive, the intoxicating scent of sugar and baker's yeast all take me back so many years. I can't escape the feeling that the bench has been holding on through the decades, fighting off the elements, the rain, the sun, the graffiti, the gentrification—waiting for me to return.

But something *is* different. It registers seconds later than it should. A man stands at the edge of the patio, coffee in hand, talking quietly on his cell phone in French. He's dressed too elegantly for this time of morning—navy suit, red cashmere scarf, telltale lapel pin, *trois couleurs*. I glance around the parking lot, noticing a black Peugeot, diplomatic plates. He slides the phone into his pocket, meets my eyes, glances at the writing on my sweatshirt. And so it goes.

2

Ranchers in Wyoming, tired of losing sheep to wild coyotes, implemented an aggressive plan to cull the coyote population. Ten years later, after dozens of successful hunts and hundreds of kills, the coyote population is more than an order of magnitude larger than before the slaughter. In a 750-word essay, discuss the folly of conventional wisdom and the power of expecting the unexpected.

Rory has assimilated to this strange new place much better than I expected. Greenfield is so unlike New York, where we raised him to have the freedom of a city kid, at home in the noise and the chaos, navigating the subway, the park, the occasional crazy street scene. And yet, despite his skills, tenth grade at his tony new public school has him a little baffled.

"Like private school, with a better stock portfolio," one of the moms whispered to me during Winter Networking Night.

He'd been all set to return to his public school on the Upper West Side, and then the unthinkable happened. Staying in New York didn't seem feasible—too many reminders of his dad in our tiny apartment, too many reminders of his dad in every shop front along Columbus and Amsterdam, all over Central Park. It wasn't good for Rory. It wasn't good for me.

If I'm honest, there were other memories too, buried across New York, that I wanted to escape. The one case, the one source, the one mistake for which I can't forgive myself.

Before Fred's accident, I'd planned to take a couple of weeks off, come to my dad's house alone, handle everything in one fell swoop—settle the will, clean out the house, put it on the market. Now, everything has changed.

"Just for one semester," I told Rory.

"How can you make me leave my friends right now?" he exploded. "What kind of mom does that?" Then he retreated to his bedroom and didn't speak to me for three days. But that was the end of it. The fact that he accepted his fate so easily, with so little resistance, made life easier, but it also broke my heart. I sensed he was trying to take care of me, to protect me somehow, when I should, of course, be taking care of him.

My father's house has never ceased to surprise me. Complicated and enormous, it is as incongruous with my father as the town of Greenfield itself. Population 10,231, average income astonishing, minimum house size three thousand square feet, minimum lot size one acre. According to a school pamphlet that appeared in the mailbox the day after Rory enrolled, "Families are strongly encouraged to donate a minimum of $5,600 per child per year to ensure excellence." I've been trying to figure out how I'll manage that. This town is not meant for midlevel civil servants.

"I don't have any actual classes," Rory tells me over tacos at the end of his first day. We're sitting at the kitchen table, bowls of meat, cheese, guacamole, and shredded lettuce arranged on the lazy Susan. "At least, not regular classes, math, science, whatever. Instead, the day is divided into seminars focused on the Wonder Test."

"Never heard of it."

"It's apparently the gold standard of standardized tests. It happens in the spring of tenth grade, and every public school in Silicon Valley is obsessed with it. The kids have been preparing since day one of freshman year. According to our assemblies, which are more like pep rallies, the test is crucial to the teachers, the principal, the parents, the whole town."

I take a sip of my Modelo. "What about the kids?"

"I'm not sure anyone asked them." He reaches into his backpack and pulls out a thick yellow booklet, which he slides across the table. *Wonder Test Prep* is printed in red on the cover. "We have to do one question per section each day at home, and we spend the first half of each school day analyzing our answers."

I flip to the table of contents:

Part 1: Analogies

Part 2: Ethicalities

Part 3: Diagrams and Analyses

Part 4: Theories of Global Patterns

Part 5: Future Functionalities

I turn the page and skim the introduction. "According to research published in 2012, well-constructed multiple choice questions trigger a retrieval response that can help encode memories of correct information." Footnotes reference various articles on the subject, ranging from the impressive (Harvard) to the questionable (Global Institute for the Advancement of Academic Assessment).

I glance at the first question and read aloud: "'Mars drilling is to Chopin as: (a) polyatomic ions are to mollusks, (b) blue is to brown, (c) Berlin is to Belgrade, or (d) reinforced concrete is to steel.'" The next few pages include complex diagrams and graphs to explain why three of the proposed answers are incorrect.

"Why is it called the Wonder Test? That sounds so new agey."

"I think it's the opposite of new agey," Rory says. "More like Silicon Valley on steroids. 'Disrupting the educational paradigm: Learning through testing.' At least that's what the posters say. All I know is that I need to figure it out. The test is the first week of March. Our school has had the highest scores in the country for the last five years." He takes a giant bite of his taco, spilling shredded cheese all over the table.

"Whatever happened to chemistry and world history?"

"Mom, that is so ninth grade."

I consider my next question. Is it wise? I'm not sure, but Rory could use a distraction, and I could use his help. "I have a covert mission for you."

His eyes light up: "Go on."

"At school, you might meet a French girl."

3

Orange and green are considered more complementary
in European cultures than they are in the United States.
Discuss the geographic and socioeconomic implications
of global color theory.

When I drop Rory off at school the next morning, I have to run a
gauntlet of Range Rovers and shiny new Teslas. As Rory exits our
Jeep and wades into the crowd, I envy his ability to blend so easily.
Somehow, he's wearing the right jeans, the right shirt, the right
backpack, even the right hairstyle.

I'm the one who doesn't fit in. Black pants at the volunteer
signup meeting where tennis whites prevailed. A dress to the school
board meeting, where everyone was wearing designer jeans and
stilettos. This morning, I chose jeans and a silk blouse for the
superintendent's coffee, but as I join the stream of women entering the library, I realize my error. Apparently, the event calls for
workout gear.

Inside, I head straight for the coffee and pastry table. A woman
sidles up to me. "You didn't get the email about the uniform?" she
asks, lifting a scone from the artfully untouched display.

"Pardon?"

Her dark hair is gathered in a ponytail, and she wears a blazer with a pencil skirt and navy pumps. "The mom uniform," she whispers. "There's some kind of code. I've been here six years and still haven't figured it out."

"Glad to know it's not just me." I pick up a croissant, leaving an obvious dent in the perfect row. "Lina Connerly. New in town. My son, Rory, is in tenth grade."

"Brenda Mills. Eleventh grader, tenth grader, and, surprise! A third grader." She reaches into her purse and pulls out a business card, which she presses into my palm. She's VP of research and development at a space tech firm. "Text me. We'll have lunch."

A tall, handsome man strides up. "Kobayashi," he announces, thrusting his hand toward me. Is Kobayashi his first, last, or only name? He has wavy black hair, onyx cuff links, an air of authority.

"Lina, correct?" Firm handshake. Intense gaze. Southern accent. "We're so pleased to have Rory. I looked at his transcripts and test scores from freshman year. Quite impressive. He'll be a real asset to the school. If I can do anything to smooth the transition, let me know."

He turns and walks to the center of the room and raises his arms to quiet the chatter. "Welcome, everyone. Shall we begin?"

I turn to Brenda and whisper, "Does he always read the new kids' transcripts?"

"Read them?" she says. "He *studies* them. You'll find this school leaves nothing to chance."

Back at my dad's house, I take my old boom box into the garage to continue unpacking, wondering for the umpteenth time about the wisdom of my decision to move us here. I leave the garage door open to air the place out. The first indication that the Cure's

"Lovesong" is cranked up too high is the angry glare from a woman pushing a stroller by the house, golden retriever in tow. The town probably has an ordinance against the open garage door, another one against the Cure.

I've made scant progress when a black-and-white pulls into the driveway. An officer, no more than a kid, steps out and walks over to the garage. With his short blond hair, scrubbed skin, and perfectly pressed uniform, he could star in a commercial for laundry detergent.

"Lina?"

"How did you know?"

"Your dad talked about you a lot."

"Nice to meet you, Officer . . ."

"Kyle."

"Officer Kyle."

"Just Kyle. Sorry for the bother, but I noticed you'd moved in." He takes a step inside the garage, nearly shouting to be heard over the music. "Your dad hoped you were going to live here. Are you?"

"For a little while."

I glance at the chaos around me. Not only Rory's and my stuff, but my dad's things too. Decades of it. I used to hound him for not giving me a sibling, "somebody else to clean out the house when you're gone." That was back when I was in grad school, and I couldn't imagine him actually being gone.

I reach over and turn down the volume on the boom box. "Sorry for the noise. Did someone complain?"

"First rule of Greenfield: somebody always complains. Clearly, you didn't grow up here?"

I point east, down the hill, in the direction of the tiny bungalow in San Mateo where I lived as a child. "Two miles south and a world away. Maybe Dad told you, he was a mechanic, had a Jaguar place on North Amphlett. He worked night and day, said that's what it would take to move up the hill."

"And he succeeded!" Officer Kyle smiles.

"Yep, a few years after I moved away."

I don't tell Kyle that my dad had recently been pressuring us to come live with him, to escape our cramped, junior two bedroom on Ninety-Second and Columbus. I don't tell him Fred wanted to take my dad up on the offer, give Rory the good life, the sunshine and fresh air, the trees and the ocean and the bright promise of Silicon Valley. I was the one who never wanted to move back. I was the one who couldn't imagine life without my squad, my work in New York City.

"So, I hear you're FBI. Your dad said you're a profiler?"

"Actually, I've spent my entire career in foreign counterintelligence. Behavioral analysis is a collateral duty. But yes, I've been profiling for twelve years now. Taking a break at the moment."

"From the profiling?"

"From all of it."

"Sure. Understood." He doesn't understand, of course, but I don't want to go into the details.

He glances around at the mess in the garage, as if he's formulating a plan for it. I get the feeling he could clear this whole place out in a single afternoon. "If . . ." He hesitates. "If I, like, hypothetically, needed a little help on a case, would you mind me running something by you?"

"It would be my pleasure," I say, surprised. And it would be. I never minded the work. At the moment, I just can't take the rest of it: the office, the questions, webTA, Sentinel, Delta, the meetings, quarterly firearms, FISA training. The work itself I always loved. The bureaucracy not so much.

"All righty, I'll leave you to it. What day is good for you?"

"Any day. I'm right here until this garage is cleared."

He turns to walk back to his car. "Kyle, what's the second rule?"

"Pardon?"

"You said, '*Somebody always complains* is the first rule of Greenfield.' What's the second?"

He points to the sky. "Property values only go one direction: up."

4

True or False: Circles are more efficient than triangles.

At night sometimes it rolls through my head—"the love of my life, the love of my life." From the moment we met, nineteen years ago, I never went a day without feeling grateful for the grand luck of having met Fred, the great coup of having *landed* him. And when the love of your life is gone: what then?

But he was more than that, of course. He was also the center of our family, the grounding force, the anchor that held us in place.

When Rory was three years old, Fred quit his job as a data engineer at a Fortune 500 company to open his own one-man firm. After a shaky start, he built a strong business and did pretty well. He had boom years and bust years, but overall it worked. He was the one who coached soccer and attended PTA meetings when Rory was small, the one who shepherded our son through doctors' and dentists' appointments, the one who was free on Saturdays for a movie and pizza, the one who gave the sex talk, the drug talk, the respect-for-girls talk, the one who was fully *there*.

If I was obsessive-compulsive about work—the travel, the late hours, my head often buried in a case even when I was at home

—I told myself Rory didn't suffer. After all, he had his father. Until, one day, he didn't.

With Fred, it was unexpected. There were no warning signs, no lengthy disease, no period of getting used to it. One morning he was there, and later that same day, he wasn't. He didn't have time to "prepare," and Rory and I didn't have time to say goodbye. The abruptness was the worst part, I think: the sense of simply going about our lives, everything according to plan, until, suddenly, it wasn't.

A car accident on the West Side Highway. A law school student, texting, crossed the divider and hit Fred's car head-on. "Your husband died instantly," the coroner said, as if that somehow would ease the pain. It didn't. It doesn't. The word "instantly" is misleading, anyway. Did Fred see the Ford Taurus barreling toward him? Didn't he know it was coming, if only for a second? Wouldn't he have understood, in that moment, that he was about to leave everything behind?

So cruel, swift, and random.

My father, on the other hand, knew for months that he was dying, although he kept it hidden from me. He promised the doctors had it under control. I have a gift for sussing out lies, half-truths, obfuscation. But with my father, somehow, my instincts failed. I think I didn't want to believe the truth.

He must have spent hours during his final weeks writing notes on orange Post-its, placing them strategically around the house. He obviously planned for me to spend some time here. I imagine Rory's kids will still be finding their great-grandfather's Post-its years from now. The thought of Rory's kids makes me smile, but the thought that Fred won't be around to meet them makes me cry. This is part of why I'm not working.

Of course, I want to be here for Rory, to try to fill some part of the void Fred left in his life. But there's more to my hiatus than maternal concern. I don't want to be *that agent*. The one who breaks down in the office, the one who can't cut it, the one for whom others have to take up the slack. I was always good at compartmentalizing, focusing on the task at hand, zeroing in on a complex problem and solving it methodically, fearlessly, no matter how many months or years it took.

But when Fred died, I discovered my limitations. Days after his accident, I made a mistake for which I still can't forgive myself. That's when I understood that I needed to step back, recalibrate, get my head together.

In the garage, on a cabinet filled with leather polish and car wax, my father has left a note: "Don't hesitate to throw my things away. I know how you hate stuff. But keep the Jaguar. Her charms will find you. She needs a little TLC before she's roadworthy. Go to John's Jaguar in San Francisco. Now that I'm gone, he's the best."

On the box of coffee filters: "The best coffee is at Philz on Primrose." On the desktop monitor: "Router password is your birthday. For Wi-Fi or other issues, call Mr. Beach. Good guy."

Above the phone: "This place is not like where you grew up." And beneath that one: "Subscribe to www.Greenfield-Neighbors. org. Wildly entertaining. An education in the strange ways of the affluent."

"Thanks, Dad," I say out loud, half expecting him to answer. When I was growing up, anytime I found myself in a funk, he always came up with a way to distract me. I guess he decided to offer me one last distraction.

I recline in his leather chair in the living room with my phone, navigate to Greenfield-Neighbors.org, enter my email address, and hit Subscribe. My phone pings: Gray cat missing. Last seen on Hayne. Answers to "Jeeves" or "Mister Fancy."

I click on the link and fall down the rabbit hole. For the next hour, I immerse myself in the passionately narrated dramas of the bored and entitled. Okay, maybe unfair. Like my dad always said, "There are good people everywhere, and no one passes through this world without suffering." But the message boards do point to a certain level of insularity.

> Yellow water bottle left rudely in the Designated Beautification Area on Black Mountain Rd. Does anyone know who the culprit might be? SAD that some people do not respect our public spaces! -heather22

> Egyptian cotton towel embroidered with the name "Stefania." Gently used. Paid $95 at Kashmere Kids, asking $70. -TatyanaA
> Reply: My daughter is named Stephanie with a ph, which is of course the traditional spelling. I will give you $30 if you can have the monogram altered. -AshleySykes

> Seeking backup SUV for nanny, seven years old tops, preferably black, kindly contact Marlene. I do NOT feel safe with my nanny driving children in her Honda. -mrscharbonnet

It goes on. For every post selling used linens or sniping about unsightly mailboxes, another offers nice furniture or paving stones "free to a good home." Colleen Tanner and her sisters are collecting donations for the homeless shelter, and Maggie Stringer is giving away firewood. I can see how Greenfield-Neighbors.org could become addicting.

I turn off my phone, return to the garage, and crank up Social Distortion. While trying to decide which of my father's tools to keep, I find myself worrying about Jeeves, aka Mr. Fancy. Is he okay? I have a soft spot for cats.

"Get yourself a dog," Dad used to say. "Nobody trusts a cat person."

5

Should efforts be made to contact life on other planets, or
do the risks of contact outweigh the rewards?

We live only a mile and a half from campus, but school policy
prohibits students from leaving school without a parent or guard-
ian. When Rory tried on his first day, he was stopped by a mom
wearing a neon-yellow T-shirt and visor. Several such moms keep
watch after final bell every afternoon. The Visor Brigade, Rory
calls them.

When I pull up to the curb, Rory is standing with a girl. He
opens the front door and drops his backpack into the passenger
seat. "Okay if Caroline comes home with us?"

"Of course."

Rory shuts the front door and the two of them climb into the
back seat. I glance into the rearview mirror, noticing a look of fascination on Caroline's face, as if she has heard of old, clunky Jeeps
but has never before experienced one firsthand.

"Hi, Caroline."

"So nice to meet you," she says in a pronounced French
accent.

Well done, Rory. I'm impressed. I only gave him the task last night. Perhaps he's cut out for the family business after all.

Caroline is an awkward girl. Glasses, long brown hair arranged in a complicated braid. I surmise she isn't popular, something of a loner, quirky but confident in her tastes, still trying to find her place in the elaborate hierarchy of an American high school. As we pull out of the traffic circle and approach the intersection, we pass one of the neon-shirted moms keeping watch over the sidewalk. "What's with the Visor Brigade?" Rory asks Caroline. "Why aren't we allowed to walk home from school?"

"This is because of Gray Stafford," Caroline explains. "Last year he disappeared, but now he is back."

"What do you mean, disappeared?" Rory asks.

"He claimed he was kidnapped," Caroline announces. "But no one believed his . . . comment dites-vous . . . tel?"

"Tale?" I offer.

"Yes, his crazy tale."

"How long was he missing?"

"About two weeks. After he returned, his parents started giving him school at home. No one ever explained what happened. And now, he is back. Before, he was a friend to everyone, you know? Always talking, laughing, big personality. Now, it is like he is not there anymore, like he has been—" She pauses, searching for the right word. "Efface?"

"Erased?" I suggest.

"Yes," she nods. "Erased."

I make a mental note to ask Officer Kyle what the real story is behind Gray Stafford. Sounds like a runaway or perhaps a secret stint at drug rehab.

When we get home, the kids dump their backpacks in the entryway and head for the stairs. Rory stops midway up. "Mom, can we have grilled cheese?"

Of course, Rory is old enough to feed himself, but at his age, there's so little I can do for him, this small task feels like a gift—not to him but to me.

From the kitchen window, I can see the kids crossing the breezeway. My father's house is set on a hillside and shaped like a barbell, with the bedrooms, living room, and movie room on one side, the kitchen, dining room, office, and more rooms on the other. The breezeway connecting the two ends of the barbell is made of concrete and glass. If the house weren't so secluded, surrounded by trees and shielded by an imposing front gate, the glass breezeway would be uncomfortably exposed. It bothered me when we first moved in, the same way that having my back to a room bothers me.

But this is Northern California, not New York City. I've left my work behind. I should do the same with the paranoia.

When I bring the grilled cheese sandwiches to the movie room, Rory and Caroline are sitting on opposite sides of the sectional. It's the episode of *Seinfeld* in which George introduces himself as the architect Art Vandelay. When Fred and I first met, we watched *Seinfeld* every night on the only channel his television could pick up in his tiny cabin in the Hudson Valley. Before Fred died, he and Rory had been watching reruns together. Every night, I'd hear them laughing, pausing the TV to get snacks or to talk. They'd made it halfway through the fifth season when Fred died. Rory hasn't watched it since.

The night of the funeral, I heard Rory swearing and slamming his fists against the coffee table. I found him on the couch in front of the broken table, tears pouring down his face, his eyes wide open in shock and disbelief. When I tried to comfort him, he pulled away. "Who am I going to watch my show with?" he wailed. I felt helpless, so ill equipped to meet the fact of Fred's profound and inescapable absence.

I'm surprised to see Rory watching it now. It feels like forward momentum.

At five past seven, Rory and Caroline come downstairs. "Stay for dinner?" I offer.

"Thank you, but I have to study."

"Need a ride home?"

"No, thank you. Our driver is on his way."

Rory waits outside with his new friend. Gray clouds have moved in, and from the kitchen I can see the kids standing in the rain, their backs to me, their body language already so much more familiar than it was a few hours ago. Headlights appear, casting the two of them in a halo of light. Another black Peugeot, diplomatic plates, bigger than the one I saw at the Royal Donut Shop, rolls into the driveway. Rory steps toward the car, reaching out to open the door for Caroline. She kisses Rory quickly on both cheeks before disappearing into the vehicle.

Maybe this isn't such a good idea. I'm happy that Rory has befriended Caroline, impressed that he made such quick work of my request, but worried that, given time, she just might break his heart.

6

Explain the relationship between retrieval practice and increased performance using Gates's theories of recitation. Identify and diagram a cohesive structure in your own learning that has been formed as a result of focused testing.

I'm in my father's library, boxing up books to donate, when I hear the doorbell ring. Through the window, I see Officer Kyle's cruiser.

I motion him inside. "We can talk out back." I lead him through the house to the covered patio, where my dad installed a minibar, grill, and coffee station. I put coffee on to brew. Kyle doesn't relax until he's sitting at the table under the heat lamp, gazing out at the expansive green canyon.

"This place is amazing. If you don't mind my asking, how did a mechanic afford it?"

"My dad had a way with British cars, and he had a way with people. His clients were loyal. Eighteen years ago, one of his best clients, a retired stockbroker, decided to return home to Long Island. He knew my dad loved his house and had been wanting to move 'up the hill' for years, so when it came time to sell, he quoted him an absurdly low price. The place was in bad shape, but the bones were good. My dad welcomed the project."

"Everybody needs a project," Kyle says.

The coffeemaker beeps. I pour coffee into two mugs and join Kyle at the table. "Tell me about your case."

"Actually, it's my first."

"Is it this thing with the cat, Mister Fancy?" I joke but regret it when I realize how condescending it sounds.

"No." Kyle doesn't sound the least bit offended. "Jeeves turned up this morning. This is more complicated."

"I like complicated."

He sips his coffee. "Has your son by any chance mentioned the business at school? The kid who went missing—"

"Gray Stafford."

Kyle nods. "Right. He vanished on the way home from baseball practice."

"When?"

"Last February, sophomore year. He used to cut through the woods and follow the canyon back to his house. His coach and one of his teammates saw him jump the fence after practice ended at four thirty p.m. At a quarter past seven, his mother called the station in a panic."

"She waited more than two and a half hours to call?"

"She wasn't worried at first. If he walked straight home, it took him twenty minutes—"

"But he didn't always walk straight home."

"No. Sometimes he'd horse around in the canyon, playing on his phone, whatever, or stop by a friend's house. So it wasn't unusual for him to arrive home an hour or two after practice. That evening, Mrs. Stafford took Gray's sister to dance class. The mom and the sister didn't return home until seven, which is when they realized Gray wasn't there. The mother called a few of his friends, the coach. No one had seen him. She went down to the canyon and found his backpack sitting on a rock by the stream. That's when she panicked."

"But he came back, Caroline said."

Kyle raises his eyebrows. "Who's Caroline?"

"My son's friend from school. She said the school wasn't too concerned about the whole thing."

"Well, that's a different ball of wax, but he did come back, eventually. My predecessor, Crandall, thought the kid had run away, but it never made much sense to me."

"Why not?"

"For one thing, the backpack. If you were planning on running away, wouldn't you pack a few supplies and take your backpack?"

"What if he wasn't planning it? Spur of the moment thing. Teenage boys are impulsive. What about money?"

"According to Gray's mom, he always carried a hundred dollars in his wallet."

"What's a tenth grader doing with a hundred bucks? Was Gray using?"

"Unlikely. He was a star athlete. And a hundred bucks is pocket change here. You ever try to buy a green juice on Burlingame Avenue? Anyway, the wallet and the money were still in his backpack."

"What about his phone?"

"Gone."

"So if he had his phone, he could use mobile payments."

"Possibly, but there was the thing with Uber. Gray's phone had been used to summon an Uber to the Crystal Springs Shopping Center at five nineteen p.m."

I picture the shopping center in my mind. "That's what, two and a half miles from the canyon? Tenth-grade kid, athletic, he could have easily gotten from the canyon to the shopping center in just under fifty minutes." I think for a second. "But you didn't say he called the Uber, did you? You said an Uber *was summoned.*"

"Yep."

"You think somebody else did it to mislead everyone. You talked to the Uber driver?"

He nods. "Thirty-six-year-old divorced mom from Foster City. She never saw Stafford. When she arrived at the location, she couldn't find a passenger, which checks out. She entered him as a no-show. Crandall guessed Stafford was staying with a friend in San Francisco, tried to convince the parents as much, but they weren't buying it. They called SFPD, put up flyers, the works. Nothing panned out."

"How long exactly was the kid gone?"

"Eleven days."

"Who found him?"

"That's the thing. *Nobody* found him. He just reappeared from out of nowhere, wandering along the beach in Half Moon Bay."

"Half Moon Bay? That's a weird place for a kid from Greenfield to pop up. Did he have any connection to it?"

"None. His parents said they only went to Half Moon Bay once a year for the pumpkin festival."

"Was he hurt?"

"Gaunt, scratched up, traumatized for sure, but other than that, he seemed . . . not fine, exactly, but mostly unharmed."

"Traumatized how?"

Kyle frowns. "You'll have to read the file."

"How did he get home?"

"Seriously, I think you need to read the file. I don't want to contaminate your thoughts with my version of the story."

"Well, what did Gray say after he reappeared?"

"*Nothing.* He came back mute, didn't utter a word for months."

I'm stunned. "A kid goes missing, reappears under mysterious circumstances, skeletal and mute, then returns to school this semester, and it doesn't even come up at the parent meetings?"

Kyle glances down at his immaculately manicured nails. "This town likes to keep things quiet. There are sensitivities. Decisions, you know, above my pay grade."

"When did you finish the academy, Kyle?"

He scratches his chin, a little embarrassed. "Twelve weeks ago, give or take."

"And the first case that lands on your desk is a missing child. Doesn't it strike you as odd that they didn't push this one a little higher up the food chain?"

"Technically a 'found' child, but, yes, I thought so too."

"Do kids disappear here very often?"

"Hardly ever."

I'm not sure I heard him right. "*Hardly* ever?"

Kyle takes a long drink. "The year before Gray Stafford. Two other kids, twins."

"How old?"

"Fifteen."

"Same school?"

He nods. "There are only five schools in this town. Three elementary schools that all feed into one middle school, which feeds into the high school."

"Who was on that case?"

"Crandall."

"Is Crandall helping you with the Stafford case?"

"No. He got a job in Montana, on the border somewhere, left in a hurry. I hear he got an offer too good to refuse."

"Surely you're not handling this case alone?"

He shrugs. "I'm told that's how we do things here. We're a small department."

In my office in New York City, if a stranger abducted a child, it prompted an instant, frantic buzz of activity, all hands on deck. Dozens of agents immediately stepping into their roles, a machine moving together in concert, a freight train rolling. And that was in a city of two million kids. How can a town this small afford to drop the ball when *three* of its own go missing?

Kyle seems so young and so lost. "Can you help me?"

"Of course. Do you have the file?"

He nods.

"With you?" I prod.

His face lights up in understanding. "Oh, you mean now. It's in the car. I'll go grab it." He races out to his cruiser and runs back carrying a banker's box. He isn't even breathing heavily.

Kyle has the slim lower body and oversized arm and chest muscles of someone who recently spent time at a police academy. There's something different about him, though. In my class at Quantico, when we went around the room on the first day of training, forty-seven of the fifty candidates said that being an FBI agent was a lifelong dream. And then there were the other three—those of us who fell into it, who came to the organization sideways, not by any grand design but almost by accident.

Kyle seems to have come to police work sideways too. It could be the hair, shorter than a civilian but probably twice the length of the next kid in his academy class. Or maybe it's his easy smile. A lot of people in law enforcement think they have to be serious all the time in order to earn respect, so they adopt a rigid, humorless persona.

He sets the box on the table. I remove the lid. "Out of curiosity, what made you want to be a cop?"

"To protect and serve," he says with a faint smile.

"No, really."

Kyle glances down at the box, then back up at me. "Man, you're good. I don't know what it is, but I feel like I can't lie to you. You've got to teach me that."

"Seriously, why did you join?"

"Would it make you think less of me if I said student loans?"

"Absolutely not."

"What about you? Why'd you join the FBI?"

"I'll tell you another day."

"Fair enough."

I push my coffee aside and look into the box. Kyle and his predecessor have produced a lot of paper. A file, like an encyclopedia, consists of multiple volumes. Each volume is contained within two cardboard covers. The bottom cover has two metal prongs, and the first piece of paper in the case—usually the initial incident report— is the first to go in the volume. I always enjoy the moment when I begin a new file. There's something satisfying about it: the frisson of possibility, the promise of the investigation.

A case file builds historically, from the first document to the last, with the oldest documents at the bottom of the first volume.

Once the metal prongs have reached capacity—about one ream of paper—you begin a new volume.

This box contains three volumes, each one numbered and dated, with the words "Gray Stafford" printed in black Sharpie on the front.

I pick up the latest file and flip to the middle, Kyle's write-up of an interview with one of the Staffords' neighbors. The write-up is surprisingly well written, descriptive in a way that belies his recent arrival on the force. A similar report from a veteran tends to be unilluminating, filled with jargon, clichés, and shorthand, mostly written in the officer's head before the interview has even begun.

"Nicely written. You read a lot?"

"Everything I can get my hands on."

"College really messed you up. Left you with student loans and a bad reading habit."

He gives me a wry smile. "Ivy League education isn't what it used to be."

Kyle is a strange bird. I like him. "Can I spend some time with the file?"

"Here?"

"Yes, here."

I sense that Kyle is racking his brain for the appropriate department regulation that governs the possession and location of files. "I don't know."

"Who assigned the case to you?"

"Don Jepson, chief of police."

"If you're worried about chain of custody, tell Chief Jepson that you've formed an informal task force, enlisting the help of an FBI profiler?" I suggest.

He frowns. "I'm not sure how that would work."

"Just run it by him." Usually, small police departments with a complex investigation and a limited budget are happy to get help from the FBI, but maybe the GPD doesn't have a limited budget. Maybe they're eating caviar in the break room.

"You on sabbatical, officially?" he asks.

I can't help letting out a little laugh. "I'm a midlevel federal government employee. We don't get sabbatical. I'm on LWOP, leave without pay. Still a special agent, though, if that's what you're worried about."

His face relaxes. "I don't see why not. Can you read quickly, in case someone goes looking for it?"

"Come by day after tomorrow, same time. You can grab the file, and we'll discuss the case."

He stands to leave. "Awesome. Thanks a ton. I'll let myself out."

Before the front door closes behind him, my attention has already drifted back to the box.

I pick up the first volume, the one that was started by Kyle's predecessor, Crandall. I thumb through it, skimming. In this line of work, files can be deceiving. Size rarely matters. I've seen files over fifty volumes containing almost no useful information, filled instead with administrative fluff—travel vouchers, irrelevant phone records, skeletal write-ups of poorly executed interviews.

The early reports are like that, plentiful but sloppy, the information cursory at best. Volume two shows the same utter lack of finesse, not to mention a level of detachment that goes beyond the usual professional boredom. Either Crandall was a lousy investigator, or he knew he was leaving.

7

Orange, Yellow, Singing, and Velvet. Identify the four countries in which these revolutions took place and explain the origin and meaning of the names. Create a logical name for your own country's next revolution, incorporating current sociopolitical trends.

Although volume three of the Stafford file is half as thick as the other two, it's packed with solid interviews, surveillance, focused records checks. The best work is from the last few weeks, since Kyle got the assignment. From the looks of it, he might turn out to be a natural investigator.

I'm tempted to get lost in volume three, but the only way I'll truly grasp the case is to work my way through the file systematically, bottom to top. While some people tackle a file from the most recent documents to the oldest, I prefer to start at the beginning to see the whole picture. I need to watch the story unfold in the same order it unfolded for the investigator.

For me, each file is a narrative. Some constitute a short story, some a novel. In complex cases, a file is often disconnected, confusing, the real clues buried deep within. I was a graduate student in English literature before I was an FBI agent, and I tend to think of these files as a literary genre. To be honest, the files are probably the reason I stayed in this business for so long. When I was hired out of grad school, I only meant to stick with the FBI for three years, five at most. I wanted the experience, the novelty. I wanted to step behind the curtain, if only for a minute.

But in my first month on the job, I inherited an old espionage case, ten volumes magically appearing in my cubicle at 26 Federal Plaza in Manhattan. Instantly, I was lost in the story, and soon I was absorbed in the investigation. So many interviews, everyone telling his or her version of events, contradicting accounts, hundreds of stories blending together to form the larger narrative, the novel that became the case, the case that turned into a strange adventure. A few months later, another case appeared, then another, and one day I looked up and sixteen years had passed.

Long past lunchtime, I'm still on the back porch reading volume two when I hear another car pull into the driveway. It's not the American rumble of Kyle's cruiser but rather a low vibration.

When I walk through the house to the front porch, I see a small man standing at the bottom of the driveway in front of an orange Bentley SUV. He's wearing pink shorts, pressed and pleated. His white oxford shirt and bow tie look as if they were purchased from the boy's section at Barneys.

He walks toward me purposefully, hand outstretched. He could be Asian American and forty, South American and fifty, or he could be a small, tanned, midwestern teenager. His entire being is an optical illusion. His face is such an unusual amalgam of heavily edited features, it's impossible to place. The obvious Botox, chemical peels, cheek implants, and fillers, along with some nipping and tucking around the mouth and eyes and follicle implants at the hairline, only make his face more confusing. The eyes are too flawless, the widow's peak almost contrived.

"Harris Ojai," he says, pulling me into a firm, enthusiastic handshake. "Ojai with a *j*. I sell houses." His voice is deep, very FM radio, his accent vaguely South African.

"I'm Lina. Thank you, but I already have a house."

"Ha!" he exclaims, breaking into a huge grin to reveal gleaming white teeth. He reaches into his pocket and pulls out a business card, which he presents to me with two hands. White linen cardstock bearing the words: "Harris Ojai, I sell houses."

"I understand you inherited this lovely home from your father."

"I did."

"I understand you are thinking about selling."

"Well," I say, caught off guard. "I haven't really decided. I suppose I have to move in before I can move out."

"Decision beats indecision, my friend. When I say I sell houses, I mean I *sell* houses. Last year in Greenfield, fifty-two houses were sold. Do you know how many of those transactions were shepherded by me and my firm?"

"You tell me."

"Forty-seven." Harris makes a flourishing motion with his hand, and the sun reflects off his green diamond ring. I imagine he's practiced that move in the mirror a few thousand times.

"Impressive."

"In the last quarter, I did two hundred and eight million dollars in sales volume. I guarantee you a good price. I have overseas buyers." He leans forward on the word "overseas," eyes narrowed and gleeful, as if to imply that it has some sort of magic. Then he turns and skitters down the driveway and back into his Bentley.

8

In humans, the HBB gene influences how hemoglobin is made. If someone inherits two of the "s" version of the gene, they develop sickle cell anemia. If someone inherits two of the "S" version, they have a higher susceptibility to malaria. If a new planet had to be colonized, should we send only humans with two of the "S" version, only humans with two of the "s" version, or some of each? Why?

Caroline has a new blue streak in her hair. She's standing at the curb in front of the school with Rory, wearing baggy chinos, Puma Clydes, and a Patti Smith T-shirt—a reproduction of the iconic cover of *Wave*. Unsettling. The album's first line drifts through my mind, "Jesus died for somebody's sins, but not mine."

The sight of Patti Smith immediately sends me into a mental funk. Fred was the fifth in line to bear his Christian name, Frederick. In college, I was a huge Patti Smith fan, so when I first met him, her song "Frederick" instantly came to mind. It's an intoxicating love song, dreamy and loud.

Pulling into the driveway of my dad's house, I glance at Caroline in the rearview mirror. "Do you like Patti Smith?"

At first, she's confused, then she realizes I'm referring to the shirt. "Oh this. Sure, she's a friend of my dad or something."

"Cool," Rory says. "Six degrees."

Caroline frowns. "What does that mean?"

"You haven't seen the movie?"

"What movie?"

"We're totally watching *Six Degrees of Separation* this afternoon," Rory says.

Rory and Caroline drop their backpacks in the foyer and put a bag of popcorn in the microwave, filling the kitchen with its buttery smell. Then they head upstairs to the movie room. From the kitchen, I watch them race through the breezeway, jostling each other like puppies. I love seeing Rory so happy. I wish Fred were here to see it too.

I sit down at the table with a cup of decaf and return to the file, getting lost in the story once again. It's dark when Rory goes outside with Caroline to wait for her driver.

"Hot dogs for dinner?" he suggests after she's gone.

"Absolutely."

After Fred died, I made a concerted effort to maintain stability in Rory's life. Every night I came home from work by six and put dinner on the table at seven. I tried dishes I'd never made when the three of us were together—risotto with truffles, delicate white fish in foil with zucchini, even beef bourguignon. It was as though, in the absence of our third party, the anchoring member of our family, I had to up the culinary game.

One night, poking at a burnt pot roast, Rory said, "Mom, I appreciate what you're trying to do, but since when do you cook? Besides, sitting down to dinner without Dad is too depressing."

"You have to eat."

"Yeah, but we don't have to make it a big ritual."

Since then, Rory and I have only sat down together for a formal dinner a handful of times. We eat together, yes, but in a haphazard way, with takeout from Panda Express, messy tacos, or crackers and cheese in front of the TV. Am I a bad mother? Am I doing everything wrong? All signs point to yes, but it seems to work for us. Some days, just getting by feels like a major accomplishment.

I push the files to the side and set the hot dogs and condiments on the table, along with a bowl of sliced strawberries and a can of Reddi-wip.

Rory eyes the file box. "What are you reading?"

"Case file."

He slathers one hot dog with sauerkraut, another with shredded cheese and ketchup. "I thought you were on leave?"

"It's unofficial. A local policeman brought it by. Officer Kyle? Blond, young. You've probably seen him at the school."

"What's the case?"

"The boy Caroline was talking about, Gray Stafford."

"I heard he'd just been at his grandparents' house in Tahoe." Rory devours his first hot dog in three bites.

"I'm only halfway through the file, but I don't think that's how it ends."

He takes a swig of Fanta. "You really think he was kidnapped?"

"I don't think he was with his grandparents."

"Like, he got nabbed by a pedophile or something?"

"In noncustodial kidnappings of children, unfortunately, that's the most likely scenario, but his age makes that less likely, and I don't see any evidence pointing that way."

Years before we became parents, Fred and I attended a mandatory religious weekend at Yosemite National Park, a hoop we had
to jump through in order to get married in the tiny chapel in the
valley. The pastor who led the seminar had copious instructions for
how we needed to live our lives; most of his advice involved raising
children. At the end of the weekend, we decided that when we became parents, we would simply be ourselves. And being ourselves
meant we would always tell the truth.

On the day we brought Rory home from the hospital, swaddled
in the giraffe-themed blanket, with that tiny blue cap on his fuzzy
head, Fred reminded me of the pact we'd made years before. When
Rory started asking questions, we agreed, we would answer truth-
fully. It was easy enough in the beginning, when he was a toddler,
then a preschooler, then a kindergartner, asking questions for which
we had answers.

But the older he got, of course, the more complicated his questions became. And the answers weren't always happy or age appropriate, especially where my work was concerned. Although I omitted
the classified details, when he asked me a question, I answered
as honestly as possible. If he asked follow-up questions, which he
usually did, I answered those too.

Now I'm the one with questions. "Do you see Gray around
school?"

"Sometimes at lunch, but we've never talked."

"Does he fit in all right?"

"Sure, he has friends. I heard he was super popular before the
whole disappearing act."

"And now?"

"Kids kind of give him space. They don't make fun of him, nothing like that. It's not like he sits alone at lunch eating his dandruff, but he's quiet. He's always in a group but never involved. Things just happen *around* him." Rory shakes the Reddi-wip can, covering his strawberries in whipped cream. "I'm glad you took the case."

I shake my head. "Didn't take it, just glancing at the file."

"Mom, if a kidnapper is on the loose, you have to *do* something."

"We can't be certain there's a kidnapper."

"If I disappeared, you'd want someone to get to the bottom of it."

"You won't disappear. Anyway, who's going to deal with this?" I motion to the house around us, which feels colossal and impossible. "The furniture, the books, the dishes, the tools, everything."

"The house can wait. This is all just stuff. Remember what Tyler Durden said about owning things?"

"What?"

He squirts Reddi-wip directly into his mouth from the can and talks through a mouthful of foam. "Mom, have you been living under a rock?"

"Enlighten me."

" 'The things you own end up owning you.' Anyway, you *need* to work."

The way he says it, I know he's not talking about money. He's talking about me: who I used to be versus who I've become. This new, always-around version of Mom who is a shadow of the old, somewhat absent, laser-focused version of Mom.

"I'm not sure I'm ready."

"You're beyond ready."

When Fred died, I thought I could get past the grief by throwing myself into my job. When Rory needed me most, I burrowed into the familiar comfort of sources, meetings, reports. Grief wasn't in my skill set; the spy game was. I couldn't solve the problem of Fred's death, my son's wrenching sadness, but I could solve cases, recruit sources, work the difficult angles, drawing strength from the tangled complexities where I felt most at home. Work offered a sense of control.

But then I fumbled. Distracted by a grief that, after all, refused to yield to my demands, I made the worst mistake of my career. A major case went sideways. I lost a friend. As abruptly as I had returned to work, I took a self-imposed leave of absence, my confidence truly shaken for the first time.

I know Rory is right. I *need* to work. I've been absent for too long. I'm getting skittish, allowing one day to morph into the next without accomplishing anything. I've lost my way. I have to snap out of it.

9

Kierkegaard once said that the Pythagorean theorem could be applied existentially to the problem of Schrödinger's Cat. Explore.

At four in the morning, a clear voice wakes me from a dead sleep. For a moment I think I might have dreamed it, a trick of the subconscious on that plane just below waking life. But the voice was clear and loud. It sounded like it was coming from inside the room.

"This town sure is strange," the voice said. "Seems normal, but it isn't."

My eyes search for a figure in the darkness, my hand instinctively reaching inside the drawer of the bedside table, fingers curling around the frame of my SIG Sauer. The room is empty. I stop, motionless, listening. Nothing.

I slide out of bed, my socks moving silently across the floor. At the door, I move slowly, slicing the pie, like I learned all those years ago at Quantico, a lesson that never leaves you. A quick glance to see if someone is in the long hallway. Nothing. I move toward Rory's room. The door is open. Rory is sound asleep, breathing quietly. I look in the adjoining bathroom, the closet. I feel a bit ridiculous now, but I'm still on high alert.

Here's the thing: I *don't* hear voices in my sleep. I never have. "Seems normal, but it isn't." The words were clear, unmistakable.

I move through the rest of the house. The enormity of the place unsettles me. Truth be told, I felt safer in our small New York apartment, despite the crazy upstairs neighbor. I tiptoe through the breezeway, my neck prickling. Moonlight pouring through the glass walls makes me feel exposed. In the foyer, I edge behind the door and glance out the window.

In the middle of the driveway, a big gray cat with a white throat and paws sits on his hind legs, gazing straight at me.

I have a strange thought: it was the cat who spoke those words to me in my sleep. "This town sure is strange." I relax, chuckling, unnerved. I lower the gun and stare at the cat for several seconds, a full minute. He doesn't budge. I have to go back to bed. I need to sleep.

At the stairs, I glance back, only to discover he's still staring at me. It freaks me out. He looks familiar.

I peek in Rory's room. He hasn't moved. I listen for the steady rise and fall of his breath, just as I did when he was a baby—still relieved to hear it after all these years. The room has a tangy teenage smell—vinegar and sweat. I sit in the plush chair in the corner, holding the SIG Sauer in my lap. I watch my boy—at fifteen, still a sweet, angelic child in his sleep.

The next morning, while we're eating cereal in the kitchen, I say to Rory, "I think Mister Fancy was in our driveway last night."

Rory has his spoon in one hand, his iPhone in the other, scrolling.

"I think he spoke to me in my dreams."

Rory glances up from his phone. "What did he say?"

"He said, 'This town sure is strange. Seems normal, but it isn't.'"

"He's right about that," Rory mumbles. I love that about him. He has no functional constraints; he is open to all possibilities. Most adults have a fully formed idea of exactly how the world is; we're so quick to dismiss any detail that doesn't fit into our understanding or our expectations. Not so with Rory. Once, when I confided to him that I'd sensed Fred's presence after he died—not in a general way but at a precise moment, in the room with me—Rory replied, "Yeah, he does that."

"Does what?" I asked.

"Stops by."

10

Genetically modified fruit will either save or destroy the planet. What makes this statement true, false, or irrelevant?

GRAY STAFFORD

Volume 3, page 6

Subject: Jennifer Delacroix

Interviewer: Officer Kyle Ramsey

Date: December 17, 2018

At 10:30 a.m. on December 1, an interview was conducted with Jennifer Delacroix at her place of residence, 120 Pepper Court, Greenfield, California. Mrs. Delacroix was made aware of the identity of the interviewer and the purpose for the interview: to discuss the disappearance of Mrs. Delacroix's neighbor, Gray Stafford.

Mrs. Delacroix advised that her home backs up to property owned by Bill and Lacey Stafford. The Delacroix and Staffords have been neighbors for five years and nine months. Prior to that, the

Delacroix family lived in a home three blocks
west on Cedar Avenue. As the properties in this
area are all one acre or more, the Delacroix do
not have much interaction with their neighbors.
Mrs. Delacroix did indicate that the Staffords'
two chickens, Helga and Heloise, once got loose
in her yard. Heloise was killed by the Delacroix
dog, Gunter, but the Staffords seemed to harbor
no resentment. The Staffords have since repaired
the fence. In the months since the chicken incident, Mrs. Delacroix occasionally finds a con-
tainer with fresh eggs on her porch.

Mrs. Delacroix indicated that Gray Stafford
was rambunctious and prone to distraction. Maisie
Delacroix, one of the top students in her junior
class, tutored her younger peers three times a
week during Enrichment Hour. In this capacity,
she had been assigned on occasion to help Gray
Stafford prepare for the Wonder Test. His most
challenging subject areas were Analogies, Future
Functionalities, and typing. By the middle of his
tenth-grade year, he was typing at a speed of only
67 words per minute, and Gray's school adviser
was concerned that his poor typing skills would
negatively impact his performance on the test.

What Gray lacked in academic prowess, he com-
pensated for in athleticism. Dickie Delacroix,
Maisie's brother, was on an all-star baseball
team with Gray Stafford last season. Although Gray

was a year younger, he was athletically advanced for his age and was their starting pitcher. The coach was Ron McCrory, who could vouch for Gray's exceptional skills on the mound.

I've just flipped the page to the Ron McCrory interview when I hear Officer Kyle's cruiser pull up. My dad taught me that every car has its own distinctive sound, like a fingerprint. The make and the model have a lot to do with it, of course, but it goes beyond that, down to the specific vehicle, the maintenance schedule, the anomalies in its exhaust, the way its tires and weight, its own personal history, respond to a particular surface at a particular speed. My father taught me how to listen for a car's "voice."

Okay, maybe it sounds kooky, but when a new person enters my life, one of the first things I instinctively commit to memory is the sound of his or her vehicle.

I'm at the door before the doorbell chimes. Kyle is holding two cups of coffee and a bag of doughnuts. "Have you been to the Royal Donut Shop yet?"

"Once or twice." I push aside papers and files to clear space for him at the kitchen table. "I was just getting to the interview with McCrory."

"Stafford was a great pitcher. McCrory coached him on four different teams, beginning in Little League. Every year, the coaches hold a draft, and they pick the kids in order of talent. McCrory said Gray Stafford was tops every year. Mostly, McCrory was just mad that the incident caused Stafford to miss half the season."

"A kid went missing and he was worried about his Little League team?"

"This town is serious about baseball."

I'm still trying to form a picture of Stafford in my mind. After years of profiling adults—primarily diplomats and spies—it's difficult to switch gears and think about someone his age. Kids are tricky. While adults remain largely unchanged through the years, kids are a moving target.

"I don't know what to do next," Kyle says. "While he was missing, the department got dozens of leads. After the news got hold of the story, the leads piled up, but most came from outside: San Francisco, San Jose, as far south as Cabo and as far north as Calgary."

I sip my coffee. "Anything promising?"

"Not that I could tell. I tracked down every last one. Since then, the leads have dried up."

"What does Chief Jepson say?"

Kyle mimics a gruff cop voice: "Let's see if we can get this closed out. Last thing we need is people in a panic."

"What do you know about the two kids who disappeared the year before Stafford?"

"The Lamey twins? That case is inactive."

"What?"

"Crandall isn't exactly a hard charger. He followed up, sort of, but when the leads ran dry and the Lamey family moved east, he decided to shelve it."

"Don't tell me the Lamey twins showed up on a beach somewhere."

"You're going to want to see that file too. I'll bring it by tomorrow."

"What's the story?"

"They were one grade ahead of Gray Stafford, lived less than a mile from him. They disappeared in the spring, the previous year. Like Stafford, they showed up almost two weeks later, but not in Half Moon Bay."

"Where?"

"Marin Headlands."

"Seems related, no?"

"Of course," Kyle says. "But we never found any evidence to connect them. I hate to say it, but the fact that the twins are on the spectrum complicated things. Everyone assumed they had just walked off. When they reappeared, unharmed, unable to articulate where they'd been, it confirmed what a lot of people wanted to think. This is Greenfield. If a crime can be explained as a misunderstanding or, better yet, kids being kids, if it can somehow be kept out of the annual statistics, that's what happens. Kids wandering off on their own? That's just bad luck."

"Have you talked to the Lameys since they moved?"

He shakes his head. "They dropped off the map. Supposedly they went to Boston, but I couldn't find them. Got any ideas?"

"Not sure. Can I see the beach where Stafford reappeared?"

Kyle doesn't hesitate. "Yes ma'am. How about now?"

"I have a lunch commitment. Does tomorrow work?"

"Absolutely."

As he's heading back to his cruiser, I ask, "Hey, do you know a little guy named Harris Ojai? Shorts and a bow tie?"

"Real estate agent," Kyle replies. "He sells a *lot* of houses."

"Dumb question: Where is he from?"

Kyle gives me a funny look, and I regret asking the question. Totally inappropriate, but I'm too curious to stop now. Being a profiler,

I'm always trying to figure people out. "Like, nationalitywise?" I clarify.

Kyle smiles. "Sorry. Didn't understand. Harris is a strange dude. Sometimes I wonder if he's from this planet. Whatever you think he is, he's not. Even the accent is phony. His family goes back a long way around here. His great-great-great-grandfather was one of the original founders, railroad baron. He grew up on that huge estate on Robin Road. Went to Vista School."

"But," I say, "the face?"

"Plastic surgery. Chief Jepson has a theory that he's trying to look like all different ethnicities and nationalities in order to attract more clients. Wouldn't put it past him. I did hear, and I think it's true, that Elton John played one of his birthday parties. Huge donor to the school."

11

Compare and contrast comparison and contrast.

The front door of Brenda's house is ajar. I follow the sound of voices and find a group of women in the dining room serving themselves buffet-style from an impressive spread of salads. On the dining room wall, a beautiful photograph hangs: an enormous pool surrounded by snow, a single swimmer slicing through the expanse of blue, the word "Helsinki" scrawled across the bottom of the photograph in red.

"You came!" Brenda exclaims. "Everyone, this is Lina. Lina, this is everyone!" I notice there's no uniform today. One by one they say their names, and I commit them to memory: tall Elaine in the serious pantsuit, wispy Mary in yoga pants, redheaded Tina, Amanda in hospital scrubs.

By the time I've poured myself a mimosa and filled my plate, the women have moved to the living room, where they're sitting on sofas and ottomans, plates perched on their knees. I sip my mimosa, eavesdropping—kids' sports, college applications, home remodels, spring break plans. When I overhear Elaine complaining about the school pickup policy, I slide down to the end of the sofa to join her conversation. "They're high school students, for God's sake," she says.

Mary pipes up. "I'd rather pick Olivia up than leave things to chance."

"Leave things to chance?" I ask.

The room goes silent, and the women exchange glances, as if they're deciding how much to tell me. "You haven't heard?" It's the redhead, Tina. "A student went missing last year on his way home from baseball practice."

I nod. "Gray Stafford. I did hear about him. What do you think really happened?"

"We all have our theories," offers Amanda. "But I feel better knowing that Danny is accounted for in the afternoons."

"What theories?"

"Well, hell, if no one wants to mention it, I will," says Brenda. "Gray's dad used to be in gambling before he moved here. Sports betting. He got busted and served two years in some country club up north, then returned mysteriously as a pardoned man."

"But what about the Lamey twins?" I ask.

Elaine dabs at her lips with a napkin. "That's different. The twins wandered off. That's on the parents, in my opinion. Could've turned into a real tragedy."

There's so much that these theories don't explain, but the fact that Gray's dad did time certainly changes things. Especially if it involved organized crime, it's not unusual for that kind of entanglement to reach the family.

I want to hear more, but Brenda taps her knife on her glass as if calling us to order. "Sorry to interrupt gossip hour, ladies, but we need to talk about Saturday morning study group. Does nine a.m. still work?"

Nods all around.

"Okay, then." She passes around a chart she's printed in four colors. "Matthew will take the Ethicalities discussion this week, Olivia has Future Functionalities, and Hannah is in charge of Theories of Global Economics. That just leaves Analogies, plus Diagrams and Analyses. Lina, do you think Rory would be interested in leading a discussion?"

"Wait, your kids voluntarily do this on *Saturday mornings?*"

The looks of consternation passing among the women indicate I've just committed some sort of blasphemy. "I think you'll find the kids take the Wonder Test very seriously," Tina says. "We *all* do."

Early in the evening, the Lamey file appears on my doorstep, and I retreat with it to the library, my favorite room in the house. I love the comfortable leather chairs and walls of books, complete with a rolling ladder. It feels like something out of a Hollywood set.

Rory sits across from me, reading. He's at that transitional age when he no longer wants to share every detail, yet he still likes being around me. I don't want this phase to end.

The Lamey file is all boilerplate, random copies, travel vouchers, and other useless administrivia. The investigation is cursory, the interviews short and unrevealing. I get the feeling it was conducted by a sloppy detective on his way to lunch.

I look up from the file to watch Rory. He's reading intently, but I can't see the title. Each night, Rory has three types of homework—questions from the test prep book, reading, and typing. Because the test is administered entirely online, all answers have to be typed. Last week, Superintendent Kobayashi emailed a link to a report about the correlation between typing and test performance. Fast typing may not make kids smarter, Kobayashi argued, but it does allow them to "communicate their intelligence more effectively. An improvement in typing speed by ten words per minute results in a four percent increase in test scores."

Four percent can apparently be the difference between living in Atherton and scraping by in Daly City. That may not mean anything to the general public, but it does to Greenfield parents. No one wants to live in Daly City. Atherton would be nice.

Every night, I hear Rory's hands flying over the keyboard. After that, he spends two hours reading. Students may fulfill their reading requirement any way they choose, so long as they record it. *Time + quantity = success!* Of course, I'm all for reading, but the school's approach seems to miss the point.

"They encourage us to read the same book twice or even three times," Rory has explained. "According to Kobayashi, reading the same text repeatedly improves reading skills twenty-one percent better than reading something new. When you subtract your interest in the actual material, it helps you focus on the pure skill of reading and improves speed."

"I call BS."

Rory just gives me an annoyed look. He's not buying into this Wonder Test stuff, is he?

"Hey, I had lunch with some moms from the school today. They invited you to join a Saturday study group, but it starts at nine in the morning. Prime weekend sleeping time."

"Who are the kids?"

I tick the names off on my fingers.

"They're cool. I guess I could do it, since Caroline already has a study group."

"Why don't you join hers?"

"Can't. It's more formal, mandatory for students who are struggling."

"Caroline's struggling?" I say, surprised. "She seems pretty smart to me."

"Yeah, but she's terrible at the test."

"I was terrible at tests too."

He turns the page of his book, not looking at me. "Mom, you don't have to do that."

"Do what?"

"Try to *relate*. It's so obvious."

"Well, at the risk of being obvious, what are you reading?"

Rory holds up his book. The cover is an illustration of space, seven planets against a black background, bright clusters of stars. The title is printed in tiny letters against a glowing blue orb. *Martin in Space*, by Anders Svarlbard. "I rescued it from the recycle bin at the school library."

"What's it about?"

"The narrator is this teenager in Stockholm who cuts school one day and wanders around the city, gets lost in a confusing section of Old Town, meets some other kids who have beer, drinks with them, and then falls asleep in a park."

"Oh, a bit like *The Catcher in the Rye*."

"Sort of, but there's more to it. Martin has this dream that he's in a spaceship, moving eighteen thousand miles per hour through empty, dark space, all alone. The Earth is gone, and somehow he's on his own, with enough food and fuel to last forever, a bed, and only a small window. He thinks of his parents, who he'd been fighting with, who he didn't like much, or so he thought before the planet was destroyed, and he thinks about his former life that he once resented . . ."

"And now he wishes he could have it all back?"

Rory nods. "There's more. The instruments in Martin's aircraft don't work. Because they're out in space, the instruments have no way to define his position. They have no anchor. You know, like a compass needs the North Pole."

"It's a metaphor, then?"

"Yes, a metaphor for modern life. Martin can't know where he is without something to compare it to. So, a million miles from Earth, that's a location. At this very moment, you and I are at latitude 37.5741 degrees north, longitude 122.3794 degrees west. All locations are defined in relation to other locations. No place is only a place, everything is relational."

Work is an anchor, I think. Fred and Rory are anchors. Not long ago, I knew where I was in relation to my crucial points of reference. Then my dad was gone, and Fred, and soon thereafter, work. If not for Rory, I'd be like *Martin in Space*, free-floating, lost without an anchor. Only Rory is tethering me to Earth. It's an enormous burden for a kid. It's not fair to him.

Rory runs his hand through his hair, a gesture that reminds me so much of Fred I feel twin stabs of pain and joy in my heart. "I wish Dad was here. It's totally his sort of thing."

"How does the book end? Does Martin find his way back home? Does life return to normal?"

"I think in the end it turns out that Martin didn't just cut school and wander around Stockholm. It turns out that *Martin in*

Space is really about Martin *in space*. He actually is floating through space, unable to define where he is, and so he sleeps away his days, dreaming of when he was a child, dreaming of that day when he wandered around Stockholm, drinking a beer, trying to figure out who he was."

12

Are Christmas trees good or bad for the planet?
Furthermore, are they good or bad for the soul?

It feels strange to be sitting in the passenger seat of Kyle's police cruiser. I observe the equipment: the shotgun attached to the ceiling, the radio, the bulletproof glass partition between the front and back seats. B-cars are more subtle, with all the real gear concealed in the trunk.

"I was watching a documentary on NBC last night about an important spy case," Kyle says. "You were in New York at the time the case was going on. Maybe you know it. There was a book too." I know what he's going to say before he says it: *Blue Squared.*

Because so much of the case is classified, the writer didn't know my real name. Despite the requests from Public Affairs, I never granted an interview, and the writer got plenty of things wrong. I remember everything from the actual case, but all I recall from the book is a description of an arrest, a sentence about me in my Royal Robbins pants.

"Did you know the woman who solved it?"

"We were acquainted, yes."

A bug smashes against the windshield, and Kyle turns on the wipers to remove it, leaving a grotesque smudge on the glass.

"Hey, you promised you'd tell me how you ended up with the FBI."

"When I was young, I planned to be a professor of literature. In grad school, a friend dared me to apply to the FBI. I did. It was nothing more than a lark. I never expected to pass the written test, which is heavy on math. After that, I didn't expect to pass the endless rounds of interviews and assessments. And then I didn't expect to pass my seventeen weeks of training at Quantico."

"So why'd you stay so long?"

"Fame and fortune, obviously," I deadpan.

Years ago, when my father asked why I had stayed with the FBI for so long, I realized it wasn't the cases, the intellectual challenges, or even the occasional adrenaline rush that made it difficult to leave. Instead, it was a feeling of belonging to something worthy.

The organization doesn't exist for the pursuit of money. No one joins to get rich. Because agents work out of sight of the press and the public, the FBI doesn't tend to attract self-aggrandizing types. Thanks to the excruciatingly detailed background checks, the office has a uniquely open atmosphere. Everyone is an open book. Questions are usually met with direct and unqualified honesty, even when the answer may not be something you want to hear. I tried to explain it to my dad but ultimately couldn't find the right words.

Instead, I told him this: With searches and arrests, the call is usually for 4:30 a.m. Driving to the meeting spot, I'm tired, cold, cradling my coffee, navigating empty streets while the world is sleeping. I pull into the corner of a parking lot in front of a big-box store, and I sit drinking my coffee, listening to quiet music, headlights off, hidden in the darkness. Then I see them, two by two—headlights pulling off the highway, onto the side streets, slowly moving toward me. In minutes, my car is joined by another. The two cars become four; the four quietly become eight. Friends, coworkers, or sometimes strangers who will become friends all standing around in the cold and dark, talking and laughing, relaxed, preparing to complete the serious task at hand.

Of course, I don't explain all of this to Kyle. I just say, "When I arrived at Quantico, I was such a fish out of water. Now, the FBI is home."

We veer onto 92 and head over the mountain in silence. Soon we're enveloped in fog. I power down the window, and the fresh smell of the ocean blows in. I take a deep breath, filling my lungs. In Half Moon Bay, we turn left onto Cabrillo Highway. We follow the highway for half a mile before turning right onto a one-lane road littered with potholes.

"What do you know about Mr. Stafford's priors?" I ask.

"You mean the stint at Lompoc?"

"Precisely."

"He did his time, appeared to get out of the business."

"What does he do now?"

"Sells software for a start-up that's about to go public. Why? You think what happened to Gray is somehow connected?"

"Don't know."

"Doesn't square with the Lamey twins, though," Kyle observes. "It would mean the two cases aren't connected."

"Agreed."

At the end of the road, we come to a parking lot. The temperature has dropped twenty-four degrees since we left Greenfield. We get out of the car, passing a small red house set into a flat patch of ice plant. The paint is peeling, and plastic toys litter the patio. Stones have been stacked in rows in a futile attempt to keep the sand at bay. The truck in the driveway is green, the California Fish and Game logo painted on the side. In front of the house, the sandy path narrows. We follow it another few hundred yards down to the beach, where the surf is pounding the shore.

"Where are the surfers?"

"It's because of the layout." Kyle gestures toward the ocean with both hands. "Sets splitting both ways, a dangerous shore break."

"You surf?"

"Dude, I live in a mobile home in Pacifica. Of course I surf." He narrows his eyes playfully. "What, it wasn't in my file?"

"You think there's some warehouse in DC filled with files on regular citizens?"

"Isn't there?"

"There's a warehouse, all right, but it's not in DC. It's called Google." I look up and down the beach both ways. It's eerily deserted. "Tell me the story of the day Gray came back."

He points south. "Stafford was walking from that direction. And Nicole was alone, over here on a piece of driftwood when she saw him."

I do a double take. "I don't remember a Nicole from the file."

"She asked to be kept out of it, and Crandall agreed. He didn't think it was relevant. I had to really work to get it out of him."

"So he just omitted her from his write-up?"

61

"Pretty much."

"What was her deal?"

"Tech exec from the city. Originally from Chattanooga, Tennessee, went to Stanford."

"So why did she want to be anonymous?"

"This isn't what you'd call a popular beach. The parking lot is sparse, lots of privacy. You remember that Explorer with the blacked-out windows when we pulled in?"

"Yes."

"On cold days, at lunch time, there's usually a car or two off in the corner." He's trying to put it delicately, which is, to be honest, a little insulting.

"Nicole was screwing someone in the parking lot?"

He blushes. "Something like that."

"You just said she was alone when she saw Gray."

"She was. She met the guy in the parking lot. When they were finished, he left, and she went for a walk alone on the beach."

"Anything else Crandall left out of the file?"

"Probably plenty."

"I want to talk to her."

I regret it as soon as the words leave my mouth. Do I really want to get more involved? Reading files is one thing. Doing interviews is something else. As soon as your name appears on a write-up, you're in it, you're on the 6(e) list, you're a case participant. It can be a slippery slope, leading to an appearance at grand jury, an unwelcome stint at trial, all of it. But Rory was right when he said, "You need to work." In fact, I *want* to work. I feel a familiar tug, anticipation, the magnetic pull of the unsolved case drawing me in.

"Sure. I'll call her. She'll be thrilled."

Kyle pulls out his phone, goes through contacts, dials a number. After he introduces himself, there's a long pause. When he asks to meet, there's an even longer pause. "You could come to the station instead," he says in a voice I haven't heard him use—more Officer Kyle than Apprentice Kyle. It seems to do the trick, because the next words out of his mouth are: "No, I've got your address. See you in half an hour."

He slides the phone into his pocket. "Up for a ride to the city?"

13

Economist and former Federal Reserve chairman Alan Greenspan famously endorsed the theory that sales of men's underwear (the Men's Underwear Index, or MUI) served as a valuable economic indicator. Plot your MUI predictions for the years leading up to and following the next recession.

Nicole is waiting for us in the lobby when we arrive. Before we even say hello, she enters our names into the reception desk computer. The machine spits out badges bearing the words INDUSTRY CONTACT. We slip the lanyards around our necks and follow her into the elevator.

As we walk the long hallway past the beanbag chairs and dining areas, I get the feeling that this famous, feared, mildly respected tech company is really just a stock symbol and a slick website being run out of a building that resembles the food court at a shopping mall.

We step into a café, quiet save for the clicking of laptop keyboards. Nicole leads us to a dimly lit booth, and Kyle and I slide in side by side. She returns moments later with three coffees and slides into the seat across from us, attempting to shield her face from prying eyes. It's no use. Two young men pass our table, greeting her cheerfully. She doesn't want to be here with us, but now that she's been seen by her colleagues, she has given up her defenses. She tells us about the morning on the beach, the "sandwiches" in the car, the strange figure in the distance, shuffling toward her. Her eyes are almost frantic. I can tell she hasn't been sleeping well.

"And when did you realize it was a boy?" I ask.

"I don't know." She shudders. "I mean, I knew in that last ten feet it was human, but it was so white. So bluish white, and the completely bald head, the lack of hair anywhere. His skin was translucent, shivering, so cold, I could see his veins through his skin. He was tall enough to be fifteen or sixteen, I guessed. But he was so gaunt and weak he struck me as much younger."

"What did you do?"

"I asked the boy if he was okay, even though it was obvious he wasn't. He didn't reply. Then I took off my coat, wrapped him up in it, and called nine-one-one. The operator said to stay right there, so I just held him in my arms, trying to warm him up. He was trembling, his lips blue. He didn't meet my eyes. He was humming, this terrible, high-pitched noise. The firemen arrived within six or seven minutes. But still, those minutes standing there with that frozen, traumatized boy felt like hours."

"Did he say anything at all?"

"No, he just kept humming, shaking."

"Could you see where he came from?"

"Somewhere down the beach." She bites her lip. I wait for her to fill the silence. Several seconds tick by. She shifts uncomfortably in her seat. "Is he okay?"

"He's with his family," Kyle says.

"But is he *okay?*"

"Hard to tell, but at least he's back in school."

Nicole lets out a deep sigh, almost as if she has been holding her breath all these months. "Thank God." She swipes a tear from her face, sits up, looking first at me, then at Kyle. "Did you catch the guy?" The tiny twitch of her mouth, barely perceptible, gives me pause.

As we're getting into the cruiser, I ask Kyle: "Why doesn't it mention in the file that Stafford had no hair when he appeared on the beach?"

"I asked Crandall the same thing."

"What about the Lamey twins? Also hairless?"

"No, but they did have an unusual smell."

"I didn't see that in the file."

"Crandall wasn't big on details, as you've noticed."

"What kind of smell? Sweat? Feces?"

"The opposite."

"What's the opposite of feces?" I say, laughing. I can't help it. In the Behavioral Analysis Program, BAP—a special division of the Behavioral Analysis Unit focused on counterintelligence—we used to laugh at the most inappropriate things. It was a way of releasing tension, or maybe it's just that inappropriate things are funnier.

"It was the absence of smell. Like a cloak of *unsmellability*. At least that's how the nurse described it to me."

"What nurse? I thought Crandall handled that case?"

"Yes, but when I got to the job, I was curious, and the Lamey case hadn't been officially closed yet. I tracked down one of the nurses who'd received the twins at the hospital right after they were found. When she told me about the absence of smell, it sounded like a clue."

"Or the absence of a clue."

"Have you ever heard of Febreze?"

"The cleaning product?"

"Not a cleaning product, a deodorizing product, invented by a chemist at Procter and Gamble. A pretty amazing feat of chemistry really, it's an inorganic compound, microscopically small, shaped like a doughnut. And it doesn't smell like anything. The shape traps the odor molecule, blocking it so that the smell is undetectable. But when Procter and Gamble first sold the product, it was a total flop. In cleaning products, it turns out, people don't want clean so much as they want the *smell* of clean. Anyway, long story short, P&G relaunches the product with a trademark scent, and it makes millions."

"So are you saying the twins were doused with Febreze?" I ask.

"All I know is, both kids had a rash over their entire bodies, which cleared up within days of their return. The doctors found traces of beta-cyclodextrin in one of the twin's urine."

"The key ingredient of . . ."

"Febreze. Though, apparently, it's not unusual for people to have that chemical in their urine."

I'm beginning to wonder how much else was missing from the Lamey file. "Did the kids mention anything about it? Or were they mute, like Gray Stafford?"

"Not mute, but they hadn't talked much before and they certainly didn't start after they returned. Eventually, their mother was able to surmise that they had been kept in a room with bunk beds, wherever they were."

"Were they fed?"

"It was hard to tell, because they were extremely picky eaters. They'd lost a dangerous amount of weight, but that might have just meant they didn't eat what they were given."

"Anything else?"

"They didn't hear any human sounds." He glances over at me.

"What do you mean? Were there pets? Machines? Road noise?"

"There might have been horses."

"Really?"

"One of the twins was afraid of horses when she returned. Never had been before. I know the file says 'learning disabled,' but that's not quite accurate. Someone who knew more about these things, someone not like Crandall, in other words, would probably have asked the parents if the children had Asperger's. The twins gave us nothing. In fact, they seemed totally uninterested in shedding light on anything that had happened to them. And unlike Gray, they didn't seem overly traumatized, except for the horse thing."

We wind back along 92, heading inland, emerging from dense fog into sunshine. "There was a news story a few years ago," I say, "about a father and his twelve-year-old son who survived overnight in the Atlantic Ocean after their fishing boat capsized. The father was terrified, but the boy seemed to think the whole thing was a great adventure. He had autism, and his neurological difference allowed him to stay calm. It saved their lives. He didn't sense the danger. Could that be what happened with the Lamey twins?"

"Possible. The Febreze thing is just my theory. Their mother thought the rash could be from something else. She said they were both allergic to black walnut trees. Before Chief Jepson told me to leave the case alone, I wasted an entire weekend researching black walnut trees. I had this vision of myself solving the mystery, you know, finding the villain camping out in a tent in a black walnut orchard."

"With horses."

"Exactly. But it doesn't really work that way, does it?"

"Sometimes it does. I can't tell you how many weekends I've spent on details like that. Occasionally, it pans out."

Kyle takes the Black Mountain Road exit, cruising into Greenfield, slowing to take the hairpin curves. On Robinwood, a deer darts out in front of us. Kyle swerves and brakes expertly, not too hard, the stunned deer staring at us for several moments before leaping into the brush. As we pull up in front of my dad's house, I have one more question for Kyle. "What reason did Chief Jepson give you when he told you to quit investigating?"

"He insisted there was *no there there*. Chief said my primary job as a new officer on the force was to be, and I quote, 'a comforting presence for the good citizens of Greenfield.'"

14

Government employees must manage natural resources
according to the principle of "maximum sustainable yield."
Would a similar perspective be productive for parenting?
Why would Malthus agree or disagree with your answer?

It's four in the morning and I can't sleep, so I pull on a windbreaker
and shorts, grab my bike, and roll out of the garage. The momentum of the hill pulls me down the same path. I feel like a ball on
an unleveled billiard table, always rolling toward the same corner.

It was my father who suggested the bike rides, back when I
was an anxious kid. It started with the paper route, but over time
it morphed into a kind of ritual, an almost-spiritual practice, a
way to settle my mind. In the years since—in California, Florida,
Arkansas, New York City—I've logged tens of thousands of miles,
maybe hundreds of thousands. I once calculated that I had biked
the six-mile loop around Central Park nearly four thousand times.

I don't have fancy gear or a racing helmet. I don't wear a ridiculously tight onesie bearing the name of an Italian coffee company.
I do, however, own a top-of-the-line bike. It's orange, with yellow
tires, a fine leather saddle, handmade by a highly sought-after craftsman in Vermont, whose signature graces the crossbar. It arrived

via FedEx nine days after Fred died, at our fourth-floor walk-up at Ninety-Second between Columbus and Central Park West. The delivery guy buzzed up: "You'll have to sign for this one." I pushed and wrangled the huge box up all sixty-five stairs. I had no clue what could be inside. No card, no invoice. Just this sleek, beautiful bike, smelling of rubber and leather.

Fred and I had admired a similar bike in the craftsman's shop in Burlington more than a year earlier. Rolling it around the living room, I knew this purchase had been months in the planning, and I also knew it was the finest thing I owned—more expensive than my engagement ring, possibly even our car. Fred must have worked feats of financial magic in order to purchase it. One day, if I ever dig myself out of this mess, I'll balance the checkbook, organize the credit card statements, and discover exactly how much he paid. But for now, it remains a mystery: a beautiful, bittersweet mystery and the final reminder of a wonderful, imperfect marriage.

Inside the Royal Donut Shop, the guy at the counter recognizes me.

"Hey," he says. "It's the FBI lady. What can I get you?"

"One old-fashioned, please, and two raised chocolates." The old-fashioned is for me, the raised for Rory. I fish around in my pocket for the twenty-dollar bill I always keep there, but I can't find it. I glance over at the ATM, but of course I don't have my card. I start to apologize and say I'll come back later, but he hands me a bag—it feels like four or five doughnuts—and interrupts my apology.

"Don't worry about it."

On the ride back up the hill, I pass the Shirley Jackson house on Forestview, the one she memorialized in *The Road Through the Wall*—a novel about a seemingly perfect town full of dark secrets.

I never even realized she'd lived here until long after I moved away. At some point in high school or college, most students read Jackson's short story "The Lottery," a classic horror tale about the evil committed by ordinary citizens in an ordinary town. Perhaps you remember it: each time the lottery comes up, a citizen is randomly selected and stoned to death by his or her friends, neighbors, and children.

Minutes later I'm in Greenfield, pedaling toward the cul-de-sac where Gray Stafford lives, my bike tires gripping the smooth asphalt. There are five houses on the cul-de-sac. As I roll past each home, telltale blue lights illuminate the lawns and driveways, motion sensors bringing the security cameras to life. I imagine the lenses following me from house to house, street to street. I don't even recognize the Stafford home from the photograph; a tall wooden fence has been erected around the property. I think about Nicole's story of the day she found Gray Stafford on the beach. I turn the story over in my mind.

I roll back along Eucalyptus beside the golf course. From here, I can see the back of the Delacroix place. It stands out among the neighboring houses, with its concrete fence, glass walls, and oversized sculptures holding court over the expansive green lawn. I pedal the mile uphill to my father's house, leaning into the pain, legs burning.

15

In Mexico during the late 1990s and again in Serbia in
the fall of 2005, frogs fell from the sky. How might this
be possible? How might it be impossible? In your answer,
discuss whether the intersection of science and religion is
moving, and, if so, in which direction.

I'm clearing out a file cabinet in my father's study Saturday morning when my phone starts ringing downstairs. I feel that Pavlovian
panic I've had ever since I got the call about Fred—something must
be wrong—but then I remember Rory is at his study session. He's
fine. By the time I reach it, the call has gone to voicemail. It's my
friend and colleague George Voss.

"There's a bench on a path behind the Embassy Suites in
Burlingame," his message says. "Meet me at noon?"

George and I were in the same class at Quantico. Later, we
spent eleven months together on a major case in the woods of North
Carolina. It was George who recruited me to the BAP team. We've
worked together off and on for my entire career. We've always liked
similar locations—off-the-beaten-path towns where the best motel
has a "6" in the name and you'll miss Main Street if you blink—so

when a case comes come up in, say, Big Spring, Texas, we often end up working it together.

There's one unspoken rule in this organization: when a colleague asks for help, you show up. See you then, I text.

I find George on a bench behind the Embassy Suites wearing a sweaty Seahawks T-shirt and green running shorts. His black hair is damp, his face flushed.

"How far?"

"Eight miles," he says, rising from the bench. I've spent so much time with George driving around in cars, every time he stands to his full height—six foot four—I'm surprised by how tall he is. At five foot five, I have to crane my neck to talk to him. "Felt amazing. Weather has been shitty in New York."

"Meeting someone?"

"Airport at three."

"Shall we walk?"

We stroll along the path toward the abandoned Burlingame drive-in. The flat, gray water of the bay stretches toward the city skyline, blanketed in fog.

"Who's your guy?" I ask.

"Eurasian diplomat coming in through Luxembourg. We haven't seen each other since an awkward pitch at the UN seven years ago."

"Must not have been *too* awkward. He's meeting you again."

"He doesn't exactly know he's meeting me. Hopefully, this time it won't turn into an international incident."

George bounces some ideas off me, and we talk about the best way to draw the guy in—how to make the approach, what to say and how to say it.

"I sense that's not the only reason you're here," I say after we've hashed the whole thing out.

"Come back to work. Things are heating up with Russia. We need you."

A plane comes in low over the bay, drowning out our voices. After it passes, I stop and turn to George. "I can't."

"Why?"

"If I had a clear answer, I'd tell you. It's just . . ."

"Just what?"

The wind picks up, small waves slapping the silt and rocks. "How much do you know about Yellow Beak?"

"Enough to know you're not to blame."

"You heard what happened?"

"Lina, it wasn't your fault. It wasn't even your op at that point."

"That's the problem. I shouldn't have passed it off."

"I don't know a single agent who would have made that meeting under the circumstances. And you somehow managed to follow procedures to the letter. Jesus, you wrote up the 1023 and the USIC referral the day after you buried your husband." Another plane passes overhead, causing the ground to vibrate beneath us. When the noise subsides, George puts his hand on my shoulder. "We all want you back."

"Thanks, that means a lot." My eyes water. George squeezes my shoulder and gives me a tender look. "Damn salt air," I mumble.

I get the feeling they've been talking about me back in New York, and everyone decided George would be the best person to approach me. I appreciate the effort. I've been feeling so isolated out here, so far from my friends and my normal life, it's comforting to know someone still has my back.

I point out an abandoned boat several hundred yards out. "That was a fish restaurant in the late seventies. My parents used to bring me here after the school talent show."

"How was the food?"

"Terrible. But it was dinner on a boat!"

I loved those evenings with my parents—the thrill of going out to dinner on a school night, the Naugahyde booths, the little red candle, the squares of butter in waxed paper, our discussions of the more questionable talent show acts. My dad used to make my mom laugh so hard she'd have tears pouring down her face. It was the best part about being an only child: the complete attention my parents gave me, the way they included me in their conversations, as if I were their equal.

That was before my mom took off, before my dad moved up the hill. When I became a parent, I tried to emulate that model three-some with my own family, the way I remembered it from the best years, at least. And it worked. Rory enjoyed being an only child. He never once expressed the desire for a sibling or asked why he didn't have one. But two isn't the same as three. Two is a straight line, not a triangle, as I know so well from my own adolescence. With Fred gone, the balance is off. If I'd been able to see the future, I would have had another child.

"How's Rory?" George asks, as if he can read my mind.

"He kind of amazes me." I smile. "He's made a good friend already. Her parents are in the French foreign service."

George raises his eyebrows in surprise. "That's random!"

I give him a guilty look. "Not really."

We turn and begin walking back toward the hotel. "I've got a puzzle for you." I tell George about Kyle and the case of the Stafford boy.

George is intrigued—not just by the disappearance but also by the way the local cops are handling it. After college and before his master's in psychology at UW, George worked as a police officer in the Northwest, so he understands small-town department politics. He asks me twenty quick, intuitive questions about Greenfield, Kyle, Crandall, Gray Stafford, and the Lamey twins. The efficiency of his questions, the way he gets to the heart of the matter so quickly and precisely, brings me back to my former life.

I miss the collaboration, the way the back-and-forth helps me put words to ideas that have been subconsciously percolating. George narrows in on the fact that the Stafford boy had no hair and may have come out of the ocean. "The baldness seems related, somehow, to the lack of smell, the rash on the twins," he says.

"I thought so too."

George nudges me with his elbow. "Only you could step away from the job and find yourself embroiled in a triple kidnapping case with a side of the seriously weird. I think you might have a professional on your hands."

"Yes, but—"

George finishes my sentence: "A professional who kidnaps kids never gives them back."

16

Columbus discovered the New World in 1492. What is
wrong with this statement? What is right?

Before going into counterintelligence, agents spend six weeks at
Quantico in BCI, the basic course. It's mostly legal training, surveillance detection, and case studies, along with hours of filler. When
I was in BCI, the instructors were an eclectic mix of veterans who
wanted something slower, SWAT guys angling for more workout
time, or agents on the bricks spending time in the penalty box.

Sometimes, they surprised us with something more interesting. One afternoon we came back from the cafeteria to find
an agent I'd seen around the New York office. A funny guy with
a pronounced Southern accent, he was there to talk about a Russian recruitment he'd pulled off years earlier. An analyst who had
never spent a moment in the field had made a name for himself
by writing a book about it, then hiring himself out as a consultant
on cable news. I'd read the book, which reeked of self-promotion,
as those books by "former agents" and "former analysts" so often
do. The presentation was much grittier than the book. The agent
pulled back the curtain and showed what the case was really like
from the inside.

At the end of his presentation, he said something I've never forgotten. "Because success in this job is rare and fleeting, agents who achieve something noteworthy are usually remembered only for that one success. People call me the Nine Fox guy, because it was the code name of that case. But when I think about my twenty-year career, Nine Fox is only a small piece of the pie." Then he listed more than a dozen espionage cases in which he failed. "Those are the ones I remember," he said.

At the time, I thought he was just trying to make the new agents feel better about how little we had accomplished, how much we had to learn. But over the years, I've realized how honest his words were. When people see me in the hallways at 26 Fed or down at HQ, they often just refer to me as the agent from Blue Squared or the Cuban thing or Rocky Asphalt. "Hey, it's Blue Squared," they'll say, giving me a smile and a nod.

Yet those aren't the cases that stick out in my memory. I think only of Yellow Beak. And not even all of Yellow Beak. I don't think of the recruitment, the hotel room meetings in Panama and Finland and Kishinev. No, I think of one decision I made just after Fred died. It's there in the file, though you'd have to read all the way to volume eight to find it. Somewhere among the write-ups, the records checks, the travel vouchers, and the gift reimbursements is a long 1023 about a surprise meeting at a New York City hotel.

When I reflect on my career, I am haunted by the decisions I made that day. Everything I did was proper, legal, exactly what regulations required. One hundred percent by the book. Yet, even then, I knew I was doing everything wrong.

17

Is artificial intelligence truly artificial? Is it intelligence?

I arrive ten minutes early for the quarterly budget meeting at the school and wait outside for the auditorium doors to open. It's not the sort of event I'd normally attend, but Brenda's text this afternoon intrigued me: You don't want to miss it. I glance around, looking for Brenda, but I don't see her. Tina Rennert and Elaine from the lunch at Brenda's house are standing in a foursome with their husbands. I try to catch their eyes, but they're busy talking. I'm relieved when the doors finally open and the crowd filters in.

A PowerPoint presentation is projected on a big screen at the front of the room, the title slide declaring: "Excellence + Empathy = Extraordinary!" I take a seat at the end of the last row and unlock my phone, only to realize I intended to compose a text for Fred. We used to text a dozen or more times during the day—little stuff, gossip, jokes. It was such an integral part of my daily life, I still get that gut-punch feeling every time I start to text and realize there's no one there to receive it. I should remove Fred's number from my phone. And of course, I should give up the cell phone number he had for almost two decades, remove his phone from our family plan, but I can't stand the idea of Rory dialing his dad's phone one day and hearing a stranger's voice.

By the time the lights dim, it's standing room only, so I move over to free up the end seat. The guy to my left is talking loudly to a man two rows ahead, something about their upcoming trip to Palm Springs to golf with the lieutenant governor. The crowd is noisy and jovial, lots of air-kissing and firm handshakes. It seems everyone is happy to be a part of this exclusive club.

"Mom," Rory said last night, when I remarked on the slick patina of wealth that coats everything in this town. "We inherited a mansion from Granddad. I looked it up on Zillow. Do you know how much it's worth? You don't get to play the working-class card anymore."

"Shut up and eat your mac and cheese," I said.

A woman in a maroon suit sits down next to me, placing her Louis Vuitton bag on the floor at her feet. I'm certain I've seen her before, but I can't place her. Sleek blonde bob, pearl drop earrings, and Botox that makes her look shiny and surprised.

"Hi, I'm Lina."

She glances up from her phone. "Laura Crowell."

"What grade are your kids in?" I ask.

"No kids. I'm with the Davenport Team."

Ah, now I remember: her face graces the shopping carts at Safeway, an ad for her real estate group. She must be Harris Ojai's competition. "Where do you live?"

"Betancourt Drive."

She turns off her phone and turns her attention to me, suddenly friendly, her broad smile revealing a gap between her front teeth that makes her look vaguely glamorous. "Oh, the Pellner house!"

"Pardon?"

"Your father's place. The five bedroom, four-and-a-half bath with the glass-and-steel breezeway designed by Stuart Pellner. I've been meaning to get in touch with you."

This town is way too small.

"Good light," she continues. "Odd embankment in the back. The flat properties are more desirable, as you know, but your canyon and bay views compensate for the hillside location. When you decide to sell—" She reaches into the front pocket of her blazer and pulls out a business card, which she thrusts into my hand.

At that moment, the room goes dark. A spotlight swoops overhead and finds the stage, illuminating a tall, striking man in a well-cut black suit.

"Welcome." Kobayashi speaks into the microphone, his baritone voice echoing off the walls. "I think we all know why we're here, but first we have a few housekeeping items."

The housekeeping bit is an update on surplus funds this semester. Apparently, there has been a debate about whether the money should be invested in new laptops or an additional language teacher. I'm preparing to vote—language teacher, obviously—when Kobayashi announces that there will be no need for further discussion. The pledge drive has exceeded all expectations and the school's investments and endowment have enjoyed a banner year.

"I'm pleased to announce that we will be able to procure new laptops and not one but *two* full-time language teachers." A murmur of appreciation goes through the crowd.

"Based on parent input, research, and district needs, we have reached a conclusion. Special thanks to the Davenport Team for funding an exhaustive study." The Davenport logo appears on the screen above Kobayashi's head. "Extra special thanks to parents Dave and Celia Byrnes from Intel for donating the code to crunch the data. The Byrneses could not be with us this evening, but if the members of the Davenport Team will please stand—"

Laura Crowell is quickly out of her seat, followed by three other women in identical maroon suits. The room erupts into applause again.

Kobayashi continues, "The two new languages we will be offering, in addition to our current Mandarin requirement for all incoming freshmen, will be Ruby, of course, and Hungarian. Simply put, Hungarian has been proven in longitudinal studies to enhance key neurological connections, thus complementing students' preparation for the math and analogy portions of the Wonder Test."

Approving murmurs go up from the crowd, despite the glaring absence of Spanish in the curriculum. I lean over and whisper to Laura Crowell: "Ruby?"

"The programming language!"

Kobayashi makes more announcements. He seems miffed by the fact that Miss Townsend has gone and gotten pregnant, creating "continuity issues" with the freshman Rhetoric for Testing program. The talk goes on for another fifteen minutes.

I've completely zoned out by the time Kobayashi takes a deep breath and declares, "The time has come." The air buzzes with excitement. A drone's-eye view of Greenfield is projected on the screen, and rousing orchestral music emanates from the speakers. Laura Crowell edges forward in her chair. Palm Springs man pounds his feet on the floor, and a drum roll rises up as others join in.

"And now," Kobayashi announces, "I am honored to share with you the results of last year's Wonder Test."

The principal appears from stage left, clad in a tailored black dress and knee-high boots, carrying a silver tray. She lifts the tray, from which Kobayashi plucks a red envelope. He takes his time opening the envelope, holding it in front of the mic so we can hear the paper tearing. He lifts the flap, gazes at the audience. "Before I announce the results, I want to thank the students, the parents, the community, and our amazing teachers for so willingly adopting my vision: Prepared for the test, prepared for life, every student counts."

The motto appears in bold black letters on the screen, imposed over a photograph of students sitting in a classroom, faces aglow in the light of their computer screens. People in the audience mumble the line with him, not fully committing.

Kobayashi raises his eyebrows in mock surprise. "I can't hear you."

The audience chants the lines again, louder but still tentative.

Kobayashi smiles coyly, leaning toward the audience, his hand cupped around his ear. "What's that you said?"

"Prepared for the test, prepared for life," the audience says, more confidently this time. "Every student counts!"

It feels more like a Tony Robbins seminar than a budget meeting. But when I look around, everybody seems to be taking it in stride. I can't tell if they're just accommodating Kobayashi, having a bit of fun, or truly indoctrinated.

Amid the pandemonium, Kobayashi stares directly at me. He appears to have noticed that I'm not joining in. He makes a small waving gesture with the envelope. Laura Crowell turns to me and whispers, "Just say it."

"What?" She's not kidding. Kobayashi is still looking at me, and several audience members have turned in their seats, following his gaze.

"Just say it," Crowell whispers again.

"Every student counts," I mumble. Not for my sake but for Rory's. If there's one thing I know about school, it's that you don't want to attract any attention to your kid. It's better to flow with the stream than to block it, even if the stream is flowing in the wrong direction.

A tiny smile from Kobayashi, a nod, and then he breaks eye contact with me.

He holds the silence for several moments, palms out, messiah-style, and leans into the microphone. "Every student counts," he whispers, more seriously this time. "They say, 'Oh, it will all average out.' They say, 'Oh, what does it matter?' They say, 'In every district, in every school, a few kids are bound to have a bad day. In every district, in every school, a few kids are bound to be off their game, behind the curve. Perhaps they're sick or unfocused. Perhaps they just don't care.' Am I right?"

"Yes," a woman's voice answers.

Kobayashi shakes his head sadly. "We've all heard it. It's human nature, they tell me. It's the law of averages. 'Kobayashi,' they insist, 'not every student will ace the test. Not every student is up for the challenge. Not every student can be a winner. Some kids are wired for other things.'"

Kobayashi peers into the half-opened envelope, teasing the audience. "I get it. I do. Law of averages. With a hundred and sixty-eight kids in tenth grade, how much can one student really affect the overall score? Simple math, right? Glaringly simple, my friends, and it does indeed average out. One distracted student, one bad day, one errant key stroke—"

He takes the mic out of the holder and paces back and forth. *"One* bad day for *one student* can drag the school's average down by *2.03* points . . . *2.03 points."*

The guy next to me whips out his phone and types numbers into the calculator. Kobayashi motions to the stage manager. "Bring it down a little bit, Andy." The spotlight dims. "Can I tell you all a little story? Can I tell you a story about a friend of mine?"

He surveys the crowd, pretending to wait for an answer. "I have this friend from Stanford, brilliant mathematician. I won't use his name, you know, protect the guilty. He's in Vegas right now, loves to play blackjack. In graduate school, he learned how to recalibrate the odds based upon what cards are still left in the deck and bet accordingly. On a good day, he says, when his eyes are keen and his mind is nimble, he can shift the odds in his favor by nearly three percent. Three percent. Doesn't sound like much, right? Pennies on the dollar, not even the tax on a cup of coffee." Kobayashi steps down from the stage and begins walking down the center aisle. "Right now in Vegas, do you know what he's doing? He's sitting at a table, counting cards, making his bets, keeping a low profile, riding that three percent. Do you know how much he made yesterday? Sixty-two thousand dollars. Do you know how much he made the day before that? Seventy-one thousand dollars. He's not greedy, my friends, but he's practical. Every day he adds to his assets, cushions his nest egg, makes life a little easier, a little more secure, for his wife and kids, and yes, even for his future grandkids. All because of that three percent advantage. A little can mean a lot. A little," he repeats, "can mean *so much* for the future of your children."

Kobayashi chuckles to himself, shakes his head. "The funny part is that the guy actually owes me money, but that's a different story." He has reached the back row now. He looks straight at me, and for a moment it seems he might actually wink. Then he breaks our gaze and turns to the opposite row. "Anyway, where was I?"

He paces to the front of the room, mounts the stage, places the microphone back in the stand. "Just 2.03 points on the Wonder Test is the difference between the winners and the runners-up. It's the difference between this brilliant, beautiful, unparalleled, safe, coveted, affluent town, and"—he pauses, pretending to choose his next words, although it's clear this whole performance has been well rehearsed—"it's the difference between this town and our neighbor to the south, Belmont." The room is silent. He shrugs. "Belmont isn't so shabby, right? Twelfth in the country last year. There are some smart kids in Belmont. Good schools. Excellent test scores. It's a nice place, Belmont. So"—long pause—"would you rather live in Belmont?"

And with that, the audience comes alive. "No!"

Kobayashi shrugs. "So perhaps Belmont isn't too worried about one of their kids having a bad day. Not for me to judge." Then, in a somber voice, like a pastor concerned for his flock, Kobayashi asks, "How many of *our* kids are going to have a bad day?"

"Zero!" The crowd shouts in unison.

"How many of *our* kids had a bad day last year?"

"Zero!"

"What kind of kids do we have?"

"Winners!"

He lifts the envelope, pulls out a white card, and takes a moment to read the text. "Twenty-two thousand, four hundred, eighty-nine," he announces into the microphone. "Twenty-two thousand, four hundred, eighty-nine," he repeats slowly, confidently. "First in San Mateo County, first in California, first on the coast, first in the western region." Long pause.

But no one is smiling. Palm Springs is chewing his fingernails, and Laura Crowell is holding her breath.

Kobayashi turns briefly to the principal, who gives him a nod. Then he pivots back to the room and breaks into a megawatt smile. "And, once again, first in the nation. Congratulations parents! Congratulations staff! And most of all, congratulations to our students!"

The audience bursts into applause. There's a palpable sense of jubilation and something more: relief. Kobayashi leans down to high-five a few people in the front row. A school band appears from stage left, brass and winds, playing "Eye of the Tiger."

Laura Crowell has closed her eyes, a huge smile spread across her face. Kobayashi stands there, head bowed, soaking up the applause.

"We have a band?" I whisper to the guy to my left.

"Of course not," he laughs. "Who has time for band practice? The band is from Belmont."

18

Provide evidence from Butler's 2010 experiments demonstrating that repeated testing (a) increases retention of facts and (b) is more effective than simple studying in increasing transfer of knowledge to new concepts.

My cell phone rings at 7:30 a.m., unknown number. "Good morning," a voice says smoothly. "Laura Crowell here. What time works for you today? I'd like to discuss how I can help you sell your home."

"Thanks, but I'm not ready to sell—"

"No time like the present! The month following the announcement of the test scores is the hottest sellers' market of the year. We have many interested buyers, foreign and domestic."

"We?"

"The Davenport Team! When you sell with us, you sell with the best. I can have the stagers, landscapers, and photographers out today. We could do a showing on Sunday, and I guarantee we'll have a bidding war with at least twelve extremely favorable offers by end of day."

"Now isn't a good time." I hit End Call. The whole thing puts a bad taste in my mouth.

Later, as I'm exiting the school drop-off line, I see Kyle sitting in his cruiser at the curb. I pull up next to him. "Any new leads?"

"No, Captain's got me on school duty and department outreach all week."

A car pulls up behind me, and I inch forward. "Come see me on Friday?"

"I'll be there."

The disappointment I feel on Friday when Kyle doesn't show makes me realize how much this case has sucked me in. I want to ask more questions, dig deeper. My mind is stuck on Nicole, her story about the day she found Gray Stafford on the beach. I need to pay her another visit.

On Saturday, there's a parade to celebrate the Wonder Test scores. Since the announcement, I've received letters from three real estate firms asking if I want to sell. Harris Ojai even sent a balloon bouquet—eight helium monstrosities shaped like dollar signs, anchored by a catalog of Ojai's recent sales.

In the house, I'm making steady progress. Each week ends with two trips, one to the Goodwill and another to the Mussel Rock dumps in Pacifica. Each journey leaves me with a feeling of accomplishment and a corresponding sense of dread. Though I'm still thirteen rooms from completion, every week leads me one step closer to facing the prospect of the future. I can't put it off forever, but as long as there are rooms to clear, I can avoid making decisions. I never thought I'd say it, but I have begun to see some positives in this town. Maybe it's the quiet and the clean air, the guilty pleasure of Greenfield-Neighbors. org, or the fact that much to my surprise I belong to a group of moms for the first time in my life—coffee at Philz every other Wednesday and occasional walks with Brenda at the beautiful Sawyer Camp Trail.

Although I feel myself relaxing into life here, returning to California has done nothing to cure my insomnia. Most nights, sleep comes easily at first, but my internal clock wakes me at precisely 3:57 a.m. I wander downstairs and lurk around the house, checking the driveway for Mister Fancy. He never disappoints. We have an unspoken nightly rendezvous.

"This is a strange town," I remember him saying that first night. "Seems normal, but it isn't."

Around 4:30 a.m., I usually get on my bike and roll down the driveway. The neighborhood suits me better before sunrise—empty streets, tall eucalyptus trees creaking in the wind, the hiss of sprinklers turning off and on. No one around, just me and the little blue cameras, continuously in motion.

And then one night, I'm not alone.

When I get to the intersection of Eucalyptus and Newtown, I see someone running—a thin guy, bushy haired, wearing only running shorts and a red T-shirt despite the chill in the air. Out of curiosity, I turn in his direction. It takes me longer to catch up than I expect. He must be doing a sub-six-minute mile. Lean legs, long stride. As I pedal up behind him, I realize he's not from around here. The dated Asics are a giveaway.

"Morning," I call out as I roll by. He doesn't notice me at first. He's got his earbuds in, the music loud. Then he sees me out of the corner of his eye. He seems startled, jolted from a state of nirvana. He nods but never slows from his brisk pace.

He seems so familiar. Do I know him? He resembles the actor Edward Norton but older, taller, and more aerodynamic. I want to linger, to get a few words out of him—maybe the voice will sound familiar—but he wants none of it. Past Floribunda, the runner's face stays with me, but I still can't place him. Later, at the breakfast table, Rory remarks, "Doughnuts three days straight."

"And eggs," I say, pointing to the pile of scrambled eggs on his plate.

"What's up? Can't sleep?" He's got a chocolate cruller in one hand, *Martin in Space* in the other. I'm not sure how he does that, reading and talking simultaneously. Perhaps it's a new technique he picked up from the school's "reading technician."

"Hey, I saw a runner this morning, older, red bushy hair, flying. He may have even been running a five-minute mile," I say incredulously, "in these worn-out Asics."

"That's Mr. Beach," Rory says, his eyes still moving over the text.

"Who?"

"He teaches honors trig. He also runs the Bitcoin mining club and, of course, he coaches track."

Why does the name sound familiar? I can't place it. "What's his first name?"

Rory shrugs. "How would I know? He's a teacher."

Mr. Beach. And then I remember: that's the name my dad wrote on the sticky note attached to his computer monitor. He's the person I was supposed to call if I had Wi-Fi issues. "Good guy," my dad's note said. But I'm certain that's not where I know him from.

My first Bureau supervisor called me borderline OCD, said I couldn't stop pulling on every little thread. He claimed that was why he gave me the tougher cases. Of course, I hated him for it. I always wanted one of those dull, open-and-shut securities-fraud cases, all wrapped up with a nice bow, the ones where you could write the opening, closing, and stat all in one. Then again, if I'd been stuck riding those kinds of cases, I would have quit long ago.

On the drive to school, I turn the question over and over in my mind. Who, exactly, is Mr. Beach?

19

Crocodiles and alligators. Discuss the importance of small differences.

I'm sitting on a bench in the company's modern lobby. Beside me is an engraved copper plaque explaining the bench's "origin story," how the company founder chopped it down in a Brazilian rain forest and then planted a thousand better trees in its place. The bench is comfortable, elegantly molded to accommodate the human form, but the tangle of phone and laptop chargers sprouting from the end ruins the effect.

Tech workers pass by, each one dressed more casually than the last, toting their designer coffees and stylish messenger bags. Nicole is three steps past me when she stops in her tracks. After a few seconds, she turns, walks back, and sits down on the bench next to me. She looks resigned.

"I knew you'd be back," she whispers. "So, now what?"

"It's up to you."

"The fourth-floor cafeteria does a killer breakfast burrito. You're not vegan, are you?"

"Tried it once. Lasted a week."

Nicole prints out a badge for me at security: INDUSTRY CONTACT. I slip the lanyard around my neck and follow her into the elevator, where she punches the button for the fourth floor. The doors close behind us and we stand side by side at the back of the elevator, leaning against the wall.

"How did you know?" she asks.

"When I asked where the boy had come from, your expression changed and you bit your lip."

"That simple?"

"No, there were other tells. Your fingers turned in slightly, you tucked your feet under the seat, you scratched your arm. With deception, it's never one thing but a combination of behaviors that add up. There's a whole thing with the eyes, but I won't bore you."

Her shoulders slump. "It flew past the cop kid, but I knew you knew."

The bell dings to indicate our arrival on the fourth floor, the elevator doors open, and Nicole leads me through a maze of hallways. By the time we arrive at a café that serves only breakfast burritos and Blue Bottle Coffee, I'm completely turned around. The place reminds me of a book I once read about a labyrinthine prison in the middle of the Nevada desert. We're the only ones here.

"This café just opened for beta testing," Nicole says. "Staffed entirely by robots. Access is limited while we work out the kinks."

Nicole scans her thumbprint, we punch our orders into a machine, and we settle into a corner booth. The table lamp is turned low, the sound on the video monitor beside us set to mute. A headless robot wheels up to our table bearing a black lacquer tray. "Your order, sir," intones a disconcertingly smooth voice.

Like Siri without the sex appeal. "Your order sir your order sir," it repeats more rapidly.

Nicole takes the tray and the robot whirls around, racing back to the kitchen.

"Like I said, they're still working out the kinks."

The coffee is delicious. So is the burrito. "I'm not sure whether I should be nervous about the future or optimistic," I say.

"We should all be nervous," Nicole replies. "How does this work?"

"Why don't you tell me what else, *who* else, you saw that day on the beach?"

She takes a deep breath and forges ahead. "As I was wrapping my coat around the boy, I noticed something out in the water. Dark gray, moving away from shore. At first, I thought it was a shark. But then I noticed it was undulating, so I thought it must be a sea lion."

"How did you know it wasn't?"

"Just as it crested the wave, I saw the flash of red. A swimming cap. After college, I had a thing with a swimmer. Female swimmers have a unique shape. To someone who doesn't know the sport, they look chunky, with their broad shoulders, thick arms and hips. But they're in better shape than all of us. Whoever was out there, she was a real swimmer, not a hobbyist. She'd have to be a high-level competitor to hold that boy, carry him all the way to shore."

"Did you actually see her bringing him to shore?"

"No, he was already out of the water when I saw her swimming out."

"She could have just been out for a swim, totally unrelated."

"That boy definitely came from the water. When he got to me, he was still wet. He could barely walk. In the condition he was in, there's no way he could have survived the surf alone."

"You never told anyone?"

"No," she says miserably.

"What exactly did you see?"

"Red cap, dark-gray wet suit. That's all. She swam so fast."

"Did you see a boat?"

"Yes, but it was *way* out there. It could have been a crab boat. It had branches coming up on either side. That's all I could see."

"Color? Size?"

"No idea. I was worried about the swimmer. I mean, I was mostly worried about the boy, of course, but I couldn't figure out how the swimmer was going to make it all the way to the boat."

"What happened next?"

"Just what I said before to you and Kyle. The fire truck showed up, there was a huge commotion, an ambulance, and when I looked back out, the swimmer was gone, the boat was gone, no little red head bobbing up and down in the waves." Her voice is tinged with regret. "For a while, it kept me up at night. But I saw how that girl swam. I saw how strong she was. I believe she made it."

"Why didn't you tell anyone?"

"If I could go back in time, I would. I panicked. I figured once the paramedics arrived the kid was safe, and that was the important part. I just wanted to get out of there, avoid more questions. I didn't want to have to explain to the cops what I was doing at the beach, where I worked, who I was with."

"Sandwich guy."

She cringes. "Yes, sandwich guy."

"Is that such a big deal?"

"He's married, two kids, high up at a rival firm."

"Name?"

She bites her lip. "I can't tell you that."

"Look, I've got no interest in outing your affair—"

"It wasn't an affair. It's over."

"Regardless, I need to know his name so I can rule some people out."

She sips her coffee, seems to be considering her options, then blurts out a name. I don't write it down, just commit it to memory.

"It would have been on Valleywag, Recode," she rationalizes. "Forever after, I would have been the tech exec who meets up for quickies in cars. This industry isn't exactly female-friendly. Once the public gets the scent of a scandal, things can go sideways. There would be repercussions for the company." She peers at me from red-rimmed eyes. "I know," she says. "So freaking predictable, a Silicon Valley techie with no moral compass. I'm sorry. I really am."

She's getting defensive, so I dial it back, try to reestablish the rapport. "Whatever happened to your swimmer from college?"

"Ah," she says. Her eyes dart up and to the left, honestly recalling the memory. "I fucked it up. I panicked and split. Seeing a pattern here?"

"We all have regrets."

"She got married, had children. I went back to my old boyfriend. Shithead lawyer, good on paper, bad in bed. Then I got married. Then I got divorced. I should've stuck with the swimmer. I see that now. She looks fantastic."

"You still hang out?"

"No. She does the Ironman Triathlon every year. I DVR it. Sometimes I check out her Instagram." The hint of a smile. "So on top of it all, I guess you could say I'm a stalker."

20

Kinshasa is one of the most dangerous cities in the world. Why, then, are the diamond sellers able to travel the downtown streets daily, carrying bags of expensive diamonds, with no fear of theft?

Caroline's eyes are red and puffy from crying. I hope it's not something Rory did.

They slide into the back seat, sitting close together. "We got the results back from the Wonder practice test," Rory says before I even ask.

"You have a very smart son who has a very dumb girlfriend," Caroline mumbles.

I don't even know where to begin unpacking that sentence. Girlfriend?

"Tonight is movie night at the school," Rory announces cheerfully, trying to distract us all from what Caroline just said.

"Movie night?"

"The fundraiser. Remember, they made us buy tickets?"

"Right." I've written so many checks to that school, I have no idea what I've bought.

"Can Caroline come with us?"

"Of course. Parents out of town?"

"Yes," Caroline says.

"Where?"

"Vienna, I think."

"Your father is a diplomat?"

"Yes," she says. "My mother is"—she pauses—"a diplomat too." The way she meets my eyes in the rearview mirror, I suspect she knows they're more than diplomats.

"That's interesting," I say.

"Interesting for *them.*"

When we return to campus at six thirty in the evening, the soccer field is decked out in twinkling lights, a movie screen showing the candy factory episode of *I Love Lucy.* Rory and Caroline head to the food line. I watch as they make their way across the field, arms touching. Caroline's hand reaches for Rory's, their fingers interlock, and she stands on her tiptoes to plant a quick kiss on his cheek.

I have one goal tonight: to find Gray Stafford's parents. This afternoon, I ran Bill Stafford's name and checked out the shady business dealings that led to his stint at Lompoc. I also looked into his software start-up, but nothing came up. In photos of Bill and Lacey from charity events over the last several years, they look like a typical Greenfield couple. They're about the same age, probably met in college or grad school. He's well dressed and tan, a little thick in the jowls. Her long platinum hair, smooth forehead, and toned physique point to countless hours in barre class and the aesthetician's chair.

Scanning the field, I locate the two of them sitting on a plaid blanket. I weave through the crowd and wedge my blanket in beside them. By the time the movie starts, the night is dark and cold. Rory and Caroline have disappeared. I try to make conversation with Lacey, but she's not interested. She looks considerably older than she did in the photos taken just two and three years ago, her forehead etched with deep lines, her hair brittle. After a tortured attempt at small talk, I offer, "I'm Lina, new in town."

"I know who you are," Bill Stafford replies.

Although I instinctively dislike Bill Stafford, the way he exudes arrogance, my gut tells me that Gray's disappearance wasn't related to his dad's business dealings. Lacey ignores the exchange, sipping wine from a plastic cup and scrolling through her phone.

At first, I don't recognize Gray when he returns to sit with his parents. With hair down past his shoulders and a San Francisco Giants jersey hanging off his thin frame, he barely resembles the photos of the bald, rescued boy. The only empty spot on his family's blanket happens to be right next to me. When his mother tries to switch places with him, pointing out he can't see the screen from there, he replies, "I don't care."

His tone isn't rude, just jarringly emotionless—the same flat affect I've witnessed in so many trauma victims over the years. His plate is nearly empty, just lettuce and watermelon, a few green beans. Any armchair psychologist might speculate that the once-promising athlete, in the aftermath of his ordeal, is protecting himself by changing his body, making himself less noticeable. I could be wrong, but the whole vibe—the long, straggly hair, the ill-fitting clothes, the whiff of body odor—seems to be a wall he has built purposefully.

"Did you catch the Giants game on TV last night?" I venture, ignoring Bill Stafford's glare.

Gray doesn't look me in the eye. "I watch all of them." Then he talks about Gorkys Hernández batting leadoff, Johnny Cueto and his hair.

A shadow of the kid he once was is still visible in Gray's strong shoulders and his height, attributes he can't hide no matter how much he tries. His vocabulary and sentence structure, however, are not as finely formed.

"Are you a Warriors fan too?" I ask.

His dad stands abruptly. "Son, let's go."

"What about Ben?" Gray wants to know.

"He's spending the night with James," Lacey replies.

"He should come home with us," Gray says, a note of panic in his voice.

Lacey puts an arm around her son's shoulders. "Your brother will be fine, sweetheart."

Gray stands up and steps off the blanket, holding the paper plate in front of him, as his mother quickly folds the blanket and his father gathers their things.

Gray leans down to pick up a compostable fork that he has let drop to the ground. "You're Rory's mom, right?" he whispers.

"Yes."

There's something haunted and intense in his green eyes. "Rory will be fine."

Or, at least, I think that's what he says. But I can't ask him to repeat himself, because his mother is tugging him away.

I watch them threading their way between the blankets and food trays, this tragic family, every mother and father glancing up at Gray as he passes, some more obvious than others.

* * *

In the car, as we're driving Caroline home, I ask if they have plans for the weekend.

Caroline frowns. "The school has me seeing a math tutor on Saturday, typing tutor all day Sunday, the reading technician Sunday night. That stupid test is all anyone cares about." And then she launches into a tirade against the Wonder Test, the school, and the American system of education. "In France the school system is so rigid, everyone tells me it will be better in America, but c'est la même chose!"

When she's angry, Caroline's French accent becomes even stronger, a bit of French peppered in with the English. She directs me *left* on Forestview, and then *droite* on Oakhurst. Her home sits behind a huge iron gate with brick columns rising up on either side. A mail slot is cut into the left column, above it an engraved gold plate bearing the name Donadieu. As we approach the property, she pulls out her iPhone and presses a few buttons. The imposing gate yawns opens. The wide, tree-lined driveway goes on for half a mile, the trees ultimately giving way to a view of a massive turn-of-the-century stone mansion.

"*This* is your house?" Rory says.

"I know. It's a little, how do you say . . . a little beaucoup."

The house is famous around here. Even by Greenfield standards, it's grand. It was built by the French government for their ambassador more than a century ago. The architecture is stately, the shrubbery indigenous to the French countryside, the clay in the driveway mined in Bordeaux. It was all designed to be a French refuge on the edge of America—to make the ambassador and his family feel at home, even when they weren't.

The house is dark except for a sconce on the porch and a dim yellow light emanating from a corner room on the third floor. A window must be open, because I hear Edith Piaf's "Non, je ne re-grette rien" spilling into the night.

"Someone's home?" I ask.

"Blandine. The house manager. You do *not* want to tangle with Blandine."

Caroline thanks me for the ride, gives Rory *les bises*—left cheek, right cheek, left, plus a peck on the lips—and hops out of the Jeep. As she approaches the porch, the massive front door swings open, and she disappears inside the mansion.

21

A twenty-foot boat is being rowed by ten men, a ten-foot
boat is being rowed by five men, and a twenty-nine-foot
sailboat is being sailed by two women. Which boat is
moving faster and why? Illustrate your answer.

A text message arrives from George: Have to pay my new friend,
can you witness?
　　Am I allowed to do that on LWOP?
　　LeSaffre says yes.
　　When?
　　1 p.m., same bench? BTW this guy knows me as Damien.
　　See you then, Damien.
　　I park on a residential street near Coyote Point and walk the
path toward the meeting spot. Instinctively, I double back twice to
make sure I'm not being followed. The tradecraft is second nature.
You don't just stop looking over your shoulder after sixteen years
in the business. I arrive four minutes early and wait on the bench.
　　At 12:58, I spot George walking toward me with a slender man
in dark slacks. From their body language, I understand that George
has made significant progress in the relationship. As they approach,
the source puts his arm around George's shoulder. George tilts his

head, confiding something. The source smiles. I stand and walk toward them.

"This is my friend Anne," George says.

The man reaches out to shake my hand. Firm handshake, damp palm. "Nice to meet you, Anne. Damien speaks highly of you."

"Likewise."

I feel George slide something surreptitiously into the side pocket of my purse.

"Anne was kind enough to bring something for you," George says.

I reach into my purse and pull out the envelope George just deposited there. From the thickness and weight of the envelope, I can tell it's about five thousand dollars. George and I have done this many times. I open the envelope, pull the blank receipt out, and hand the envelope to George, who passes it to his new friend. The friend quickly slides it into his coat pocket. He does what they always do, some more discreetly than others: runs his hand over the envelope, squeezing to feel the size. The motion is almost imperceptible. He's done this a few times himself.

George gives me a pen and a small notebook. I initial the receipt, using the notebook as a surface, and George does the same. As he gives the pen to his friend, he says to me: "Where are my manners? My friend here is known as Wheeling."

"Yes," the man says, understanding, writing the word "Wheeling" on the source code name line.

For years, George has chosen his source's code names from a poetry anthology he keeps at his desk. As Wheeling folds the paper, I remember others who came before him—Quartet, Raven, Red Wheelbarrow, many others. The source names I devised were more playful: surfing terms suggested by Fred—Over the Falls, Pointbreak—or the names of candy bars no longer in production: Marathon, Hi-Noon. Sometimes you choose a name for someone you think will be a minor source, and seven years later, when you're still in the weeds of a case that won't go away, you wish you'd given it more thought. Maybe one day I'll tell you about Nickel Naks.

I hand George the receipt, nod to his friend. "Thank you, Wheeling."

"No," the man replies in his halting accent. "Thank *you*, Anne."

22

David Bowie once said that it's not who does something first that matters, but rather who does it second. Explain why he was right using historical examples from the hard sciences.

Pedaling through the streets of Greenfield before sunrise, I have a clear purpose beyond the ride and the doughnuts. I pedal all over town, including around the golf course, looking for Mr. Beach. My shirt is drenched in sweat, and I'm about to give up when I get a glimpse of the bushy hair and electric-blue shorts on Forestview.

He's really moving, even faster this time. I hold back, tailing him from afar as he turns up Oakhurst and loops back toward Ripley. I set the stopwatch and odometer on my phone. If he senses me trailing him, he doesn't let on. It's when I'm checking the numbers—a five-minute pace on wet tarmac, uphill, forty-eight-degree weather—that I realize where I know him from.

My father ran track in high school. Even into his sixties, he took regular runs down California Drive to the track at Burlingame High. On Saturdays, he always had the TV tuned to a track meet. Every four years, he'd camp out in the living room and watch the Olympic track and field events. He got me interested in running when I was in high school, long enough to show me I had inherited some of his genes, long enough for me to win a few races. Ultimately, I gave it up, opting for a good bike ride instead.

For years, I listened to his lengthy monologues on the current state of track, absorbed trivia about the latest big star in the mile or 1,500. How many times did I sit side by side with him in our house in San Bruno, kicking back in matching recliners, watching old videotapes of Olympic events and other legendary races? Dave Wottle, Jim Ryun, Lasse Virén. He had them all in a box beside the TV. I bet that box is still around here somewhere.

Why do I tell you this? Because I'm certain that Mr. Beach is not Mr. Beach. Sure, he is Mr. Beach to the students and everyone else in this town, but not to me and not to a smattering of track fans who remember a race from a wet January day in 1983. The Kezar Mile. Maybe you've heard of it.

Before metrics, the mile was *the* race. Arguably the most important track event in history was that day in Oxford, England— May 6, 1954—when Roger Bannister ran the first four-minute mile. An even better race took place months later in Vancouver, the Miracle Mile, when Bannister and his Australian rival, John Landy, met. More than 100 million people listened to the live radio broadcast. On a work trip to Vancouver a couple of years ago, I drove out to the stadium to see the famous statue from the race: Landy in bronze, forever caught looking over his left shoulder while Bannister flew past him on the right, a potent reminder never to lose focus, never to take your eye off the finish line.

Anyway, by 1979, dozens had run a four-minute mile, but no one had done it in San Francisco. So the Golden State Brewing Company planned a race to bring the first four-minute mile to the city by the bay. A one-time, one-off event to promote their new brand of beer. They called the race the Kezar Mile. They offered a huge cash prize, so the race attracted all the big names. But the day of the race, it rained, crazy rain, sideways rain, whipping over the ocean and straight up Irving Street. Because the prize money would only be awarded to a runner who broke four minutes, most of the big-name competitors scratched. There were rumors the company would cancel the event, but the ticket refunds would have been too expensive. They postponed it from 10:00 a.m. to 11:00 a.m. and then to noon, waiting for the storm to let up. It never did. By 3:00 p.m., when the first runners started to gather on the track, most of the crowd was long gone and the remaining few were drenched and shivering.

Just as the race was finally about to start, the organizers discovered that the rabbit they'd hired had disappeared. A rabbit, if you don't know, is paid to set the pace for the real runners, keep things moving, break the wind, help everyone else go faster, and then pull off right before the final lap.

At the last second, some guy steps out of the stands and offers to be the rabbit. The announcers don't even get his name. He has bushy red hair, and he's wearing ripped-up shorts, old waffle trainers, and a T-shirt from Glen Park Hardware. As the cameras pan in on the real runners, you can see they're skeptical of his abilities. The mic even catches one of the announcers asking his cohost: "Is that the rabbit or just some homeless guy?"

But they need a rabbit, and this guy has volunteered, so the organizer puts him out there. When he takes off in a flash, the other runners fall in line behind him. There's the Olympian, Mike Torre, and the Brit, Gavin Telfer, Florent Briand, and this Finnish guy I loathed, Ute Vironnen, with his sharp spikes that came up too high and his sharper elbows that swung far too wide.

My father's video of the race is burned into my memory. When the rabbit is still leading the pack after two straight fifty-nine-second laps, the announcer stops referring to him as the rabbit and starts referring to him by the name on his shirt, Glen Park.

"Glen Park, Ute Vironnen, Mike Torre, Gavin Telfer, Florent Briand, down the back stretch . . ." The announcer was an Irish guy who was famous for his hysterical shouts following soccer goals. To this day, his call of the Kezar Mile is more famous than the race itself—the hyperbole, the screaming, the final home-stretch narration that was used for years in the opening credits of ABC's *Wide World of Sports*. "Glen Park, drenched in rain, the wind threatening to blow these runners off the track, Ute Vironnen, Mike Torre fading, Briand all but washed away in the flood . . ."

As they approach the final lap, their time is surprisingly great, a four-minute mile still possible. Puddles fill the track, wind whips water into the runners' faces, Vironnen and Torre are on Glen Park's shoulders, ready to kick it into high gear, and then a funny thing happens. Glen Park doesn't peel off the track the way the rabbit should. No, he sticks with it. He just keeps going. Vironnen appears confused, and Torre appears dazed, both of them beaten down by the weather. Vironnen starts yelling at Glen Park, but Glen Park keeps running. As they head down the backstretch, Torre and Telfer drop back, and it's just Vironnen and Glen Park, giving it everything they've got.

Vironnen is now visibly angry. Who is this guy, this unknown rabbit who dares to race Finland's single greatest athlete? Vironnen, struggling, pulls around Glen Park to pass. As he's passing, he clips Glen Park in the face with a high, sharp elbow. Blood spurts out of Park's nose and pours down his face, the streams of rain making it look even worse. Blood flows from both sides of his face, scattering out behind him dramatically, painting the track with blood.

At the final turn, Vironnen is a man racing nothing but the clock, aiming for the four-minute purse. What he doesn't realize is that with each step Glen Park is gaining on him, blood still streaming down his face, staining his shirt, his shorts, his beat-up waffle trainers. Incredibly, halfway around the final turn, the mysterious rabbit tucks in just on Vironnen's shoulder. The announcer is going crazy, yelling out the names, the time on the clock, counting it down, the four-minute mile still within reach, despite the crazy conditions, the miserable track, the huge puddles, the insane wind. Vironnen's elbows are punching the air as he pushes out into lanes two and three, trying to stop Glen Park from passing.

And then it happens, just like Bannister's famous moment, immortalized in the bronze statue in Vancouver. Vironnen glances over his shoulder, and Glen Park passes him silently on the inside. His eyes are focused, his feet gliding over the drenched track.

The announcer is screaming, the bad public address system distorting his words beyond recognition. Thirty yards, twenty yards, ten yards. There is no pain on Glen Park's face. No, he looks almost beatific, ecstatic. At the line, the PA system goes out, and there is only a stunned silence, nothing but the sound of rain and wind, and then the sparse crowd out of their seats, screaming, going wild, beers flying, the drenched, faithful fans jumping up and down, surging toward the track.

I'm not sure how I remember the last few steps of the race. Is it from my father's grainy video or the words he used to describe it? His pure awe and disbelief, his sheer joy at the triumph of the common man over the preordained titan of sport. Nothing made him happier, and his elation, every time we watched the video to-gether, filled me with happiness too.

There's a famous photograph. I bought a copy from the archives of the *San Francisco Chronicle* for my father's fifty-fifth birthday. It still hangs on the wall in the living room. Ute Vironnen forever in shock as Glen Park breaks the tape in front of him, the huge num-bers above them displaying the impossible time: 3:57.

But I haven't yet told you the most amazing part of all. At the finish line, Vironnen collapses to the ground, into a puddle, end over end, and medics rush out to help him. Torre and Telfer struggle for third, just over four minutes and painfully out of the money. In the commotion, as the camera focuses in on Vironnen and the doctors surrounding him, one thing escapes the camera's eye: Glen Park.

Back then, without digital cameras and phones, it took nearly a week to locate the footage that showed what actually happened. Glen Park burst through the finish line and just kept going. Some say he even sped up after the race was over, pushing past the view-ers, into the tunnel, straight out of Kezar Stadium, onto Stanyan Street, never to be seen again.

It's one of the greatest mysteries in sports. Glen Park. Who is he, and why did he disappear? Why did he never return to claim the adulation, the trophy, the prize money? Of course, there were theories. He was wanted by the law, he was on some superdrug that eventually killed him. Some say it never happened, that Glen Park is only an urban legend, the story concocted, the footage fake.

The most likely scenario? Glen Park was trying not to be iden-tified in order to maintain his amateur status. At the time, you had to maintain amateur status to qualify for the Olympics. For a young runner, the Olympics was always the ultimate goal. A year or two later anticipation ramped up in the running world, everyone waiting to see if a tall, thin guy with a big red afro would show up at the Olympic time trials. But he never did.

These days, in the ever-shrinking circles of people interested in track and field, the mystery of Glen Park still comes up every now and then. Every year, on the anniversary of the race, a reporter writes a story about that crazy 3:57 mile, complete with a photo of the mystery runner in his bloodied Glen Park T-shirt.

I switch my bike into a higher gear and push forward. The wind in my hair, I feel a flush of exhilaration, freedom, something I haven't felt in a long time. The mysterious runner in front of me is now less than 200 yards away, 150. He picks up his pace, pulling away.

I click one gear higher, head down, closing in. The bike gets quieter, smoother, and steadier, the belt drive system purring, tires clutching the road. I see Fred alone at the computer on the day he ordered the bike. I hear him answering the designer's questions, selecting from dozens of options—hydraulic disc brakes, Rolhoff internal gear hub. Secretly scheming, designing the bike to be better and faster than I could ever need. When it arrived, I ran my hands along the frame, feeling unworthy. I thought I didn't need a bike this good, this strong. Yet somehow Fred knew that I did.

Mr. Beach turns left onto Eucalyptus, around the third fairway, and I pull in close behind him. He's flying gracefully, not even winded, gliding over the quiet streets, ageless, his form unchanged over the decades.

When I pull alongside him, he glances at me, startled, but he doesn't miss a step. In one quick motion he pulls his earbuds out of his ears, nods.

"Morning," I say.

And that's it. Left on Forestview, right on Chateau, up Ralston. I'm flying now, pumping my legs as fast as I can, moving swiftly through the wind and now a light rain, pushing the bike onward, trying to find its limits. Although I move faster and faster, the feeling of exhilaration and freedom fades until it's completely gone.

I want to thank Fred for this brilliant machine, to thank him for knowing me so well, to thank him for loving me.

And I want to tell my father what has just happened. Glen Park, I would say, Glen Fucking Park, in the flesh, right here on Eucalyptus Avenue, right here in our town. And he's still going, never slowing down, never giving up, still steps ahead of Ute Vironnen, still steps ahead of the doubters, the detractors, still running that amazing, unexpected four-minute mile.

23

Insights from Vygotsky's concept of the "zone of proximal development" have been useful to Tiger Woods and the US Department of Education. Why does the Irish potato famine suggest that such insights will be useless in the field of agriculture?

"I spoke with Nicole again," I tell Kyle. We're sitting on the patio behind the house, sipping coffee. "She remembered something else."

"What, she just suddenly had a flash of insight?"

"Maybe it took a little prompting."

"What did she remember?"

"A swimmer in a red cap and a crab boat way off in the distance. The swimmer is probably a woman, fast in the water."

"So Gray Stafford *did* come from the water."

"I think so."

He leans back in his chair, gazing at the canyon. "Do you know how cold that water is? The riptide is a beast. Not to mention sharks."

"Does the red cap ring a bell?"

He shakes his head. "I've got nothing."

With the new information, we have two potential leads to chase down, the swimmer or the boat. Personally, I like the swimmer. No real reason, just instinct.

Kyle leans the other way. "My money's on a crab boat. Most of them dock at Pillar Point Harbor."

"Want to check it out?" I feel myself pulling the threads, drifting further into the case, against my better judgment.

"Definitely." But then he checks his watch, smacks his hand on the table. "Shit. I've got to be at East School in seventeen minutes for some PTA thing."

"They're really keeping you busy with the Mayberry stuff, huh?"

"An officer retired last week. With the personnel shortage, Chief Jepson insists we'll need to focus more on presence and less on investigations."

"Seems like a waste of talent."

Kyle doesn't respond, but I can tell the compliment pleases him. "Some other time," I say. "Mind if I do a little digging on the swimmer?"

"Hell, no. That would be awesome." He stands to leave.

"I should probably tell you I talked to someone else."

"Who?"

"Gray Stafford. Met him at movie night. I met the parents too, sort of."

His eyes widen in surprise. "They let you talk to him?"

"They didn't want me to. They whisked him away pretty quickly."

"The family therapist warned Mr. and Mrs. Stafford that talking to investigators too much could impede Gray's recovery. We did two brief interviews with him, and then they shut us down, said he'd told us everything he knew."

"Gray said something strange. At least I think he did."

"What's that?"

"He said, 'Rory will be fine.'"

"What's that supposed to mean?"

"I don't know, but it was unsettling. Why *wouldn't* he be fine?"

Competitive female swimmer, red swim cap. Not much to go on, but it's something. After Kyle leaves, I google "Bay Area swim teams," but the results are for high schools. Intramural and college teams are a better starting point. I think about the local colleges and their colors. Berkeley is blue, SF State is purple, Santa Cruz doesn't do sports. Then it occurs to me that Stanford's official color is cardinal red. I do an image search, disappointed to discover the Stanford swim team cap is white, emblazoned with a red S.

I search "Half Moon Bay swim team," but I only get pictures of a high school swim meet. The school colors are orange and green. I try the other towns along the coast: Pescadero, nothing; San Gregorio, nothing; Moss Beach, no luck.

My search for "El Granada swim team" brings up an article about the annual Escape from Alcatraz Triathlon. Every June, two thousand athletes begin the triathlon with the grueling 1.5-mile swim from Alcatraz to Marina Green in San Francisco. For decades, the myth prevailed that no one could escape the infamous prison because the bay is too cold, the currents too strong, the sharks too plentiful. Yet now, every year, thousands of people voluntarily make the swim in a series of popular races.

The article mentions a woman from El Granada who won the swim portion of the triathlon seven years ago. There's a photograph of her in the bay, facing the shore, one arm out of the water, one arm in. The photo was taken seconds before she won the race. She's wearing a white bathing cap. Behind her, however, beneath the splashing water, I count three red dots, neck and neck.

I scan the rest of the article but find no mention of the swimmers who won second, third, and fourth place. I search for the race results from that year, women's division. There she is, first place, the words "Montara Swim Team" beside her name, followed by an incredibly fast time. Beneath hers, three other nearly identical times are listed, but they're not identified by name or city. Instead, it says "Dolphin Club." Bingo.

24

Many older cities are built at the base of a mountain. Is this a wise model for modern city planners to emulate? Support your argument with two quotes from Italo Calvino's *Invisible Cities* and one example from John Summerson's *Heavenly Mansions and Other Essays on Architecture*.

Caroline rings the doorbell at 9:45 p.m., unannounced. Wearing jeans, a plain black sweater, and bright-white sneakers, she somehow manages to look chic and very French. The word "effortless" comes to mind.

"Sorry it's so late," she says. "I got stuck at school. Kobayashi brought in a guy from LA to meet with my study group."

"A tutor?"

"No, more like a motivational speaker. He's an Olympic pole-vaulting champion who visits schools and corporations to tell people how to be better, faster, smarter versions of themselves."

"Sounds expensive."

"Harris Ojai paid his fee. He pays for *lots* of stuff at the school."

That would explain the banner surplus of funds this year. Maybe Ojai isn't all bad.

"Rory's in the library."

From the hallway, I hear the kids talking. "How'd the indoctrination go?" Rory asks.

"Endless. Embarrassing. Boring."

Caroline does an impression of the speaker, her soft voice transforming into a gruff baritone with a heavy Southern drawl. "The Wonder Test, kids, is nothing more than a glass of water. And you are a packet of Alka-Seltzer, little fizzy tablets, bubbly magic. You gotta rip that packet open and drop those fizzy tablets into the water, feel the magic, be the magic!" she bellows.

Rory is laughing—long, genuine, careless laughter—the way he used to before Fred died. It's a beautiful sound, all too rare these days. Later, Rory comes barreling down the stairs, Caroline on his heels. "Do we have any art supplies?" he wants to know.

"Poster board, markers?" Caroline chimes in. "Tomorrow is the student government election. I talked Rory into running for minister general."

"What exactly does the minister general do?"

"We'll find out when he wins."

"There's money in my purse," I tell Rory. "Walk down to Walgreens and get whatever you need."

When I drop Rory off at school the next morning, his signs line the breezeway. While the signs for other candidates are sleek and professional, with four-color printing on giant banners, Rory's are just block letters drawn with marker on neon poster board:

RORY FOR MINISTER GENERAL

BRING BACK THE CANDY!

"What do you have in there?" I ask Rory, pointing to his bulging backpack. "A body?"

"Twix, Snickers, and Swedish Fish."

"Buying votes. I approve! Not original but effective."

"'Bring back the candy' was Caroline's idea. They banned candy from the cafeteria last year because the current minister general, Sophie Parker, is a food Nazi."

"Is she your only competition?"

"No. There's also Dopey Barrett, but he can't win. Everybody hates him."

Caroline is standing in front of the breezeway, handing out candy. As Rory walks toward her, a boy with bright blond hair comes up alongside Rory and slaps him on the back. "Dude, I'm so voting for you."

25

Proponents of inexperienced candidates who win a major political election often argue their candidate will grow into the job over time. If the term is for four years and, by month thirty-one, the elected official has shown no signs of improvement, what are the chances said official will be prepared for the job by the time his or her term ends?

I drive to San Francisco, park at Marina Green, and wander through Fort Mason to Aquatic Park. I love the way it smells here, seawater and fish, both rank and pleasant at the same time. My parents used to bring me to Fort Mason on summer days when it got too hot on the peninsula. Sometimes I wonder if the happiness of those days was a mirage, if my mom was just pretending, biding her time until she could leave, start her real life far from us.

The side of a two-story white clapboard building is marked with a boat-and-oars insignia and the words DOLPHIN CLUB—ESTABLISHED 1877. The door is locked. I ring the bell, wait, ring again. The door opens. A leathery-skinned woman with broad shoulders fills the doorway. "Need something?"

"I'm interested in joining. May I have a look around?"

"Come back tomorrow. Fridays are members-only days."

She's already shutting the door in my face when I ask, "How do I become a member?"

"We accept new members four times a year. Next application period is in two months."

I walk around the back of the building to the beach, a narrow spit of sand abutting Aquatic Park Cove. I kick off my sandals and dip my feet into the frigid water. A few dozen yards from shore, a lone swimmer floats faceup, arms akimbo, a thick patch of gray hair covering his barrel chest like a pelt.

What am I doing here? Maybe I'm wasting my time, trying to distract myself from the tasks at hand: combing through all of my father's things, coming up with a plan, deciding when to go home—if New York really is even home anymore. In this state of limbo, it's too easy for grief and anxiety to set in. I prefer dwelling on outside problems rather than my own. The complex counterintelligence cases served as a kind of refuge long before Fred died. Few of us make it to adulthood without a few demons to stuff in the closet. I think of my mother, that old wound, and how the work gave me focus, purpose, a family I could count on.

I go back to the car and sit, radio off, windows down. I feel empty, directionless. It's an awful feeling. I've been many things in my life—ambitious, obsessed, even reckless—but until recently, I've never been directionless. Fred and I always had a plan. We set goals for every phase of our lives: marriage, work, parenthood, vacations, Rory's college, our retirement. In addition to personal goals, I always had at least half a dozen cases going at work. Until now, I was always making progress in at least one area of my life. I always had forward motion, something to look forward to. I loathe stasis, this feeling that I'm going nowhere.

Without warning, the tears come, slowly at first, then gushing. I rummage in the glove compartment for tissues, but who am I kidding? It was Fred who stocked the glove compartment with tissues and other sundries. I used up the last of them months ago.

A guy pushing a Bugaboo stroller down the sidewalk is staring. He looks both ways and crosses the street. Then he's standing by the Jeep, gazing through the driver's side window. Warm brown skin, two-day beard, Zendesk hoodie. "Are you okay?"

"I'm fine, thanks, just allergies."

What's a guy with a baby doing checking on a strange, sobbing woman in a car? For a moment professional paranoia kicks in, and I wonder who sent him. Then I see a movement in the stroller, a furry head peeking up. It isn't a baby but a miniature schnauzer.

"This is Miranda." He turns the stroller so I can get a better look. "I got her in the divorce. Then she got a fibrocartilaginous embolism, so now I drive a stroller."

"Sorry about that."

"The divorce or the embolism?"

"Both. I hope she's not in pain."

"No, she's blissfully medicated. She'll be fine in a couple of weeks. So, this is abrupt, but do you want to grab a glass of wine sometime?"

"Thanks, but I'm—" I was about to say I'm married, but I'm not, am I? "My husband—"

He glances at my left hand on the steering wheel. "Oh, right, sorry, didn't see the ring at first."

"Don't be sorry. It was a nice gesture. Woman sobbing in the car and all."

"So it's not allergies?"

"Nope."

"If it's any comfort, I sobbed in the car a few times after the divorce."

"And now?"

"Now I use a dog in a stroller to pick up women, so . . ."

"How often does it work?"

"About half the time?"

"If we run into each other again," I say, "will you give it one more shot?"

"That's a promise."

I smile, start the car, and pull away. In the rearview mirror, I take one last look. He's ridiculously good-looking in that casual San Francisco way. The dog is cute. Fred would find it hilarious: the first guy who asks me out after my husband dies is pushing a dog through the Marina District in a thousand-dollar stroller.

On the way home, I activate voice text and send a message to George on the encrypted app. Ever heard of the Dolphin Club?

Swimming? he texts back. Good for you, clear your head.

No, it's about the kid. Caught a thread.

Give me a minute.

I'm cresting Skyline when he texts again. Membership at the Dolphin Club is tough. Long waiting list, but I have a friend. He'll give you a tour Saturday, says you have to swim with him beforehand. 5:30 a.m. His name is Timofey.

5 WHAT?

Good luck!

More than I bargained for. Typical George. I just wanted to get into the clubhouse to have a look around, ask questions. I never intended to actually swim in the bay. Although I'm tempted to cancel, I resolve to take Timofey up on his offer. What's the worst that could happen? Death, I suppose, by drowning or maybe even sharks. I could be dragged out to sea, screaming, bleeding, embarrassed. To be honest, even that doesn't worry me. I've never feared death, but I do fear leaving Rory alone.

One last text comes in from George. I'll be in town again next week. Can you witness? Same place. Monday. 1:30 p.m.

I'll be there.

At pickup, I glean from the fake smile on Rory's face that the election didn't go in his favor. He climbs into the front seat, Caroline into the back.

"That jerk Dopey Barrett!" Caroline blurts before the doors are even closed.

"No big deal," Rory says, but I can tell he's disappointed.

"It doesn't make sense," Caroline protests. "I polled more than thirty students, and I couldn't find a single person who voted for Dopey."

"People lie," Rory says, "especially in exit polls."

"No, there's something else going on," Caroline insists. "Something fishy. I hate that kid." She takes on an upper-crusty accent, "On my passport, it reads Edward Douglas Barrett, but you can call me Dougie. If you need me, you can find me up Superintendent Kobayashi's ass."

I catch Caroline's eye in the rearview mirror. "You think the election was fixed?"

"Definitely. But that's not even the big news of the day." She taps Rory on the shoulder. "Tell your mom what Gray said in gym class."

He shoots her a look, like maybe he wasn't planning on telling me right away.

"*Tell* her."

"First of all, he said you interrogated him at movie night. Not cool, Mom."

"I wouldn't exactly call it an interrogation. We talked about the Giants. What else did he say?"

"Gray said to tell you he's not going to be the last one."

"What?"

"He looked at me in this crazy way and said, 'There will be others.' But the way he said it, I couldn't tell if he was for real. I thought he might just be messing with me because you were all up in his business."

"What does your gut tell you?"

"All I know for sure is that kid is messed up."

26

True or false: rare earth minerals are neither rare
nor mineral.

At 5:15 a.m. on Saturday, I pull into the near-empty parking lot at Aquatic Park, strip off my sweatshirt and sweatpants, struggle into the wet suit I rented yesterday at the surf shop in Burlingame, and walk over to the beach behind the Dolphin Club. I dip a toe in and shudder. I detest the cold.

George's friend Timofey turns out to be a fit, muscular Russian guy in his sixties. His two friends are younger Americans, one bald, one bearded. Timofey wears two rings on his left hand. I suspect one ring represents a family back home, abandoned though not forgotten. Next time, I'll ask George how they met. The few other agents with George's rare talents refer to their counterintelligence sources as targets, recruitments, even conquests, but for George, they are all simply friends.

"You are as lovely as the picture George painted for me," Timofey says. In the thick wet suit, "lovely" is a stretch, but I thank him anyway. Russian men of his age, in our business, have a natural ability to charm.

I hold up the long fins I rented with the suit. "Is this cheating?"

"Not if they keep you alive, my dear."

His friends and I exchange brief, silent nods. I struggle into my fins, and we wade into the freezing water. The three men are smiling, enlivened by the cold. My feet and hands are instantly numb. When I put my face to the water and plunge in, the water shakes my brain awake, and I lift my head, gasping as the salt water burns my nose. We swim and swim and swim, farther than I've ever gone before into the bay. The water is choppy. I struggle to keep the pace. I fall behind. I catch up. I'm nervous about drowning, more nervous about sharks and boats. My legs are aching, my face freezing. Every stroke is a challenge, and I'm tempted to turn around and go back when I raise my head and see the three of them treading water, waiting for me.

As I swim in closer, arms burning, I take a moment to get my bearings. I kick myself up higher to get a view over the swells, lungs tight with the cold. I see Alcatraz in front of me, the Golden Gate Bridge on one side, the Bay Bridge on the other. I try to focus on why I'm here: Gray. Is it possible that he did some of the swimming himself while the swimmer with the red cap towed him through the water? He was a star athlete before the kidnapping. In his condition, would he have been able to kick and hold his head above water? When he was found, he was naked. But surely the kidnappers didn't throw him into the bay naked. How could he have survived the cold? The Polar Bears do it, of course, and so do many of the experienced open water swimmers who brave the journey from The Rock, so it's possible, but Gray was already in such a weakened state.

I swim up beside Timofey and his friends, panting, trying not to panic, trying not to think of the billion gallons of water that pour straight out of the bay twice a day underneath the Golden Gate and into the wild Pacific. I hope low tide isn't anytime soon.

"Unfuckingbelievable," the bearded guy says to Timofey, as I join their circle.

"These are my old friends Bobby and Luther," Timofey says. "And this is my new friend Lina."

"What was unfuckingbelievable?"

"The shark. Have you ever seen anything like it?"

"Shark?" I echo. The two friends burst out laughing, and I realize they're messing with me.

"You'll pay for that," I shoot back, grinning.

We tread water. My lungs fill with cold, clear air. "So, how do you like it?" Timofey asks. "Swimming so early in the morning in this beautiful bay. Is good for the soul, yes?"

"I'm not sure that's how I'd describe it," I pant. But the icy water does make me feel strangely alive, shocked to alertness. I see how you could get addicted to the swim, the smell, the weight of the water against your legs.

Timofey motions back toward shore. "Let's introduce Lina to the Dolphin sauna."

The return swim feels endless, each stroke more difficult than the last. I keep looking up, expecting to see the shore fast approaching, but it never seems to get any closer. I fall into a rhythm of exhaustion, the pain giving way to numbness, my vision adjusting to the murky water splashing against my goggles. This is a thousand times harder than cycling.

I feel it before I see it—the sandy bottom brushing against my legs. Relieved, I drag myself up onshore.

Timofey extends his hand to help me stand. "Good workout, yes?"

"Wonderful. Now how about that sauna?"

I follow them up the beach. Bobby and Luther exchange hugs with Timofey before disappearing through the back door of the clubhouse. Timofey leads me toward the women's locker room. The same woman who turned me away a few days ago is standing outside the door, ruddy cheeked after her swim. "Good morning, Margaret," Timofey says. "I realize it's members-only day, but this is my dear friend Lina. I'm sure you'll make her feel welcome."

Margaret beams at Timofey. It's a total transformation from her surliness the first time we met. "Take as long as you like. Wander around. Clean towels over there. No bathing suits in the sauna, please."

I thank her. My legs are still jelly, struggling to hold me upright.

Timofey pats my cheek with the palm of his hand. His attention feels paternal, comforting. "Please, make yourself at home. We swim every Monday, Wednesday, and Saturday. Same time, same place. Join us anytime. If you would like to become member of club, I make this happen. For you, no waiting period."

"Thank you, Timofey. You're a doll."

He takes my hand, holds it between both of his, as if we are old, dear friends. "Until next time, Lina." I imagine that whatever he did before he met George, in whatever capacity he worked for his country, his natural charm paid off in spades and made him dangerously good at his job.

The locker room is clean and smells of chlorine and shampoo. The blue metal lockers and tile floors probably haven't changed since the 1920s. There's still a pay phone on the wall outside the locker rooms. Old San Francisco is getting harder and harder to find these days, but this club is a reminder it still exists. I hang my wet suit on a hook, wrap the thin towel around me, and wander into the empty sauna. I love the smell of the sauna—cedar and heat. I scoop some water onto the rocks and the room fills with steam. The bay has frozen me to the core, and the heat feels like heaven. As my body slowly thaws, I drift off, thinking about Gray, the woman in the red bathing cap, the trawler, trying to fit the puzzle pieces together in my mind.

I don't know how many minutes have passed when I hear a hiccup. I open my eyes to realize a woman is sitting on the lower bench opposite me, legs and arms splayed, staring at me unabashedly. How long has she been here? How did I not hear the door? She's ginger-haired, blue-eyed, attractive in a sturdy Viking way. The thin layer of fat covering her from head to toe and those broad shoulders tell me she's a competitive swimmer.

"The boys sure worked you out this morning. I saw you out there. Awesome. A shark too? You should become a member. We need more women."

"So there really was a shark. I thought they were messing with me."

She winks. "There are always sharks."

"I'm Lina."

"Christine."

Christine is thirty-eight, a dermatologist at Kaiser. I ask about the club, the swimming, and eventually steer the conversation in the direction I want it to go. It takes a lot of conversational gymnastics to get us there, but eventually I ask, "Does anyone in the Dolphin Club wear a red bathing cap?"

"That's random," she says. "I have a bunch of them in my locker. You can always borrow one."

"You have red ones?"

"No. They do have some neon-green ones at the commissary, though. Safer, more visible to the sailboats. It gets crowded in the late summer."

"A college friend of mine had a red one. She told me it was a special Dolphin Club thing."

"Hmmm." She studies me with her frank expression. "Did she? I haven't seen that. We did sponsor a swim team from Half Moon Bay for a while. They wore red. That was years ago, though. Funding has been sparse lately."

I make a mental note to check out the Half Moon Bay swim team. Maybe it's nothing, but maybe it's something.

After the sauna, I stand on the deck and take in the view one last time, enjoying the cool air on my skin. Out in the bay, cargo ships move along the shipping channel. The kayakers bobbing in the waves look so small, so vulnerable. And this is only the bay. I think of Gray Stafford in the open ocean. I think of the woman in the red bathing cap. I think of what Gray told Rory in gym class: *There will be others.*

27

The recipe for chocolate chip cookies requires 2.25 cups flour, 0.75 cups sugar, 0.875 cups brown sugar, 1 teaspoon baking soda, and 1 teaspoon salt, to yield thirty-one cookies. If you only had three measuring instruments—one cup, one half cup, and one teaspoon—what is the fewest number of cookies you could accurately make? If you made forty-eight cookies, how would the taste differ from a batch of thirty-one?

On Sunday evening, Rory and I relax in the lounge chairs behind the house. The sun is setting, mist settling over the trees. An aircraft is idling on the runway at SFO, the roar of the engines echoing down the canyon. I'm posting items for sale and for free on Greenfield-Neighbors.org. Rory is reading *Martin in Space*, but he's distracted, his eyes darting back and forth between the book and his phone.

"Read me something," I say.

Rory flips to a dog-eared page and reads aloud: "The dial on the control panel spins endlessly, the pinprick of green light bouncing right and left and back again, scanning for a signal, a radio wave, a sign of life. I search for my own center, my anchor, a clear point of reference, but I find only boundless space."

His next question surprises me. "Do you ever feel that way?"

I think about it for a moment. "Sometimes. Do you?"

He lays the book facedown on his knee. "Yes, ever since Dad died. It's like Dad was the anchor for our family, and now we're just sort of floating."

It feels like an opening to a deeper conversation. I want to reassure him, to promise we won't be floating forever. But before I can respond, Rory checks his phone again and mutters, "This is so weird. Caroline was supposed to come over tonight. I texted her three hours ago, but she didn't respond. She always texts right back."

I close my laptop. "I'm sure she's just busy."

"No, she had her final Wonder practice test today."

"On a Sunday?"

"She had one yesterday too. She was supposed to text me on her walk home today. We had plans to watch a movie."

"The test probably went long."

"Impossible. Nothing about the test ever goes long or short. Everything is precise. Nothing is left to chance. If any teacher went off script today, especially with Caroline's group, they'd have to answer to Kobayashi."

"What do you mean, especially with Caroline's group?"

"She's struggling to improve her score. Which tells you how arbitrary the test is. She's one of the smartest kids I know."

"Why is today so important?"

"Mom, what planet are you on? The Wonder Test starts tomorrow. We have it every day this week, then again on Monday and Tuesday of next week. Haven't you read any of the emails from Kobayashi?"

I groan. "What did I miss, aside from the date?"

"I'm supposed to be taking omega-3 supplements, eating high-protein, high-fiber breakfasts before school every day, and sleeping at least ten hours a night."

"Sorry, I'll make you an omelet for breakfast tomorrow. We must have some omega-3 supplements around somewhere. Grandpa was really into vitamins."

"Those regular brands are crap according to Kobayashi. He wants us to take a proprietary blend, the Wonder Pill, which was created by a neuroscientist whose kid graduated from the school."

"That sounds unethical," I say. "Bordering on illegal." Still, I feel guilty. Have I put Rory at a disadvantage by not keeping up with these details? "I'll start opening the emails, I promise."

"Don't worry about it. Kobayashi means well, but he's obsessive. Actually, the pill makes kids break out. Most of them just throw it away." He types into his phone again, frowning.

I weigh my words before suggesting, "You might want to give Caroline some space."

Rory wrinkles his brow, bewildered. "Why?"

"Girls need space."

"Not Caroline. She says it's different in France. She says when you go out with someone, you're exclusive."

"So she really is your girlfriend?"

"Mom, yes, she's my girlfriend, okay? Can we stop talking about it?"

"Okay, no more questions, I promise." I mime zipping my lips. "Want to make chocolate chip cookies?"

"Sure," he says, glancing at his phone one more time before sliding it into his pocket.

* * *

The cookies were Fred's specialty. He made them almost every week, tweaking the recipe, experimenting with different brands and ingredients, different temperatures and cooking times, different pans. It was an obsession for him, a kind of Zen meditation. In the weeks after his death, the mere smell of chocolate chip cookies brought me to tears. For more than a month, I didn't dare bake.

Then, one weekend when the kitchen was empty, save for Fred's cabinet filled with high-priced vanilla powder and muscovado, Rory suggested we try to re-create the recipe. As the first batch came out of the oven, I felt a blip of joy. It felt almost as if Fred were there cheering us on. Since then, we've made the cookies once a week. We don't go to church, and we don't go to therapy. At my insistence, Rory did try therapy after Fred died, but it made him uncomfortable. It felt false, he said, a violation rather than a consolation. He didn't want to dwell on the sadness. So we make cookies. It works for us. It's a way to honor Fred, to keep him with us.

Between cracking eggs and measuring and stirring, Rory keeps checking his phone.

"Did you argue?" I ask.

"No, we talked on Snapchat this morning before she left home. She was in a great mood. She told me she's been really happy lately." He blushes. "She said *I* make her happy."

That does sound serious.

"Maybe she lost her phone."

"Caroline doesn't lose things. She doesn't need space. She doesn't play games. She's not like that."

The first batch of cookies comes out. While I'm transferring them to the cooling rack, Rory polishes off three warm cookies and a glass of milk. I put the second batch in.

"Does Caroline have a group of friends she hangs out with?"

"No, just me."

"Where does she go when you're not together and she's not at school?"

"She takes walks around town, sometimes she goes for a run at Crocker Lake. She always texts me, like, a dozen times while she's out walking, and she posts tons of pictures on Instagram. She also tells me if she's going to the lake, just so someone will know where she is."

"She tells you instead of her parents?"

"They never have a clue where she is. They're totally absentee." He swipes the screen of his phone again and looks at me, helpless.

"Want me to drive you by her place?"

28

Is it better to do the right thing for the wrong reason or the wrong thing for the right reason? Using diacritical logic, chart your answer.

"How are you feeling about the test?" I ask as we pull out of the driveway.

"Good. I finally figured it out this week. Every question has two answers, the correct answer and the answer the test wants. Sometimes, the two are the same, but not always. You have to fight the urge to give the answer that's technically more correct than the answer they want."

"That sounds like a nightmare."

"Not if you think of it like a game. They use AI to grade it. AI, at its heart, is just an algorithm, so if you can figure out the algorithm, you can beat the test. Every answer doesn't have to be correct. It just needs to *sound* correct and be organized logically. And there are tricks."

"Such as?"

"Using the word 'thing,' for example, gets you docked 1.4 points, but using the word 'preponderance' adds 2.2 points. The basic rules of essay writing apply: work from general to specific, use examples, insert quotes whenever you can. But in the case of the Wonder Test, more obscure quotes are better. So you'll get more points for a Mozi quote than a Confucius quote. Montaigne is better than Mother Teresa but worse than Heraclitus, that sort of thing."

"Who's Mozi?"

"His main idea was that disorder in society is the result of the absence of mutual love. So if we could love groups of people who are unlike ourselves, order would be restored."

"I like this Mozi fellow. What class is that from?"

"No class. I learned it on YouTube. Anyway, there are more tricks. Like compound-complex sentences are good, but sometimes the data conflicts. So, for example, you can override the automatic deduction for too many simple sentences if you use repetition correctly."

"If they teach you all that, why doesn't everyone ace it?"

"Not everyone has the patience, but also, they don't teach us all that. I got a little obsessed, so I did research. Any student can log into the portal to see the anonymous results of every practice test for your district. I spent hours reading the answers and analyzing how they're scored. I wanted to figure out how to *think* like the AI. Of course, the AI is always evolving. The right answer this month won't be the right answer next month."

"Impressive. So why aren't you tutoring Caroline?"

"I tried, but mandatory test prep takes up most of her time. Anyway, she's French. We get about five minutes in and then she protests the injustice of it all. She threatened to show up on testing day in a yellow vest."

"You've gone and gotten a revolutionary for a girlfriend. Dad would be proud."

"Unfortunately, school isn't designed for revolutionaries." Rory rolls down his window. "Sometimes I think the goal of school is to take a bunch of kids and herd them into the middle. Catch the stragglers, slow down the leaders, get everyone in line. Make sure everyone writes the same, talks the same, and thinks the same."

"That's harsh."

"But it's true! Tell me one real thing you learned in school. Not how to diagram a sentence. Something *useful.*"

I slow down for a tiny gray-haired lady in tennis whites and copious gold jewelry walking three giant poodles down Barroilhet.

"Never sit in the front row if you want other kids to like you," I say. "Never sit in the back row if you want the teacher to like you. Raise your hand often enough to show you're listening but not so often that you look like a know-it-all. Smile but not too big. Laugh but not too loud. Make allies in every social group. Identify the mean kids, and don't be their friend but don't be their enemy either. Be open, don't be a cynic, let the readings and lectures wash over you. The important knowledge will take root and the detritus will drift away."

I glance over to see Rory staring at me. "You're smarter than you look, Mom."

"I hope you were taking notes. That was some of my best material."

We wind through lower Greenfield. On Ralston, a family of four is loading suitcases into a Range Rover. Rory cranes his neck to look. "That's strange. Why are Marc Rekowski and his family packing to leave the night before the Wonder Test?"

"Maybe they don't care about the test."

"They definitely care. Marc has had a tutor since the beginning of the school year. He takes the mandatory study class with Caroline."

"Maybe they arranged for him to make the test up."

"Nobody makes it up. You're either there or not there."

When we pull up to Caroline's estate, Rory jumps out of the car and punches a code into the keypad. The gate opens and he runs ahead of the car down the driveway. As I approach the house, I see a lone light burning in a corner room on the third floor, the same light that was on the first time we dropped her off.

My mind flashes to the first arrest and search warrant I ever went out on. It was an estate in Westchester, New York, similar to this one. I remember a long hallway flanked by half a dozen doors. The house was huge, and our arrest team was small. Standing before the first door in the hallway, I kept yelling, "Need one!" But the team had already dispersed, and no one came. I took a deep breath and burst into the room. It was a teenager's bedroom. There were clothes on the floor and a single book on the shelf, *The Worst-Case Scenario Handbook.* For some reason, the presence of that particular book on an otherwise empty shelf struck me as terribly sad. I had the strange sensation I would experience dozens of times over the ensuing years: the sense of having walked into the middle of someone else's life, at once exposed and secret.

By the time I park and get out of the car, Rory is already ringing the doorbell. It chimes through the house, orchestral and grand. When no one answers, he grasps the giant iron knocker and bangs on the door—once, twice, three times.

"Rory," I say. "Manners."

He waits a minute before pounding on the doorbell again.

The light from the third-floor bedroom begins to spread, window to window, across the third floor, then down to the second, to the foyer. The exterior sconces illuminate, and the heavy door opens to reveal a trim, middle-aged woman in a navy uniform, slightly out of breath. Caroline said her name is Blandine. The house, her uniform, the way her chestnut hair is wound tightly upon her head give the impression we've stepped back in time.

She glances at Rory, registers recognition, and addresses me. "Bonsoir, Madame."

"Bonsoir, Madame," I reply. "Excusez-moi de vous déranger."

"Puis-je vous aider?"

"Oui, merci. Vous êtes la directrice de la maison?"

She nods, suspicious.

"Je suis la mère de Rory," I say, gesturing at my son. "On cherche Caroline. Est-elle ici?"

"Non," she says, pursing her lips.

I ask if Caroline came home after the practice test today.

She glances at her watch, as if I've already taken too much of her time. "Peut-être, non."

I ask if Blandine knows where we might find her.

"Je ne sais pas."

I ask if I may speak to Monsieur et Madame Donadieu.

"Ils sont absents."

I ask how I might reach them.

"Je ne sais pas."

Finally, realizing I'll get nowhere with Blandine, I thrust a business card into her hand with my personal cell number written on the back. "S'il vous plait, telephonez moi quand Caroline retourne."

Usually, the FBI calling card makes an impression. Not so with Blandine. "Bien sûr, Madame." With that, she closes the door. I can hear her heels echoing on marble floors. The lights go off, one by one, in the same order they went on minutes ago.

Rory stares at me, dumbfounded. "What was that, Mom? Since when do you speak French?"

"Remember when you were five and I worked in Tunisia for a couple of months?"

"No."

"Well, I did. They gave me some Berlitz tapes before I left. I used to listen to them in the car on the way to work. Traffic on the West Side Highway is no joke. I spent *a lot* of time with those tapes."

"So what did she say?"

As soon as we're in the car, doors closed, I translate. "Caroline never came home after the practice test today. Her parents are away. Do you know if they're still in Vienna?"

"No, Caroline says they go on work trips a lot." The massive gate opens as we approach. "Back to France, but other places too, somewhere in North Africa. Always out of the country. Sometimes she doesn't even know where they are and has no way to reach them."

The gate closes behinds us. "I thought you said he was the consul general."

"Maybe the first consul?"

"There's a big difference between consul general and first consul, especially a first consul and wife who go on lengthy, ill-defined trips."

He frowns. "Could Caroline be in some sort of international trouble or something?"

"No. My point is that an unexplained absence isn't surprising, considering her father's position."

"Okay, but if she had to leave, she'd *tell* me. She wouldn't just disappear."

Of course, it's possible Caroline just found a new friend to hang out with and didn't want to hurt Rory's feelings. Or maybe her parents called and told her to go to the airport and meet them in Paris or somewhere else. But if that were the case, wouldn't Blandine have seen the driver pick her up? If Caroline is constantly texting Rory, wouldn't she have texted to let him know she was leaving?

It doesn't feel right. Something else is nagging at me: the timing of the Rekowskis' getaway. We drive back by their house. They're just about to pull out of the driveway. I stop the Jeep, blocking their way. Mr. Rekowski honks the horn.

"Mom, what the hell?" Rory hisses, ducking down in the seat.

"Just sit tight."

I get out of the Jeep and approach the driver's side of the Range Rover. Mr. Rekowski rolls down the window, clearly annoyed. Mrs. Rekowski leans over the middle console. "Can we help you?" Her tone is polite, not entirely friendly.

Two kids are in the back seat. The younger one, a girl of about twelve, is on her iPad. The boy from Rory's grade, Marc, is scrolling through his phone.

"Sorry to bother you. I'm Lina Connerly. My son, Rory, is in tenth grade at the school."

The mother manages a smile. "Nice to meet you. Actually, it's not a great time. We're just on our way out, going to spend a week in Dubai."

"Sorry, it's just, we're looking for a friend of Rory's, Caroline." I speak directly to Marc. "She was in the practice test with you today, right?"

Marc glances up from his phone. "Yes."

"Has something happened to Caroline?" Mrs. Rekowski asks, a note of genuine concern in her voice.

"Rory can't find her, and he's worried. He thought Marc might have seen where she went after school. Her parents are out of the country."

Mr. Rekowski addresses his son in the rearview mirror. "Did you see Caroline at the practice test?"

"Yeah. When I left school she was in the breezeway, arguing with some lady. She seemed upset."

"Could you tell what she was upset about?" I ask.

"The lady told Caroline not to come to school tomorrow, to skip the whole week."

Mrs. Rekowski turns around to look at Marc. "They were trying to *prevent* her from taking the test?"

"Looked that way."

"How did Caroline respond?" I ask.

"She was pissed. She said she'd been working really hard and she was going to take the test, no matter what. The lady said that wasn't a great idea. That's all I heard. I just wanted to get home and pack."

"Did you recognize the woman?" I ask.

"I couldn't tell. Blonde, tall."

His little sister speaks without glancing up from her iPad. "That describes half of the moms at the school."

"Are they going to let you to make up the test?" I ask.

"No makeups. They're super strict about that. I only took the practice test today to get an extra excused absence."

Mr. Rekowski adjusts the rearview mirror, eager to get on his way.

"Just one more question. Did Kobayashi give you a hard time about being absent for test week?"

It's Mrs. Rekowski who answers. "Actually, I was pleasantly surprised. When this opportunity came up for a family trip, they were completely understanding. I'm sure Caroline is fine. She's probably just being a teenager." She glances at the dashboard clock. "Sorry, but we really do need to catch our flight."

I thank them for their time, wish them a great trip, and move the Jeep out of the way.

"I can't believe you did that!" Rory says, still trying to cover his face. "That's so embarrassing."

I sit with my hands on the steering wheel, frowning. "Marc claims he saw a woman trying to convince Caroline not to take the test."

"What do you mean? Who?"

"Could it have been Caroline's mom?" I wonder out loud.

"I'm telling you, her parents have been gone for weeks." Rory cranes his head to watch the Rekowskis pull out of the driveway. "All this work, all this preparation, and now they don't want her to take the test? *Why?*"

29

From the perspective of Adam Smith, construct an argument for restoring the gold standard. Restrict you answer to 114 words or fewer.

We drive back to the school and search the campus. Rounding a corner, we nearly bump into Kobayashi. "It's our very own Wonder Test whisperer!" he exclaims, resting a hand on Rory's shoulder. "I don't know if your son has told you, but his scores on the practice tests have been off the charts. We're lucky to have this young man."

"We're looking for Caroline Donadieu," Rory blurts. "I was supposed to see her after the practice test today."

Kobayashi lets his hand fall from Rory's shoulder. "She's probably home resting up for tomorrow, as you should be."

"Did you see her on campus today?" I ask.

"I was in the city all day. I just stopped by to make sure all systems are go for tomorrow." Kobayashi reaches up to scratch his left temple. Is he nervous? Hard to tell. Sometimes touching one's face is a sign of deception, but just as often it's the natural response to an itch.

"Speaking of tomorrow, I notice you haven't been opening my emails, Lina. Rory needs a minimum of ten hours of sleep to be ready for the test. Complex carbs tonight, we recommend sweet potatoes, and equal ratios of fat and protein in the morning, along with a half cup of oatmeal. Don't forget the cinnamon! And a cup of coffee each morning. We'll have a Philz cart on campus to provide the students with free coffee at lunch."

"Rory will be ready tomorrow," I assure him.

"Great! Prepared for the test, prepared for life, every student counts!" He turns to Rory. "Now go home and get some sleep. We're counting on you."

Our next stop is Laney Park. Empty. We cruise through the golf course, then up to Crocker Lake. I park in front of the closed gate, open the glove compartment, and take out my flashlight. I don't tell Rory about the young woman who disappeared from South City in 1987 and was found dead beneath a pile of leaves at this very lake.

The park has changed a lot since my high school days. Beside the gate, a wooden sign says, "Crocker Lake is proudly maintained by the Greenfield Beautification Committee." A few yards down the path, two wooden benches sit side by side, and a bed of flowers has been planted within stone borders. The well-tended path curves toward the lake. Beyond the path, the vegetation remains wild and dense.

"Watch out for mountain lions," I tell Rory.

"Yeah, right."

"I'm not kidding. One of them killed a deer on Robinwood Lane right after we moved in. You're not in New York City anymore, kiddo."

"Caroline?" I call, as we make our way along the two-mile loop.

Rory joins in. "Caroline?" It's eerie, the sound of our voices cutting through the silence as twigs snap beneath our feet. By the time we get back to the Jeep, we have a few bug bites but no answers.

We drive around for another half hour. It's just past eleven when we finally give up. At home, Rory is jittery. Realizing we never had dinner, I make him a tuna melt, a bowl of strawberries and cream, and a glass of milk. I slide the sandwich across the counter. "Here, omega-3."

He eats the sandwich with one hand, typing on his phone with the other. At 11:29, his phone pings with a text.

"Caroline!" His face lights up with joy and relief as he reads aloud, "I'm fine. Something came up. Talk soon." His shoulders relax, his face softens, and he is himself again.

Where have you been? he texts back. Can we talk?

Ping. Don't worry, Friend. All is well.

He sets his phone on the counter, Caroline's text still visible on the glowing screen.

"I guess I overreacted," Rory says. "God, the Rekowskis must think you're insane." He takes his dishes to the sink. On his way out of the kitchen, he stops and turns around. "Thank you, though, for helping me stalk my girlfriend."

"Anytime."

30

When time travel is finally invented, who will be in the most danger? Provide a plausible timeline and supporting scientific data.

At traffic circle Monday morning, the A team is out directing cars and greeting students for day one of the Wonder Test: Miss Hartwell, the dainty English teacher with a shock of white hair; Mr. Cartwright, the science teacher who moonlights as the lead singer in a ska band; and Kobayashi. Rory points out Dopey Barrett, the kid who defeated him in the student council elections, standing beside a table covered with blue paper bags. A banner hanging behind the table declares, BLUBERRY: THE PERFECT BRAIN FOOD.

"What's that about?" I ask Rory. "And why'd they misspell 'blueberry'?"

"It's the name of his dad's software start-up. They also own an organic blueberry farm near Clear Lake. They've been passing out berries every day as a publicity stunt."

Kobayashi stands next to Dopey, waving at parents, greeting students. Rory gets out of the Jeep and scans the crowd, looking for Caroline.

At 1:25 in the afternoon I arrive at George's designated spot on the Bay Trail. I sit on the bench, waiting. I've been looking forward to the meeting, but now I'm distracted, worried about Caroline, running her text message through my mind: Don't worry, Friend. All is well. It has been nagging at me. It doesn't sound like Caroline. Call it instinct, call it statement analysis, call it what you will: one thing I know for certain. Something is off.

At 1:29, George appears on the path, alone. He sits down beside me. Without a word, he hands me the envelope to count.

"What, no run today?"

He points at his right foot and cringes. "Plantar fasciitis is a bitch."

I quickly thumb through the stack of fifty-dollar bills. Like me, George pays his sources in fifties whenever possible. I'm the one who turned him on to the idea. Every time you pay a source, regardless of the amount, you create goodwill and generate personal equity. Since most people don't carry around fifty-dollar bills in their daily life, if you pay them with a stack of fifties, then you get a little bonus bump every time they spend one. Even if it's just a flash, a quick memory of the moment you paid them, it fosters a positive association with you.

On the crudest level, some agents measure the strength of a relationship with the equation: "number of contacts" multiplied by "total amount of time on target." But the equation is too simplified, overlooking myriad subtle methods for strengthening the bond. Since personal contact is limited in a clandestine relationship, the noncontact methods are key. For me, paying in fifty-dollar bills is just one way to spark repeated, safe memories of the relationship, thereby creating additional relationship equity.

I count $9,950, just under the reporting limit for outbound US passengers. I pull out the receipt, write in the amount and the date, and initial.

"I told him one forty-five, so we have a few minutes to talk," George says. "Good news. LeSaffre said we can't have you working for free. He sent a memo asking personnel to reactivate you part-time."

"I didn't ask you to do that."

My tone must have been harsher than I intended, because George looks slightly hurt. "I thought you'd be pleased."

I touch his arm. "I am. Thank you. I just feel like I'm not finished here. And Rory seems to like it."

"I knew you'd say that. LeSaffre says you can work from here. He said to get him something on the French diplomats."

"French diplomats aren't exactly the big white whale, George."

"No, but this fellow Donadieu is still a valuable target, and he has some interesting contacts in Moscow. No pressure. You in?" George has a velvety smooth voice that somehow wills a person to agree with him.

"Of course I'm in."

A figure appears in the distance, walking toward us. Wheeling.

"Bastard is always early," George mutters.

"How's it going with this guy?"

"He's producing a ton."

"Good stuff?"

"Excellent. I'm getting tired of typing. Twenty-three IIRs last week alone. Let me know if you could use a hand on the French diplomat."

"As a matter of fact, I need to track him down."

George gives me a confused look. "Wait, you're already working on it?"

"It's more of a personal matter. As I mentioned before, Rory is friends with his daughter. Donadieu suddenly dropped off the map, but so did the girl. I don't know if it's related."

"Sounds like a job for Malia Lind at HQ."

Wheeling is a few dozen yards away. "Quick, before he gets here, how'd you decide on the name Wheeling? I don't know the reference."

"Joy Harjo, from *In Mad Love and War*." He recites, "I don't know the ending. / But I know the legacy of maggots is wings." Wheeling is a few steps away now. "The poem is set in Wheeling, West Virginia," George says. "It fits him perfectly, don't you agree?"

"Too early to tell about the wings."

We stand together to greet Wheeling. "Let's do this, *Damien*," I say.

Wheeling shakes George's hand and gives me a sweaty hug. Either he likes me or he just likes the money that materializes whenever I'm around. After the exchange, the two of them walk off together.

Being in this familiar triangle, going through the familiar motions, is comforting. It reminds me that everything's still ticking, that this whole world, just below the surface, is still there for me whenever I'm ready to return. I'm not sure I'd know how to do any other job. Every time I see George, I'm back in my element, a fish returned to water.

I take the long path back to the car, feeling more optimistic, recalibrated. It's good to reengage with that other person I was, not so long ago—not quite a maggot sprouting wings, but not quite a caterpillar emerging as a butterfly either. In this line of work, we live somewhere in the middle, between two extremes: ugliness and beauty, life and death.

31

Provide examples to illustrate the term "diminishing returns" without providing so many examples as to achieve diminishing returns.

"How did the test go?" I ask when Rory climbs into the front seat, alone.

"Good, I think. I wrote an essay on modern alienation in *Martin in Space*."

"So why the gloomy face?" I ask, although I'm afraid I already know the answer.

"I haven't heard from Caroline since that text last night."

"Why don't we swing by her house again?"

As we cruise through the wrought iron gate of Caroline's estate, I have a knot in my gut. Instinctively, I turn down the music on the car stereo, bracing for bad news.

When I first received word of Fred's accident, I was in our apartment, washing dishes, taking the morning off after a long night at work. I had turned the music up loud to drown out the thoughts in my head. I've always found it difficult to get to sleep after operations, no matter how exhausted I am. Usually, I end up cleaning the house until I'm sufficiently relaxed to go to bed.

Most agents have a similar post-op ritual, for two reasons. First, ops like search warrants and arrests create adrenaline spikes, and you need time to come down from them. Second, search warrants have taught me that American homes are dirtier and more cluttered than you would ever imagine. Combing through jumbles of paperwork, rank-smelling shoes, broken toys, used batteries, abandoned projects, and far worse will inspire any agent to get her own house in order.

That day, Rory was at school and Fred was in a cab, headed downtown for a meeting. My phone rang. I remember the moment with startling clarity, like when you press Pause on a streaming video and instead of pausing, it moves forward slowly, one frame at a time, frozen but not frozen, forward motion interrupted but not entirely stopped. The stereo was playing a Mendoza Line song, "Love on Parole." As I reached to turn the volume down, preparing to answer the phone, I listened to one more line: "The room readied itself for that transfer of power / When you rode right through in your penultimate hour."

I can hear the song so clearly, even now. I can see my hand reaching toward the volume knob, the cell phone buzzing on the kitchen counter. Looking back, I understand how completely unprepared I was for that moment. Since then, every time I hear that song, or when the lyrics unexpectedly flit through my mind, unwelcome but unavoidable, everything comes flooding back: the horror of that moment, the collapse of our world, the avalanche of grief. In behavioral analysis, it's called a linguistic trigger.

I'm not sure what will happen in the coming hours or when Rory and I step up to that door. But I feel dread welling up, a certainty that things are going to get worse. I don't want some Dylan song to be a land mine that triggers Rory's sadness for the rest of his life.

At the door, Rory hesitates, as if he too has suddenly been struck by that wall of inexplicable dread. I press the bell. The orchestral chime carries through the house, and we stare anxiously at each other. Rory bounces up and down on the balls of his feet. He rings the bell again, then lifts the knocker and pounds the iron against the heavy oak door.

We hear footsteps in the foyer. The door opens a crack to reveal Blandine in her pressed navy uniform. I speak with her in a rapid-fire stream of French that belies my story of Berlitz tapes and the West Side Highway.

Blandine tells me she last saw Caroline yesterday morning before the practice test, but that doesn't mean Caroline hasn't been home since then.

Wouldn't she have known if Caroline came home? I ask.

"Cette maison est très grande, et la fille est très calme," she responds. No matter how big the house or how quiet the girl, it seems unlikely that Caroline could be in the house without Blandine knowing.

The first consul and his wife and daughter come and go at odd hours, she says. They do not always inform her of their schedules. She is here to maintain the estate, nothing more. A personal assistant tends to other family affairs, but Caroline's mother fired the assistant three weeks ago and she hasn't been replaced.

"Pourquoi?"

"Elle manque de savoir-vivre."

Bad manners? Judging from Blandine, the bar seems low. Either the assistant's manners were atrocious, or there's something Blandine isn't telling me.

"Peut-être," she says, "la fille rejoint ses parents lors de leur voyage."

"She says Caroline might have joined her parents on their trip," I tell Rory. "Did she ever mention that she might meet them?"

"No." His forehead creases with worry. "If she planned to meet them, she would have told me."

"Could they have summoned her?" I ask in French.

Blandine shrugs. "Je ne sais pas."

"Caroline is missing," I say. "Aren't you concerned?"

"Ce n'est pas grave."

If a missing teen isn't serious, I wonder, what qualifies as serious? And what about Caroline's parents? Don't they have a right to know she hasn't shown up? After several minutes of stonewalling, Blandine pulls back her shoulders and declares, "Je travaille pour mon pays. Je ne travaille pas pour cette fille. Maintenant, vous devez aller!"

And then the door slams in our faces.

32

A force F acts at point P on a rigid body, as shown in the figure below, where R is the distance from point O to point P, and θ is the angle at which the force acts. What is the torque exerted on the rigid body about point O?

Two streets over, beyond the range of the security cameras on Caroline's estate, I park the Jeep.

"Why are we stopping?"

"I need to send a quick message."

Malia Lind has inhabited the same tiny, windowless office on the fourth floor of headquarters for twenty-three years. Before she was an analyst, she was an intelligence officer in the navy. With an admiral from New Jersey for a father and a forensic pathologist from Brazil for a mother, Malia has service and curiosity in her blood. She is left to her own devices, tasked with researching all of the historical, unsolved espionage cases.

Malia is brilliant, maybe on the spectrum. She gets obsessed, looking at each case from dozens of angles, searching for the elusive nugget of information that will finally break it open. Usually, this means finding the exact guy who would know an exact piece of information, tracking him down, finding the perfect agent to do the pitch, and creating the extensive, complicated op that might make it all coalesce into a recruitment.

Malia's passion for these forgotten cases is infectious. In the past, when she asked me to meet someone, I always said yes. It often meant I had to drop everything and be on a plane to some far-flung location within hours. Each time Malia's number flashed across my phone screen, I felt a rush of nervous excitement. I knew I'd soon be packing, making excuses to Fred and Rory, to my boss and my coworkers, apologizing to everyone whom I was surely going to disappoint in the coming days.

The last time Malia called me for one of these last-minute gigs was Iceland. The trip went well, but now, whenever I see a news item or travel ad for Iceland, I think of the hours I wasted in that northern outpost when I should have been at home with Fred, enjoying our time together during what would prove to be his final months. The most difficult part of the equation is this: if I hadn't gone to Iceland, the calendar might have shifted, time altered in some unknowable way, and he would still be here now. Rory would still have a father.

Asking for a favor means I have to be willing to return it. At the moment, there's probably only one thing Malia needs from me: she needs me to go back to Iceland, do another meeting, and finish this thing we started.

We're approaching the anniversary of the last meeting, and I'm certain the source has been expecting an email from me. On paper, he's known as Red Vine. I open the encrypted messaging app Confide and type: I need you to check some "diplomats" for me discreetly. Also, let me know if the interest and money are there for another Red Vine trip.

Seconds later, her response arrives: Money and interest always there if you're willing. I've been saving part of my budget for you.

I send Malia what I know about Caroline's parents: Official surname Donadieu, French first consul and his wife assigned to San Francisco since last year, frequent travel to Vienna and North Africa. Can you find out where they are now?

On it, she replies.

Rory cracks his knuckles. "Are you worried?"

I can't lie to him. "I'm not *not* worried," I admit. I think of Gray Stafford's cryptic message to me on movie night. I think of the blonde woman telling Caroline not to show up for the test. Of course, there's also the personal assistant fired by Caroline's mother three weeks ago, but my gut tells me that has nothing to do with Caroline.

We drive the streets of Greenfield again, searching. Then, in concentric circles, we widen to Burlingame, San Mateo.

"Has Blandine ever seemed hostile toward Caroline?" I ask Rory.

"No, she's almost invisible. She doesn't pay any attention to us unless we go into the kitchen. She thinks snacking is a mortal sin."

Rory's texts to Caroline's small group of girlfriends produce no information. He reads their responses aloud. They don't even sound like friends.

"Is it possible she just didn't want to face the test?" I ask. "That she took the mystery woman's advice?" I want to ease his concern, but the more I think about the single text she sent last night, the more it bothers me.

"Not a chance. She really wanted to do well, and she's worked so hard to try to improve her score. The fact that someone told her not to show up would have only made her more determined."

After nearly two hours of searching, I pull into the Rodeo Pizza in Foster City and hand Rory my wallet. "I'm going to try to reach Officer Kyle. Why don't you run in and get us a pepperoni to take home?"

When Kyle doesn't answer his work or personal cell phones, I call the station. The dispatcher tells me he's out sick. I call Kyle's personal cell and leave a message. "A friend of Rory's didn't show up to school today. Maybe unrelated, but I don't like the timing. Her name is Caroline Donadieu. Can you get the CCTV footage from the school for this past Sunday?"

Inside the pizza joint, Rory is the only customer. He seems worn out, not quite here. He hands me the wallet. "I didn't pay yet."

A tatted-out skinhead stands behind the counter, tending the metal ovens. He looks me up and down, a creepy grin spreading across his face. He's spindly and greasy, tall, a buck fifty at most, probably in his late thirties. He pulls the pizza out of the oven, cuts and boxes it. Instead of handing it over the counter, he walks around to where I'm standing and edges up close to me, so close the box touches my stomach. The look in his eyes, the way he presses the box against me, pisses me off.

I take the pizza and hand it to Rory. "Go wait in the car. I'll be out in a sec."

I don't relax until I hear the door closing behind him.

"How much?"

"Seventeen ninety-five. But for you I'll work out a discount. I get off in twenty. If you want to wait for me, I'll make it worth your while."

"No thanks." I reach around him to place a twenty on the counter.

As I turn and move toward the door, he sidesteps in front of me, blocking my way.

"Wait, mama. You're the only pretty customer I've had all day. Let's talk this through." He's on something, I'm not sure what. An upper, something that makes him unpredictable, probably even to himself.

"You need to move. Right now."

"Come on. It'll do you good, wake you up to possibilities."

A prison tattoo runs the length of his left arm. He wears a flannel shirt, sleeves torn off. He smells like smoke and a bad apartment, days spent playing video games and watching porn in a dark room. He places his hands on my shoulders, positioning himself between me and the door, his thumbs digging into my skin. I smell pizza burning in the oven.

I force his hands off my shoulders. "Final warning. You *do not* want to do this."

He grins and reaches around me, sliding a bony hand up my back.

Disgust surges through me. I feel my eyes narrowing, tunnel vision coming on. The training comes back instinctively. I lower my center of gravity by a couple of inches, planting my right foot behind me. I mumble something he can't hear, drawing him in closer. It's about balance. He expects me to push him back, so I pull him in instead. With his weight leaning forward, his mind momentarily relaxed, I have the advantage, even though he's much taller.

"What?" He tilts forward. "Was that a 'yes' I heard, mama?"

I put my palms on his chest. I feel his bones, no muscle tone. I let loose with a burst of focused energy, pushing him backward. In Quantico they taught us about the torque that comes from your planted feet, the twist of your waist, how it's an especially effective tool for women facing off against bigger guys. Of course, this target is a walk in the park compared to the rock of an agent who served as my DT partner.

Pizza guy is even lighter than I expected. He loses his balance and falls backward. As his hands grab for the table behind him to break his fall, I lunge forward, twisting my core. I swing my fist low and fast across my body and slam it into his left cheek. His eyes are wide open, stunned; clearly, he didn't expect things to go this way, this fast. His hands scramble for the table beside him, but his balance is all off, his body spinning away from the punch, blood streaming from where my ring caught his cheek. He hits the ground hard and the flimsy table falls over him.

Adrenaline pulses through my body. I fight the urge to kick him once in the face or neck. Eliminate the threat. But it's uncalled for, really, and I know that all this rage I'm taking out on the pizza guy isn't just about him. It's about Fred. It's about my dad. It's about not knowing how to fix anything for Rory. It's about Gray and the Lamey twins, three kids who went missing and showed up a shell of themselves, and it's about Caroline, this sick feeling I have in my gut that she's in serious trouble.

I watch for a moment, my center of gravity still low, arms and hands poised to fight. I pause to make sure he's still breathing, but also to make sure he's not going to pop back up and reengage.

"Bitch," he whimpers, his hand hovering over the cut on his face. He moves slowly to push the table off of him, but he has no strength.

I take several deep breaths, take a few moments to compose myself. When I step outside, I realize Rory is standing just outside the restaurant, still holding the pizza, staring in the window, wide-eyed.

"What the hell, Mom."

"Get in the car."

Once we're inside the Jeep, I lock the doors and turn the key in the ignition. "How much did you see?"

"All of it."

"I'm sorry. I lost my temper."

"Mom, you don't *have* a temper." Rory stares at me as if it has just occurred to him that he doesn't entirely know me.

"The guy was a jerk, but I could've talked my way out of it. I should have handled it differently, obviously."

"How did you even know how to do that?"

"Training. Practice."

"Did Dad know you could do that?"

"I suppose."

"Did he ever see you do something like that?"

"God, no," I laugh.

Rory doesn't pursue the subject any further, but I can tell from the way he stares at me, mulling it over, that we'll return to this conversation.

In the middle of the night, a message arrives from Malia:

Your son seems to be dabbling in the family business. The girl's parents are the real deal. A posting to Kiev, then one to Sofia, back to Paris for two years, then San Francisco. Not clear if they're Asian or Eurasian Directorate. CD-2 wouldn't sneeze at it if you bring them around. Definitely a team. The wife's credentials are legit. She speaks Mandarin. He speaks Russian and Farsi. The two of them may have been in Algeria since last Wednesday, under different names and passports, completely off the grid, but you didn't hear it from me.

33

A ten-meter-tall tree can have leaves ranging from one millimeter to one meter in length, but a hundred-meter-tall tree can have leaves ranging from only ten to twenty centimeters in length. Why does natural selection sometimes give the underdog a boost?

On Tuesday morning, day two of the Wonder Test, Rory is out of sorts, still checking his phone obsessively. On the way to school, he clicks the door lock up and down, up and down, an old nervous habit. The relief of that single text from Caroline has faded. The strangeness of last night's failed search and the ugly incident at the pizza joint casts a pall over everything.

At school, he lingers in the car for a moment when we reach the curb. "Aren't you going to tell me to do my best or something?"

The car behind us honks.

"I know you will."

"Yeah, but you're still supposed to *say* it."

"Okay, kiddo," I say, tapping his knee. "Do your best."

The truth is I don't give a damn about the test. I'm distracted, hoping he'll hear from Caroline, almost certain that he won't. I think back to Kobayashi's speech that night in the school auditorium. *One student, one bad day, one errant key stroke* . . .

Moments after I walk in the door at home and set the coffee to brew, my phone rings, no caller ID.

"Lina? It's Nicole. Can we talk?"

I'm surprised. I hadn't expected to hear from her again. "I can be at your office in forty-five minutes, give or take."

"No, not the office. Do you know Louis' Diner in the Outer Richmond?"

When I arrive, the waitress is clearing the corner booth in the back. It's my favorite seat in the place, windows on two sides. The place has the best view of any restaurant in the city, spanning the ruins of Sutro Baths, Seal Rock, down the long stretch of Ocean Beach. I take the left side, my back to the window overlooking Kelly's Cove, so I can see the whole restaurant, leaving the panoramic ocean view for Nicole.

I order coffee and wait. I have a nervous buzzing in my gut. My phone beeps three times, but it's just Greenfield-Neighbors.org, mostly people going back and forth about the burglary on Marlborough yesterday. The intruders entered through a sliding glass door, took jewelry and electronics, the usual. Located just a quarter mile from the 280 exit, Marlborough is a favorite target of burglars—easy in, easy out. Thieves rarely venture down the winding labyrinth of roads where grand estates stand behind iron gates or down steep, narrow driveways. I scroll the texts for posts about suspicious vehicles, lurkers, anything unusual that could be linked to Caroline but find nothing. Mister Fancy's owner is on the hunt again, but I saw Mr. Fancy just this morning, and he seemed perfectly happy in our front yard.

The restaurant clears out, tourists with places to go. Someone turns up the music, "Box of Rain." It feels like the San Francisco I once knew. Sometimes when you least expect it—amid the fog, the tech workers and tourists, the noise of traffic and MUNI buses—1970s San Francisco pokes its head through to say hello. The song ends and someone hits Repeat.

Nicole appears at the door, clad in a gray cashmere sweater, dark skinny jeans, riding boots. She walks over and slides into the booth. "Sorry for dragging you out here. I didn't want to email. Does that make me paranoid?"

"Makes you smart."

Nicole must have put her makeup on in a rush. A streak of foundation is visible at her jawline, black dots of mascara scattered across her eyelids. Every time I see her, she looks more exhausted than the last. Something is keeping her up at night. Is it the business with Gray Stafford or something else?

"Everything okay?"

"Not exactly. Boy troubles, you know."

Nicole seems too old to be dating boys. Maybe that's her problem. Still, the way she says it is unconvincing. The waitress brings coffee. Nicole orders an egg-white omelet with mushrooms and bell peppers, hold the cheese.

"Same for me," I say. "Except I'll take the whole egg and extra cheese." The Dead song grows louder, the spiraling guitar and harmonies wrapping around my brain.

The waitress walks away. Nicole picks up the salt shaker, puts it down again. She's not hiding her nervousness very well. When I first took the job, I used to underestimate the effect my presence had, the stress people feel when they meet with me. It doesn't matter that Nicole called me. I'm still FBI, and that freaks her out. "Any progress with the case?"

"No. In fact, there's been a big setback."

"What kind of setback?"

"Another kid has disappeared. Same school."

Nicole's hand goes to her mouth in horror. "You think it's connected? Oh, God, is it my fault?"

"You're here now."

"Did you find the swimmer?"

"Not yet."

Nicole starts fumbling inside her bag, looking for something. I see a laptop, a Kindle, phone, billfold. She pulls out a blue Moleskine notebook and places it on the table. "That day, when it happened, my first instinct was not to get involved. Later, after I let myself think about it, I knew my silence wasn't justified, but I forced the reservations out of my mind." She raps her fingernails against the side of her coffee mug. "Do you do yoga?"

"I've tried but I get antsy. I can't turn my mind off."

"I go to this place in Cole Valley. It's mellow, more of a workout than a way of life, you know. But it has feel-good quotes painted all over the walls."

The waitress brings the food, refills our coffee. The sourdough toast is crunchy and slick with butter. Nicole takes one bite of her omelet, then pushes the plate away.

"At the yoga studio, I always get a spot in the back row. There's this quote in big letters on the back wall. When we do some of the poses, the quote is directly in front of my face, and I'm just stuck there staring at it. I'm sure you know it. 'If not me, who? And if not now, when?'"

"Hillel the Elder. 'If I am not for myself, who will be for me? If I am for myself only, what am I? If not now, when?'"

"I guess it got a little watered down over time," she says, mulling it over. "Point is, I've stared at that quote a hundred times. The day after I found the boy on the beach, I went to yoga. And when I went into warrior pose, there I was, staring at the words on the wall. I felt that they were speaking directly to me, accusing me. But by then it seemed too late. How could I go back and revise my story?"

"What changed your mind?"

"I met you. We're about the same age, maybe similar backgrounds. Obviously, *very* different trajectories but still." She shakes her head. "Here I was, doing nothing, not getting involved, while you were doing the opposite. And I just keep thinking, 'If not me, who?' But I knew the 'who' was *you*, and it made me ashamed."

She pulls a pen out of her bag and tears a piece of paper from her notebook. She starts writing, transcribing from the notebook onto the torn-out page. Her cursive is elegant, old-fashioned. When the waitress comes over to refill our coffee again, Nicole covers the paper with her hand. As the waitress walks away, she returns to copying the information. "If," she says, "hypothetically, you knew that someone broke the law, but you also knew they broke the law in good faith, in pursuit of important information, are you required to report it?"

I crunch into my toast, considering. "I broke ten traffic laws on my way here."

Nicole smiles, the stress fading from her face for just a few seconds. For an instant she looks younger, transformed, and I wonder if this is the way she always looked before that day on the beach and her subsequent silence changed her, forcing her to see herself in a harsher light. She slides the paper across the table. I open it and read. She has drawn a vertical line down the middle to form two columns. In the first, she has written the following:

Seaside Fresh Seafood
650-393-5921
Owner: John Murphy
Boats: Rock Crawler (Princeton) &
    Left Wing Preacher (Ferndale)
1900 Main St.
Half Moon Bay, CA

In the second column, she has written:

Ivy Blankenship
415-575-7979
DOB: 12/12/1991
670 Pacific Way, B
Moss Beach, CA

I can feel her gaze on me as I scan the information. She is so nervous, so eager to please. "You should eat," I say.

I glance over my shoulder, out the window. A massive cargo ship, stacked high with orange shipping containers, is slowly making its way out of the mouth of the bay, into the ocean.

"That's a lot of shit going somewhere," Nicole says.

"They're all empty. True fact. It's from Shanghai. The boats come in filled to the brim, but most of them depart the Port of Oakland empty."

"How do you know?"

"A case I once worked." I examine the names and addresses again. "Apple or Google?"

"Google."

"Secret's safe with me."

"My friend Susan had a party last night," she explains, even though she doesn't need to. I don't care where she got the information. I'm just glad she got it. "There was this guy. Not too attractive, interesting, though. Google coder. He just broke up with his girlfriend, caught her cheating with some guy from Square. So I asked him how he found out. He wouldn't tell me at first, but I badgered him until he did. He was depressed, a little drunk. He said he ran a script at work that let him track her phone. Did you know that nearly every single Android phone in the world pings back to Google headquarters as often as every fifteen minutes?"

"Yes. Everybody's worried about the government spying. It's silly. They *should* be worried about big tech. For me to get that kind of information requires a hundred-page FISA warrant, eleven approvals, a day in a pantsuit, and a judge in a giving mood."

"Well, this guy tracked his girlfriend's phone to a hotel bar in Berkeley when she was supposed to be at work. It went downhill from there. But when he told me the story, it gave me an idea. I asked him if he could do the reverse, if he could tell me all the phones that pinged from a certain location at a certain time. He said that he *could*, but he probably wouldn't."

"So how did you convince him?"

Nicole moves a mushroom around on her plate, not looking at me.

"You didn't sleep with him?"

She gives a look of feigned innocence. "I didn't?"

"You said you found him unattractive!"

"No, I said he was *not too attractive*. Totally different."

I smile. "I hope he didn't have dirty dishes in the sink. Old bedsheets for curtains. Don't tell me he vapes."

"No and no and no," she says. "He was really sweet. I woke up at four in the morning, and he was on his laptop. He wrote a geolocate script with lat/long fences and then ran it against the historical pings for the hour before and after my encounter on the beach."

"You told him about the sandwiches?"

"I did. Honesty. It's something new I'm trying. Apparently, the fact that the boat was offshore made it easier. Not many cell phones ping from the Pacific Ocean. Those were the only two Android phones in the area at the time. He said the geolocate isn't always exact."

"Yes, there's a give-or-take of a hundred and fifty yards. Sometimes more in the fog. The signal skews off moisture."

"So these could be phones from other boats," she says.

"Could be. These are also just Androids, so if there are iPhones present, we wouldn't know. On the other hand, right place, right time. It could be our man, and it could be our swimmer."

Nicole sips her coffee. "Too bad I don't know any engineers from Apple." Maybe she's joking. Probably not.

"Are you going to see your coder again?"

"If you need me to, I will. He texted me twice this morning, invited me to some hipster peewee golf slash bar in the Mission for a drink tonight."

"That sounds painful."

"Not really." I think she means it. "You'd be surprised. You should try it sometime. Hooking up, I mean."

"What makes you think I don't hook up?"

The truth is, I can't imagine hooking up with anyone. Not now, not ever. I had Fred. *He* was my hookup.

34

Square feet is to cubic feet as time is to what?

Moss Beach is just a blip on Highway 1, so it's no surprise when I miss my turn and find myself driving past a field of artichokes. Although the area is famous for the annual pumpkin festival, it's the artichokes that pay the bills. When I pull onto a dirt road to turn around, the farmworkers pause, look up, and immediately return to their business. The farmworkers are on edge these days. There was a time, not that long ago, when they could simply do their jobs and not worry about an unfamiliar car passing by. That's not the only thing that has changed here. When I was growing up, the fog provided a protective layer of moisture on this stretch of coastline nearly year-round, but the day, like the year, is hot and dry, not a wisp of fog in sight.

The house at 670 Pacific Way is squat and run-down with a dead lawn and an empty driveway. A plywood board nailed to the fence, 670A displayed in red spray paint, points around back. I go through the gate and take the gravel path to a guest house, even smaller than the main house.

I knock on the door, but there's no answer. Through the window, I see an unmade mattress, clothing littering the floor, an open box of Life cereal, three empty packages of Sudafed. Orange Home Depot buckets sit beside the back door, along with a funnel and an empty propane canister, signs of amateur hour in the meth trade. Ivy Blankenship doesn't live here anymore. She probably hasn't for a while.

I walk across the street to the fancier place, the one with the balcony overlooking the ocean, with a bird's-eye view over Ivy's former home. A woman in a loose white linen dress opens the door. She's speaking into a headset—something about a warehouse, shipments, and then the conversation turns to Swedish. She raises her finger to tell me it will be one minute.

She finally clicks off the headset. "Crazy day. May I help you?"

"Sorry for the bother. I wanted to ask you about the people who live across the street?"

"I don't know them at all. Haven't seen them in a while." She speaks in a nervous burst. "Are you a friend of theirs?"

"Not exactly." I slide my creds out of my pocket and angle them up in her direction.

"Oh!" She glances from my face to my photo and back again. "Wow, I've never seen those in person before. Come in."

Her house is spotless and impeccably decorated. Black-and-white photos line the walls of the living room. Music is playing somewhere else in the house.

She gestures to a white sofa. "Have a seat. Coffee?"

"Yes, please."

While she's in the kitchen, I survey the room. A collection of Fan Ho photographs on the coffee table, weighted down with a white conch shell. Rows of cameras, from the simplest Holga to a top-of-the-line Nikon DSLR, line the shelves of a corner bookcase.

An ivory sheet hangs from the ceiling along one wall. The space is so beautiful, so calming in its well-ordered minimalism, it makes me want to throw away even more things when I get back to my dad's house.

She returns with the coffee. "I'm Elsa."

"Lina." I take a sip. "Thank you, this is really good coffee."

"Lina? That's a fine Swedish name. Are your parents Scandinavian?"

"Nope. Scotch-Irish. Oddly enough, I was named after the German runner Lina Radke or the American silent film actress Lina Basquette. Depends on who you ask."

"I don't know either."

"Lina Radke was the first Olympic champion in the women's eight hundred. As for the other, my mother was a silent film buff. When she was pregnant, she discovered that Basquette was born in San Mateo. She liked the legend that Basquette had once kicked Hitler in the balls. My dad wanted to raise a runner, and my mom wanted to raise a little ball kicker. So here I am, Lina with an *i*."

"That's fantastic!" Elsa says, breaking into a wide grin. It's been a while since I told that story.

"You're a photographer?"

"Indeed." She sits down in a wooden chair facing me and puts two white mugs on the oak coffee table, casually marked with coffee rings. I think of something George once said to me right before we made entry on a search warrant at a residential address in Riverdale. "Inside every house, a new adventure."

Elsa opens her mouth to say something but then stops. She stares at my face for several moments. "I like your cheekbones," she declares. "Good angles, great for black and white. You are rather unusual looking. Have you ever modeled?"

I laugh, caught off guard. Fred used to tell me I looked unusual. No one has ever asked if I modeled.

"Can I take your picture?"

"I actually just wanted to ask you about the neighbors."

"Of course, I will tell you about the neighbors. Just one picture first." She stands and glides over to the shelf, where she picks up a Leica and a light meter.

"Do you know them?" I ask.

Elsa is distracted, adjusting the buttons and dials on the camera. "Not really. Those guys were bad news. I avoided them. But now they're gone, thank heavens." She presses a button on the light meter and glances at the result.

"What about the woman who lived there?"

Elsa hovers over me with the camera. "The swimmer, Ivy?"

"Yes."

"She lived there before the last renters. My husband and I like her."

"So you know her."

"No, no, I mean we liked to look at her." She glances down at her light meter again and then back at me. "Just one picture. With the coffee cup."

The agency psychologist I often worked with on the BAP team used to say, "Every interaction is an exchange. A little give, a little take." I pick up the coffee cup and begin to raise it to my lips. Just then, Elsa presses the shutter release several times in rapid succession, then glances down at the Leica's screen.

"Ah," she says, pleased. "I was right!" She turns the camera toward me to show me a photo, but I only give it a quick glance. I hate pictures of myself. I remember exactly when I started hiding from cameras: My dad took a picture on my fourteenth birthday, just weeks after my mother left. The face that stared out at me from that photo was such a sad, lonely face. I didn't want to have a record of that girl.

Satisfied, Elsa sets the camera down. "Bill, who lives down the block, said Ivy almost made the US Olympic team. She seemed like a good girl. Her boyfriend, though, was a loser. No job. Bad friends, always playing music too loud, drinking. The girl was driven, though. Every morning at five she was up and out of the house. She would go swimming in the ocean! Can you imagine?"

"How did you know she was swimming in the ocean?"

"I asked her. I'm an early riser too. The light here is better in the morning. I would always see her getting into her car while the whole neighborhood was still asleep. So one time I just walked over and asked her: 'Where do you go so early every morning?'"

"What did she say?"

"Montara Beach. Insane, yes? I told her those currents would kill her, but she didn't seem to care."

"Do you know where she lives now?"

Elsa shakes her head. "She told Bill she was moving to Pescadero. But one morning, I was out at Montara Beach taking photos, and I saw her car. I think she still swims there. If she lives in Pescadero, why would she drive all the way to Montara to swim?"

"So you think she was lying?"

"Yes. She isn't in trouble, is she? My husband always said that boy was dragging her down. I think that's the reason she lied to us about where she was moving, in case he asked us. I think she was afraid of him."

"What makes you say that?"

"There were noises in the house sometimes. Yelling, things crashing around. Of course, he was scrawny, out of shape. In a fair fight, I'd put my money on the girl, but he was mean."

"You know his name?"

"No, we never did meet him. Never did want to, either."

I finish my coffee and stand to leave. "Thank you. I'll let you get back to work."

"Wait. I might having something else for you. Follow me."

Elsa leads me through the kitchen into the back of the house to a room with fifteen-foot ceilings. Light shines down through a dozen skylights. The music is still on. Photo equipment is lined up along the walls. She sits down at an iMac Pro with a twenty-seven-inch monitor.

She clicks through several file folders and stops on a folder labeled "Ivy." The screen fills with hundreds of tiles, each one a photograph of Ivy, all taken from this house. Some pictures are up close and others are far away, different lenses, different weather, different days: working in the yard, bringing in groceries, checking the mail, climbing into her silver Suzuki Samurai. In each picture, Ivy seems totally unaware that she is being watched. In many, she wears sweatpants and a sweatshirt, the straps of her bathing suit peeking through. I'm struck by the calm focus in her expression. And also by how nonchalant Elsa is about letting me in on the secret of her surveillance.

Elsa plugs her Leica into the computer, and I watch the screen. Scanning the photos, I see the telltale dot of red.

"Wait," I say, pointing to the tile. "Can you pull that one up?"
She clicks on the photo.

There she is on the huge screen, the last photo in the folder, maybe taken the day Elsa saw her at the beach: Ivy Blankenship in a red bathing cap.

"Can I have a copy of that?"

"Of course."

Elsa hits a button, and a printer across the room comes to life. I walk over and take the photograph from the tray, the slick paper still warm. When I return to the computer, Elsa has pulled up the picture she took of me. She is fiddling with the contrast and the light, blurring the background. "See," she says. "You're unusual, like I said. Beautiful even."

Looking at the screen, I don't see a beautiful woman. I see myself, only older, more tired. I see the brutal effects of a terrible, horrible, no-good, very bad year.

At home, a pamphlet from Harris Ojai has been stuffed into the mailbox. On the front, he has scrawled the words: "Time is running out. I will get you an excellent price!"

I make coffee, open my laptop, and do a deep dive on Ivy Blankenship. I get 1,037 hits, mostly articles from her days swimming at Oregon. There are also a few mentions of her in national newspapers leading up to the US Olympic trials for Beijing. She had the best time that year in the thousand-meter freestyle and was expected to easily clinch a berth on the team. Then the trial results: fourth-place finish, 0.07 seconds away from making the team, a photograph of her standing poolside, looking up at the clock, stricken.

That defeat was followed by ten years of nothing. She has no social media profiles, at least not under her name. There's more on her brother. A few years ago, he landed a job with a fourth-tier VC firm, and he apparently made the most of it. His Twitter feed is populated by earnest notes regarding rising tech firms, earnings reports, kudos to this person and that person for various business achievements. No mention of his sister. I set up Google alerts.

I take out the piece of paper Nicole gave me and place it on the table beside my laptop.

A search for John Murphy and his two boats produces even less satisfying results. Both boats are crab trawlers with a long history of registrations in Eureka and later El Granada. The name John Murphy is so common it takes hours to narrow the search. He first went bankrupt in 2009 and again in 2015. No-cost divorce. A short, failed business as a seafood purveyor. Murphy owns three properties: a cheap townhouse in Fortuna connected to a possible son, a pricey house in El Granada where the ex might live, and a condo in Pacifica. In the single photo I find of him online, he looks unremarkable: close-cut beard, graying hair, the deep tan and leathery skin you expect from a guy who has spent his life on boats.

But there's something else. John Murphy has kind eyes. I can't describe them beyond the color—pale blue—but if you saw the photograph, you'd think so too. How could a guy like this and a woman like Ivy be connected to the disappearance of high school kids from Greenfield? It doesn't add up. Maybe I'm on the wrong track. Maybe those pings from the middle of the ocean at the same time Gray Stafford appeared on the beach at Half Moon Bay mean nothing.

It doesn't add up: *unless.*

Unless you factor in the unfortunate truth that bears itself out again and again, a grand human theme on endless repeat: some people will do anything for money.

35

Demonstrate Chan's theory of retrieval-induced facilitation. Complement your response with three answers you have given that were aided by this retrieval-induced facilitation.

As I pull up to the curb at school, Kyle approaches my Jeep. I'm surprised to see him. I roll down the passenger-side window. "You're sure looking healthy. Dispatcher told me you were sick."

"Nope, I just decided to take a personal day." The way he says it, the spring in his step, tells me there's either a woman or a surfboard involved, maybe both.

"What's her name?"

"Holly."

"Is it serious?"

"It used to be. She's visiting from Michigan, second chance. I'm trying not to mess things up this time."

Now I understand why Kyle wasn't answering his phone. He's protecting his time with his girlfriend, protecting his home life, avoiding cross contamination. It's likely he sees Holly as the best thing life has to offer, and he thinks he can keep his two worlds separate. I want to tell him it's a worthy goal but impossible. If you let this job in, it can be insidious, quietly invading everything you hold close.

He props his elbows on the window and leans into the car. "About that video footage you asked me to look into? Turns out there isn't any. CCTV has been out at the school for a few weeks. They're doing an upgrade. I asked around while I was getting coffee in the teacher's lounge. The proctor for Sunday's practice test said Caroline seemed like her usual self. She also said a few of the kids had family trips and were going to be out all week. She wasn't certain if that was the case with Caroline, but she assumed so."

"Family trips, huh?" I think of Marc Rekowski's family packing up their SUV, getting out of town.

"I checked with the registrar too. Caroline *has* had several unexcused absences in the past. The registrar said the parents never return phone calls."

Kobayashi is waving the cars forward, giving Kyle impatient looks, so I have to pull through. I don't tell Kyle about the meeting with Nicole, not yet. It's tricky. The information Nicole provided is critical and useful, but in a courtroom, its provenance could create challenges for a prosecutor and endless fodder for a defense attorney.

As Rory climbs into the front seat, Kobayashi approaches the window and hands me a red paper bag. "Our parents and friends have provided us with an embarrassment of riches," he explains. "Vitamin Central and our district nutritionist have collaborated to create a unique supplement cocktail for each student, in order to help them meet the rigors of the test with confidence and vitality. As the great Japanese warrior-poet Hiraku once said, 'In battle, preparation / In preparation, battle.'"

I nod to Kobayashi and finish off the quote: "Know in your heart, young one, / the war has been lost or won / before the first

footprint on the battlefield." I'm not sure I'm remembering it correctly, but Kobayashi's wry smile tells me I got it right.

"Show-off," Rory says after we pull away. His tone is different,
though. He's relaxed, in a much better mood than this morning.
"Good news," he says. "Dave Randall told me Caroline's parents
surprised her with a last-minute cruise in Norway."

"Reliable source?"

"Dave is student council president. He seems on top of things."

"So, why does he know about Caroline's trip if you don't?"

"According to Dave, knowing where everyone is during Wonder
Test week is part of his job description. He also said Melissa Madsen
is touring elite music programs, and Jordan Kingsley is spending a
week on the set of a Martin Scorsese film. He won a contest from
a movie studio or something."

"Wow, maybe it's time for us to start entering contests."

But in my mind, I'm mulling over the strange timing of the
vacations and why Caroline didn't tell Rory she was leaving. Still
no text from her since the last one on Sunday night: *Don't worry,
Friend. All is well.*

"Do any of those kids happen to be in Caroline's study group?"

"I don't know. She did mention a Melissa once, but I'm not
sure which Melissa."

Back home, I toss the supplements in the trash and make Rory
a grilled cheese sandwich and a mango smoothie. He polishes it
off in a few gulps. "Do you believe Caroline's really in Norway?"

As much as I want to put Rory at ease, I can't lie to him. "There
are some details I should probably let you in on, but they don't go
beyond this room."

He frowns. "What details?"

I tell him about Gray Stafford's appearance on the beach that morning last year, the trawler, Nicole and our conversation. I leave out the part about sandwiches in the parking lot.

"Android phones ping back to Google every fifteen minutes?" he says.

"Yup."

"Then why doesn't everybody use iPhones?" he wonders.

"That doesn't solve the problem, kiddo. Those ping back to Apple."

I tell him about the woman in the bathing cap, Ivy, her early-morning swims at Montara. I watch his face as he mentally connects the dots. "You have to find Ivy."

36

Investigators of animal reproductive behavior note the existence in mammals of paternity uncertainty and maternity certainty. Is there a winner? Is there a loser?

It's 5:00 a.m. on Wednesday, day three of the test. I leave a note for Rory on the kitchen table and toss a collapsible beach chair in the Jeep. Ten minutes later I'm pulling onto Highway 92. I pause at the top to look out over the sprawling Skylawn cemetery before plunging down the other side of the mountain and into the fog. I drive past the horse farms and pumpkin patches, artichoke fields and trailer parks and stop for coffee at Three Sisters. The place is already filled with farm laborers, tech workers, and aging Half Moon Bay hippies.

Montara Sate Beach is two and a half miles south of Devil's Slide. Due to the limited parking and the difficult climb down the steep hill, it's far less popular than Pacifica State Beach and Rockaway Beach to the south. The towering cliffs, golden sand, and the fog layer hovering over the deep blue water make it feel like a hidden, undiscovered gem.

I climb down the precarious path and set up my chair at the peak of a small berm with a clear view of the entire beach. It's just before 6:00 a.m., and the beach is deserted, chilly, the sun glowing softly on the hillside to the east. I pull out my binoculars and paperback, *Martin in Space*. I finally drove down to Kepler's and bought a copy for myself.

I sip my coffee, keeping my eyes on the two paths leading down to the beach. The water looks deceptively smooth and glassy, but the turbulent shore break announces to anyone paying attention that this is no place for children and tourists. With the severe drop-off, infamous riptides, and northern currents, it's not safe for swimmers or surfers either. Ivy is either crazy, as Elsa suggested, or self-destructive. My bet is on the latter.

At 6:10, I notice movement in the parking lot. Two guys appear on the northernmost path, carrying fishing poles and ice chests. After that, nothing. I open the book and read. I'm three chapters in, the part where Martin slips into the lobby of the Grand Hôtel in Stockholm to escape the rain. He meets an American businesswoman, Grace, and they have an amusing, vaguely inappropriate conversation. It's a great scene, but I understand why Rory never mentioned it to me.

At 6:34, I see headlights approaching from the highway. The motor whines and the brakes squeal as it pulls off into the dirt lot. I peer through my binoculars. The car, a silver Suzuki Samurai, disappears from view. I shift my gaze to the far path. Several minutes pass, and still no one appears. I text Rory: You up?

Yep

There's a plate of biscuits and bacon in the fridge. Zap them in the microwave for thirty seconds. Good luck on the test!

I feel a little guilty for not being there this morning. He has a ride set up with a kid named Bradley and his mother, but no one should have to start the day with that pair. The mom talks a mile a minute, and Bradley doesn't seem to have discovered deodorant.

A woman appears at the top of the path and begins the descent. She's wearing sweatpants and a baggy green hoodie with a big letter O on the front. She skitters down the path with the agility of a mountain goat. She drops her bag, shimmies out of her sweatpants, and yanks the Oregon sweatshirt over her head, revealing shoulder-length brown hair and a swimmer's body clad in a one-piece bathing suit: broad shoulders, muscular build, all enveloped in a thin layer of fat.

For several minutes she stands staring out over the water, apparently unfazed by the biting wind. I imagine she's studying the tides and currents, mentally preparing herself for the swim. Over the years, I've visited this beach dozens of times, but I've never seen anyone go in past their knees. It's too dangerous.

I'm starting to wonder if she's changed her mind when she reaches into her bag for a wet suit. She works the wet suit up over her legs, hips, and arms, then grabs the long tail to the zipper and pulls it up over her head. She stops for a moment, head turned in my direction. Has she noticed me? I drop the binoculars into my lap. She's definitely looking this way. One count, two counts, three.

She takes a step in this direction, hand raised over her eyes. Did she see the binoculars?

Several seconds pass, but then she turns back toward the water and whips her mass of hair into a ball atop her head, quickly fastening it. She reaches into her bag once more and pulls out something small and red. As she stretches the red cap over her head, tucking in the loose strands of hair, I know I've come to the right beach on the right day.

193

She moves her big hands along the smooth red surface of her head, affixing her goggles. I pick up the binoculars again, more careful this time. Watching her, I understand Elsa's fascination. Ivy Blankenship isn't beautiful. She isn't even striking by any traditional definition. When she wandered onto the beach in her dingy sweats, she was nondescript, like so many of the longtime residents of the coast—people who are drawn to the ocean, hiding from something or someone, moving around inconspicuously under bulky layers of clothing to shield them from the coastal fog, damp air, and unpredictable weather. The appeal of Ivy Blankenship is in the transformation. Standing on the beach, gazing out over the water, compact and chiseled, she is the caterpillar that turns into—not a butterfly, that's wrong. A caterpillar that turns into a warrior.

She bends her knees deeply, explodes into a single jump-squat, and jogs toward the shoreline. No hesitation as she hits the water and dives headfirst into an imposing wave breaking just short of the beach. She disappears for several seconds, emerging in a flash of red on the other side of the wave, midstroke, powering through the cold, relentless tide, out past the second set of breakers.

She swims toward where the sharks are known to congregate, fearless, before turning north and working her way up the coastline, against the currents, against the shifting wind. She never speeds up, she never slows down, she never changes her stroke. It's amazing to watch. Eventually, she reaches the far outer edge of the cove, and her red cap pops up to survey the situation. She stops swimming, treading water as the current swiftly carries her back down the beach.

I will her to turn back, worried she won't make it. Maybe she's taken it to too far this time. Maybe she misjudged her strength.

But then, at the last moment, just before the currents would push her out toward Devil's Slide, north past Pacifica, east to the Farallon Islands, then beyond—Hawaii, Japan, Vladivostok—she ducks under the water and swims powerfully for the shoreline. I watch the red cap plunging and lifting, plunging and lifting.

That cap, moving inexorably through the water, tells me she'll be fine. And it tells me something else: it could have been her. She could have done it. She could have carried a weak, gaunt, terrified teenage boy through the punishing waves back to shore.

Finally, she emerges from the ocean. Mist rises off her body, the morning sun casting her in a golden glow. She looks eerie, unreal, like some comic book hero come to life. I glance at my phone, startled to realize it's 8:05. She was out there for more than an hour.

Pretending to read my book, I watch her pull off her suit, towel off, and pull on her sweats. Seamlessly, she transforms back into a caterpillar. When she reaches the bottom of the path and steps out of sight, I grab my bag and chair and scramble up the other path. Just as I reach the parking lot, her Suzuki pulls out. I climb into my Jeep and follow her.

I can't say how, but somehow, I know for certain: Ivy Blankenship *did* carry Gray Stafford out of the ocean.

She saved him. But from whom? And why?

Was she involved in his disappearance or only his recovery? Was she doing a good deed or making up for a bad one?

More important: what, if anything, does she know about Caroline?

37

An algae plant the size of Algeria could eliminate all CO_2 emissions from air travel, while also producing enough carbon fiber for a productive electric car plant. Is there hope for the future, or is it too late?

Two miles south of Pescadero, Ivy turns left and up into the hills. She stops at a deli and reemerges a few minutes later with coffee and a bag of groceries. As we wind into the mountains, I struggle to keep a safe distance and still maintain an eye. If she noticed me on the beach, she doesn't seem to notice me now. Fortunately, my beat-up Jeep fits right in.

She turns right toward La Honda. In the early seventies, with the arrival of the Merry Pranksters, La Honda earned a reputation as a weird, wild, and occasionally wonderful place. Eventually, the ideals of free love and chemically expanded minds gave way to disenchantment and a far more sinister drug culture. Today, many of the old, run-down cabins have been reclaimed by the forest, inhabited by bikers, or turned into meth labs.

A mile up the winding, narrow road, Ivy pulls into an unpaved driveway beside a tiny cabin. There are no other cars out front. I note the fading address on the leaning metal mailbox. Ivy grabs her duffle and gets out. There's no way to stop or turn around without drawing attention to myself, so I drive past, glancing in the rearview mirror to see if she notices me. She looks up, her gaze lingering on my Jeep until I round the next curve.

I drive down to an abandoned trailhead, park, and pull a notebook out of my bag. After jotting down her license plate and address from memory, I call in to the New York comm center. The rotor from my old squad answers the phone. I ask after the kids, we talk about the Mets, but then I hear a commotion on the other end, so I get to the point.

"I need some info on an address." I worry that my current status is too tenuous for such a request, but he doesn't miss a beat.

"Sure, ready to copy."

I give him the address of Ivy's cabin.

"We don't have CLETS access here, so I'll have to connect to SF and email you the info."

"Thanks," I say, feeling grateful, for the umpteenth time in my career, for a helpful voice on the other end of the line. The organization is a family—albeit dysfunctional—and once you belong, well, you belong. For better or worse.

More than once, Fred accused me of prioritizing my FBI family over our own. He even joked, not always kindly, that George was my real husband. I denied it, but there were times when I'd find myself out in the middle of the night working a case and realize I hadn't had a real conversation with Fred in weeks, that all of my most meaningful interactions had, indeed, been with George. Invariably, I tried to dial it back, spend more time at home, but the job always pulled me back in.

I drive back up the hill and find a spot where I can watch Ivy's house from a safe distance. An hour passes and nothing happens. I settle into the familiar groove of boredom, listening to a podcast on my phone, watching. My phone pings with an email. The address comes back to Ivy as of six months ago, give or take. The car is registered to the brother with an address in Campbell, California. He has two decade-old DUIs, a nasty domestic dispute, and one D&D, but he cleaned up his act after starting the job at the VC. Ivy's DMV is the surprise. It's from a few years ago, and she doesn't look so great. The girl in the photo in no way resembles the warrior from the beach.

Finally, at 11:05, Ivy emerges from the front door in shorts and a T-shirt, spends a few minutes stretching, then takes off. As soon as she crests the hill, I get out of the Jeep and move quickly toward the house, determined to get inside. It's risky. I have no search warrant, and who knows how long she'll be gone. But what choice do I have? Although the chances of Caroline being in the house are small, I have to check.

At the abandoned cabin next door, I slip down the driveway and into the woods behind the houses. I watch for movement inside Ivy's place. Seeing nothing, I sneak out from behind the tree line and up the stairs leading to her back deck. A lounge chair with a bright-red cushion sits next to a portable Coleman grill. The door is locked, but the shade is open. The cabin is no more than six hundred square feet, and I can see nearly all of it, but the bathroom door is closed.

The place is tidy, spartan, a twin-size bed against the wall, a pine table and small dresser, two wooden chairs, and bookcase. There are no pictures on the walls, nothing on the counters, no dishes in the sink. The kitchenette contains a coffee maker and an old toaster. If not for the shiny silver laptop on the table and the Steve Prefontaine biography on the bed, it would look like a monastic room at one of those Buddhist retreats near Big Sur.

No sign of Caroline. Still, I need to get inside.

The tools in my wallet are enough to pop the aging lock. I open the door, pause on the doorstep for several seconds. I've done some things in my career that I needed to do to get to the truth, things that might not look great on paper. Until this moment, breaking and entering wasn't one of them. I step inside.

I cross to the bathroom, hand on my gun, and open the door. Empty. I pull the door closed, go to the table, and open the laptop. It's on sleep mode, and it boots up in seconds. No password protection.

I do a quick search of Ivy's files. I open up Word and scroll through the file names, but nothing stands out. I open the iPhoto tab, but Ivy doesn't take many pictures. There are just a few dozen a year dating back to 2014, including shots from the Hardly Strictly Bluegrass festival, a picture of her in front of Amoeba Records, a coyote at Crystal Springs. Nothing of note. I try to access Facebook, Instagram, and Gmail, but find no automatic logins.

I run my palms under the mattress, behind the few books on the shelf. I rifle through the dresser and under the bathroom sink, careful to leave everything exactly as I found it. Nothing. Outside, I step off the porch and retrace my steps back to the Jeep. I put the car in neutral, rolling down the road, the smell of pine and tar rising up through the open windows. As soon as I'm far enough away for the neighbors not to hear, I turn the key in the ignition.

38

The category is music. What do the white keys tell us? What do the black keys tell us?

At pickup Wednesday afternoon, Kyle checks both ways before leaning down to talk. "Update on the French girl. When I talked to the registrar yesterday, remember, Caroline had no excused absences on the schedule. But today, she told me Caroline has excused absences all week."

"Why the discrepancy?"

"She said the call from the parents came on Monday, and the message had been misplaced."

"Does the registrar seem like the kind of person who misplaces things?"

"No, but a substitute answered the phone call and put the message on a Post-it instead of in the book. Anyway, I wanted to let you know I'll be out of commission for a few days."

"Again?"

"Chief put me on training, a car-stop in-service, starting tonight down in Santa Cruz. I'll let you know when I get back."

I thank him and pull forward. Rory climbs into the front seat. "How'd the test go?"

"Easy. Tomorrow is the long essay part. Kobayashi says this is where we really distinguish ourselves." Rory mimics Kobayashi's prayer hands, his monotone, Zen-like voice: "The long essay is the difference between mere success and everlasting greatness. Reach for the stars and you will pierce the clouds."

As we pull out of the parking lot, the levity quickly fades.

"No word from Caroline?"

He shakes his head. "It doesn't make sense. If she were really on some cruise, she would *definitely* text me." He pushes the door lock button up and down, over and over, *click-click-click*. "Did you find the swimmer?"

"Yes. I made a visit to her house."

"So, what did she say?"

"I haven't talked to her yet. You only get the element of surprise once. As soon as I talk to her, it's out there, things change, evidence gets destroyed."

Of course, there's another reason I hesitated before talking to Ivy. It's just bad opsec. You shouldn't do a conversation like that without backup. People are unpredictable, especially those with nothing to lose. Of course, I took a lot of chances in the past, but that was before Fred died.

"But you have to do something," Rory insists. "It's not about evidence."

"In the end, it's always about evidence." I pull into the driveway and kill the engine. "Beyond that, I need to decide who to talk to first, Ivy or the boat owner, Murphy, or someone else altogether. Once I talk to someone, they're going to alert the others."

Ideally, I would interrogate the one who planned the Gray Stafford and Lamey twins kidnappings. You want to go as far up the food chain as possible. Certainly not Ivy, probably not Murphy—but who?

"You just have to choose," Rory says. "Remember what you used to say? Action always beats reaction." His face is red, as if he's going to cry. I haven't seen him cry in so long. I know he still does. I've heard him, late at night in his room.

But he's right. I have to choose. What started with reading files and interviewing a reluctant witness, dipping my toes in to a defunct investigation, is about to get real. A brief, off-the-record stakeout is one thing. Confronting the suspect is another level entirely.

Years ago, I worked a case with the Israeli internal service, Shin Bet. It was a real lesson in getting things done. With them, there was no such thing as scheduling meetings or appointments. If something was worth doing, you did it then, no wasting time. At their core, they believed that the world would probably be here tomorrow, but then again maybe it wouldn't.

"You're absolutely right," I say. "I'll go talk to her." And with that promise, I'm all in. I've let him down in so many ways. I can't let him down on this.

39

You are on an island where sheep outnumber people by more than three to one. The temperature is cold and a breeze blows in from the north. Fish are the greatest natural resource. You could be in Calais by tomorrow night if the seas are calm and a ship's captain is willing to take you on. Where are you?

On Wednesday night and Thursday morning, my texts to George go unreturned. He's probably off the grid. I have no case, no authority. I also don't know anyone from the San Francisco office well enough to call in a favor of this magnitude. In the afternoon, unwilling to wait any longer, I go upstairs and get my gun. I throw my handcuffs, baton, pepper spray, and small green notebook into my messenger bag. I pull my drop phone out of the safe and use the slipstream to make up a nonattributable email account.

I find Rory in the library, reading *Martin in Space*, again.

"I'm going out. I'll be out late."

He looks up from his book. "You're going to talk to Ivy?"

"Yes."

"Good." I can see there's something else he wants to say.

"What?"

"Do you think of yourself as a protective parent?"

"I suppose, but not overprotective, I hope. Why?"

"Three kids went missing, and now this thing with Caroline. You're worried about Caroline, but you're leaving me alone. Which means you're not worried about *me*."

"Go on."

"So I've been trying to figure out *why* you're not worried about me. Why we're not on the next flight out of this town where kids keep disappearing and nobody wants to talk about it. Nobody even seems that concerned. It's weird. And then I had this crazy idea."

"What's that?"

"Caroline, Gray Stafford, and the twins share one important thing in common, don't they?"

"Technically, they have a lot in common."

"Yes, but the other day, you asked me something that got me thinking."

I get the feeling that we're being watched. I glance out the window, and there's Mister Fancy, sitting in our backyard, staring in. "Whatever's on your mind, Rory, you can say it. But only here. Only with me. Do you understand?"

"It's about the test, isn't it?" Rory waits for me to deny it. I don't.

He continues. "Marc Rekowski took off with his family. Jordan Kingsley won a contest to spend ten days on the set of a Martin Scorsese film in Bucharest, and Melissa Madsen is auditioning for music programs way out of her league. You wanted to know if those kids were in the special class with Caroline, so I asked around. They were. Every kid in that study group got called away during the test.

And the blonde mystery woman tried to talk Caroline out of taking it, but Caroline refused."

I look at him, waiting.

"The only kids who go missing," he says, "are the ones who might fail."

40

Does the economy reward honesty or dishonesty? Design four strategies that a simple shop owner might devise that would tip the balance in his or her favor. How might this apply to literature?

I wind into the hills of La Honda, dimming the Jeep's headlights as I round the bend toward Ivy's place. Her car is parked out front, and there's light glowing in the cabin's small windows. I park up the hill and roll down my window. The night fills with the sound of barking dogs and other, unseen creatures. La Honda is teeming with raccoons, skunks, foxes, coyotes, mountain lions. And biker gangs. Always biker gangs. A party is raging somewhere up the road, but right now, it's Ivy I'm worried about. With her chiseled frame, her bare home, her lack of internet presence or ties to anything or anyone, her treacherous morning swims, she's an unknown quantity. She appears to have little accountability and no fear of death, nothing to lose.

I consider how I should approach her. With the weak, it's always best to base your approach in strength. With the strong, it's more complicated. Strong people thrive on having an opposing force to confront.

I grab my messenger bag and slide my gun into the small of my back. It's in the tiny holster I brought back from my temporary deployment to Tel Aviv. The firearms unit hates it, but it's the most effective way to conceal the weapon without sacrificing speed or flexibility. I exit the Jeep, close the door softly, and walk down the street, grateful for the cover of darkness. At Ivy's cabin, I move up the stairs and stand to the right of the door.

I knock. Several seconds of silence followed by the sound of bare feet moving across the wood floor. The porch light comes on, two locks click, and then the door opens. Ivy is wearing her green hoodie, a big O on the front.

"Special Agent Lina Connerly," I say, flashing my creds.

She squints to see into the darkness, glancing past me, probably to see if I'm alone, calculating her options. Then she takes a deep breath. "So," she mutters, resigned. "This is how it happens."

"May I come in?"

She's still trying to decide her next move. In any encounter, this is the crucial moment. Her breathing has slowed.

"It won't take long." I try to sound relaxed, nonthreatening.

"Do I have a choice?" She steps aside, cracking the door farther.

"Everyone always has a choice. The best one for you, right now, is to talk to me."

Inside, she sits on her bed, motions me to the chair. "I've been expecting you." She motions with a hand toward me. "Okay, maybe not exactly *you*."

"What *were* you expecting?"

"Somebody bigger. No offense. A SWAT team maybe." She chuckles, but in her laughter, I can hear the trace of fear, maybe defeat. "I guess that's just television."

"I know some guys who *would* send the SWAT team, but I prefer this." The door to the bathroom is open. Ivy is alone. "Maybe we can just talk."

"I expected you guys to show up a year ago. Every morning, I waited. I heard that people always get arrested at six a.m., something about warrants and the court. For a couple of months, I set my alarm for five forty-five every morning, got dressed, and just sat there, waiting."

"But nothing happened."

"I figured it was a matter of time. But after a few months, when no one showed up, I felt relieved. Maybe I wasn't in any trouble after all. That's when I got back into swimming."

"Montara, no less. Jumping into the deep end."

"Maybe I was secretly hoping to drift out to sea one day, go so far I couldn't fight my way back."

"But that didn't happen."

"Not in the cards, I guess."

"Or, maybe you're just too good of a swimmer?"

Ivy slides her hand across the quilt. I can see almost all of her possessions from my chair. Six books on the shelf, two button-down shirts hanging on wall hooks, a bathing suit drying by the space heater, a wet suit on a hook. In the dresser, I know there are three T-shirts, one sweatshirt, two pairs of sweatpants, one pair of jeans, underwear, and two more bathing suits. One pair of red Nikes waits by the door. I've never before known a woman to have only one pair of shoes.

I pick up the Prefontaine biography on the table. "Good book."

"You read it?"

"Years ago. I liked the movies too."

Ivy leans back against the bed pillow. "As a kid, I tacked a quote of his on my wall. 'Anything less than your absolute best is an insult to the gift you were given.' Sometimes it inspired me, but sometimes it made me feel rotten."

My father dreamed I would be a track star is the thing I almost say, but then I don't. In these situations, the ring of truth is always preferable to the actual truth. "Track seems easier than swimming," I say instead.

"Don't know about that."

"With track, if you run out of steam you don't drown."

"True." She breaks into a smile and unfolds her arms, slowly letting down her guard.

I want to ask her about Caroline, but I don't. Not yet. From a behavioral perspective, it's complicated. There are two trains of thought, and most people in the intelligence field subscribe to the first: if you need to ask a critical question like something about WMD or counterterrorism, you must ask it as soon as possible, because you may not get another chance. While I understand the logic, I tend to go the other way. I never ask a question until I know I'll get a truthful answer. If you ask too early, while your subject's defenses are up, if you ask before you build rapport, you're more likely to get a nonanswer or an outright denial. Once someone lies to you, it's hard to walk it back. The lie, in some form or another, will sit there for a long time, maybe forever, an unmovable obstacle to a genuine relationship.

"I like your place."

"Not much to it."

"Minimalism. There are loads of books about it now. People are making a fortune writing books about having nothing."

"It wasn't by choice. I had lots of stuff, but then, well, I had to get out of a situation in a hurry."

I nod. "I've been trying to get rid of stuff too."

She tilts her head. "How's that working out for you?"

"Fine if you don't look in my garage."

"At first, having nothing bothered me. For a few weeks, I missed my stuff. I'd wake up thinking I was going to put on a certain shirt or pair of shoes or drink my coffee out of my favorite mug, or I'd want to write something down and realize I didn't even own a pen. But I came to appreciate it. When you don't have any money and you don't have any stuff, you can focus on what's important."

She gets up from the bed, walks over to the table, and sits across from me.

"What do you miss most?" I ask.

"I had a little orange thumb drive with all of my photos. Thousands of them. My mother liked to take pictures. She's dead now."

Ivy's words hang in the air. There's something on the tip of my tongue, something I want to say, something I would say to a trusted friend or a colleague, certainly not something I should say here, to Ivy. I say it anyway.

"My husband died a few months ago."

Ivy looks up at me, surprised, her sympathy battling with her curiosity. I wonder if she'll ask it. One beat, two beats, three. Then she does, because some people can't help themselves: "How?"

"A car accident in New York City. The guy who hit him was texting. Twenty-four years old."

She cringes. "Did he live? The guy who hit your husband?"

"Yes, but he'll never walk."

"That must be satisfying, in a way."

"No, it isn't." I don't tell her how he sent a letter asking to meet me two weeks after Fred died. How I couldn't read the whole letter, never even got through the first paragraph. How I stuck the letter back in the envelope and put it in the bottom of a desk drawer back at my office in New York. How I haven't opened it since, but I know it's there in my desk. And when I return to my desk, at some point, I'll have to decide what to do with it.

I shake my head, trying to erase the image of the letter in the drawer. I focus on Ivy. It feels strange to be talking about Fred here, mildly inappropriate, although I know he wouldn't mind. "Happy to be of use," he would say. With someone strong like Ivy, showing vulnerability is an effective way to defuse tension, reducing the likelihood of a physical confrontation.

"I like to think my mother's death was an accident too," Ivy says, though she doesn't explain.

I reach across and put my hand on top of hers. She stiffens. I sense she hasn't had physical contact in a long time. "I have to ask you a question."

She doesn't pull away.

"Do you know where the girl is?" My voice is low, almost a whisper. Quiet brings people together. It's less confrontational, more conspiratorial.

There's a flash of confusion on her face. "What girl?"

This clearly wasn't the question she expected. But she knows something, and she's calculating how much to reveal. I don't take my hand from hers. It's not easy for me—I've never been big on touching—but it is elemental. The physical connection, if done in the right way at the right time, is just one more key to building bonds, creating an atmosphere where the truth becomes possible. I wait for her to fill the silence.

She shakes her head, looking at me as if I'm the one who's confused. "But, it was a boy."

I know in that moment that she wasn't involved in whatever has happened to Caroline. "You mean Gray Stafford."

"His name was Gray?"

"Yes."

She pulls her hand away, stricken. "They never told me."

"Were there others before him? After him?"

Her head snaps up, and she looks me directly in the eyes. "No, God no!"

"The twins?"

She looks confused. "Twins?"

"Have you heard of a girl who went missing recently?"

"A girl? No." Ivy covers her mouth with her hand. She stands abruptly and moves away from the table. My hand instinctively moves to the small of my back.

She stops at the kitchen counter and gets a paper towel to blow her nose. Her shoulders shake. She turns to face me, her back against the sink. I can't see her hands. The redness around her eyes, spreading across her cheeks, makes her seem like less of a threat. Still, I can see her lean muscles, her strength.

"How is he?" she asks. "The boy."

"Gray is okay, physically at least. He's back in school."

"I think about him. A lot. I was so happy that woman was there on the beach. The boat owner—"

"Murphy?" I venture.

She nods. I wait.

Ivy drops the paper towel in the trash, stalling. But she doesn't stall for long. She's obviously been wanting to tell her story for a while, just waiting for her confessor to show up.

"Murphy wanted me to drop the kid at San Gregorio, but when I saw that woman on the beach, I told Murphy that was the place to do it. Once I got back to the boat, Murphy was determined to get out of there as fast as possible. I stood on the deck with the binoculars, watching the boy standing on the beach with the woman. Later, I wanted to track her down, thank her in some anonymous way, but I had no way to figure out who she was. I kept looking online, waiting to read about the boy who appeared naked on the beach, but I never could find anything. Strange, right? How does that not make the news?"

"How did you get involved? Was it Murphy?"

"God no. He knew less than I did." She comes back over and sits down. "I always assumed Murphy would slip up and get us caught. He was in a bad way after it went down. I don't think he knew what he signed up for any more than I did." She frowns. "Was it Murphy who gave you my name?"

"No."

"Who, then? Travis?"

"Travis?"

Ivy catches herself and gives me a look. It's one I've seen many times, that look of dismay people get when they catch themselves talking to me fast and casual, as if we're friends. You need to spot it quickly and pull the conversation back before they correct themselves and stop talking.

"Can I get a glass of water?" I ask.

"Help yourself. Cups beside the sink."

I pour water for both of us, keeping my eyes on her the whole time. I return to the table.

Ivy is biting her lip, contemplating how much to tell me. "Travis," she finally says. "I got involved through Travis."

"What was his role?"

"He owed a guy a favor. He was terrified, and he said he needed me to be there. He needed me to do the hard part, because he didn't know anyone else who could swim in the ocean. And he didn't know anyone else who would care enough to do it right."

"So he had something resembling a conscience."

"No, no." She dismisses the idea with a wave of her hand. "Travis only cares about Travis. He said if the kid drowned, the guy would come kill us all." She hesitates. "I shouldn't be talking to you, should I? I always told myself that when this moment arrived, I would hire a lawyer before I said a word. I even picked one out on the internet, guy in Petaluma. I put his number in my cell."

"Who's the attorney?"

"Duane Lipinsky."

"The guy with the commercials? If you need an attorney I'll help you find a real one. But for what it's worth, in my experience, every person who talks to me straight, no bullshit, ends up far better for it."

She narrows her eyes at me. "Will I need an attorney?"

"You can always get one. Anytime. Hopefully, though, if we do this right, we can avoid that. It will be tricky. You have to trust me."

Ivy sits in silence for several seconds, calculating. "Travis and I went to school together."

"Oregon?"

She nods. "We were on the same dorm floor my freshman year. We weren't great friends or anything, but we saw each other around a lot. We hooked up a few times during college and again the year after. A few years after graduation, I got injured, and I needed surgery on my shoulder. Coach wanted me to see this doctor at Stanford, best in the country.

"I heard Travis had been living out here for a while. I didn't know anyone else in the area, I was broke, and he'd always wanted it to go further than it did with us, so I emailed and asked if I could stay with him. It was a big ask, with my surgery and all. Maybe I was using him, but he didn't mind. He said it was no bother, he had plenty of room."

"What brought Travis to California?"

"He had degrees in engineering and chemistry and had come here to do research at Applied Materials. In school, he was the smartest guy I knew."

"Where's the house?"

"Four acres in the hills over Montara, a big rancher that he was renovating. He put in a gorgeous new kitchen, new bathrooms, a whole new foundation, turned out the old one was rotten. And he had goats, lots of goats. In the beginning, I'll admit, it was amazing. It was close to the city and the hospital but felt like the country, so it was a great place to recover from my surgery."

"Was he different than when you'd known him in the dorm?"

She picks up the Prefontaine book and thumbs through it, sets it down again. "Sure. He used to just be this super-smart Oregon hippie nerd. He grew up along the coast, had normal parents. He's a brilliant chemist. He loved the work at AMat. He told me he made a lot of money those first couple of years, and he put it all into buying and fixing up his property. But it's a big piece of land, and the renovation turned out to be crazy expensive, so he had to take out a huge loan. When I moved in, he told me he'd been laid off from his job a while back."

"Did he say why?"

"He didn't elaborate, but I got the feeling he wasn't getting along with his coworkers. Which didn't surprise me, because he can really rub people the wrong way. After he lost his job, he was at risk of going underwater with the property. So he borrowed more money but not from a bank. And once he'd borrowed the money, things went downhill. He had to do someone a favor; that's how he presented it to me."

"Why did you agree to it?"

She sighs. "Look, I owed Travis, okay? He didn't only let me stay at his place. He took care of me. Cooked for me, helped me get up and walk around. For a few weeks there, it was like we were married, like we'd skipped the whole dating phase and transitioned into domesticity. He made me *soup*, fluffed my pillows. No one had ever done anything like that for me."

She frowns, activating the parallel lines between her brows. "But eventually it went sour. He set up a lab for the guy he owed. Travis just needed to cover the debt, he said. Then he started to like it. After that, he turned into a dick. It happened so fast. The drugs brought out this huge ego."

"He was taking meth?"

"No, he said meth was for losers. He did coke. He liked being productive."

"What about you? Did you ever do drugs with him?"

She shakes her head adamantly. "Hell no, I was too smart for that, or so I thought. I'm an athlete. But the doctor prescribed Oxy after the surgery, and she kept prescribing it. The surgery hadn't gone exactly as planned, and she had to go in a second time, so I was on Oxy and Dilaudid for nine months. Totally messed with my mind, up and down, blissful highs and crushing lows. I was always tired and jittery, my muscles shrank, I lost my appetite. I got scary thin. I was in bed for months, watching TV. In the beginning, Travis was so nice. I couldn't have recovered without him. But later, when I stopped medicating and my body had begun to heal, and I started talking about running and swimming and getting my life back together, he got weird."

She bites her lip. She doesn't like remembering this, doesn't like showing her vulnerability to a stranger.

I get up to refill our water glasses, give Ivy a little space. "Weird how?" I ask from the sink.

"One night, when I told him I wanted to move back to Eugene, he started threatening me. I'd been helping package the product, as a way to repay my debt to him. Then he started to need me. He didn't want me to leave. So when I told him he didn't have a say in the matter, he beat the shit out of me. It was bad. It was embarrassing. I wasn't like I am now. I could barely move my arm. I weighed a hundred and seven pounds. Oxy will mess you up."

I return to the table. Ivy takes a long sip of water.

"How did you get out?"

"That beating was my wake-up call. After that I cleaned up my act, got healthy, waited. Then Travis had a situation. A disagreement about money with some guy you *don't* want to have a disagreement with. It was scary. We had to leave the house, lay low, stay in this crappy cabin in Moss Beach for a while. Travis slept with a gun under his pillow. Then the thing with the kid came up, and the guy told Travis that if he did him the favor, they would be clear."

"Where does Murphy fit in?"

"Murphy was one of Travis's first clients, owed *him* a bunch of money. Travis wanted me to do the real work, get the kid back to shore, make sure we didn't get caught. If I did that, Travis promised he would consider us even. If I did him that one favor, I'd never have to hear from him again."

I'm silently diagramming in my mind, keeping track of favors granted and favors owed, and how it all leads back to an emaciated, shivering Gray Stafford on the beach.

"He called it an opportunity," Ivy continues. "I didn't know anything except that I was returning the kid. Honestly, he made it sound like a good deed. Somebody needed to get the kid back to his family. Once I did my part, the kid would be safe and I'd be off the hook."

"Were you?"

She rubs her face with both hands. "I never went back to the house to find out. The whole thing scared the shit out of me. I slept in my car for a couple of weeks. I was lucky to find this place. I work online all day, graphics, web design, virtual assistant, you name it. I'm saving up to go back to Eugene. I want to show up fit and healthy, with some money in the bank."

"So, do you know who asked Travis for the favor? Who did Travis owe?"

"No idea. He didn't tell me or Murphy anything. It was all supposed to be anonymous."

"Where was Gray Stafford coming from?"

"I'm telling you, we had *zero* information."

"Did you get paid?"

Ivy wipes some imaginary crumbs off the table. "What do you want me to say?"

"Never mind. I don't need to know. If you asked Travis who set it up, would he tell you?"

She lets out a hard, cold laugh. "If I saw Travis, he'd probably shoot me. He's a wreck. Paranoid with a capital P. He gave up the business entirely, and now he just sits on his land with his stupid goats. I'm telling you, he's not the same guy I used to know."

I sense Ivy has no more to tell me. She looks at me with the rare kind of intensity you see in certain people, the kind of intensity she demonstrated when she swam against the current at Montara Beach. I understand how she almost made it to the Olympics. Although she has given me a lot of information, she hasn't told me the one thing I really need to know: Who orchestrated the kidnappings?

Ivy is staring at me, red-eyed. "I will do absolutely whatever you want. I will make this right. If it kills me, I don't even care." Tears are rolling down her cheeks now, but she doesn't look away. "I am so, so sorry."

I take my notebook and pen out of my bag. "I need you to tell me everything you know about Travis. I need his address, phone numbers, email, spending habits, where he gets gas, where he shops, date of birth, personality traits."

She tells me everything, and I write it all down.

"Lunch," I say. "Where does he go for lunch, and when?"

"He used to eat lunch at noon every day at La Bamba in Mountain View. He's a creature of habit, picky eater, so I bet he still goes there."

"I need photos."

She opens her laptop, pulls up Travis's photos on password-protected sites, and emails them to me.

I stand to leave. "Thank you. You're doing the right thing."

Ivy looks confused. "That's it?"

"That's it. We'll talk. We'll work it out. Don't say anything to anyone. Seriously. No one."

Driving back along 280, I have a feeling of something accomplished, something gained. But too many questions remain: Who took Gray Stafford and the twins? Where were they kept? Who was Travis working for?

And the most important question of all: Where is Caroline?

41

Two houses in Florida share a back fence, yet the residents must drive more than seven miles to go from one house to the other. In 250 words or fewer, describe how this situation reflects both the most significant advances and the greatest challenges in urban planning over the past century.

It's a quarter past midnight on Friday morning when I get home. Mister Fancy is sitting on the porch. I leave the front door open, but he doesn't follow me inside. When I return with a bowl of milk, he gives me a dismissive look. If I could hear him speaking again, I imagine he would tell me to get my head in the game.

Rory is asleep beneath a blanket on the living room sofa, television on. I shake his shoulder gently to wake him. "You're home," he mumbles. The way he says it, I realize he was worried about me.

He sits up, making room for me on the couch. "Mom, I keep looking at that last text Caroline sent me. *Don't worry, Friend. All is well.* It doesn't sound like her, it's not something she would say. Tonight, when I was rereading *Martin in Space*, I realized it's a line from the book."

"It is?"

He pulls the blanket around his shoulders. "At one point, Martin has dinner in Stockholm. One minute he's eating potatoes with chives and sour cream, and the next minute he wakes up alone in an unfamiliar room. The room is all white and it has no door, no windows. There's just a bed, a chair, and a desk with a note on it. The note says: *Don't worry, Friend. All is well.*"

"Was Caroline reading *Martin in Space* too?"

"I gave it to her a couple of weeks ago. The book is so long, so strange, the line didn't stick out until I read it again. What could it mean? Do you think Caroline was trying to send me a message? Is it some kind of code?"

I don't know what it means. But it gives me chills. I put my arm around Rory's shoulders. "We'll find her."

"Do you promise?"

"I promise." And I realize, as I say it, that it's the first time I've made a promise to Rory I'm not sure I can keep.

A few hours later, over a breakfast of bacon and biscuits, Rory complains, "I'm so tired of the Wonder Test."

"Just do your best."

He looks up and gives me a look I can't read. "Like my life depends on it?"

When I get home from dropping Rory off at school, our street is crowded with parked cars. I realize the culprit is an open house three doors down. A Mercedes is blocking my driveway, so I double park and walk up to the open house.

The grass is so green, the trees so manicured. Everything is almost too perfect. A woman with long black hair greets me at the front door. Her suit is well cut but revealing, more automobile expo than high-end real estate. I'm about to ask her if she knows who

222

the owner of the Mercedes might be when she thrusts an iPad-size gadget into my hands. "Here's your personal walk-through with Harris Ojai," she says brightly. "You can pause it whenever you like and swipe left on any screen to call an attendant." The screen is blank. I feel around, but I don't find a button to turn it on.

"Oh, you've never used one of these?" she asks.

She leans over and speaks into the screen. "Begin the tour." In response to her command, a hologram pops up from the screen, six inches high, full color. It's a mini Harris Ojai, doing a little dance to some techno-beat music. The hologram declares exuberantly, "I'm Harris Ojai. Welcome to my open house!" His feet tap on dots that appear on the screen as he instructs: "Press here for a 3D layout of the house, press here for listing details, and press right here to send me a message!"

"Nothing better than having your own little Harris Ojai to walk you through!" the woman exclaims.

I wander through the foyer into the living space. The house is like a centerfold from *Architectural Digest*. Two dozen prospective buyers are walking around with their brokers. In the kitchen, a chef I recognize from local television is arranging appetizers on a platter. A young man in a catering uniform hands me a glass of champagne.

Beyond the dining area is a media room, where the 49ers' old Super Bowl victory is playing, larger than life. Steve Young is nearly nine feet tall. As Dwight Clark makes the catch, the room comes alive on all sides.

I wander upstairs and then upstairs again, the champagne buzz heightening the sense that I've wandered into a dream, Alice in Real Estate Land. I'm not even sure why I'm here. It's as if Harris

Ojai willed me up the block and into the house. But I feel drawn to it, as if the secret of Caroline's disappearance, the secret key that will unlock this town, might be somewhere in this mansion.

After seven bedrooms, a slew of marble bathrooms and cedar closets, I try to find my way out. A concrete staircase leads down to what Harris Ojai unapologetically calls the maid's quarters. I escape to the backyard with mini Harris Ojai looking up at me and imploring, "Error! Don't you want to see the wine cellar. Error!"

"Stop," I command, but I can't turn him off.

A chorus of elementary school children in matching green outfits sings "California Dreamin'" beside an enormous, glittering swimming pool. The real Harris Ojai materializes beside me. He's wearing the same shiny suit as his hologram. "Error!" mini Harris repeats. "Don't you want to visit the wine cellar?"

The real Harris Ojai takes the gadget and speaks to his doppelgänger as if to a disobedient child. "Go to sleep," he says, and the hologram disappears.

He points to the children's choir. "Listen to the way their voices echo off the marble inlays on the patio!" He cups a hand to his ear. "Beautiful, yes?"

"Yes, but I'm surprised they're here on a school day."

"Ah, it's the unique synergy of our little town. What is good for Greenfield is good for the children. What is good for the children is good for the town. Strong property values lead to strong schools. Strong schools lead to strong property values. We are all in this together! Selling houses is my art, Lina. One day, you and I will make a masterpiece."

42

Which major American rivers have been least addressed in American literature, and how has this lack of recognition influenced local cultures and economies?

La Bamba is located in a strip mall in Mountain View. Ivy told me Travis eats lunch here every day at noon, so I arrive at 11:30. Judging from the line of workers in fluorescent orange vests stretching out the door, it must be good. I wait in line and order a burrito with chicken, black beans, cheese, guac, no rice.

I take my tray out back to a corner table with a view of the entire place. At 12:10, I spot a guy who looks like the photos Ivy showed me, minus twenty pounds, give or take. The odd ridges in his face hint at mental illness, palpable paranoia. He finds an empty table, peels the aluminum foil from his burrito, and digs in. He eats like a feral animal. I imagine he's a shadow of the University of Oregon chemistry student he once was.

I walk over to his table and set my drink down. "Mind if I join you?" This is the ideal place to engage. It's public, and he's not expecting me. If he goes off, the situation will be easier to contain than if we were alone.

"Yes, I mind."

"Thanks, I'll sit anyway." Confused, he sizes me up, determines I'm not a threat, and returns to his burrito.

I pull out the chair and sit. "Travis."

Now he meets my eyes. "Do I know you?"

"You're going to need to focus, Travis. I'm going to say something, and then I'm going to ask you some questions. This conversation will have a profound impact on the course of your life. Do not underestimate me. Understand?"

Fear flashes across his face. He's made so many bad decisions in the last couple of years, he's probably trying to figure out which specific bad decision brought me here.

"One year ago, a person asked you to arrange the return of a teenage boy."

The fear morphs into panic. "What?" He looks around frantically. "Is this a joke? Did someone put you up to this?" He sets down his burrito, breaking into nervous laughter.

"Up here." I snap my fingers to get his attention, waiting for his eyes to meet mine again. "We don't have much time."

It's crucial to set parameters for any confrontational conversation, especially with someone who has a limited ability to focus. "This meeting ends in only one of two ways. One, you answer my questions, all of them, you answer honestly, then you go home and you never mention this conversation to anyone, ever."

"Yeah, what's the second way?"

"Federal agents, search warrants, you in jail, and Mom and Dad trying to scrape together two million for bail."

Travis leans back in his chair and crosses his arms, appraising me. My suburban mom outfit seems to throw him off. "Who the fuck *are* you?"

I reach into my bag, pull out my creds, badge side up, and slide them across the table underneath my palm, uncovering them only long enough for Travis to see. His eyes dart down to the badge, back up at me. "How do I know it's real?"

I slide the creds back into my bag. "I suppose you don't, but you'll definitely know the gun is real."

He's silent for several seconds, trying to figure out what to say, but his brain is shot. He's not who he used to be. "You won't find shit at my place."

"Okay," I say, standing. "So you're going with the second option. Good luck with that."

"No, no, no." Panic rises in his voice. "Sit down."

A big guy next to us in a Sharks jersey gives Travis a withering look. I can tell Travis wants to run, but he's too scared to make any sudden moves. I sit back down.

"It's possible your place is clean right now, Travis. It's possible there's no paraphernalia, no residue, no incriminating emails on your laptop, no text messages on your phone, no documents under your bed, no tax problems, no hair fiber, no DNA, no plants, no ashes, no cash, no weapons. It's possible but unlikely. More importantly, did you pay for any part of that property with drug proceeds? I'd hate to see you lose it. Forfeiture is a bitch."

He folds the tin foil from his burrito, hands shaking, and sips the last of his drink. He pulls at his shirt, scratches at his forearms and chest. A trail of red moves up his neck. Hives. "Go ahead. Ask your questions."

"The missing boy. Who wanted you to return him?"

"I don't know what you're talking about."

"Good luck with the raid." I scoot my chair back as if to leave. "Be sure you avoid any sudden moves. And maybe think about getting some slip-on shoes and elastic pants. They don't allow ties and laces at Dublin. Federal prison is weird that way."

"Whoa, lady." He reaches across the table to grab my forearm. "Relax."

The guy in the Sharks jersey jumps to his feet. He's six five, at least three hundred pounds. "Is this guy bothering you?"

I look at Travis. "Are you bothering me, Travis?"

Travis puts his hands up in a gesture of surrender. "Naw, man, just having a conversation."

"I'm watching you," the guy says. He sits down and returns to conversing in Spanish with his friends.

"I never even saw the kid."

"What did you see?"

The hives are spreading to his face. "Someone asked me to take the kid from one guy, and, well, return him."

"Return him? Like a pair of pants?"

"The guy said to do it however I wanted, just make sure the kid didn't wind up dead. So, I asked a friend to do it. And then it was over, case closed. I never heard another word."

I stare at him, waiting for more, but he is silent. "Yeah, Travis. That's not really going to work."

"It's the truth, swear to God."

"I need specifics. Who asked you to do it? Who gave you the boy? Where had he been? Who 'returned' him? Have you done similar things since then? Do you know where the girl is?"

"Whoa! I don't know anything about a girl." Like Ivy, he appears genuinely surprised at the mention of a girl. "No, no, no. I'm

228

telling you: *One time.* I only did it once. I got that boy back where he was supposed to go. That was the beginning of it and the end of it. I'm no freak. I was asked to take the boy from some dude and return him. That's all she wrote, man."

"Who asked you?"

"Um," he says. "Not a 'who,' but more of a 'what.'"

"Okay."

He leans forward, nearly whispering. "Let's say a person needs to move a bit of product, okay, a lot of product. Here, there aren't a lot of options when it comes to—"

"Distribution networks?"

"Right."

"Who is your distribution network?"

"These people don't exactly use first and last names," he says. "One of their runners, when he's picking up my shit, he passes me a note. A phone number, simple instructions, date, times, meet a guy, get a boy, return him safely. For some reason, the boy has to be left on a beach, alive. I'm telling you, it was clear we were sending the boy back home, *not* the other way around. All I knew was, we were getting a boy back to his parents. Guess I should have told them to fuck off."

"But you didn't."

"I wasn't exactly in a position to tell them to fuck off. And I'm being straight here. I doubt there's any proper way to say no to these people."

"So how did it go down?"

"I know this guy Murphy, owns a boat. I bought crab off him a few times, loaned him money here and there. I knew he was in a bad way, businesswise. He had two bad crab seasons, back to back.

They wanted the kid returned to a beach, and it couldn't be traced back to anyone, to any car, plates, address. So I'm like, how the hell do we get the kid there without a car? Are we supposed to hike? And the runner, some guy with a stupid haircut, says, 'Just figure it the fuck out.' Murphy needed money, and it didn't hurt that he owed me. So I gave him a drop phone and the number."

"What happened when Murphy called the number?"

"The guy on the other end arranged to meet him at Pillar Point Harbor. At four thirty in the morning, Murphy is sitting on his boat, waiting for a couple of Asian gangbangers. Instead, this white dude shows up. Six foot two and fleshy, wearing plaid pants and a pink Gucci shirt, thousand-dollar shoes. He walks up the pier, whistling, pushing a big wooden crate on a flatbed dolly. He heads straight for Murphy, gets up in his face, and whispers in his ear, 'Hello, darling.'"

Travis cracks a smile for the first time, as if he still can't quite believe the story.

"The guy is wearing latex gloves. He orders Murphy to help him load this heavy crate onto the boat. When they get it down below, the plaid guy pulls out a set of pocket tools and pops the top."

I'm getting a sick feeling, listening to Travis. I don't want this story to go where I know it's going.

"Inside the crate, there's this pale, skinny kid. Murphy thinks the kid is dead and starts freaking out. Plaid Man grabs him, pulls him in close, and says, 'Please don't tell me this is your first rodeo.' The guy has Murphy's head in his hands, so close Murphy can smell Cheetos on his breath. And the guy is *huge*. He looks Murphy straight in the eyes and says, 'Can we maintain?'"

"Murphy is scared shitless, blabbing, 'Yes, yes, yes.' Plaid Man puts his mouth on Murphy's ear and says, 'If you do not maintain your shit, I will burn this motherfucker down.' Plaid Man, still in his gloves, pokes at the kid's shoulder. The kid wakes up. Murphy is so relieved he almost pisses himself. The kid's alive. But he's groggy, not really there."

"Had he been drugged?"

"Maybe."

I think of Gray Stafford sitting beside me on the school lawn at the movie. Gray Stafford, a normal high school kid before all this happened, star athlete, a little cocky, well liked. It breaks my heart. It gets under my skin. Somebody's got to deal with Plaid Man.

"What about his hair? What was the condition of the boy's hair?"

"The kid was completely bald. Murphy asks Plaid Man why, and Plaid Man starts singing, 'Not my first rodeo, dear, not my first rodeo.' They lift the boy out of the box. He's groaning. Murphy's trying to be gentle. One thing you should know about Murphy, he loves kids. He wants to get the kid as far as possible from this dude.

"They get the kid out of the crate, and Murphy wants to make him comfortable, but Plaid Man has all these rules. He insists on laying the boy out on a plastic sheet. Murphy's seen enough *Law and Order* to know a plastic sheet is not a good sign. Plaid Man tells Murphy to fetch the fire extinguisher, then he hoses the boy down." Travis mimics a fire extinguisher with his hands. "Whoosh! While the boy lays there shivering, coughing, Plaid Man breaks down the entire crate, *boom-boom-boom*. Then he packs up all of his stuff in a giant vinyl zipper bag."

The baldness, the fire extinguisher, the vinyl bag, hosing it all down, Plaid Man's methodical ways. He must have shaved their heads to eliminate hair fibers, DNA. He was covering his tracks.

"What happened next?"

"He orders Murphy back up to the deck. Plaid Man says, 'You should know, Mr. Murphy, *John* Murphy, I am a very busy man, and I would hate to have to spend time burning this motherfucker down. I would hate to burn down your boat, your other boat, your condo, your house, your place up north, your wife, your sister's kids.'"

Travis is lost in the story, imitating Plaid Man, almost enjoying it. The guys next to us have turned to stare.

"Plaid Man left with his big vinyl bag, Murphy took the boat out, and a little while later, he left the kid on the beach."

"That's it?"

"That. Is. It." He throws his hands up in a gesture of surrender. "I swear."

"How did the boy get from the boat to the beach?" Of course, I know the answer, but I'm curious to know if Travis will rat Ivy out.

One blink, two, three. "Murphy had a blow-up raft."

"He told you that?"

"Yeah, he had one of those little boats with oars, and he put the kid in it, and he told the kid to row to shore."

"The boy was in terrible shape. He couldn't even stand on his own. How could he row himself to shore?"

"Don't know, wasn't there." Interesting. He's protecting Ivy. Is it possible Travis has a heart?

I switch gears. "When Murphy was at Pillar Point Harbor, did he see Plaid Man's car?"

"No. Plaid Man materialized out of nowhere and vanished into nowhere. Murphy said he thought Plaid Man must've walked there with the crate on the dolly."

"From where?"

"Don't know. Anyway, as soon as Murphy dropped off the kid, he docked the boat and drove around for hours, trying to calm down."

"When did you next see him?"

"That night, I promised him the cash as soon as the job was done."

"And have you seen Murphy since then?"

Travis shakes his head. "Never. That was the end of it. I got paid, he got paid, case closed. Can I go? Are we good?"

I can tell he's about to try to make a run for it, so I reach across the table and grab his wrist. "No."

Travis winces. "I told you everything."

"Who runs your distribution network? Who's your contact?"

He tries to pull away. "Are you trying to get me killed?" He mumbles to himself: "Every decision I made was the right one, but now they've all added up to one big fucking mess."

"Who does your distribution?"

Travis is quiet for a second, playing with the foil from his burrito. "I just have a phone number. It's never the same runner. I call the number, someone shows up."

"Name?"

"It's a crew from Daly City. They call themselves the Kenji Boys. One of them hinted they're connected to the Triads. Maybe he was blowing smoke, but they *are* connected to somebody. They fronted me a shit ton of start-up cash."

"Okay, I need those phone numbers." I let go of his wrist, take a notepad and pen out, and slide them across the table.

Travis sits several seconds, head in his hands. Then he pulls out his phone. He looks at it for nearly a minute, considering. He swipes the screen, scrolls through the contacts, and writes down two numbers, a K over the first and a PM over the second. He pushes the notebook toward me. "Can I go?"

"Don't do anything. Don't say anything. Don't tell anyone we talked. And stop selling drugs. That shit destroys everything and everyone around you. You're a smart man. You should know that."

"Yes, yes, yes." His eyes narrow, he looks directly at me, and I sense the focus he must have had back when he was a star student, the focus that landed him the fancy job and helped him buy the property.

"You remember what happened to Walter White?"

"Yes."

"You want to end up like that?"

"It's a little late to be asking that question, don't you think?"

"Do yourself a favor and get a real job. You earned an engineering degree from Oregon. Act like it."

He shakes his head. "Damn," he chuckles.

"What?"

"If I had someone like you busting my ass every day, maybe I wouldn't be in this situation."

"It's not too late."

"I don't think you heard anything I said about the Kenji Boys. I hope you find the girl, whoever she is. I really do. Can I go?"

"Go."

"One thing. Before you track those numbers, can you give me four hours to get the fuck out of Dodge?"

"Two."

Without another word, he bolts from his chair.

43

Home ownership has long been a cornerstone of the American dream. Weighing the risks and rewards of home ownership, as well as the sociopolitical implications of class disparity, explain why we as a society should continue or dismantle this way of thinking.

The New York office comm center has nothing on either phone number. My public records search yields no clues. I open Confide and send Malia the numbers and the name Kenji Boys. Daly City connection, I type. May be connected to the Triads.

Nothing on the numbers, Malia messages back minutes later. As for the Kenji Boys, you're right about the Asian OC. There's a Daly City operation plus Chinatown connections. Despite the plucky name, they've got serious cash flow and even more serious muscle.

As I'm typing *thanks,* another message arrives from Malia: Don't get yourself killed before you can go to Iceland.

I message Nicole on WhatsApp. You there?

She responds immediately. Howdy.

How's your love life?

She replies with a thumbs-up emoji.

Can your relationship handle two additional phone numbers?

We'll see.

I send the two numbers, adding: It's urgent.

Under normal circumstances, I would file the paperwork, request the court order. But if Plaid Man has anything to do with Caroline's disappearance, I can't wait for the process to work its way through the courts.

Rory is in a surprisingly good mood when I pick him up from school. The student council president, Dave Randall, invited him to a swimming party at his house next Wednesday to celebrate the end of the Wonder Test.

"Isn't it cold for swimming?"

"They have an indoor pool. But the important part is, Caroline will be there."

"What?"

"Dave said she'll be back on Wednesday."

"How does he know?"

"Someone at lacrosse practice told him. Do you think we've just been paranoid all along?"

"Is Caroline friends with anyone on the lacrosse team?"

He frowns. "Well, no. But why would Dave lie?"

Rory has a point. Why *would* he?

"How did the test go today?"

"Hard to tell, but I think I'm in good shape. Dave's mom, who's on the school board, read the report from the first day of the test, and I had the top score for the school."

"Wow, congratulations."

"You sound surprised."

"I'm not surprised you aced it. I'm surprised a member of the school board can access your scores."

After dinner, my phone pings with a text from Nicole. That was fast. Only the second number was an Android. Registered to Leonard Blake. The phone was purchased a little over a year ago at a Best Buy in Windsor and hasn't been powered on in 361 days. Final ping was from 20107 Armstrong Woods Road, Guerneville, California.

So, 361 days. The last time Leonard Blake, aka Plaid Man, used the phone was just days before Gray Stafford showed up on the beach in Half Moon Bay. Which means there's a good chance Leonard Blake was keeping Gray somewhere near Guerneville.

I need to go to Guerneville, but I don't want to go alone. With George still out of the country and Kyle in Santa Cruz, I don't have many options. I try a few other numbers, including two friends from my Quantico class, but no one is in the area. I try an old friend at the Palo Alto office, but from his outgoing message I realize he has moved on. Getting other agents involved is tricky. I'm in the gray area now, that period between your first hunch and the opening of the case. Between the two, there can be days or weeks of legwork, painstaking research to determine the validity of the lead. Once you open a case, start the official file, and put the machinery of the federal government into action, there's no going back.

At 4:37 a.m. on Saturday, running on fumes but unable to sleep, I go down to the kitchen, make coffee, open Google Maps, and survey the area around 20107 Armstrong Woods Road. I compile a list of the properties within a three-hundred-yard radius: ownership, social media posts, taxes, crime records. Geographic pings have a variance of about one hundred yards due to complex rules involving national security. Still, the last ping on the phone could be a red herring. Leonard Blake could have taken a long drive and dumped the phone as a precaution.

Mister Fancy is in the driveway. He lifts his head and stares into the kitchen window. I pour milk into a saucer and set it on the front porch. He walks toward the bowl, sniffs, laps up a few drops, and loses interest. He rubs against my leg as he enters the house.

"Ah, coming inside, are you?"

In the kitchen, he jumps up on a chair and watches me pop a bagel in the toaster. I'm probably misreading his cat language, but I imagine he considers us to be fellow travelers, both of us on the outside, peering into the snow globe of this strange town.

On the map, Armstrong Woods Road stretches three miles, from the town of Guerneville to a sprawling state park known for its eight-hundred-year-old redwoods. There are two small resorts, a store that sells tables and clocks crafted from redwood burl, a church, a library, residential cul-de-sacs, and a trailer park. The redwood grove has more than fifty miles of trails, hundreds of acres of wilderness. The kind of place a person can hide . . . or be hidden.

Another possibility: Maybe Dave Randall was telling the truth, and Caroline really did tell someone she'll be home on Wednesday. Maybe, despite the coincidences of time, place, and poor academic performance, Caroline's disappearance is unrelated to Gray Stafford and the Lamey twins. Just because two things *seem* connected doesn't mean they are.

I'm deep into research when I hear footsteps on the stairs. Mister Fancy and I both turn. "Rory, what are you doing up?"

"Can't sleep. I was thinking about what you said about the lacrosse team. Caroline hates the whole jock thing. I've never seen her talk to any of those guys." His hair is sticking up in the back where he slept on it. I feel a gut punch of love for this kid who has changed so much in the last year, who will change so much more before I send him off to college.

He plods into the kitchen and peers over my shoulder. "What's this?"

"I asked a friend to run a phone number on someone I think was involved in Gray's disappearance. It's a long story. She located him, or at least who we think might be him, in Guerneville."

He sits at the table opposite me, stroking Mr. Fancy's fur. "You don't believe Caroline is on a Norwegian cruise with her parents, do you?"

"I don't think she is, no."

"You think this guy took her?" he asks, panic rising in his voice.

"We have zero evidence of that, but I do think he was involved with what happened to Gray."

"Can't you call Caroline's parents?"

"I tried. They're impossible to find."

"They must be somewhere. They can't just fall off the map."

"That's the thing, Rory. People like them are extremely good at falling off the map."

"But you don't disappear without your kid knowing where you are."

"I'm afraid people do." I don't tell him about the times I did it myself. But I always knew if something happened to me, Rory had Fred, and as long as he had Fred, he would be okay.

Rory reaches across the table, pulls the laptop toward him, and types. "Ninety-seven point four miles to the Russian River," he says.

"It's not that simple."

"Why not?"

"If I had my squad here, or even *one* colleague I know and trust. Or even Kyle. But this isn't the kind of situation you go into without backup."

"Do you have a better idea?"

Before I can reply, he's heading up the stairs. "I'll be ready in ten minutes."

Mister Fancy sits there gazing at me. "The boy's right," he seems to be saying.

"I'll go alone," I call up the stairs. "It's too dangerous."

But by the time I get dressed and brush my teeth, Rory is already standing at the front door, backpack slung over his shoulder, holding the car keys, waiting.

"No, Rory. You're not going."

"Yes I am."

"You're *not*." I reach to grab the keys out of his hand.

But Rory is quicker. He darts out the door, gets in the passenger seat, and slides the keys into the ignition.

It's cool outside, dew on the ground. I stand in the doorway and call to Mister Fancy. In no hurry, he slinks past me out the door, and I shut it behind me. In the car, I try to reason with Rory. "You can't go."

"She's *my* girlfriend."

"Having you there will change things. I'll be too worried to do what I need to do."

"If I don't go and something happens to her, I'll never forgive myself." He glares at me, a teenager who has made up his mind.

"Fine," I relent. What the hell am I doing? No parenting handbook in the world, no agent, no expert, would say that bringing your teenage son on surveillance is a good idea. "You might want to bring a book, some music. These things can drag on."

He holds up the CD folio Fred gave him on his twelfth birthday. Every time I see the case, it brings back a flood of memories, all of those nights after Rory had gone to sleep when Fred would retreat to his computer. He burned him eighteen discs, counting down the three hundred best songs he believed Rory needed to know. The case holds all eighteen discs, plus a notebook with Fred's personal thoughts on each song.

As we pull down the driveway, I'm searching my brain for any other option. Yet I know if I leave Rory behind, it will cause a tear in our relationship I might not be able to repair. His girlfriend is in danger, and he won't be satisfied until we find her. The hardest part of parenting is the gray area that falls under the heading of "trust." I want my son to trust me, and in my eagerness to make that happen, maybe I don't always make the best call.

Rory opens his CD case and asks, out of the blue: "Do you think Caroline knows her parents are more than diplomats? Do you think she knows they're in *your* line of work?"

"Caroline is smart. I'm sure she does."

He slides a disc into the player. We've listened to all of them so many times I know the songs by heart, Fred's notes too: "Disc 7, Track 1, Little Steven and the Disciples of Soul, 'Inside of Me': So many words here and not a single one hits a wrong note. Little Steven never made another album like this, but he didn't have to."

We pull onto 280 North. By the time Lou Reed's "Halloween Parade" comes on, I feel so guilty I'm tempted to turn around and go home. This world I know so intimately is exactly what I'm supposed to protect Rory from. But then, when Lou Reed gets to the colorful verse about the girls from pay dates, I realize Fred and I were never that protective. Maybe we both could have been more vigilant about insulating Rory from this dangerous world.

44

You are twenty-eight times more likely to be killed by a dog than by a shark. Explain why, and then rank the following states in order of likelihood of being killed by an animal, insect, arthropod, or human: Texas, Wyoming, South Dakota, Florida, and Oregon.

"I need to ask you something," Rory says as we drive toward the city. "Why did we *really* come to California?"

"Because of Grandpa. To get his things in order."

"You could do that this summer. Why now? Why did we have to leave New York in the middle of the year? Why did we have to give up our whole life?"

"You know Dad always wanted to move here. He loved Northern California, the clean air, the big beaches and hiking trails, this whole other life we couldn't give you in New York City. He thought our noisy apartment with the crazy upstairs neighbor and the cramped little rooms was too stressful."

"I *liked* our apartment. I liked my school. You loved your job. All those years, Dad wanted to leave, but you talked him out of it, so why now?"

"It's complicated."

"Really," Rory insists. "Why did you leave your job?"

"I had to."

"*Why* did you have to?"

"I made a mistake. A big one."

"Did you get fired?"

"No, no, nothing like that. After I made this mistake, I couldn't trust my judgment."

"Mom, I need more than that."

I'm thinking about how to word it and, of course, how to say it in an unclassified way.

"I had this friend," I begin.

"Friend, or"—Rory raises his fingers in air quotes—"*'friend'*?"

I smile sadly. "He was a *'friend'* who became a friend."

"So what happened?"

"The night after the funeral—"

Rory flinches. I'm not sure I've said the word "funeral" aloud to him in all these months. "When you dropped me off at Marcus's house?"

"Yes. I had to go meet my friend at a hotel."

"Which hotel?"

"Doesn't matter. He was in town for only one night. He came specifically to see me. I said I couldn't get away. I told him that we'd buried your dad the night before, but he still insisted, so I knew it was an emergency."

"So you went."

"Yes." The memory resurfaces in my mind, images I don't want to see. "A long SDR—"

"Surveillance detection route?"

I nod. "Up to Yankee Stadium, down to the village, around in circles, and then to the hotel."

"What did he want?"

"He needed to tell me he might have been compromised."

Rory sits up straighter, frowning, trying to follow. "Compromised? Like he thought his people knew he was your friend?"

"Yes."

"And a friend to America."

"Exactly."

"How did he end up on our side?"

"It's my job. Making friends. Believe it or not, sometimes I can be pretty persuasive."

"How do you persuade someone to do something they don't want to do?"

"You listen to them, you pay attention, you put yourself in that person's shoes. You figure out what they want or, more importantly, what they need, what motivates them. The most successful people in the spy game are the ones who don't just exhibit empathy but actually *feel* it. Empathy is something you can't fake."

45

"The more identities a man has, the more they express the person they conceal."

—John le Carré

Part 1: Address the tradition of split identities in literature.

Part 2: In order to succeed, should one strive for an attitude of concealment or of exposure?

I arrived late to the meeting with Yellow Beak at the Lucerne. That was a first. I'd never been late. It was raining, and I was sick with a fever and terrible cough, in no state to meet a source.

I had dozens of questions for him, questions prepared by a twenty-four-year-old analyst from the DI who didn't have a clue about the nuances of source recruitment. I had a wad of cash. The room was too hot. Normally, I would have booked a suite with a separate sitting area, but because of the funeral, I had asked a new agent on the squad to get the room and leave the key at the desk under my undercover name. He tried to get a suite, but none were available, so he booked a deluxe courtyard room. He didn't know about my friend's claustrophobia. That's on me. I should have told him.

Yellow Beak was waiting in the corridor outside the room when I arrived. Big mistake: He knew it. I knew it. But I wasn't there when he arrived, and he didn't want to miss me. We slipped into the room, and as soon as he saw the courtyard through the window, he stiffened. I apologized for the room and for being late, but he just waved off my apologies. "I am very sorry to interrupt your—"

He didn't know what to say. My grieving? My postfuneral funk? His English was spotty but I don't think the right words exist in any language. He put both his hands on my shoulders, looking into my eyes. He never did that. Usually, he gave me a quick cheek kiss at the door, a hug at the end—"in case we never see each other again," he always said—and nothing more. This time was different. "I am worried, Lina," he said. "I am nervousing."

So we sat, me on the foot of the bed, him in the uncomfortable chair. Although we discussed a few things, the main reason he had called was to tell me about a penetration. A man from his internal branch appeared on a delegation list for a trip to the US the following week. Yellow Beak was familiar with the man's work, so when he saw the itinerary, he knew something was wrong.

I told him I would handle it. That's what pushed me to go into the office and upload the write-up the night after Fred's funeral.

The memory still pains me. After the meeting, I picked Rory up from his friend's apartment. We went home, and I heated up a dish of chicken and rice that had been left by one of Fred's coworkers. We sat face-to-face at the table for the longest time, saying nothing, listening to music. I wished Rory would fall asleep, because I needed to get this done. It sickens me to think of it now. We had buried his father the day before, and I just wanted him to go to bed, so I could go to work.

Finally, about half past eleven, he did. I heard him brushing his teeth, changing into pajamas, plugging his phone into the charger. Then I heard him crying. I went into his bedroom, sat on the edge of his bed, brushed his hair from his face, and asked if he wanted to talk, but he turned away and said, "I just want to sleep."

"Do you want some milk?"

"No," he said, his voice collapsing in grief. It was Fred who offered Rory milk every night before bed. Sometimes he accepted, sometimes he didn't, but the offer itself was part of the ritual, had been since Rory was small.

"I love you." I wanted to say so much more: *We'll be okay, we'll get through this.* But I didn't, because I didn't know that we *would* be okay. I didn't know how we would get through this.

I went back to the living room, waited half an hour, then checked on Rory again. He was curled in a fetal position, blankets pushed to the foot of the bed. I kissed his cheek, pulled up the covers. Then, feeling like the worst mother in the world, I left a note on the kitchen table. Had to go out for a bit, I'll be home before you wake up. If you're reading this, sorry, you already woke up ☹. Love, Mom.

I was in the office for less than ninety minutes. I filed the write-up, put it in the system, sent leads to the appropriate divisions, and sent out an email notifying our liaison people. I requested that the guy's visa be rejected. If he couldn't get into the country, he couldn't find my friend. Then I locked up and left. I was so sick on the way home that I had to pull over on Tenth Avenue and vomit into the gutter.

As it turned out, I explain to Rory, State didn't see my request until it was too late to block the man's visa. My CBP contact was on vacation, so he sent the request to his deputy. The target had changed his itinerary by two days, and the deputy didn't do more than a cursory search, so he missed it. The new agent on my squad found the record and was able to get a surveillance team out at the last second. Unfortunately, it was a Saturday, so the team was abbreviated—too many newer agents, not enough senior members. They were able to keep eyes on him out of the airport but then lost him on the Van Wyck.

"They never caught up with him," I tell Rory. "There's a video from a week later, showing the guy driving a rental car across the Canadian border near Trout River."

Of course, I relay only some of the details to Rory. I don't tell him the name, Yellow Beak, and I don't tell him about the glass of milk. I don't tell him how I watched him sleep or how I rushed my write-up, eager to get back home to him.

"Wait, back up," Rory says when I'm finished. "What happened to your friend? Was he okay?"

When I promised all those years ago to always tell him the truth, I had no idea how complicated it might become. "No, he wasn't."

I explain how the lookouts didn't see Yellow Beak come in for work the Tuesday morning after the guy entered the country or any day after that. I kept waiting for a message from him, but it never came. A month later, our squad received notice from his embassy that Yellow Beak had died "of natural causes."

"Was it my fault?"

"Oh, Rory, no. Of course not."

"If you hadn't been worried about me, you wouldn't have had to come home. You could have seen it through."

"Rory, no, no, no. *No.* It was my fault, not yours. Nothing having to do with my work could ever be your fault. Ever."

He thinks for a minute. "You said we had to leave New York City because of it, but I still don't understand. You did everything you were supposed to do."

"Yes," I say. "I followed the rules, I checked off the boxes, I filled out the paperwork and the requests. I followed protocol to the letter."

"So what's the problem? You can't get in trouble if you follow the rules."

"I *didn't* get in trouble. I did everything I was required to do, but not everything I *should* have done. The *correct* thing to do and the *right* thing to do aren't always the same. You want to know why we left New York City. The long and the short of it is that I couldn't trust myself after that."

Yes, our apartment was too expensive without Fred's salary. Yes, New York City holds too many memories. And yes, I felt guilty for never making good on Fred's wishes to move to California.

But the truth is we could have carried on, Rory and me. We could have found a way to stay in New York City, make the best of the life we had built there. What I really couldn't face was work. I couldn't walk into my squad area, feeling all those eyes on me. I couldn't sit at my desk, looking at my computer, where I'd filled out my reports and sent all of the appropriate emails, through all of the proper channels. The office was a painful reminder of everything I hadn't done. A reminder that I had failed, and my failure had cost a friend his life.

46

"What? Is man merely a mistake of God? Or is God a
mistake of man?" Identify the author, answer the question,
and then answer the question that the author has not asked.

The sun is lifting hazily over the horizon as we cross the Golden
Gate Bridge, fog snaking around Angel Island. Rory is still sleeping
in that way only teenagers and babies can, stone-like and dead to
the world. Gliding through the hills and canyons of Marin County,
I turn off the music and GPS. I know the way. When I was a child,
when we were still a family, we spent two weeks every summer at
an old-timey resort on the Russian River, the kind of place where
the kids run free during the day and everybody gathers at picnic
tables at night for potato salad and cold chicken, the parents drinking beer, the kids playing hide-and-seek among the trees.

The Russian River is a world unto itself. Originally a vacation
wonderland for San Francisco cops, in the sixties it was overrun
by hippies. Ten years later, the biker gangs arrived. In the eighties,
it became a gay vacation mecca, a place of wild abandon and, later,
deep sadness, populated by men vacationing from San Francisco,
their ranks dwindling from one summer to the next. Since then,
the holdouts from each of those groups have blended together into

a unique mix you won't find anywhere else in the world. I haven't visited in a long time, so I'm not exactly sure what we'll find.

At Rio Nido, we wind along the river, past cabins, the hardware store, all the way to Guerneville. From a distance, not much has changed: the post office, the River Inn, Lark Drugs, and, off beyond the old bridge, Johnson's Beach. I turn onto Armstrong Woods Road and pull in at Coffee Bazaar. I kill the engine. Rory stirs but doesn't open his eyes.

Inside, Bob Marley's "Stir It Up" pulses through the speakers, the barista dancing behind the counter. He's five foot ten and wiry, midthirties, a Sideshow Bob mop of a hairdo, tie-dyed pants.

"Hellllooo," he croons. "What can I get you?"

"Morning. One latte and one hot chocolate with extra foam, please."

"Righteous." As he steams the milk, he stares at me as if trying to place me. His body is still gliding to the music, his lips mouthing the words. "Last night, I was eating at that new Chinese place in Forestville. Been there?"

"Nope."

He spoons chocolate syrup into a paper cup. "It was excellent, five stars. And, at the end, they gave me a homemade fortune cookie. Do you want to know what it said?"

"What?"

"I kid you not. It said, 'Tomorrow, you will meet a mysterious lady.' By chance, are you that mysterious lady?"

"I don't feel very mysterious this morning."

"And yet, you are indeed a mystery to me. I love the color of your hair. What do you call that? Strawberry blonde?" He slides the drinks across the counter. In the foam on the hot chocolate, he has created a Volkswagen bus. "My name is Curtis, but my friends call me Sunshine."

"Nice foam art, Sunshine. How much do I owe you?"

He rings up the drinks, and I stuff a big tip into the jar. I might want to talk to him later. "Goodbye, Mystery Lady," he calls as I walk out the door.

Rory is standing by the door, stretching, looking around. I hand him the hot chocolate, and he glances down at the VW bus foam art. "Where *are* we?"

"Guerneville."

Once we're back in the Jeep, doors closed, I instruct him: "Sit up, be alert, open the camera on your phone. If we see anything unusual, I want you to get a picture. If we see any unusual cars, you need to capture their plates."

"What are we looking for?"

"A panel van, maybe a transit van, and a colorfully dressed white man in his forties, tall, overweight, imposing."

"Okay," he says, tapping the camera icon on his phone.

"We belong here, right?"

"Right."

"Say it."

"We belong here," Rory echoes.

"And don't let anyone see you take a picture."

We slowly drive down Armstrong Woods Road, past the auto repair shop, the church, the library. We pass a boarded-up motel with an ancient FOR SALE sign out front. The other resort is a cute set of five cabins surrounding a retro swimming pool. The cars in the parking lot—TTs, 328s, Mini Coopers—tell me it's popular with hipsters from the city.

A couple of miles down, we pass the address where the Leonard Blake phone last pinged—an empty lot across the road from a fenced-in field. An old Mustang on cement blocks sits rusting against a backdrop of towering redwoods. Rory raises his phone to the window and quickly snaps pictures. I turn left into a cul-de-sac. No vans here, just tidy houses with neatly kept yards. I complete the circle and continue up Armstrong Woods Road, slowing as we pass a dirt road cutting between two huge redwood trees.

"Trailer park," Rory observes.

"Yeah, fatal funnel. One way in, one way out, narrow, trees on both sides."

"Are we going in?"

"Not yet."

We continue east, where the road dead-ends at the parking lot for Armstrong Woods Park. "I used to come here with my parents," I tell Rory. "Up for a walk?"

We grab our backpacks and fall in behind two women headed toward the entrance, wearing matching Dykes on Bikes T-shirts from the 1997 parade. Rory is determined, alert, his eyes registering everyone on the trail, in the parking lot, near the restrooms. I'm not sure what I'm looking for, not sure this is how we should be spending our time.

Nearly three hours later, we end up back at the car, no closer to answers. Every road leads to two more roads, every trail leads to more trails.

Rory kicks at the tire. "What now?"

"Let's do another loop on the main road."

As we circle in and out of cul-de-sacs, Rory jots down the addresses of the three houses that stand out. We choose the most suspicious, a yellow rancher with a white van in the yard. A tall locked fence encloses the yard, a fifteen-foot shed standing in the corner. We park down the street.

An hour passes. Rory keeps an eye on every house on the cul-de-sac, making notes in his notebook every time we see a new car or person.

"It's amazing how much you can see when you sit still," he says.

After two hours, we drive to Safeway to pick up some lunch. Rory suggests we play "spot the shoplifter." It was Fred's game every time we went to Sloan's or Gristede's in New York. The first one to spot a shoplifter in the act got to buy any frivolous item in the store. I'd usually see three or four before I said anything, just to level the playing field.

Russian River shoplifters are less discreet. We aren't even past the cashiers when Rory taps me on the shoulder. Halfway down the aisle, a guy is stuffing a jumbo pack of Twizzlers into the pocket of his oversized army surplus coat.

"That was too easy," I say.

"Deal's a deal," Rory insists. "Now for my prize." At the deli counter, he orders two pounds of fried chicken tenders.

We wander the aisles and select more food than we need: Oreos, bananas, mango kefir, Havarti and crackers, sparkling water. By the time we get to the checkout, we've spotted four more shoplifters, including a pregnant woman in bulky parachute pants.

Back at the yellow house, the van is still across the street, but the lights are out. We eat the chicken tenders and Rory inhales a dozen Oreos. We wait and wait. We listen to music. The air gets colder, and I turn on the heater. I think of Gray Stafford shivering in that box. I think of Caroline.

"You do this a lot?" Rory asks.

"I used to. It can be Zen if you just roll with it." How many hours of my life have I spent on surveillance, sitting in cars, watching and waiting?

At 5:33 p.m., a white Volkswagen Jetta pulls up to the yellow rancher, and a well-dressed woman emerges with a toddler, who chats happily as they go inside and shut the door. "We can cross that one off," I tell Rory.

"We have to go to the trailer park."

He's right. We do have to go to the trailer park. Leonard Blake's phone pinged from the empty lot down the road, but allowing for the variations in range, the cell phone could have also been in the trailer park, or even in the empty field. If Rory weren't with me, I would have started in the trailer park—more nooks and crannies, more opportunities for concealment.

"Driving is a bad idea," I tell him. "We should walk."

"Because of the fatal funnel?"

"Yep. Never drive into something unless you're certain you can drive out."

47

James Joyce once wrote: "Whatever else is unsure in this stinking dunghill of a world, a mother's love is not." W. D. Hamilton would disagree. Why?

As we walk up the street, staying close to the tree line, I slide my gun out of the knapsack and tuck it into the small of my back. What was I thinking bringing Rory? Despite his size and strength, he's still a kid. I chose this career; he did not. I've never felt fear going into a dodgy situation, just curiosity and adrenaline. Now, with my son by my side, I feel a sense of dread.

We move along the wet embankment, the earthy smell of the redwoods drifting up around us. I consider all the things I should have taught him—the difference between cover and concealment, the fact that when someone says "get down" in a shooting situation, you don't get all the way down. Bullets don't bounce, they travel along the surfaces they strike. You never lean against a wall for the same reason.

"Act natural," I say.

Rory rolls his eyes. "How else would I act?"

The muddy dirt road descends through the two giant redwoods into a deeply wooded area. It looks like there might be about twenty-five trailers. The park is arranged in two concentric circles, surrounded by dense brush. A few of the trailers have curtains in the windows, but most of the windows are covered with sheets and towels. A mess of wires connects each trailer to a haphazard grid.

Rory walks quietly with his hands in his pockets. When I nudge him and glance toward two vans parked side by side, he takes out his phone and pretends to be texting while discreetly snapping pictures of their plates. No one is out, but I can hear televisions and voices through the thin walls. Someone is playing Bon Jovi, someone is watching *Friends*, a baby is screaming. Passing a trailer with an ancient Dodge Dart in the driveway, I smell a strong whiff of pot. Beyond the trailers, a smaller, even muddier dirt road winds up a hill, dotted with a few more mobile homes. Behind the first one stands a neatly stacked collection of orange Home Depot buckets; the tidiness signals that this meth lab is still in operation.

A well-kept garden patch graces the trailer at the end of the road. Behind the garden is a small greenhouse with the door open to reveal hydroponic gear. The trailer itself is clean, an empty Wheat Thins box poking out of the garbage can and a new orange Wrangler in the clearing. The license plate is from West Virginia with a frame that says ALMOST HEAVEN. Across the muddy path, another trailer is surrounded by junk, the faded seat of a plastic Big Wheel filled with leaves and rainwater. A Ford Transit van sits out front.

A narrow path winds up behind the clean trailer. I motion Rory through the brush. In the clearing above, the stump of a fallen tree is perfectly positioned as a lookout. Rory and I sit on the stump overlooking the trailer and van. I check my phone, no service. The sun is gone now, the moon rising in a cloudy sky.

In my mind, I replay the facts that led us here, checking my logic. In the negative column: Caroline told Rory by text six days ago that she's fine, and Dave Randall told Rory she's on a cruise with her parents. We're a hundred miles from where she was last seen.

In the positive column: Caroline disappeared almost a year to the day after Gray Stafford, who disappeared a year after the Lamey twins, from the same town, immediately before the Wonder Test. At the same time that she went missing, three other kids who had performed poorly on the pretest suddenly left town with their families. Dave Randall isn't friends with Caroline, so he may not be a reliable source. According to my colleague Malia, Caroline's parents were last spotted completely off the grid in Algeria, a place where they would be unlikely to take their daughter. Before Sunday, Caroline texted Rory two dozen or more times a day, but since then, it's been radio silence.

As for the location, Gray Stafford was handed over to the boat owner, John Murphy, by Leonard Blake—probably not his real name—whose phone pinged to an empty lot about two hundred yards from here during the period of Gray's absence. But why here? Where do the interests of a Daly City gang named the Kenji Boys, Leonard Blake, and Greenfield intersect?

The temperature drops. The clouds shift again, moonlight flooding the camp. Rory remains quiet, vigilant. I keep going over the facts. We need to find Caroline, and we need to find her soon.

48

In some instances, one plus one equals one. Explain using the Socratic method and Goldbach's conjecture.

At 8:03 p.m., I hear a dog barking, followed by a door opening. It's the tidy trailer with the Wrangler. Footsteps, a leash jangling, a man's voice calling, "Pluto!" The voice sounds familiar.

The dog is running up the path toward us. Rory looks at me nervously. I mouth to him "don't move." We try to stay hidden, but the dog moves closer and closer, the voice right behind, twigs snapping under footsteps. "Pluto! Slow down. Where are you going, boy?"

The footsteps grow closer.

I stand and position myself in front of Rory. I slide my hand into the small of my back, unbutton my holster. Pluto sounds like a small dog, maybe a beagle. I wish it wasn't a full moon. Moments ago, it felt as though we were safely hidden, but of course that was only an illusion.

"What's the hurry, boy?" I'm finally able to place the voice. Pluto is fifty feet away, then forty, thirty. I see him moving toward us, his nose to the ground.

He stops and stands, facing us, not making a sound. The leash is long, and it takes his owner a few seconds to come upon us. "Mystery Lady?" he smiles. "Whoa."

"Hi, Sunshine."

Sunshine looks at Rory, back at me. His face registers confusion. "What are you doing here?"

I take my hand off my holster. "I'm looking for someone."

Rory stands and walks up to Sunshine, hand outstretched. "Martin," he says, without a hint of hesitation.

"Hi Martin, I'm Sunshine. This is my friend Pluto."

"Can I pet him?"

"Sure. He used to work at the airport, searching bags for vegetables and fruits. He has a whole little pension and vet insurance." I hear the tinge of a West Virginia drawl that I didn't notice this morning in the coffee shop.

Pluto wags his tail and licks Rory's hand.

"So." Sunshine winds the end of the leash around his wrist. "If I can ask, who are you looking for?"

"Just a friend."

He shakes his head. "You don't strike me as the sort of person who has friends up this way." Pluto is taking an obvious liking to Rory, and the feeling appears to be mutual. "Want to join Pluto and me for our walk?"

Pluto leads the way, with Sunshine close behind, calling out to him in a singsong voice. Rory and I fall in behind them on the path, eventually emerging into another clearing. Pluto digs under a bush, Sunshine still talking and singing. "You have to make noise when you're out here," he explains.

"To scare off the animals?" Rory asks.

"It's not the animals I worry about. You two shouldn't be up here alone. But you're good, so long as you stick close to me. They know me, they know my routine, they trust me." He frowns, looking at both me and Rory. "Seriously, you two do not want to be out here alone in the dark."

Pluto is dancing around Rory's feet, yipping, and Sunshine takes up the call again, singing loudly: "Pluto! Pluto! Time to be heading home."

He falls in step beside me. "We should get you and Martin back to your car. Where are you parked?"

"Down Armstrong Woods Road."

"So you're out for a pleasant walk and you randomly decide to take a detour into a trailer park? Looking for your ex or something?"

"Long story."

"I'll drive you back."

"We can walk."

"Trust me, Mystery Lady. You're better off if I drive you out. As soon as the sun goes down, the party starts. And it's not the kind of party you want to attend."

A small part of me wants to argue. I have my gun, and besides, this isn't the slums of Dar es Salaam. I've been in worse situations, and I never needed a knight in shining armor to escort me out of a tough spot. Then again, I've never been in a place like this with Rory.

"Okay, thanks."

Sunshine turns to walk back down the path, Pluto plodding along behind.

I put a hand on Rory's back to get him to walk between us. I don't want him in the front or back of the pack. When we get to the trailer, mist hovers over the encampment. "I just need to get my keys," Sunshine says. "Come on in."

Before I can say anything, Rory follows him through the door.

The place is clean and organized. Small but cozy, it smells like vanilla and coffee. There's a tiny kitchen, a fridge, a booth with a simple pine table, a bookshelf filled with story collections, philosophy books, and sea glass. I take in a set of chef knives on the counter, three copper All-Clad pans hanging above the stove, a fancy espresso maker. How does a guy like Sunshine end up in a trailer park like this?

Sunshine nods at Rory. "Take a seat, champ. Thirsty?"

"Yeah."

I'm not worried about Sunshine. In my mind, I've already run the "danger algorithm." He is amiable, engaging, asks questions out of curiosity, enjoys a close relationship with his dog—one of equality not control—all positives. The fact that he gets up before six each morning to run a coffee shop, something that requires responsibility and social dexterity, is also a good indicator. Of course, serial killers can also be tidy, charming dog owners with a day job, but Sunshine isn't one of those.

"I'll make you an Italian soda, my specialty."

Sunshine pulls ice and a frosted glass out of the freezer and opens a bottle of Italian vanilla syrup. A seltzer machine sits on the counter. He pours syrup over the ice and taps a button, and the machine whirs to life.

"That's a pretty serious operation."

"Can't help it. I was a mixologist in another life. This trailer may not look great from the outside, but on the inside it's a classy operation." He hands the glass to Rory, bubbles fizzing. "What can I get for Mystery Lady?"

"Nothing, thanks." I notice the Virginia Tech emblem on Rory's glass. "Were you a Hokie?"

"Nah, I actually taught there for a while. Philosophy." That would explain the books on the shelves.

Rory gulps the soda. "I love philosophy."

"Me too, brother. Me too. But, as I sadly discovered, philosophy and *teaching* philosophy are two entirely different things."

Sunshine leans up against the counter beside me, the block of chef's knives between us. He pushes it aside.

"Nice knives."

"Thanks."

"Cooking or self-defense?"

Sunshine is confused for a second. He seems like a guy who is high on peace, and I think I bummed him out. "I like to cook." He glances over at me, his face growing serious, his hippie demeanor fading. "Look, I'm not going to get into your business. I haven't survived ten months in this trailer park by asking questions. I'm only here because the rent is cheap, and I wanted to take a sabbatical from life, write a book."

"What kind of book?"

"Sort of a *Zen and the Art of Motorcycle Maintenance* but for the internet age. I bet Martin would dig it. Anyway, I doubt you're here to see me. I'm probably the least interesting person in Guerneville."

"And who are the interesting people?"

"There are some, shall we say, *business people* along this road."

"I saw them. Meth labs in both the green and brown trailers, pot grow, twelve to twenty plants, on the right, and down in the circle, some dealers. From the bikes, it looks like they might be Gypsy Jokers?"

Sunshine grins. "Mystery Lady, you are one big trip."

"What about the guy across from you? The trailer over there, with the van."

"You mean El Mayore?"

"Big white guy?" I ask. "Expensively dressed? Forty to forty-five? Maybe some loud pants?"

Sunshine laughs. "Not even close! Rafael is seventy-nine and probably hasn't bought a new shirt since the Nixon years. We call him El Mayore because he was the first one here. The original settler, if you will."

"Why the van?"

"He's been working as a contractor for Amazon. He gets us all a ten percent discount, lets us use his Prime login to watch *Ozark*. Tell me something. How is it Jason Bateman never gets one day older?"

"Deal with the devil?" Rory suggests, slurping down the last of his soda.

Outside, we pile into the truck, Rory in the middle between Sunshine and me. As we drive down the muddy road, the truck bumping along the ruts, Sunshine adjusts the rearview mirror. "I've been racking my brain."

"For what?"

"The guy you described when you asked me about El Mayore. Big white guy, forties, well dressed, loud pants."

"Yes?"

"I might know who you're looking for. He used to come in for coffee. Creeped me out. Didn't know any of the regulars."

"Do you know his name?"

"Nope. Not much help to you, but I know his drink. Medium Americano and a poppy seed muffin. Never trust a guy who asks for hot water in his espresso."

As we near the entrance, I count seven bikers hanging out in front of one of the trailers, drinking. There's a bonfire going, music blasting, Foghat's "Slow Ride." They look up, noticing us, and move toward the truck. One guy stops in the middle of the road, blocking our way. Another guy—massive tattooed arms, leather vest—walks around to the driver's side. He taps his beer bottle on the window. Sunshine rolls it down a crack, a whoosh of cold air rushing in.

Sunshine gives him a broad, winning smile. "Evening, my friend. How you boys doing?"

"We're good." Big Arms peers through the window. "Got yourself a secret family you've been hiding?"

"It's my sister and her kid," Sunshine lies, smooth as can be. "Visiting from out of state."

"What did you think?" the guy asks me. "Like our little neck of the woods?"

"It's beautiful."

"We're having a party. Y'all should join us."

"Love to, Charlie, but these guys have an early flight," Sunshine says.

Big Arms takes a swig from his beer. "Where to?"

"Denver," I offer.

"Cold out there, man. You should stay here instead." Big Arms bangs a fist on the hood.

Sunshine lets up on the brake, nudging the truck forward a couple of inches. "Mind if I join you when I get back? I just finished a new microbrew. I want you to try it, give me some feedback."

"We'll be here all night. Bring a lot, we're thirsty."

Big Arms steps back from the truck, shouts to his friend: "Hey, shithead, get outta the fuckin' road." The other guy moves, Sunshine gives him a nod, and we drive past the bonfire, past the Gypsy Jokers, through the two giant redwoods, out onto the road.

I look at Sunshine. "Charming friends you've got."

"Those guys are rough, but they've never caused me trouble. You just have to talk to them like human beings. Most of the time."

"And the rest of the time?" Rory wants to know.

"You stay out of their way."

We drive back to the car in silence. I point out our Jeep on the side of the road. "Right here."

Sunshine kills the engine, turns off the headlights. "I've been thinking. Your guy, Loud Pants? I saw him right here awhile back."

"Along Armstrong?"

"Yeah, kinda weird. His car was parked beside that big empty field just up the road. He was walking through the field in a hurry, like he had somewhere to be. He was dressed nice, like Alden shoes and Tom Ford, even though the ground was muddy."

"Alden shoes, Tom Ford? You could tell from looking at him?"

"My ex was in fashion. You don't see that on the river."

"If it's the field I'm thinking of, there's no house on the property, just a fence around some dirt."

"Yeah, but at the back of the field there's a trail leading up into the woods, up to a secluded waterfall. Nothing you should hike in Italian leather, though, mostly federal land. Pluto and I once went up there, didn't get far before we walked into some old grow sites. I heard some guys at the Pink Elephant one night talking about a compound way up in the hills there where some weird shit goes on."

"What kind of weird shit?"

"Hard to tell. They weren't specific. If a compound exists, it must be hard to get to. I've never even seen a road on this side, but the guys mentioned a locked gate somewhere beyond the field with access to an old logging road. I figured that's where he was headed."

"If you see him, could you give me a call?" I reach into my bag and pull out my business card.

Sunshine's eyes go wide. "Holy shit, you just keep getting *mysteriouser* and *mysteriouser.*"

In the Jeep, Rory turns to me. "We have to go there, Mom. Follow the path. 'Pull the thread.' Isn't that what you say?"

My mom brain tells me to take Rory home and return with backup. But the investigator part of my brain tells me Caroline could very well be up that path, on that compound. If anybody saw us poking around today, time is limited. The window can close quickly. Maybe it already has.

"What's the plan?" Rory presses.

"If I were with my squad, I'd sit on the road between the empty lot and the field and wait to see if anyone comes or goes. Then, if nothing came up, first thing tomorrow morning, when it's light out, I'd go up the path."

"So what are we waiting for?" Rory says.

We drive closer to the field. I park down the road a ways, turn the lights off but leave the CD player on, quietly playing Fred's CD. We sit, waiting. It's the kind of work a lot of millennials might not be able to handle—the boredom, the monotony. You can't check your phone, can't scroll, can't read, can't nod off. All you can do is listen to music, stay alert, watching. Some have a knack for this kind of work; most don't. Experience helps, of course, but if you don't have it, you don't have it. Rory has it.

No one comes. No one goes. Just past midnight, I tell Rory we need to get some sleep. In town, the VACANCY sign glows above the Vacation Wonderland cabins. We buy little boxes of cereal and a quart of milk from the clerk in the lobby, settle into a tiny cabin, and try to fall asleep, still high on adrenaline and nerves.

49

While common sense suggests that averaging leads to increased accuracy, does this prove true with mobile phones that do not use differential GPS? Suggest a competing method to compute location.

Sunday morning at six, I'm dressed and arranging my bag—gun, mini tool kit, water, snacks—when Rory emerges from the shower. "I'm going with you."

"You need to stay here."

"*No.*"

Rory used to be such a cautious kid, always checking both ways, thinking things through in advance, aware of everyday dangers. But since Fred died, he's different. He's more direct, less tentative. Fearless. I worry he has lost the innate fear of dying. If anything, now he only seems to fear *my* dying. He's terrified of being left behind—again. Any other risk, any other danger pales in comparison.

Outside, it's cool and gray, storm clouds moving in. In the Jeep, I tell Rory: "You have to do everything I say, exactly when and how I say to do it. No arguing with me out there."

He nods.

"As soon as we park, we need to get out with our backpacks and move inconspicuously across the field and onto the path. Fast, but not too fast. We need to look like we're going for a hike. No hesitation. Got it?"

"Got it."

"Once we're on the path, we move fast, we don't talk. Stay a couple of feet *behind* me. If I stop, you stop. If you see booby traps or cameras, grab me and communicate silently. If anything looks off, we're turning back. No complaints, no disagreement. Agreed?"

He nods.

"If anyone asks, we're hiking. We heard there's a waterfall this way. We're going to have a picnic." I reach into the back seat for the groceries we bought last night. I stuff cheese, crackers, cookies, and water bottles into my backpack.

"Waterfall, picnic," Rory repeats. I can tell he wants to ask me something.

"What's on your mind?"

"How do I even know if I see a booby trap?"

He's breaking my heart. What the hell am I doing?

"A booby trap is usually a piece of wire stretched across the path. When tripped, it signals to someone that we're in the area. It's all done electronically, so keep your ears tuned for any kind of humming or static sounds. Watch the trees for cameras or motion detectors. Anything unnatural: wiring, batteries, lights."

As we drive toward the cul-de-sac, Rory pulls on the dark green windbreaker I bought him in the fall for a school trip he never went on. He was signed up, fees paid, and he was even excited about it, but two weeks before the trip, Fred died. It only occurs to me now that he missed the trip. I'd totally forgotten about it, and he never reminded me.

I pull into the cul-de-sac and park. The street is empty. I look over at Rory. "I love you. And I want you to remember something."

"Yeah?"

"You're fast, really fast. If I say run, you run."

"Which way?"

"Toward the car." I take the keys out of the ignition and hand them to Rory. "Keep these in your pocket."

"Mom, I don't even have my learner's permit."

"Dad taught you how to drive last summer up in Woodstock."

"That was a parking lot."

"Doesn't matter. There's no traffic here, you can handle it. If I say run, you need to get to the car and drive to town. Go to the coffee shop. Sunshine will be there. You know the way?"

He nods. "Jesus, Mom. You're scaring the shit out of me."

"Good, you *should* be scared. Open the running app on your phone so you can trace our steps back." I reach over him, into the glove compartment, and pull out a plastic baggie of golf tees.

Rory smiles. "I can't believe those are still there. The last time Dad and I went golfing, I was, like, ten."

"Well, let's just consider it Dad watching out for us. We may lose cell service, so I'm going to stick one of these in the ground every time we take a turn or veer off."

"Mom?"

"Yes?"

"Do you think we're going to find Caroline up there?"

"I really don't know. Ready?"

He takes a steadying breath. "Ready."

We walk down the street, across Armstrong Woods Road, and into the field. An abandoned tractor sits on the far side of the field. Rory is focused on the perimeter, eyes noting what I've already seen: three paths—one to the left, one to the right, one heading straight up the hill. It's less worn than the others, but you can tell it gets used occasionally.

We take the middle path, zigzagging through trees, berry bushes, across streams, avoiding patches of poison oak. Heavy gray clouds block any warmth from the rising sun. I'm worried about getting back down the path if it starts raining. I move quickly, trying to beat the weather, repeatedly glancing over my shoulder to make sure Rory is still behind me. Occasionally, I feel his hand on my back, as if he's reassuring himself that I'm still here. I watch for trip wires but see none. I look for telltale slivers of smoke snaking out of the woods. I listen for portable generators.

About a mile uphill, the path splits in two. I pause and look at Rory. He nods toward the path to the right, which is more worn and provides a clearer way forward. It's the same one I would have chosen, but I want him to have a choice in the matter, to further solidify the map in his mind. I stick a red golf tee in the ground.

We ascend for another fifteen minutes. At the crest of the hill, we emerge in a clearing. No houses or vehicles, no signs of life. A jumbo jet passes overhead, a dull roar. Rory isn't even winded. The climb has energized him. Cutting through two big bushes, I plant another red tee in the soil. Rory's hand grabs the back of my sweatshirt. I stop abruptly and turn to see him glancing at a rusty, battery-powered light attached to a tree limb. It looks too old to be in use. Still, we move forward cautiously, scanning the ground, the trees, looking for anything out of the ordinary.

I stop when I see an abandoned orange bucket under a tree. The boxes next to it have been destroyed by rain and the elements, the garbage bags ravaged by animals. A few yards away, in the meadow, more garbage surrounds a fire pit. It's an old grow. Some plants remain at the edges, so I doubt the DEA knows about it.

We round a huge oak tree. The grow field cascades down the hill. It looks like no one has touched it in two or three years. Cheap equipment, dried-out hoses, and a kiddie pool litter the ground, as if someone were thinking about coming back but never did. I'd wager there's still some good product intertwined with the berries and brush.

As we keep moving, I glance back to see Rory taking it all in, fascinated. He has always loved seeing new things. The world— even this ugly piece of it, strewn with garbage, the chemical tinge of pesticides still in the air—slowly reveals itself to him, and I think he appreciates the experience.

We walk on for another hour, through patches of sunlight and periods of drizzle. We pass an abandoned cabin—no door, half a roof, the interior gutted. Only an old bathtub remains, where a riot of ferns has taken root. Ultimately, the trail turns into a creek, which we follow downhill. The creek feeds into a ten-foot waterfall. At the bottom, we sit on a downed tree trunk to drink water and eat Wheat Thins. My wristband tells me we've walked three and a half miles, but it feels longer. I check my phone. Damn.

"Do you have service?" I ask. Rory takes his phone out of his pocket, shakes his head.

"Neither do I. Your app should still work, though, in case you need it to find your way back. Remember to watch for Dad's golf tees. If you go more than a few hundred yards without seeing a tee, you're going the wrong way."

But Rory isn't paying attention. He's suddenly standing, craning his neck. "Mom!"

I stand up, follow his gaze, and see what he sees: about a half mile through the clearing, an overgrown logging road, and a vehicle making its way down the mountain.

"Stay behind me," I say.

We stop at the tree line. The vehicle rounds the corner, moving slowly along the rutted logging road—a brown vintage Toyota Land Cruiser, late 1960s, perfectly restored.

When a ray of sunlight breaks through the window, I see a Caucasian man behind the steering wheel, broad shouldered. He has a huge head and clean haircut, white collared shirt. Rory is frozen in place. "That's our guy," I say.

"How do you know?"

"I just know."

My mind flashes back to my second week on the job. The Russian Organized Crime squad had grabbed me on their way out of the office. They were doing a surveillance at Penn Station, and they needed help. On the way uptown, the team leader gave me a radio and a photograph of the subject. "We can't lose him," he said. "We probably won't need you, but stay upstairs, in case. Don't come downstairs. Don't do anything dumb."

The rest of the team went down to the train tracks, and I found a bench with a view of the top of the escalator. I hid the radio in my bag and put the earpiece in. At first, my ear filled with a cacophony of radio noise as everyone settled into position. And then there was nothing. It was so quiet, I thought my radio had gone dead or switched to the wrong channel. Still, I sat there waiting for them to do their business, catch the subject, and give me a ride back down to the office. I had piles of paperwork to do.

The next thing I knew, I saw a guy with a crew cut and a blue scarf coming up the escalator. He was in a crowd of people, and unlike in the photograph, he had a beard. Nonetheless, I sensed it was him. Chills crept up my arms, my head tingled. I was nervous and didn't know what to do. If I alerted the team and I was wrong, it would be humiliating. Yet, somehow, I just knew this was the guy. I brought the radio to my mouth and made what was probably the most tentative callout the team had ever heard.

"Um? I think maybe I have our guy? Top of the escalator. Ground floor. Heading toward the west exit?" I braced myself for the worst, expecting laughter and a short transmission: *Lina, we caught the guy ten minutes ago.*

But that wasn't what happened. The team leader came on instantly. "Alright Delta Twenty-One." That was my call sign, junior person on the team. "Move with the target. You have the eye. Everyone reposition to the west exit." The whole team fell into place, and it was soon confirmed that it was indeed our guy. That was the moment when I began to think of myself as a real agent.

Since then, I've discovered that these quick, instinctual IDs are the norm. Even if you've never seen the target before, when he or she appears, somehow you just know. Not every time, but most of the time.

"What now?" Rory asks.

"We follow the road and figure out where he was coming from."

50

In the jungles of Congo, where deforestation has
devastated old-growth forests, villagers have seen a
population of giraffes with short necks that feed on
low-hanging shrubs. Which is more likely: these giraffes
come from ancestors that have always been shorter than
typical giraffes, or these giraffes have evolved to adapt
to the lowering of the food source?

We work our way up the logging road, moving quickly along the
rocky, uneven terrain. Despite the cool temperature and the light
breeze, sweat trickles down my spine. We've climbed about two
thousand feet from the trailhead. I'm panting. Rory isn't. "You need
a minute to rest?" I ask.

"No, but you do."

We step into the cover of bushes and lean against a tree stump.
I pull out a bottle of water. It begins to drizzle.

We drink, rest for a couple of minutes, and continue on. After
a mile and change, the road dead-ends at a driveway with an imposing iron gate. This must be the place Sunshine was talking about.
Rory and I exchange glances. I'm glad we've found the compound,
nervous about what we might find inside.

The gate is ten feet tall, the wooden fence almost as high. Through the bars, all we can see is the driveway winding up the hill, bordered on both sides by mature redwood trees. The size of the evenly spaced redwoods indicates the place was established decades ago. Once through the gate, it would be easy sailing for a vehicle, but how would a vehicle ever get to this point? Is there another road on the other side, not visible on Google Maps?

My foot lands on something hard, and I look down and notice the hard green spheres littering the ground. I pick one up and show it to Rory.

"What do these look like to you?" I whisper.

"Walnuts?"

I think of the Lamey twins, who came home covered in a rash, and what their mother told the police about their allergy to black walnut trees.

I notice a camera high in a tree just inside the gate. It looks fairly new. I back up, watching the camera to see if it moves. It doesn't. I tap Rory on the shoulder and point to it. With a boost, I could probably climb over the gate, but it would have to be within the view of the camera. Our only other choice is to follow the fence around the property, look for a better entry point. There is no barbed wire, and I don't see any more cameras. Nor do I hear the static buzz of an invisible electric fence.

We walk a quarter mile along the fence without seeing anything unusual or finding an opening. The property is massive. I'm hoping for a break or some decorative feature that would allow us to peer through the fence, but there is none. Rory remains alert, his eyes scanning for traps. Finally, I spot our opportunity. A giant old oak stands in front of the fence. One of the branches has grown over the fence, and it hasn't been trimmed back. There's an outgrowth about five feet up the trunk. I point toward the limb. Rory nods.

When we get to the base of the tree, Rory interlocks his fingers and leans down to give me a foothold. I place my right foot in the cup of his hands and count off one, two, three. With a smooth, determined push, he hoists me up in a single motion.

I loop my hands around the branch and place my foot on the outgrowth. I step out of Rory's hands and suddenly I'm hanging upside down, trying to remember how to climb a tree. On my last day at the academy, I did twelve pull-ups. What I'd give for that kind of upper body strength now. I feel Rory's hands on my back, pushing me upward, and I'm suddenly up and on the branch. I reposition and reach down to grab Rory's wrists. With our hands interlocked, Rory walks himself up the tree.

One by one, we drop down on the other side. We stand, listening. Has anyone seen us? I scan the area for wires and cameras. Nothing. Slowly, we move along the fence line. There's a break in the trees up ahead. I scuttle to the opening and crouch down low. I can hear Rory's feet moving over the soft ground. He crouches beside me, and together we survey the strange view before us.

"What *is* this place?" he whispers.

51

Between good and evil lies reality. Defend or dispute
this statement.

We're looking out at a wide, green, perfectly manicured field. Just
beyond the field is a horse racing track—a genuine dirt track with
an infield, a vintage scoreboard, a winner's circle, and beyond that,
a grandstand.

The twin spires overlooking the track resemble those at
Churchill Downs. The place seems like a modified replica of the
original, from the grandstand and spires to the stadium seats. But
something is off—the size. The track itself is only a quarter mile.
There are rows of seats along the track, plus two rows of balcony
seating. On the mezzanine, there appears to be a small restaurant
and, beyond it, three betting windows. The winner's circle features
a tower, a fenced platform painted bright white, and a horseshoe-
shaped garden of red geraniums.

"What the hell?" Rory whispers.

We kneel for a few minutes, watching, listening. It is eerily
quiet, a breeze moving through the empty grandstand. The track
is freshly graded, with no hoofprints in the dirt. Is it some kind
of underground dog track? The Russian River hides many bizarre

surprises. Greyhounds? But the rail is too high, the starting gate too large. Along the back stretch is a row of several full-size carts, maybe for harness racing.

Rory and I duck into the tree line and follow the fence. At another break in the trees, we kneel down and look out again. We're on the backside of the grandstand. I see a drinking trough and two practice rings—like everything else here, on a smaller scale. A shuttered clapboard booth bears a sign declaring: TICKETS HERE. Downhill from the practice rings is a parking lot, empty except for a dusty red Ford truck.

Beyond the parking lot, a small wooden structure and series of nine miniature stables lead uphill to a big, two-story house. The house is the only thing that hasn't been scaled down. That, and the bales of hay scattered everywhere, like props. It feels as though we've wandered onto a stage set or a Hollywood back lot. Something is off, or maybe it's the opposite: everything is too perfect.

There are no cars parked beside the house, no lights on. When we were coming up the mountain, the Land Cruiser was going down, but it's impossible to know how long we have. He could be gone for hours, but he might have just run to town for a quick errand. We walk quickly past the stables. I hear a movement inside the sixth one. "What was that?" Rory whispers. We slip around the backside of the small, wooden structure, out of sight from the house. We stand still, listening, but all is quiet. I keep waiting for the familiar snort of a horse, but it never comes. We continue on. We hunch down behind the ninth stable, watching the house for movement. Rory stays close behind me.

After several tense minutes, I turn to him and whisper, "I'm going to check out the house. Make your cawing sound if you see anything."

Our first night after moving into my dad's house, we saw two big hawks circling over the canyon. At dusk sometimes, when we haven't seen the hawks for a few days, Rory will stand on the deck and make a loud, high-pitched cawing sound, like an injured animal. He only has to do it once or twice before the hawks appear, circling the sky above the canyon, looking for prey.

Rain begins to fall. I'm relieved. The rain will cover the sound of my footsteps. I move quickly up the hill, past a tractor and a row of hay bales. I notice a business card lying on the ground beside a picnic table. I pick it up, newly damp from the rain, and slide it into my pocket.

I step up onto the wraparound porch. Hunched down, I make my way around the house, peering in all of the windows. The porch is well maintained, the boards solid. Inside, the house is spotless. Farmhouse chic, refined Americana. An oak dining table bears a vase of yellow tulips in full bloom; someone was here within the last couple of days. Above the fireplace, two unfinished slabs of wood are engraved with Winston Churchill quotes:

"No hour of life is lost that is spent in the saddle."

"There is something about the outside of a horse that is good for the inside of a man."

A cry breaks through the silence—the sound of a dying animal. Rory. Startled, I race around the porch to where I can see him. He waves me over. Hunched down, I dart to his hiding spot. My thighs burn from running in a crouched position.

"I heard something."

"Where?"

"From one of the stables."

"A horse?"

"No, it wasn't an animal."

"A voice?"

He shakes his head. "I can't explain it. It sounded human." He looks scared.

The rain intensifies, the sky grows darker. Rory pulls up his hood.

"Stay behind me," I command.

The place is so deserted it's eerie. The yellow tulips on the table and the fact that the entire grounds are so spotlessly clean makes it all the more disconcerting. We stop behind the second stable. The rain is coming down hard now, pouring off my hair and into my eyes. Inching forward, I reach my hand around to the handle of my SIG Sauer. The structure is only about ten feet wide and twelve feet deep. It's made of timber, with metal joists. The roof, too, is metal. Concealment, not cover.

I go around to the front of the barn. The top half of the split door is open. I step back, moving gradually in a semicircle, slicing the pie.

My first view inside reveals a simple horse stall. But it's gated on top, with bars and a lock, more like a cell than a stable. Empty. A saddle and reins hang on the wall. The other items, though, stop me cold: inside the cell, a cooking pot, a metal cup, a plate, and silverware are arranged atop a bale of hay, all tidy and untouched. Heavy blankets are folded and stacked in one corner. A branding iron hangs from a peg on the wall outside.

I close my eyes to steady myself before going around to the back of the stable where Rory is waiting for me, watching the hill below. I do not tell him—I cannot tell him—that these aren't stables but prisons. And they're not meant for horses.

The rain is forming muddy rivulets, flowing down the hill. Rory's head is so far back under his hoodie that I can barely see him. We move quickly toward the sixth stable, where we heard a movement as we made our way up to the house. Both portions of the half door are closed and padlocked. A heavy metal ring hangs on a hook beside the door. On the ring, a single key. The rain pounding the metal roof makes it hard to hear. Still, I sense a rumbling from inside, a shuffling. I slip the ring off of the hook, insert the key into the padlock, and pop it open. I slide the padlock out of the latch and place it on the ground.

I pull the top door open just a few inches. In the darkness, I struggle to make out the details. The room is identical to the previous one: straight ahead, a few yards into the structure, the cell. On the wall beside the door, the saddle and reins, the branding iron. The smell is familiar and awful. It's the smell of damp hay mixed with shit and, I realize with horror, sweat. Human sweat.

I hear a rustling sound. Something on the floor on the other side of the bars. I reach back to the hook, grab the key, and unlock the padlock on the lower door. I open that one too. I glance back at Rory and hold up a hand. Then I slip into the stable. It's pitch-black. The floor is concrete. With my hand on my gun, I silently inch toward the back of the room. There is something on the ground, curled in a ball, tangled in a mess of hay and blankets. It's moving around, restless. A pinprick of light shines down on the creature. I think I see skin, impossibly pale white skin. I'm still telling myself it's an oversized pig or perhaps a small horse, sleeping.

I close my eyes for a moment, willing them to adjust to the darkness.

When I open my eyes, I understand that underneath the mess of hay, I'm looking at the naked, hairless leg of a human. A blanket covers the torso, so I am not sure if it is a man or a woman, but I know this: it is not a child. The leg is too long, the bulk beneath the blanket too substantial. Below the ankle, a clump of black. A boot? No, the shape is wrong. Are my eyes deceiving me? The thing beneath the ankle is shaped like a hoof.

Loud, disturbed breathing comes from beneath the blanket. Restless sleep, perhaps a terrible dream. I hear a metallic clinking. The lump moves, and the blanket slides off to reveal a long, pale arm. My gaze follows the whiteness upward, where the shoulders and head are still obscured by the blanket, and then downward. Where the hand should be, a fist, clad in a black leather glove, is attached to a horseshoe.

As I inch toward the cage, my foot hits something metal on the floor. A tray. The creature beneath the blanket stirs and rolls over. The blanket slides off, revealing a mop of long, dirty-blond hair. The hair is matted and tangled. Two eyes peek out, startlingly white in the darkness.

The eyes meet mine for several long seconds.

A voice, guttural and deep, comes from under the blanket. "What are you doing here?" The words are difficult to make out, as though the person has a severe speech impediment.

"What is your name?" The first question that comes to mind, the essential question. So much can be traced back to a name.

The figure under the blanket shifts. I hear chains rattling. "You. Can't—" I struggle to make out the words.

"Who are you?"

"You. Can't. Be. Here."

I move closer to the stall, the wrecked creature, human but not. "We need to get you out."

"No! Just. Go."

"Are you okay?"

No answer.

"I'm looking for a girl. Brown hair, about my height."

The man rolls around on the ground, struggling to climb out from under the blankets and hay. As he struggles to stand, he falls backward and into the side of the stall. On his knees, he shuffles toward me. He lifts his arms, placing the black gloves on the bars of the cage. I turn on my phone's flashlight. That's when I see they're not gloves, but wooden blocks, hoof-shaped. They make a thudding sound against the bars as he pulls himself up to his full height. He towers over me. On his head, there are leather straps, a harness. I understand why his words are so garbled: his jaw is clamped down around a bit. He wobbles on the strange, tall boots.

"You. Can't. Be. Here. Go." His face is right up against the bars. "Please. Go." His lips are unable to move properly, the sound comes from the bottom of his throat.

"Are you telling me you don't need help?"

"I. Don't. Please go."

"Okay, I'll go. But first, you have to tell me: Have you seen a girl? Fifteen years old. Please."

The man teeters, looking down at me, saliva pouring out of the sides of his mouth. His eyes look feral. "Look. In. The." The next word is unintelligible.

"In the what?" I ask desperately.

287

He leans his forehead against the bars, gathering his strength. He lifts his head, looks me in the eyes, and manages one word: "Kennel."

"Where? What kennel?" The man nods to the right, down the hill.

From outside comes the high cawing sound of a dying animal. My heart races. Rory.

52

"To exchange all the goodness and grace of every life in Omelas for that single, small improvement: to throw away the happiness of thousands for the chance of the happiness of one: that would be to let guilt within the walls indeed." Argue for or against the moral imperative of Ursula Le Guin's city of Omelas.

Rory is crouching around the corner of the stable when I come out. "A truck just pulled up to the house," he whispers.

I close the stable doors, hoping whoever is in the car didn't see that they were open. "The Land Cruiser?"

"No. A pickup truck."

"How many people in it?"

"Two."

"Let's get into the tree line. We're looking for a kennel."

I think of the smaller structure at the bottom of the hill, beside the first stable. We dart into the trees, making our way down the hill through the brush. I'm grateful for the rain. It will make getting back to the car more difficult, but it deadens sound and makes it harder for anyone to see us from the house.

At the bottom of the hill, about three hundred yards from the first stable, stands a smaller structure, half the size of the stables. The door is padlocked, but there is no key ring. Directly in front of the door, rainwater has gathered in a deep puddle. A metal cafeteria tray pokes out from a slot at the bottom of the door. I drop to the ground, splashing mud all over my jeans, and pull out the empty tray. I get my mouth as close to the slot as possible, drenching my hair and the side of my face in the filthy puddle.

"Caroline?" I say as loud as I dare. "Caroline?"

Something moves inside.

"Mom?" Rory says, his voice shaky. "Is that her?"

I look up at him. "You have to be strong right now. For Caroline."

"I will," he says, but I can see the terror in his eyes.

"Caroline?" I say again.

From inside, I hear a small voice. No words, just a quiet whimper. Human.

I take my backpack from Rory and pull out my mini tool kit. I grab the flathead screwdriver in my left hand, the Phillips in my right, and slide them through the padlock in opposite directions. Then, in a single motion, I jerk them apart, driving force onto the opposing sides of the lock. The flathead catches the wrist of my right hand, opening a gash. Blood pours from the wound, mixing with the rain, but I don't care. The lock begins to give.

Hand pulsing, I switch the screwdrivers back in the opposite direction and give one final thrust. As I do, the lock breaks apart, metal pieces thudding to the ground. I stand up, unlatch the door. Inside, it's too dark to see. I open the door a few inches to let in the light, illuminating a narrow military cot. An uneven concrete floor.

A plastic bucket in the corner. A rope hanging on the wall beside the door. The smell is intense. Urine, fear, sweat.

As my eyes adjust, I realize someone is standing against the back wall. She wears oversized shorts, a thin hoodie, no socks, no shoes. She is shivering. A chain attaches her to a bolt on the floor.

A ray of light reflects off of her pale skin. Her beautiful hair is gone. She is bald. Thin.

Just like Gray Stafford.

"Caroline?"

Her head moves slightly. "Rory?" Barely a whisper.

I turn to realize that Rory has stepped into the kennel and is looking over my shoulder, his eyes wide open in horror.

He rushes past me, past the filthy blankets on the floor, the puddles of muddy water. He throws both of his arms around Caroline, pulling her in close. In an instant, he has his jacket off, and he wraps it around her. He doesn't say a word. He stands there, holding her, a stunned look on his face. She tucks her head into his chest, sobbing.

I hear the truck coming down the hill from the house. I pull the door closed. With the three of us crowded into the cramped space, the door closed, the smell is even more intense, more terrible, the darkness magnifying everything. A mouse skitters behind the hay bale.

Even muffled against Rory's chest, Caroline's sobs are loud. "Shh." I need to calm her. I put my ear to the door to listen for the truck. I hear the noise of the engine fading. Are they gone?

I hand Rory my phone. "I need you to use this for light. Be careful. Only the screen, not the flashlight. Point it toward the floor."

He continues holding Caroline with one arm. With the other, he turns on the phone and directs the screen toward Caroline's feet. I bend down and examine the thick leather cuff around her left ankle. A chain extends from the cuff to a bolt in the floor. Sawing through the leather cuff would take time. The loop connecting the chain to the bolt, though, is old and rusted. I fit the screwdrivers through the single loop. My hand is throbbing, blood leaking from the cut, running down my arm. I jerk the tools in opposite directions several times. Nothing. I try again. Finally, the metal loop snaps, freeing Caroline from the bolt in the floor.

I loop the chain around her ankle, tucking the end into the cuff. She winces. "I'm sorry," I say. "This will keep it from making too much noise."

Rory is still holding her tight, her face buried in his chest. She's shaking violently.

"My neck," she whispers.

Rory directs the light of the phone to her neck. "What have they done to you?" he mumbles in horror. That's when I see the collar.

It is made of rubber, with an embedded lithium battery. Is it a tracking device? An alarm? I reach into my backpack for my Swiss Army knife. "I have to cut this off," I tell Caroline. "Be perfectly still." She freezes in place as I work the knife back and forth, slowly cutting through the rubber. The knife strikes something rigid—a plastic-coated wire running through the center of the collar. I continue sawing through the rubber, careful not to sever the wire. As soon as the wire is cut, it will likely send an alert.

I remove the collar, leaving the wire intact. Then I carefully wedge the knife between Caroline's neck and the wire, protecting her skin with my free hand. In a single motion, I slice outward toward myself. As the knife splits the plastic coating of the wire, a jolt of electricity surges through the wire, into my body. Caroline goes rigid for a split second, but she doesn't say a word.

I listen for an alarm but hear nothing. Does it set off a signal inside the house, or perhaps on her captor's phone?

"We need to go now," I say. "We really need to move."

She doesn't respond.

Rory pulls back from Caroline, cups his hands around her face. "Caroline, did you hear my mom? We have to go. Can you walk?"

"Yes." I see terror in her eyes. "But, I'm stuck. The chains." She's still in a state of shock.

"I've cut the bolt," I say. "You're free. We have to go *now*."

I grab the rope from the wall, loop it over my shoulder. Then I open the door a crack, glancing out. The truck is in the parking lot of the racetrack, about five hundred yards away. A man and a woman stand beside the truck. The woman is tiny, wearing a cowboy hat. The man wears a suit. They appear to be waiting for someone, but they're not alarmed. If someone received an alert when I cut the collar, it wasn't them.

I shut the door and whisper, "There are two people out there. We need to stay low and move fast."

Caroline is freezing to the touch. Her mouth is moving, but I can't make out the words.

I open the door and lead Rory and Caroline out. The people are so close I can hear their voices. Their backs are to us. They're looking in the direction of the house. Caroline is dazed, her eyes glassy. She's squinting, having trouble adjusting to the light.

I motion for the kids to follow me. We creep down the slippery hill, leaving a noticeable trail in the mud. Then we are under the rail and back along the tree line. We run along the fence until we reach the limb of the tree where we first entered. My heart is pounding. I glance back to see if the people have seen us, but they're still standing there, talking, gazing up toward the house. I feel less conspicuous here in the shadows of the trees and rain. I throw the heavy rope up and over, and Rory jumps up to reach the end dangling over the branch. He pulls it down to the ground. I quickly tie off four footholds to form a makeshift ladder. I motion for Rory to go first.

In a flash, he skitters up the rope and onto the limb, positioning himself to help Caroline over. She stands beneath the limb, dazed, shivering. She is so weak and thin. With her bald head and pale skin, she looks alien. I remember how Nicole described Gray Stafford—more creature than human, shuffling toward her on the beach.

I hear tires on gravel in the distance. Caroline hears it too, turning to look in the direction of the house, terror in her eyes. I tune my ears to the sound of the car, that music my dad taught me to listen for. It's the Land Cruiser, no question.

I put my hands on her shoulders, look into her eyes, and say, "You can do this."

She nods. I help her into the foothold and hoist her light body up the rope. Rory reaches down and pulls her up. She's out of my sight now, and I hear her landing, leaves rustling on the ground.

I use the rope to pull myself up onto the limb. Rory reaches down, grabbing my hand in his strong grip. Once I'm steady on the limb, he drops onto the ground next to Caroline. From this vantage point I can see the Land Cruiser pulling up beside the truck. The big man steps out, greeting the couple, but he doesn't even glance toward the kennel. My gaze is drawn to his pants—bright yellow, plaid. Plaid Man, in the flesh.

From their formal handshakes and the way he seems to be showing them the track for the first time, I realize the couple is probably oblivious to the kennel; they're here on separate business.

I untie the rope, hoist it over the fence out of sight, and scurry backward along the limb, dropping down on the other side.

Caroline sits against the tree, Rory hovering over her, watching for danger. Her bare feet sink into the wet leaves and soil. I take off my sneakers, put them on her ruined feet, and lace them.

"Thirsty," Caroline gasps.

Rory unzips the backpack, pulls out a bottle of water, and holds it to Caroline's lips. She drinks, water dribbling down her chin, gasping, until the bottle is empty.

Together, Rory and I lift Caroline, helping her to stand. Her arm feels so thin, just skin and bones. She is so weak, but we have to hurry. How much time do we have before Leonard Blake realizes she is missing?

We walk along the fence, back to the logging road. I look back, relieved to see our footprints disappearing in the rain. "If we hear a vehicle, we have to jump off the road and hide in the trees. Understand?" They both nod.

We cover the first half mile at a good clip. My feet slip in the mud, sharp rocks and buried roots digging into my skin. Caroline is out of breath, walking between Rory and me. Fifteen minutes into the journey, she stops and gasps for breath, bent over with her hands on her knees. She bends down farther and dry heaves once, twice.

"Are you okay?" Rory asks her, his voice anxious. He turns to me: "Mom?"

She stands up straight. "I'm okay."

She almost sounds like Caroline again. There is willfulness in her voice, but once we take a few steps farther, it's obvious she's too weak for this hike.

"We have to make it off of the logging road," I say.

Rory puts his face close to Caroline's and says a few words into her ear. She nods. He leans down and in one move hoists her up over his shoulder. We move rapidly down the logging road, along the tree line. No sign of the Land Cruiser. No sign of anyone. Rory leads the way, clearheaded, strong.

My bare feet are burning. The blood flow from my wrist has coagulated into a sticky mess. I listen for cars. We need help. We need a ride. But there's no one we can trust, and I can't even explain exactly where we are. I pull out my phone again, looking for service, but there is none.

After another quarter mile, Rory puts Caroline down, takes a moment to catch his breath, and we walk toward the spot where our path met the logging road. The air smells like pine and earth, reminding me of the camp in the Poconos where Rory used to spend two weeks each summer. My eyes scan the ground for the red tee. I pick it up and put it in my pocket. Our progress downhill is slow because of the mud. We pass the waterfall, and I'm relieved to see it, to know we're going the right way. Near the abandoned cabin, we find a protected area among the trees, and we collapse.

"You must be starving," I say to Caroline.

She looks at me blankly, still in shock.

I open the backpack and take out two full water bottles, handing one to her and one to Rory. Rory opens the bottle for her, and she gulps it down. I unwrap the cheese and break it into small pieces, handing them to her one at a time, so she won't choke. Then I open a sleeve of graham crackers. She eats ravenously for several minutes, guzzles the last of the final water bottle, then scavenges the bottom of the backpack for a few remaining crumbs. The rain pounds the ground around us, heavy drops hitting the leaves, a soothing music.

She looks up to see both of us staring at her. "Was I supposed to share?" A joke, almost. A sign of the girl Rory knows, coming back to herself.

Rory smiles and puts his arm around her, so gently. "No, you weren't supposed to share."

Finally—bruised, scraped, muddy, bloody, and wet—we reach the bottom of the trail. We're not out of danger. We still have to get across the open field, across Armstrong Woods Road, and back to the car.

Has Leonard Blake realized she's missing? Surely by now he's looking for her, for us.

Just short of the trailhead, I pull Rory and Caroline into a huddle. "You have the key?" I ask Rory.

He feels in his pocket. "Yes."

"I need you to go get the Jeep and bring it to the edge of the field there."

"Okay."

As he sprints across the field, I turn to Caroline. "You're safe now."

She tries to say something, but no words come out. After several seconds, she says, "I thought he was going to"—she shudders—"but he didn't. *Why* did he take me, if he didn't want that?"

"Did you see the person who took you?"

"No, it was so fast. I was walking home, a car pulled up behind me . . . and then, I woke up in a strange bed. I couldn't move. I think I was drugged. When I called out, no one came." She is sobbing. I wrap her in my arms. The Jeep pulls up right across the field from us. Rory gets out and opens the back passenger side door. "Ready?" I ask Caroline.

"Yes."

"Don't look back. Just run."

53

T. S. Eliot wrote, "If you are not in over your head, how do you know how tall you are?" In seven paragraphs accompanied by visual aids, illustrate this tenet with an example from your own experience.

The spires of the Golden Gate Bridge are obscured by fog. Alcatraz squats low in the bay, barely visible. I crack the windows to breathe in the cold, clean smell of ocean and fog. Caroline and Rory are asleep in the back seat. Her head rests on his shoulder, his arm draped protectively over her. Empty Gatorade bottles and sandwich wrappers are scattered around them.

Color has already returned to Caroline's face. Passing through Petaluma, she grabbed Rory's hand. "They shaved my head," she said, grief-stricken. "Why would they take my hair?"

Rory ran his palm over her scalp and said, "You look beautiful." He knew instinctively, without prompting, the right thing to do, the right words to say.

When we drive through the toll booth and make the right onto Lincoln Boulevard, Rory wakes up. He tries to readjust his arm, and Caroline wakes too.

"We should take you to the hospital, sweetie."

Immediately, Caroline's face fills with panic, her eyes tearing up. "Please just let me go home with you," she pleads. "No hospital. *Please.*"

Her voice is strong. Her appetite is good. Aside from cuts and bruises, she appears physically okay. As an agent, I know the smart move is to take her to the hospital, document the wounds, begin the chain of evidence. But as a parent, I know that what she needs right now is safety, comfort, and a warm bed in a peaceful home with people who care about her. More than anything, she needs her mother.

As an agent, I also know that a trip to the hospital means more than a simple checkup. It means implementation of the hospital's child abuse protocol, followed by the arrival of a disinterested police officer who is unprepared for a discussion of complex crimes, unknown coconspirators, and even the possibility of public corruption.

I pull up to the front door of my dad's house, so Caroline won't be visible from the street. We go inside. I shut the door behind us, lock it, and turn to Caroline. "I need to call your mother to let her know you're safe. Can you tell me how to get in touch with her?" I don't tell her that her mother hasn't even contacted the school. I doubt her mother ever knew she was gone.

"How many days have I been gone?" Caroline asks.

"Seven," Rory says.

"I'd have to be missing a lot longer than that for her to notice. But I'll call." She reaches into her pocket, but her hand comes out empty. "Merde. I forgot, he took my phone."

Rory hands Caroline his phone. She taps a phone number into the keypad. The phone rings once, followed by a voice recording on the other end, her mother's outgoing message.

"Mama? C'est moi." Caroline looks up at me, unsure what to say. "Je dois te dire quelque chose." *I need to tell you something.* She hangs up, passes the phone back to Rory, looks at me. "What now?"

"You'll stay with us until they get back."

How long will that be? Off the grid, involved in whatever they're involved in, their daughter's safety across the world in this seemingly idyllic California town is probably the last thing on their minds.

"You have to understand. My parents are—"

"It's okay. I know. They would be here if they could."

Finally, in the warmth of our home, Caroline slides her arms out of Rory's jacket. There are finger-shaped bruises across her biceps, redness on her neck. As we made our escape, I was so focused on getting her down the mountain and into the Jeep that I didn't take the time to really examine her. Her legs are also bruised, her feet caked with dirt. Leather still encircles her ankle, the small chain trailing behind.

"I need a bath," she says. In my work through the years, I've often been amazed by how quick people are to adapt, to overcome the most unthinkable things. While some victims never recover, their lives entirely shattered by what they endured, others somehow thrive, as if in defiance of their tormentors. At the moment, Caroline seems strong. But how will she be in two weeks, two months, two years?

I run water for her in the bathtub, pouring in lavender bubble bath. She stands in the doorway, watching me lay out a clean T-shirt and sweatpants. "You're in luck," I say, holding up an unopened pack of Hanes boxer briefs I bought for Rory a few days ago.

She's standing there with a blank expression, her mind somewhere else. Her right foot scratches at the remnant of leather strap still attached to her left foot.

"Just a minute. I'll grab something to get that off for you."

She looks confused for a moment, and I gesture toward the frayed strap on her ankle. She lifts her foot and stares down at it, as if surprised to see the strap. I go down to the garage and return with small gardening sheers. She is sitting on the side of the tub, still dressed in the mud-caked clothes. I gently nudge the blade underneath the strap. She winces as the cuff comes off, revealing a band of bloodied skin.

"You said you woke up in a bed—"

"Yes. I was in a room for three nights, maybe more. It had a bed and a chair. My room was attached to a little bathroom with a toilet and sink, no shower. The windows were shuttered. I couldn't tell where I was. The first day, there was food, but I was scared to eat it. Later, when I was sleeping, someone put a bottle of orange juice in the room. But they must have put something in it, because I slept so hard."

"You sent Rory a text message on Monday. A line from the book *Martin in Space*."

She shakes her head, confused. "I didn't send a text."

"It said, *Don't worry, Friend. All is well.*"

She shakes her head again. "No, it wasn't me." Her brow furrows as the realization dawns on her. "The book was in my backpack when they took me."

I think of Leonard Blake scrolling through Caroline's phone, reading the texts between her and Rory. Maybe there were messages about the book. Did Leonard Blake sit in that big house by the fire, reading her book while she was locked in the bedroom? Did he keep reading until he found the perfect line? What kind of monster are we dealing with here?

"Do you remember being taken outside?"

"Yes, I refused to eat, and I was screaming, banging on the bedroom door. I was going crazy, being in there alone. I must have been screaming for hours when the door burst open and a man came in. This huge man. He wore a stocking over his head, you know? Like in movies? He blindfolded me, grabbed me by the arms, and dragged me through the house. He said if I had just kept my mouth shut, I could have stayed in the room. 'Like being in a nice hotel,' he said, 'room service and everything.' But now I had made him mad. 'I don't like screaming,' he said. 'That really is the last straw, darling.' His voice was so calm and cruel. I was terrified."

She dips her hand in the water of the tub behind her. "That's when he dragged me outside and down the hill. He threw me in the shed and put the chain around my ankle." She shudders. "And the collar. Then he locked me in. And I was so mad at myself, you know? Because before I had a bed, and now I was locked in a shed, like an *animal*. At some point, he put food under the door on a tray. It was disgusting, beans on soggy bread, but I was so hungry."

"Was it the same man, or someone else?"

"It was him. He had this smell, a really strong smell of peppermint and Dove soap. Obviously, he thought cleanliness was important, for himself at least, so I tried to appeal to that. I told him I needed to get out to bathe, but he said that was a privilege I would have to earn. Then he left.

"That food must have been drugged too, because I tried to stay awake, but I couldn't. When I woke up there was no light coming in through the cracks. And my head felt strange. It felt so light. I reached up and touched my head and realized my hair was gone. At first I was so furious that he had taken my hair, but when I thought about it, I was relieved. I kept thinking about Gray Stafford. Gray Stafford was bald, like me. Gray Stafford came *home*."

"Did you ever see or hear anyone else?"

"No. Only him." She swirls her hand in the water. She looks so tired, so sad. "I don't want to talk anymore."

"Okay. If you need anything, just shout." I shut the door behind me.

A picture of Leonard Blake is beginning to form. He's cold, calculated, patient: the way he carried out the abduction and the scene on the boat with Gray—the plastic bag and fire extinguisher, the insistence on leaving no hairs or fibers behind. In some ways, he considers the crime to be an intellectual game: the fact that he read the book from Caroline's backpack, sent the mysterious text. He can even be thoughtful—the room with the comfortable bed. But when angry, he flies off the handle. He is in complete control— until he isn't.

I find Rory at his desk, freshly showered, wet haired, clad in jeans and Fred's old Mets T-shirt.

"How are you feeling?"

He doesn't respond. He's fighting back tears. I go over to him and wrap my arms around his shoulders. His skin is still warm from the shower. "You smell like chocolate cake," I say.

"It's this shampoo I found in Grandpa's cabinet."

Rory's face is filled with sadness. He has aged years in one day. I release him. "You were amazing today, sweetheart. Really amazing."

"Okay," he says, and that's it.

"When you're ready to talk about it—"

"No. I'm just glad Caroline is safe." He looks up at me. "She is safe, right?"

"Yes, thanks to you."

His voice stops me as I step into the hallway. "Mom?"

"Yeah?"

"The guy in the other stall, was he okay?"

After what Rory went through today, what he saw, there's no pretense of protecting any sort of lingering childhood innocence. The world is a bizarre, often ugly place. He's seen that now. "It's complicated. He didn't want to be rescued. Some people are drawn to strange things. There are whole hidden worlds, anywhere you go, just below the surface." The explanation sounds clinical, inadequate, yet my answer, for the moment, satisfies him.

"I'm nervous. About what to say to Caroline."

"You don't have to say anything. Just be there for her."

Rory's hands are balled into fists, and the sadness on his face transforms into rage. "Whoever did this, I want to kill him."

Maybe I should tell him violence isn't the answer. Some parents, in this situation, would even talk about forgiveness. But I don't know that I believe either of those things. Rory and I walked through a door together today. It's a door I've walked through many times, but in the past I always shut it behind me, walling Rory off from the harsh realities of that world.

Today, I led him right through. I don't know if he can ever forgive me, but I do know one thing: he cannot unsee what he has seen. He cannot go back to who he was before.

54

"No live organism can continue for long to exist sanely under conditions of absolute reality."

—Shirley Jackson

True or false?

The business card I picked up from the dirt at the compound is faded but legible. The front of the card is embossed with the words: "Your Home for Pony Play." Nothing else. On the back, a long string of numbers, letters, periods, and slashes—probably for the dark web.

I message Malia, knowing that each favor I ask of her leads me one step closer to Iceland, one step closer to Red Vine. Malia is the only one I trust with something like this. She knows a good contact at Amazon Web Services who facilitates her traffic in the slipstream in a way that doesn't rouse attention.

It's after 2:00 a.m. in DC, but it doesn't surprise me when Malia responds seconds later. Interest is heating up around here. Ready yet for the Northern Lights? Will check your address tomorrow—looks like a TOR address, with the password embedded.

I do some searches on the Russian River property. It's registered to a generic trust that leads back to a San Francisco lawyer who handles multiple trusts. The property was purchased thirteen years ago for a small fraction of what it's worth now. The place doesn't even exist on Google Maps.

After an hour of failed internet searches, I go upstairs to check on Rory and Caroline. They're in the movie room, asleep on opposite sides of the sectional, the television still on. The color has come back to Caroline's face, and her breathing is steady. I sit down next to her on the couch, zoning out. I want to sleep, but I can't sleep. There is still so much to do.

Caroline starts mumbling in her sleep, kicking.

I place my hand on her shoulders. "Caroline, you're safe now." She keeps kicking, her face a mask of fear. "Tu es hors de danger maintenant," I say more loudly.

Her eyes open, her arms go to her face to protect herself. "You're safe," I repeat. "You're here with me and Rory."

She's panicked at first, but then her eyes find mine and she relaxes. The terror fades. "I don't want anyone at school to know. Please don't tell anyone."

She grabs my hand, her jagged fingernails digging into my palm. I wait for her to say something else, but she doesn't. Her breathing becomes more regular, her eyelids droop, and she is asleep again.

55

When fitted with a tiny blindfold, Moorish geckos are still able to precisely match their surroundings, but when their skin is covered, their chemical camouflage reaction fails. What can humans learn from the Moorish gecko about camouflage vs. concealment?

At 7:55 a.m. on Monday, Rory wanders into the kitchen fully dressed, half-asleep, backpack slung over his shoulders. I slide bacon out of the pan onto a paper towel.

"You shouldn't go to school today," I say, dropping two slices of bread into the toaster. "Stay home. Rest. Surely you don't care about the test anymore?"

"If I don't go, people will get suspicious. It's better to just act like everything is normal. What if someone realizes Caroline is with us?"

He has a point. Nothing's going to happen to him, the star student. Missing the test would draw attention. And maybe, today, he just needs to get away. When I checked on the kids earlier this morning, they were both still asleep in the movie room, but Caroline had moved down the couch toward Rory, and their feet were touching.

I bring the bacon and toast to the table. "How is she?"

"I didn't want to wake her up." He slathers butter and jam onto his toast, grinning. "She snores as loud as Dad."

After polishing off his breakfast, Rory wipes his hands on a napkin and looks at me. "Yesterday—" he says, but he doesn't finish the thought.

I reach over to touch his arm. He pulls away. We sit in silence for several minutes until a car honks in the driveway.

"Who's that?" I ask, pulling the curtain aside.

"I got a ride with Bradley. I didn't think you should leave Caroline alone."

"Seriously, you do *not* have to go. We can make it a movie day. Sci-fi marathon. We'll start with *Close Encounters*."

Rory shakes his head. "Kobayashi said they're depending on me. If we act normal, no one will notice. And Caroline can sleep. She doesn't want anyone at school to know. She doesn't want people to look at her the way they look at Gray."

He makes sense. But I wonder too if there's a part of him that doesn't want to spend the day with her, because he doesn't know what to say, how to act.

"She's fragile right now, Rory, but you're not going to break her. You *saved* her. Did I tell you how proud I am of you? Dad would be proud of you too."

"Yeah, but he'd be really freaking pissed at you for taking me with you."

"True."

The car honks again. Rory stands and slings his backpack over his shoulder. I follow him to the foyer. An enormous black Escalade is parked in our driveway. Bradley's mom, Anita, pokes her head out the window and waves. I watch Rory get into the car, a sense of unease washing over me. He's fifteen, he's strong, he's smart. Yesterday, he proved he is courageous and incredibly capable. And he's a star student, not the kind of kid who goes missing in this town. Still, I don't want to let him out of my sight.

As I walk back inside, Mister Fancy slips out of the bushes and slides past my legs into the house. Upstairs, Caroline is still sound asleep. The room is chilly, so I pull another blanket over her.

A few minutes later, a message arrives from Malia.

I hope this guy isn't a friend of ours. From what I can tell, his true name is Wallace Russell Anderson—goes by Rusty. The Leonard Blake identity is an alias. Born in Cheyenne, Wyoming, 51, parents deceased, one sister, a doctor in Colorado Springs. Married once, divorced fourteen years ago, no kids. Regional rodeo star in the late 1980s. Misdemeanors for weed in 1991 and 1993. Domestic in Mountain View in 1995. Complainant: Jean Bismark, his wife at the time. Claims to have gone to Princeton, though no record of him there. He did three semesters at Santa Rosa Junior College. Several registered companies. In addition to the land you mentioned, he owns property in Siskiyou County. Owns five licensed firearms, three cars (F150, Merc, vintage Land Cruiser), purchased a boat in Petaluma five months ago. Donated to McCain-Palin, Romney-Ryan, and Trump-Pence, then shifted gears to donate to Michael Bloomberg. Also the Sonoma County Sheriff and the Guerneville fire department.

I scroll through the attached photos—DMV records, a few tags on random Facebook profiles, a grainy newspaper article about a Wyoming rodeo. Mixed in with the photographs of authentic horse farms and horse shows, there's some mild counterculture stuff, friends in leather and BDSM, lots of tattoos. Malia also sent a dozen photos from a biometric search, but most appear to be false matches.

Below the photos, Malia wrote,

Now for the dark web. He runs a thing called Redwoods Pony Play. You learn something new every day. Have you heard of this? It's a subculture of people who like to pretend they're horses. For a price, a very high one, he invites them to his ranch with their "trainers." I'll spare you the photographs—can't unsee those.

Anyway, the pony play isn't what concerns me. His address comes back to a hangout an agent was monitoring for a cyber case. Rusty offers a whole range of questionable services. He's expensive. It's a K&R thing, unclear if it's real or consensual. Kidnap fantasies are big business. Went down the rabbit hole. I'm so square. I've got to get out more often. I thought it was fake, until I found his dark web address in a 2703d order related to a midlevel OC case.

Outside, I hear Kyle's cruiser pull into the driveway. I shut and lock the door behind him, lead him into the kitchen. "Caroline's here," I say.

Over coffee, I quietly tell him a pared-down story of how we found her. I leave out some parts, like Ivy, Sunshine, the part about Rory being with me. I trust Kyle, but I don't entirely know him.

Kyle listens intently, not saying a word. When I'm finished, he shakes his head. "That poor girl. How is she?"

"Too soon to tell."

"Jesus, this isn't what I signed up for."

"When you sign up for this job, Kyle, you sign up for anything. By the way, your hunch about the Lamey twins and their allergy to black walnut trees?"

"Yeah?"

"There were black walnut trees on the property."

"So they *are* all linked, all three cases. Gray and the Lamey twins were kept at this property too?"

"Looks that way."

"But *why?*"

"It's about the Wonder Test."

He shakes his head, uncomprehending. "What?"

"Somebody has a stake in these kids not bringing down the test scores."

"*Who?*"

"I'm still trying to work that out."

"So, what are you not telling me?"

"A lot," I admit. "Not a word of this to Chief Jepson or anyone at the GPD."

"What are you saying?"

"I couldn't understand why Jepson didn't seem to care about the Stafford case, so I ran some checks. Turns out he controls a trust that owns a home on Vista Lane."

Kyle frowns. "He told me he lived in South City."

"He does. But he also owns this place."

"Damn, that must be worth a fortune."

"He paid five point seven million dollars, all cash, nine months ago."

"Maybe he got an inheritance?" Kyle offers, but he doesn't sound convinced.

"Listen, you can't tell anyone that Caroline is here. *Anyone.*"

"You actually think I can't trust my own department?"

"Connect the dots, Kyle. They got nowhere on the Lamey or Stafford cases. When you became too curious, the chief kept distracting you with busywork. He makes a hundred and forty-five thousand per year, his wife is unemployed and drives a Tesla, two kids in college, and he came up with almost six million in cash just a few months after Gray went missing."

"Okay. It looks bad. Worse than bad. But I guarantee you the chief didn't mastermind anything. However he got involved in this, *if* he's involved, he's not the one pulling the strings. He doesn't have a mind for complexity."

56

If moss usually grows on the north side of the tree, which
side does it grow on when you are at the exact North Pole?

Caroline spends the morning upstairs, watching TV. I do some more
digging, make some phone calls. I order Blue Line pizza for lunch.
She eats heartily but doesn't say much, staring out the window. As
we're clearing the dishes from the table, she begins talking.

"When I was trapped in that shed, do you know what I thought
about? I thought about Gray Stafford. He was so strong before he
disappeared. He was loud and fun, so alive. And later, the saddest
thing was, the boy I knew before was gone. Like he had been—"

I remember the word Caroline used when she first told me
about Gray, that day in the car. "Erased?" I offer.

"Yes. Erased. And in the shed, I kept thinking, 'I will not let
this man erase *me*.'"

After school, Rory bounds up the stairs to join Caroline in the
movie room. I can hear them talking quietly to each other. I even
hear a moment of laughter. How much of this transition back to
the normal world is real, how much of it is a brave act?

I walk down to the mailbox. Most of the mail is still for my
dad—fishing catalogs, car magazines. The stack of envelopes makes

me feel a little closer to him, as though he might show up any minute.

As I'm closing the mailbox, I see Glen Park running up the block toward me. He's moving fast, as always, wearing a University of Arkansas shirt and some expensive Hoka One One shoes. No headphones today. As he passes, I mumble, "Hello, Glen," more to myself than anyone. He's going so fast that I feel a breeze as he passes me.

Glen Park, in the flesh. It makes me smile. I wish my dad were here to see it.

When he gets about thirty yards up the hill, he does what appears to be a reluctant U-turn and slowly jogs back to me, his hands folded behind his head. He stops right in front of me at the end of my driveway, backlit by the sun. Up close, I'm surprised by how tall he is.

"Hello, Lina." I'm surprised he knows my name. He flashes a quick, pained smile. "When did you figure it out? Was it that morning by the golf course?"

"No, it was later, over on Forestview. You were doing a four-minute mile."

"No way," he says. "I'm too old for that."

"I know what I saw."

"I get carried away."

"You have no idea how sad my dad would be to miss this. He must have watched that old footage from Kezar a hundred times."

He puts his hands on his hips, does a couple of side bends. "He didn't miss it. Your dad was on to me years ago."

"What? You're kidding!"

"I ran this route by his house one too many times. Eventually, he invited me in, told me he had a VHS tape he wanted me to see. I hadn't watched that race in years. We became friends. Used to sit out on the back porch drinking Macallan twelve year, talking about old races."

I smile, thinking of my dad, holding on to this secret. "Glen fucking Park," I say. "I can't believe he never told me."

"I made him promise."

57

"But sometimes illumination comes to our rescue at the
very moment when all seems lost; we have knocked at every
door and they open on nothing until, at last, we stumble
unconsciously against the only one through which we
can enter the kingdom we have sought in vain a hundred
years—and it opens."
                    —Marcel Proust, *In Search of Lost Time*

Would the average American respond to this quote with
optimism or regret? What "kingdom" have you personally
sought and found?

I'm sitting in the car in Millbrae, on Kobayashi's street. He's not
home, of course. On the penultimate day of the Wonder Test, there's
only one place he could be. I park across the street, halfway down
the block, tucking the Jeep in behind a Porsche Cayenne. I've asked
Kyle to keep an eye on my dad's house, do drive-bys every few minutes until I return home.

    An email comes in from Malia. For Red Vine, I got you $1k for
a gift, $25k for the payment, and I earmarked whatever travel you
need for Iceland out of the IYIY funds.

I can sense Malia's excitement. This is the part of her job she loves. She'll want to know what kind of gift I selected for Red Vine, my ops plan, briefing questions. She geeks out on the details.

On the way home, I stop at the library in Burlingame. There's a public computer I like, basement level, tucked away in a corner behind the archived newspapers. I log on with a library card that was surprisingly easy to obtain in alias. I access the dedicated proton account and find that Red Vine has left two messages. I'm alarmed to discover the first one was sent twenty-three days ago: What you wanted I have found.

The second is from twelve days ago and is more insistent. For a source at this level, Red Vine is uncommonly relaxed, but even he gets a case of nerves when I don't respond. Are we not meeting on the anniversary? I think you will be happy if we meet. We should meet.

What I know is this: I don't want to go back to Iceland. I don't want to think about my time there, the time I wasted, the time I should have been with Fred. I don't want to think about the lost days, and I don't want to leave Rory behind. And yet, I made a commitment. Until I fulfill my promise, the unfinished business will weigh on me. In my head, I run through Rory's schedule. The next school break is in April. I haven't left him alone since Fred died, and I certainly don't want to leave him now.

I type a message back to Red Vine, suggesting a meeting, using our minus-nineteen code to disguise the date. I bury the schedule in a few long sentences about the weather in Moscow and the travails of a club hockey team. I hit Send. My Russian is awkward, but the important parts are clear.

At home, I call for Caroline as soon as I step in the front door. I don't want her to hear someone walking around the house and freak out. She doesn't respond. She isn't in the kitchen, the library, the guest room, the movie room. I feel a surge of panic.

But then, through the breezeway windows, I see her out back, reading, headphones on, drinking a Fanta. I go outside to join her. "It's such a beautiful day," she exclaims. "Sunshine!"

She's wearing a pair of Rory's shorts and the Cracker shirt Fred bought him at a show in Hoboken years ago. I sit next to her on the grass. There are so many questions I want to ask, but I need to ease into it.

She squints into the sun. "I talked to my mom."

"You did?" I say, surprised. "That's great. What did she say when you told her what happened?"

"I didn't."

"Oh, sweetheart."

"I wanted to, but I couldn't. I didn't want to say it over the phone. I just told her I'm in trouble, and I really need her to come home."

"Good."

"She said they'll be home soon. What do I do until then?"

"Stay with us. You're safe here." It feels important to keep saying this.

"You know what really makes me mad? Even if she knew what happened, I'm not sure she would rush home. She would call the embassy and send someone to the house to keep an eye on me, but that would be it. Her motto is 'Gardez-le dans la famille.'"

"Tough being a diplomat's kid."

"Diplomat, right." She smirks. "It sucks when your parents think their mission is to save the country. What am I supposed to say to that? Come home, I need you, I'm more important than la République?"

My heart breaks for Caroline. And for Rory.

We sit in silence for a while, the sun on our faces. She picks up *Martin in Space*. I can tell from the hot chocolate stain on the cover that it's Rory's copy.

"Rory is a real disciple of that book," I say, smiling. "What do *you* think it's about?"

"It's about the things you want, the things you need, and how hard it is to recognize the difference. Rory thinks it's about something else, but that's why it's a good book."

I notice her skin is turning pink. "You're burning." I go to the patio, grab a tube of sunscreen from the wicker basket, and bring it over to her. She carefully rubs it on her cheeks and forehead. I lean back on the grass and watch the sunlight through the top of the redwood tree. I shouldn't be sitting here with Caroline; her mom and dad should. Of course, if I'm honest, I have more in common with Caroline's parents than with any of the other parents in this town.

She rubs sunscreen across her pale white skull, where the hair is beginning to grow into a fine fuzz. Her hands move with an aggressive confidence, straight over the top, down her neck, around her small ears. It occurs to me that she is more than resilient. She's a special girl, much tougher than she looks, the years of benign neglect rendering her confident and independent. If she weathers this, there are few obstacles she won't be able to overcome.

If I had the opportunity to choose the kind of girl Rory would eventually spend his life with, it would be someone like Caroline. And yet, I want so badly to stop time and keep him with me. I want to make up for all those times I wasn't home or the times I was home but not present, juggling five different cell phones, my mind somewhere else. The stakes always seemed so high. I always thought there was so much to lose. So much could go wrong if I missed a call, if I failed at a task. Fred and Rory were doing fine without me, I thought. I was almost the third wheel—not unloved, not unwanted, but rarely necessary to the functioning of the family machine.

It was my country that needed me most, or so I believed.

58

True or false: It's safer to surf at or near high tide. Diagram.

"I want to make dinner," Caroline announces Monday afternoon. "To celebrate my liberté."

"Why don't you order from Good Eggs?" I suggest, determined to keep her inside, safe behind closed doors until her parents return. I open the app on my phone and hand it to her. "Order whatever you need."

An hour later, the delivery driver shows up with two boxes of groceries, and Rory asks Caroline what she's making.

"None of your business. Secret family recipe. Go away. I'll call you when it's ready."

In my dad's study, I continue my research on Wallace Russell Anderson, a.k.a. Rusty. Although he isn't difficult to find, there's little information beyond what Malia already provided.

At ten past eight in the evening, Caroline calls us into the dining room. The lights are low, white candles flickering in a silver candelabra. The table is set with my dad's china, the good silverware, and Waterford glasses. There's a plate piled with crusty bread, three bowls of pale-green soup. A glass of water and a half portion of red wine are arranged at each place setting. Caroline has transformed—wearing a floral Laura Ashley dress with serious shoulder pads, no shoes.

"Where did you find that? I haven't seen that dress in twenty years."

"I hope you don't mind. It was in the hall closet. It looked like it needed to be worn."

"You look great," Rory says. "But I'm so underdressed!"

She motions to our chairs and stands at the head of the table. "I begin with a toast," she says, tilting her glass toward Rory and then toward me. "Merci beaucoup. Ni plus, ni moins."

Rory and I are both waiting for more, but that's it. Simple and to the point. After the soup, Rory declares the meal delicious and begins to clear the table, but Caroline stops him. "Sit down. That was only the beginning! This is a French meal. It's going to take a while."

Dinner lasts for three hours. Every time we finish a course, Caroline goes to the kitchen for another. In the end, she brings out a plate with three cheeses. "One cheese to represent each of us," Caroline explains. "For you, Rory, a Camembert, not just any Camembert, but the king of all Camembert. Smart and smooth, like you. Then, for me, a goat cheese, bald, direct, an acquired taste. Finally, for your mother, a top-of-the-line comté, aged thirty-two months."

"Aged?" I protest.

"When I feel overwhelmed," Caroline explains, "I always return to the aged comté. A world with something like this cannot be all bad." The tears in her eyes belie the lightness in her voice.

Afterward, Rory and Caroline go out to the back patio—ostensibly to look at the stars, but because of the lights from the airport, few stars are visible. I know they want to be alone. They sit side by side, hands linked between their chairs, their voices a low murmur.

Inside, I call George. He picks up on the first ring. "Where are you?"

"Reno," he says. "Don't ask."

"Any chance you have some time tomorrow?"

"Sorry, I'm packing up tonight, taking the red-eye. I have a meeting with CD-4 tomorrow morning."

"Can you get out of it?"

Long pause. "I shouldn't."

"It's important.

"Okay, I'll catch a plane to SFO instead."

"Meet me at eight thirty a.m., same spot?"

"What's in it for me?"

"I'll buy you a burrito afterward. A San Mateo burrito. Not that Tex-Mex crap you get in New York."

"Deal."

59

Shakespeare wrote Shakespeare's plays. Shakespeare did not write Shakespeare's plays. Is the origin of a work of art relevant? Discuss modern literary criticism's fascination with the myth of the creator.

On Tuesday morning, Rory goes to school for his final day of the Wonder Test and Caroline sleeps in. After asking Kyle to keep an eye on the house again today, I drive to the meeting spot. The air is cool and crisp, the bay path busy with joggers.

I'm early, but George is already sitting on the bench waiting for me. "I'm dying with anticipation. What's the job today? I brought a change of clothes, in case this look isn't right." He stands and does a slow turn, modeling his outfit: jeans, Doc Martens, a plaid flannel shirt.

"Perfect. How long can I borrow you for?"

"I'm all yours until my six a.m. flight tomorrow."

We walk toward the parking lot. "Mind taking a ride up to Sonoma County, pay a guy a visit?"

"Love to, on one condition. I drive." George presses a button on his key. In the parking lot, lights flash on a black Alfa Stelvio SUV. "The rental guy set me up."

"Four-wheel drive?"

"Yep."

"You win."

As we drive, I explain the situation. George listens, not speaking. It's the sign of a good agent. Bad agents are always trying to stop you before you finish, certain that they've heard everything before. To good agents, every operation, every case, every source is different.

It takes me all the way to Sebastopol to get the whole story out. Only once does he interrupt: when I tell him the brutal conditions of Caroline's confinement. "Sounds like he fits in the irredeemable category," he says.

One year, George and I did seventeen arrests together. On surveillance one night, we classified all the subjects we'd brought in. As George would say, not all bad guys are criminals, not all criminals are bad guys, and not all criminals are irredeemable. Before Rusty, I had met only one other truly irredeemable person: Donald Fritz.

Fritz had attempted to assault a twenty-year-old woman seated next to him on an American East flight out of Phoenix. I happened to be at SFO for an unrelated issue when his plane landed. The call went to me. Before I could read the write-up, I was in an airport security interview room, one-on-one with Fritz. Lanky, blue-eyed, and clean-shaven, Fritz had no record and no red flags in his background. Yet before I had even opened my notebook, I knew he was a predator and a sociopath. Perhaps he hadn't killed anyone yet, but I was certain he would. I talked to him for three hours while a young Homeland Security officer stood at the door, watching us silently. I was fascinated with Fritz. A little creeped out but mostly just fascinated. He was willing to talk about anything—women, animals, sex, his violent fantasies, his childhood years with a cruel father and a distant mother—so I kept prodding, asking questions that led to ever more disturbing answers.

After the interview, the marshals came and took Fritz to lockup. As the Homeland Security woman and I watched them walk away, Fritz looked over his shoulder and winked at me. Once Fritz turned the corner, I noticed that the Homeland Security woman's face was pallid, a look of fear in her eyes.

"You okay?"

She didn't respond. I pulled a chair over, and she sat down. Finally, she managed to say, "I didn't even want to work today. I just wanted to ride my bike."

I urged the AUSA to press as many charges as he could, to get Fritz off the street for as long as possible, have him committed. It's the only time in my career I've ever yelled and sworn at a prosecutor. But, as the prosecutor said, it was a minor offense, limited evidence, no priors. When Fritz pled, the judge gave him a year and a day. Three years later, Fritz killed a woman and her seven-year-old daughter in their apartment on a reservation in Wyoming.

Donald Fritz was irredeemable. Judging from what I saw at the compound, I think Wallace "Rusty" Anderson may be irredeemable too.

I tell George my theory about the abductions, holes and all. "Am I wrong?"

He glances over at me. "The suburbs are a scary place. I'm glad I live in New York City, where crime is more predictable. What's the goal today?"

"We need to find the link between Rusty and the Kenji Boys or whoever is above them."

"A rich country boy and Asian OC? Odd. Does it matter how we get from point A to point B?"

"Not really. I saw some cameras around the perimeter, but they're old, most likely a box rather than the cloud."

"I need to know. Will today wind up in a 302?"

"It will not."

"Eventually you'll have to go one way or the other. Bring in an agent from San Francisco or make a crim referral to the locals."

"I wanted to go the local route, but I can't shake the sense that there's something off about Greenfield PD. I have a hunch there's a public corruption case there somewhere. Anyway, with what little I have now, wherever I send it, FBI-SF, GPD, or even the Sonoma County Sheriff, it's so thin it would hit the zero file before I was even off the phone."

"Agreed."

"We get the information, we move on, we were never there. My hunch is we're dealing with a sociopath. We've got a girl in a shed, her word, my word, Rory's word, but our corroborating witnesses are a meth dealer and his accomplice. Caroline never saw Rusty's face. Gray Stafford isn't talking. The Lamey twins can't. How do we prove in court that it was Rusty who put her in that shed? No way I'm putting Rory in a situation where he has to go on record against this guy. And I don't want the locals pulling Rusty in too early. I do *not* want to Donald Fritz this thing."

As we pass the old Guerneville Bridge, George turns to me and asks, "We need any supplies?"

"Like?"

"A shovel?"

It's an old joke between us. Some cases need evidence, profilers, a room full of lawyers, and a long, drawn-out plea deal. Other cases need a shovel.

"A backhoe would be good."

I direct George to the café on Armstrong Woods Road. When we park, I can hear the music from inside. Al Green, "You Ought to Be with Me."

Sunshine is behind the counter. "Hey, Mystery Lady! Didn't expect to see you." He notices George. "Hello, Mystery Lady's large, intimidating friend."

"Good to see you, Sunshine. Two coffees, please."

"I can do better than that. He pours beans into the grinder, makes a show of frothing the cream, adding cinnamon and chocolate, a touch of vanilla, and slides two lattes across the counter.

George pulls out his wallet.

"Au contraire, mon frère. Mystery Lady and friend drink for free."

George thanks him and drops a twenty into the tip jar.

"Righteous." Sunshine leans across the counter. "Your friend came in yesterday, by the by. I talked him up. He implied he was leaving town in a few days. Strange dude, gave me the creeps, and I don't creep out easily."

"What was he driving?"

"Land Cruiser. Vintage."

"Good work. Text me if you see him today?"

"Abso-fuckin'-lutely. Happy to see my taxpayer dollars at work, my friend."

Back on the road, I direct George past town. Using the aerial map from Google, I was able to find a network of unmarked roads leading up into the hills. We pull onto a gravel road that winds behind a burnt-out barn. Behind the barn is a rusted metal gate fastened with a padlock. "Looks like a job for you," I say.

George is notorious for his ability to pick any lock, a skill he picked up long before Quantico, back when he was a teenager causing minor trouble in the Pacific Northwest. He takes a kit from his glove compartment and makes quick work of the lock. Then he pulls the car through and I shut the gate behind us, refastening the lock.

The sun is out, no sign of rain. We wind our way up to the abandoned fire road. George backs in, parking behind a stand of redwood trees. The car will be well hidden here, ready for a quick exit. George pops the hatch and we gear up. I tuck my gun into my waistband and grab my backpack, containing cuffs and two magazines. George grabs two guns and his pack—long mags, flashlight, water, knife, tool pouch.

At the front gate of the compound, I point to the oversize video camera atop the fence. "Video cables," George observes. "Let's find the box first."

We move forward into the brush, following the video cable along the top of the fence. Whoever put in the security system did a half-assed job. At a turn in the fence, the cable angles down and out of sight. George scans the area and rolls a log over to the base of the fence. Using the log as a stool, he's able to get a grip on the top of the fence and pull himself up. Then he reaches down and grasps my hand. With some effort I manage to get up and over, dropping down on the other side. George is right behind me.

"I'm too old for this," I pant.

"Not too old, Connerly, definitely too short."

We follow the video cable about a hundred feet to where it enters a locked junction box. George pulls out two screwdrivers and uses the leverage to break open the flimsy lock. "Amateurs," he mutters. He shines the flashlight into the box, examining the mess of wires before disconnecting a black one and sliding the recorder box out. He pops the back off, carefully disengages the drive, and slides it into his backpack.

I lead him back along the fence, past the kennel to the row of miniature stables. I push away the image of Caroline, shivering and alone in that filthy shed. One by one, we approach tactically, clearing each stable before moving on to the next. Other than a real horse and three goats, they're all empty. We reach the third one from the house, the one where I found the man last time. Empty. The place is pristine, the floor swept, the drinking trough empty, as if no one had ever been here. Only the branding iron hanging from a hook on the wall remains.

I lead George up to the house. There are two cars in the drive-way, an Audi TT and the Land Cruiser. We step onto the porch and peer through the windows. I listen for voices, a television, a shower running. Nothing. We cautiously make our way to the front door. I turn the knob.

On the long dining room table, four identical sets of horse gear made of polished black leather are lined up in a row. Four new saddles, stiff and shiny, as if they have never been used. The saddles are too small: less horse-like, more human. Each set is labeled with a linen notecard. "Rachel and Pony David," the first card reads. "Grant and Pony Jim," says the second. And so on.

We move through the house, slicing the pie at each doorway. Between the two of us, we keep an eye on the whole room, gesturing silently. We move past the dining room and kitchen, peering into every bedroom and closet. George watches doorways while I check under beds. We come to the third bedroom—all white, attached half bath, shutters fastened from the outside. This must be the room where Rusty kept Caroline. I use my camera phone to silently snap a few photos.

The master bedroom is sparsely furnished, smelling of wood polish and leather. Twelve whips are mounted across the wall above the bed. A plaque on the dresser bears Rusty's name and beneath it the words LEATHERMAN 2001.

Beside the main bedroom is a home office with a computer. George keeps watch at the door while I snoop. The desk is covered with paperwork, mostly financial. I snap a few photos of bank statements and other papers, skimming the pages for anything that stands out. One transaction does: $150,000 cash deposited into a checking account ten days ago.

The computer monitor is black, but a blue light pulses in the lower right corner. I touch a button to wake the computer. The monitor comes to life, a screensaver of rolling green hills and a sign that says: WELCOME TO WYOMING. I pull an SSD USB drive out of my pack and plug it into the computer. No password, one drive, one TB, nearly empty. I scan and tag all but the program and OS files and copy them to my drive. I slide the drive into my backpack, and we move on to the laundry room. The lid of the washing machine is open to reveal a pile of damp clothes. George points at the honeycomb shades pulled down to cover the window. The shades rattle lightly in the breeze, the cord tapping against the wall.

A note of music strikes up outside.

George and I exchange glances. The music is old-school country. I stand by the laundry room door while George moves to the window and peers through the shades. He raises a finger to let me know there's only one person. "He's alone," he whispers.

"Our man?"

"Looks like."

We move back through the house. As we ease toward the porch, George slides his gun out of the holster. We work our way around the porch, stop at the corner, and watch for a minute to confirm that Rusty is alone. He's sitting in the hot-tub part of the kidney-shaped pool reading a paperback, *The Empty Space*. A glass of iced tea rests on the deck beside him. I scan the area. No visible weapons. No people. Rusty's cell phone sits on a table in the shade ten yards from the hot tub.

George and I emerge together from the cover of the house, guns raised. As we close in, Rusty glances up, his gaze falling first on George's gun, then on mine, then George's face, then mine. His eyes zigzag, realization dawning on his face.

I have to hand it to him: he doesn't even flinch. We're not the only professionals here. "Well, I'll be a big fat pig in shit. It's the lady from my CCTV. And, how cute, she brought her big brother."

I step closer and peer beneath the water. He's wearing swimming trunks, thank heavens for small favors. "Rusty, I presume?"

"The one and only."

I flash my creds.

"What do you know," he drawls. "Mr. Rusty's been called up to the major leagues."

60

Churchill wrote, "For my part, I consider that it will be found much better by all parties to leave the past to history, especially as I propose to write that history myself." Can history be trusted? Discuss.

Rusty looks me up and down. If he's nervous, he doesn't show it. "I've been looking forward to this, to tell you the truth. Man, I watched you and those two colts on the CCTV like a dozen times."

My skin crawls.

"Figured it wouldn't be long before you were back. Been dreaming about it." He licks his lips and sets his book down beside the hot tub. "*Real* sweet dreams. Do you want me to tell you how my fantasy goes? It's quite vivid, darling." He reaches for his iced tea, sliding his gaze up and down George's body. "Now this I did not expect. I like it, though. Nicely done. You are one big fella. Six four, two twenty, am I right?"

Looking back at me, Rusty adds, "Lady, you have outdone yourself. Thirty more pounds and some hair under the hood, and he would be one nice, fine bear. I'm gonna call him the near bear. Near Bear, I like that. I really hope he's not shaved. I hate the way the boys are doing that these days. 'Keep it natural, wall to wall,' I always say."

As Rusty closes his eyes to take a long sip of his drink, I point to the workbench across the lawn. George nods.

Rusty turns his attention to me. "I will say this, darling. You have got some sweet qualities!" His voice is big and animated. Each word is loud enough to reach the back row of some imaginary play-house. "You remind me of my ex-wife, the way you move, that ass. Shit, I do miss my ex's fine ass." He pauses, thinking, and grins. "The rest of her, I do not miss at all."

George is at the workbench now, rifling through the tools. Rusty looks over at him and smiles beatifically. Maybe he's on some-thing, something light and floaty, possibly ecstasy. "So, you never said, lady, do you want to know how I fantasized this going down? I mean, I worked it out both ways, to be honest. I kind of thought I might be the top here. That's normally how I roll." He glances over at George, eyes widening. "But this, this is cool too."

Then he says, more to himself than to me: "The lady's definitely playing chess; damn Rusty been shuffling the checkers. Should've seen it coming. Never should've climbed into the hot tub. I guess I figured you for a local GPD type, with your kid in that fancy public school and all, but you're not GPD, are you? No, sir, this fine lady is not from the suburbs."

He tips his glass toward me. "No excuses, but the hot tub has a siren's call. Things get sore after a long ride. Am I right?"

He's staring at me now, waiting for a response.

"It is hard to resist a nice soak," I agree. "Pity about your tim-ing, though."

"Heehaw! The lady done got a personality!"

He downs the rest of his iced tea and slams the glass on the deck. It shatters, cutting his hand, but he doesn't seem to notice. "So, let's get to it!" His voice takes on an angry edge. "How we gonna do this? You wanna prone me out first?"

"Not my style. Why don't you soak a little longer, answer a few questions."

"Okay, but I must warn you, I prune in this hot tub pretty quickly." He looks at his hand, noticing the blood. "Shee-it." He plunges his hand into the water. The water turns pink, bubbling all around him.

I take a few steps closer, my gun still trained on Rusty. "Tell me why you had the girl."

"No, no, no." He shakes his head. "That is *not* how this goes." He lifts his bleeding hand out of the water, pouting at the gash stretching across his palm.

"The game has changed, Rusty. We're on a tight schedule."

He holds his hand above the water, dripping blood. "Fair enough. As a sign of good faith, I'll spot you the first move."

"And what would that be?"

Rusty motions with his hands in the air, spattering blood onto the concrete, but he doesn't elaborate. His anger has turned to giddiness. He's a more extreme version of the person Travis described, more animated, less predictable. He probably has manic tendencies, even in his most sober state. "Okay, you made me say it! Here it is: I have a dungeon. First-rate. Big league. The entrance is hidden under the rug in the living room. People pay a lot to visit said dungeon. It is known far and wide."

I don't respond. When someone's talking, there's no logical reason to interrupt.

"A dungeon!" he repeats, more loudly, as if I hadn't heard. "A complete, underground, blacked-out dungeon. Fully stocked with top-of-the-line accoutrements. I possess a talent for finding affluent clients willing to pay top dollar for an authentic experience. Not a single corner cut." Several beats of silence.

"And you're telling us this because . . . ?"

"Are you not catching my drift at all, darling? Seriously." He looks at George, who has finished rifling through the tools and is now holding a power saw.

"Near Bear, enlighten her, please. Something tells me you understand. I tell you about my dungeon so that you can prone me out, cuff me, take me downstairs, and then only the Lord knows what might happen." He grins, showing all his teeth.

"I don't care about your dungeon, Rusty. Not even curious. I only need to know one thing: your connection to the girl."

"Darling," Rusty says plaintively. "That just will not do."

George places the power saw beside the pool, runs the electrical cord back to the outlet near the work bench, the orange cord snaking across the green lawn.

"A saw? Near Bear is making me nervous, and trust me, darling, that isn't easy to do. Not sure what he's got in mind, but he's definitely not following the script. It seems to me he just wants to skip to the third act. I need foreplay, honey. *Fore*play. Everyone these days wants to skip ahead. I am an old soul." He reaches for the drink, a nervous habit, but his bloody hand finds only air and broken shards of glass.

I smile. "I never skip ahead. Ruins the whole play. From your reading material there, I sense you're a man who understands the theater."

"I do, darling," he replies with complete earnestness. "Studied it, actually. Rodeo got in the way, but that's another story. Don't want to date myself here, but I was Claude in *Hair*, off Broadway."

I don't respond.

He lets out a long, disappointed sigh. "There was the thing with the girl. Dramatically speaking, that would have been act one."

Anger flares in my gut, but I refuse to show it. "In that case, this would only be act two."

"Correct," he says, a little calmer.

"And you do know what Chekhov said."

"*Everyone* knows what Chekhov said."

"So, we can save the fun stuff for later."

George scans the estate, watching, listening. He moves toward Rusty with the chainsaw.

"Well, this is what we call a leap instead of a twist. Very inelegant of you, Near Bear. I'm surprised."

Usually, George is slower, more calculated, escalating only in small measures, and only when necessary. But he's concerned, as I am, about someone else showing up. Considering the four sets of horse gear we saw on the dining room table, it could happen at any moment. A party is afoot. I don't think there is anything good that Grant and Pony Jim could add to this situation.

"Tell you what, Rusty," I say. "How about we end this act on a good note, leave a little suspense for the next time?"

"And how might we do that, darling?"

"Simple. Tell me how you came to have the girl in your shed. Enough details and I can leave you for another day."

"That's it?" He raises his eyebrows in surprise.

"For today."

He narrows his eyes. "If you're so worked up about the girl in the shed, why, pray tell, didn't you call in the cavalry?"

"I'll be honest with you, Rusty. Once you call in the cavalry, you can't hide the body."

He looks down at his pruning flesh. "This old thing?"

"Also, once the cavalry gets involved, there's a lot of paperwork. I *hate* paperwork."

He guffaws, a big, hearty laugh. "And what if I don't have any information for you?"

"Well," I say brightly, "my imagination may not be as well developed as yours, but I do see my good friend, Mr. Near Bear, standing over you with a power saw." George shoots a disapproving glance my way; he doesn't like the nickname. "I can imagine two scenarios. Neither leaves much room for your character to make any appearances in the sequel."

"Intrigued, I am," Rusty says. "What might these two scenarios be?"

"Have you ever seen a body electrocuted and waterlogged?"

Rusty smiles. "I have. But that's another story."

"What's it going to be?"

George lifts the saw over the hot tub and puts his finger on the power button. "Five seconds," George says.

"Your Near Bear is no fun at all."

"Four."

"You must understand, I—"

The saw switches on, its high whine cutting through the air, and Rusty sits up straighter, panic spreading across his face.

"I have a site on the dark web." His voice has dropped an octave.

"The pony play or the K and R?"

"No, no, those two things are just retail for the rich and curious. I mean a third business."

George turns the power saw to a low hum.

"Sometimes people contact me. I handle things."

"What kind of things?"

"Problems that others cannot."

"Who led you to the girl? What were your instructions?"

"Someone asked me pick her up on her way home from school, give her a place to stay for a little while, deliver her to somewhere else. This fellow liked to *delegate*. Strictly amateur hour. Nonetheless, the money was good, and darling, you know what they say about money."

"This wasn't the first time this fellow asked you to handle something, correct?"

Rusty regards me for a moment. George moves closer. "I might have handled a couple of other things."

"When?"

His eyes shift up and to the right. "The first time, two years ago, the second time, a little over a year ago."

"And what was his name? The one who gave you the instructions?"

"You want me to just say it?"

"That's the idea."

"His people will kill me," Rusty says matter-of-factly.

"Maybe, but he's not here at the moment, and Near Bear is very much here and very impatient."

George revs the saw again.

"Kenny Pao. The boy is named Kenny Pao. Skinny street kid. Drives a Mitsubishi Evo. A ricer, as they say, or as they used to say before everyone got so *sensitive*."

"Where might I find Kenny?"

Rusty tries to look bored, but I can see the fear on his face. Whether he's afraid of George standing over him or afraid because he divulged the name of Kenny Pao is unclear. "Tenderloin, darling, in the heart of the Tenderloin. Where nothing good happens and the homeless shit in the street. A nice girl like you has no business in the Tenderloin."

"You let me worry about that. *Where* in the Tenderloin?"

"Kenny works at a restaurant on Larkin Street." Rusty frowns. "Come to think of it, maybe he owns it."

"Anyone else involved?"

"Not in this neck of the woods. I like to keep things simple. Nobody with an entourage lasts long in this business. Kenny has other ideas, of course. Which is exactly why we're in this big old mess."

"And why did Kenny want you to handle this 'problem'?"

"Darling, please. I don't ask questions. It's the 'whats' that pay the bills, not the 'whys.'"

"Which restaurant on Larkin?"

I hear a vehicle to the north, approaching the gate, gears grinding. It sounds like a big truck or SUV. "Which restaurant?" I demand. There are voices in the distance, two men. George and I exchange glances.

"Rusty," I say. "Your friends are going to be here any minute. Unless you want this to be a group conversation, I need the name of the restaurant."

"A group conversation would be interesting."

"But bad for business," George says, lowering the saw toward the water.

"Near Bear has a point. Your average pony play fetishist won't be so eager to enlist your services if they know you have a side gig kidnapping minors."

Rusty licks his lips. "So, let me get this straight. I name the restaurant, and we pick this conversation up at a later time."

"Exactly."

"Thrill-us interruptus! Just when it was getting good."

The voices grow nearer.

George lowers the saw another inch. "You have three seconds."

"The restaurant is called Mangosteen. Vietnamese. Corner of Larkin and Eddy. Get the number thirty-two special."

George sets the power saw down beside the pool, but he doesn't turn it off. It hums there, vibrating against the slate.

"Until next time," I say, as George and I slowly back away.

"Alrighty," Rusty says, more to the air and the trees around him than to me. "Draw the curtains. Next time, I think we'll need new scenery."

61

Humans communicate fear through smell. Why does this matter? Why doesn't this matter?

At a quarter to seven, George and I step inside Mangosteen and wait to be seated. The restaurant's plate glass windows display the Larkin Street show in all its seedy glory. Across the street, several homeless people are selling random items. A gaunt woman with long gray dreadlocks is shouting: "All this shit got bed bugs!" To the south, down the hill toward the Federal Building, half a dozen addicts are shooting up, nodding out. A photographer with a big, fancy camera is snapping pictures. If we walked three minutes south, we'd be inside the headquarters of one of the wealthiest tech companies in the world. Welcome to San Francisco.

We are shown to a table with the eastern view, the bed bug bazaar. I scan the restaurant, but no one matches Rusty's description of Kenny Pao. When the server comes over, George orders the thirty-two, and I order the lamb special. As the server takes our menus, I ask, "Is there a guy named Kenny here?"

"Not yet. Kenny is an asshole."

"Because he's late?"

"An asshole in every way."

Our food arrives. George digs into his green curry chicken. "Rusty wasn't lying about the thirty-two."

We eat slowly. Then we order dessert so we can occupy the table longer. Another thirty-five minutes pass. The bill arrives. I add a generous tip to compensate for keeping the table so long. When the server comes by to refill our teapot, she whispers, "The asshole has arrived," nodding toward the southern window. A Mitsubishi Evo is idling in the yellow zone. I thank her and put another twenty on the table.

A giant kid, maybe the dishwasher, runs out of the kitchen and onto the street. He hands an envelope through the window of the Mitsubishi.

"I don't think he's coming in," George says.

We're quickly out the door and in George's rental car. We sit for seven minutes, watching Kenny talk to the dishwasher. He shoves his finger into the big guy's chest a couple of times, rolls up his window, and peels away from the curb, tires squealing.

George cuts off a Lyft driver to pull into the street. Kenny is speeding, weaving through traffic, and George pulls a few maneuvers to keep up. "Think he made us?"

"No, I think he's just an asshole, like the waitress said."

We follow the Mitsubishi up Polk, right on Broadway, through the tunnel and into Chinatown. He makes two stops at hole-in-the-wall restaurants, and both times a kid comes running out to give him something. Then he heads west, through the tunnel and out toward the avenues. I roll the window down, smelling the ocean as we drive west, the Pacific visible in the moonlight.

We follow him down Balboa, across the Great Highway, into a parking lot at the north end of Ocean Beach. He doesn't seem to notice us. Kenny sits alone in his car, vaping, talking on his cell.

"Time for a conversation?" I say.

But then Kenny screeches out of the parking lot and back onto the Great Highway. We follow him south, onto Skyline, left at the Westlake subdivision. He pulls into the driveway of a split-level Doelger house near Westlake Joe's, and we park across the street, several houses down. The place is dark, no one home. He walks up the steps and unlocks the door. The lights go on.

Curtains open. From our parking spot, we can see Kenny pacing around the living room for a full minute, letting off steam. The place is cool in a retro way, not what I expected. The front is mostly windows.

The thick fog makes the neighborhood quiet, save for the cars humming by on Skyline, the distant sound of the waves. "I could live here," George says. "It's peaceful."

We watch Kenny through the windows for a while. He pulls off his shirt, disappears into the back of the house and returns with a bowl of cereal. He sits down on the couch and turns on an enormous television. It's amazing how unaware he is, totally on display in the light of the television.

"Now or never," I say. "Watch the front door?"

"Yep. I'll start the car if it looks like he's getting up."

I get out of the car, walk down the street, and slip around the side of the house and check the gate to the backyard. Locked. A new electrical panel is attached to the side of the house, Square D, a profusion of new wiring snaking to the electrical pole. I duck down to pass through the flowerbed under the living room window. At the garage, I sniff under the door to confirm my suspicion.

Back in the car, George asks, "What did you find?"

"Grow site in the garage."

I wonder what George is thinking, whether we're on the same page. This isn't his case. It's not his battle to fight. The protocol would be to pass the info on to the locals, maybe coordinate with them to talk to Kenny when he's in lockup, play the long game, squeeze him on the illegal grow operation until he gives up his boss. Of course, George also knows that real evidence disappears quickly, and a conversation in a sterile room with a bunch of attorneys is always less productive than a more intimate discussion, alone, inside a person's house. Anyway, after what went down at Rusty's, we're certainly in the gray.

George looks at me. "You care about this guy?"

"No. I just want to move up the chain. Someone asked Kenny to take those kids. *That's* who I want."

George is silent for several beats. "We're a few steps off the reservation."

"Yes, but still close enough to walk it back."

We have no official case, nothing on paper, and our visit to Rusty was definitely not by the book. On the other side, Kyle did ask for help, and I wouldn't have a hard time painting this as a preliminary task force thing. A confrontation with Kenny at his home might be a step too far, but tracking down a kidnapper without the proper paperwork is not the sort of activity that gets you fired. Maybe a few weeks on the bricks. Months, even. I'm fine with that, but I'd rather not cause George any trouble. His wife works for a nonprofit that pays next to nothing, and they have a kid in middle school.

"Your call."

"Maybe we have a friendly talk with Kenny," George says. "But you owe me."

"Make it *two* burritos, extra guac, and I'll throw in a margarita."

George pops his door open, and I do the same. We move quietly across the street and onto the property. "I'll take the door," George whispers. I position myself at the bottom of the stairs, with a view through the window. George uses the rear end of his flashlight to knock on the door. Nothing. He rings the doorbell—still nothing. He hits the door again, feels the handle. Locked. Through the window, I see Kenny standing up.

"He's coming," I whisper. "Sweatpants, no shirt, no pockets."

The door opens. "Yeah?" Kenny says, before fully registering George's size. I move up the stairs. Kenny looks at me, back at George. "You got the wrong house, bro."

George rests his palm on the door frame. "I don't think so."

"Good to meet you, Kenny Pao."

Kenny looks shocked to hear his name. He tries to shut the door, but George blocks it with his body. "You going to invite us in?"

Kenny is still sizing him up. "No man, I don't think so. Not tonight."

"Where are your manners?" George steps closer to Kenny, towering over him. "You should probably invite us in."

Kenny backs into the house. "Who the fuck are you?"

"Someone who wants to offer you an opportunity you can't pass up," I say.

"Did Hector send you?"

"Nope."

"Man, are you with the PD?"

I sidle next to George. "Why don't you invite us in before the neighbors get too curious?"

Kenny tries again to close the door. "You know, I've got a lawyer—"

"Good for you," I say, as George wedges his foot between the door and the frame. "Now you're going to invite us in. It's not complicated. You say, 'Would you two like to come in?' And then we reply, 'Yes.' And you ask if we want something to drink, and we say, 'No thanks, this won't take long.'"

"Would you like to come in?" Kenny asks miserably.

"Nice of you to ask!" George says. We step through the door, close it behind us, and follow Kenny into the living room.

I walk over to the window and draw the curtains. "Kenny, I'm going to need you to sit down."

I take the chair to Kenny's left, George takes the couch. I can already tell Kenny is far out of his comfort zone. George uses his body well—getting into people's space, throwing them off balance. He calls it being politely menacing. I don't think he learned that one at Quantico. It's not my sort of approach—with my size, it couldn't be—but the contrast in our styles has always served us well.

"I'm not sure what you guys want," Kenny sputters. "But I'm not your guy. I'm just a small businessman."

"Oh," George says. "So you wouldn't mind me calling the DEA to take a look in your garage, right?"

"Oh man, come on, it's barely illegal. If I knew the right people to pay off at city hall, I'd be licensed."

George lifts his nose in the air, sniffing. He glances at me. "What do you think? Sixty-four plants, maybe seventy-two, close to maturity, what's that worth?"

"State or federal?"

"Both, so Kenny understands what we're talking about."

"Sentencing would depend on priors, I suppose."

"Kenny," George says. "You got any priors? Felonies, misdemeanors, a couple of domestics maybe?"

Kenny doesn't respond.

"We'll take that as a yes." George looks at me again. "What's your guesstimate?"

"Assuming the plants are mature, calculating at street value, he's looking at forty-eight months federal, sixty state, give or take."

Kenny shakes his head, miserable. "Shit. What do you *want*, man? What's this about?"

"Who asked you to do the jobs with the kids?" I say.

Kenny's blood pressure goes up, redness rising in his face, under the big tribal tattoo on his neck. He stares straight ahead, not saying anything.

"Kenny, you still with us?"

His chest is rising and falling rapidly. He makes a sudden move, his body twisting toward George, his arm flailing toward the edge of the couch, his feet sliding on the floor, trying to stand and run. In a single motion, George twists his body, slamming his elbow into the side of Kenny's head. Kenny falls back into the couch, his feet flying up, kicking the glass coffee table. He yelps in pain.

From the other room, I hear a commotion. A pit bull appears from the kitchen, sliding across the floor, his feet fighting for traction on the slippery tile. Shit. I jump to my feet, my gun out, trained on the dog. I flash back to one of my first joint arrests and the NYPD officer who told me as we were about to storm the warehouse: "If there's a dog, you're the one who has to shoot it." I had to do a double take. How did I get there? A liberal arts degree, ballet lessons until the age of ten. "Seriously," the cop said, snapping me back to it. "NYPD can shoot *people*. Dogs are different. Too much paperwork."

Just as Kenny's pit bull picks up traction and starts moving toward us, I yell, "Call him off or I'll shoot!"

Kenny screams something in Vietnamese. The dog skids to a stop and stares at us, growling. Kenny utters a few more words in a commanding voice, and the dog turns and walks back toward the kitchen.

I look over, and Kenny's chest, his white couch, the white carpet, are all covered in blood. George reaches for the towel on the table and tosses it to Kenny. He looks so small, trying to disguise his frail chest and spindly arms with the interwoven tattoos.

"I was just getting a cigarette. Fuck! You cut me."

"Nice guard dog you got there," George says. "Took him three minutes to realize there were strangers with guns in the house."

"She's hard of hearing, and she's not a guard dog," Kenny says defensively, pressing the towel to his face. "See, that's a misconception people have about pit bulls. They're a nice breed. Good with children. Sassy loves my nieces."

George tries to keep a straight face, but he breaks into a grin.

"What?" Kenny looks offended. "It's a good name, man. It fits her. She *is* sassy."

"I need you to walk over there, real slow, and close the kitchen door," I say. "I do not want to hurt Sassy. If I have to hurt Sassy, I will not forgive you."

He stands up slowly. He backs across the room to the door of the kitchen, peeks into the room, mumbles reassuring words to the dog, and shuts the door.

"All the way," I say. "I want to hear it click."

He pulls the door tighter, and the latch clicks into place.

"Good job. See? We can work together."

Kenny returns to the sofa. I can hear Sassy panting behind the door. I lean forward. "Look at me, Kenny. Who asked you to take the kids?"

"Please," he says. He's still holding the towel to the gash above his eye. "I tell you who hired me, and I am fucking dead. Dead, my body in the ocean, or in a hole behind some fucking house in the Sunset." He looks at the towel, sopping with blood. "Can I get a clean one?"

"In a minute. First answer the question."

"In Chinatown, in the Tenderloin, fuck, even in Daly City, these guys don't fuck around."

"I get it. Answer me this, though: Why would anyone in your world want some random suburban kids kidnapped? It doesn't make sense."

"I don't know. People want a lot of fucking crazy shit. The boss said it was a favor for a friend. Just a fucking favor."

"Kenny," I say. "Who asked your boss for the favor?"

"I told you I don't fucking know. Are you going to arrest me? I've got a lawyer."

"We can do that whole thing if you want," George says. "But you won't like how it turns out."

"Who asked your boss for the favor?" I repeat.

"I only saw him once for a second. Some fucking guy off 280 down the Peninsula."

"Where off 280?"

"In a parking area. I was picking up the cash. The guy was going to drop it off in the city, but then he said he was busy and could I come meet him. I asked him to Venmo it, but he said no, it had to be cash. I respect that, man. No digital record, it's better. He even gave me a tip. Big one. I fucking deserved it. Pain in the motherfucking ass."

"Remember which exit you took?"

"No, but it was by a fancy-ass golf course, and there was, like, this big lake."

"Black Mountain?"

"Yeah, that rings a bell."

"What was the guy like?"

"Middle-aged."

"Well, that narrows it down," George announces. "Thanks, we'll be going now."

"Really?" Kenny looks outright happy.

"No, not really," I say.

"Shit."

"Was he a tall, handsome Japanese fellow?"

Kenny looks at me, confused. "Naw, man, I don't know what the fuck this guy was, but he sure as shit wasn't a tall Japanese guy. Short, funny-looking dude. His face was all fucking weird."

"Weird how?"

"Like he's on *Nip/Tuck* or some shit. Like Mickey Rourke level, Charlie and the Chocolate fucking Factory. Like somebody put him through a machine and the machine was on the wrong fucking setting."

"How did he dress?"

"*Weird*. Bow tie and shit."

"What kind of car?" George prompts.

"Ugly-ass orange Bentley. Who drops a shitload on a Bentley and then paints it fucking orange?"

George catches my eyes and nods toward the door; he wants to know if we should go.

I have more questions for Kenny, but nothing good comes from us staying in Kenny's house too long.

"Kenny, I need to hear the words. What exactly did he pay you for?"

"You know what he paid me for. To take the kids and keep them out of the way, then return them. He paid a ton to make sure we did the job right. It's easy to take shit. Hard to return it."

"So he didn't want you to hurt the kids?"

"Naw, man. That would have been easier. I got a dozen guys who could do that. The instructions were to return the kids in working order, keep them out of the way until it was time to bring them back. No DNA. No injuries, no pervy shit, no trace, he made that clear. If a kid died or got, you know, *compromised*, it'd be on me, big-time. I couldn't find anyone with their shit together, and my usual guy was out of the country." Kenny is still dabbing the blood on his face. "Travis was a fucking disaster. Should have done it myself. If you're here, Travis obviously messed up."

I meet George's eyes, nod. We both stand and back toward the door.

"That's it?" Kenny is confused. "You're leaving?"

George winks at him. "Looks that way, sport."

Kenny shakes his head, panic setting in. "You can't say a word. Seriously, a fucking word. They find out, I'm totally deep-fried."

I can still hear him pleading after we close the front door behind us. Pulling onto Skyline, George says, "Man, that Kenny was a bleeder. I barely even caught him with my elbow, delicate flower." He checks his sleeve and grimaces. "This was one of my favorite shirts."

62

Following a single negative experience, starlings and
other birds can learn to avoid eating toxic insects.
Human culture, conversely, reduces the usefulness
of our instincts. Why?

When I get home, it's past midnight. Rory is asleep, TV on, sound off. I lay a blanket over him, trying not to wake him, but he rolls over and opens his eyes. "Hey, Mom."

"Hey, kiddo. Where's Caroline?"

"Her parents came to pick her up."

"Really?" I'm mildly surprised, enormously relieved. "What were they like?"

"Very French." He yawns, stretches his long arms. "Very formal, but nice."

"Was she glad to see them?"

"Yeah, I guess. Her mom was pretty."

I smile. "That bodes well."

He rolls his eyes. "Mom, it's not like I'm going to marry Caroline."

"You never know."

"I *do* know. They're taking Caroline to Paris tomorrow morning. She's going to finish the school year in France, live with her aunt."

"Sorry, bud."

"Me too."

In the morning, Rory comes down at the usual time, backpack slung over his shoulders. He pours himself a bowl of cereal and joins me at the kitchen table, where I'm nursing my third coffee.

"You *really* don't have to go to school."

"What, are you going to homeschool me now?"

"I don't think I could handle the math." What I don't say is that I feel better having him at home, where I can see him.

He stirs the Cocoa Puffs until the milk in his bowl turns chocolatey. "I hate this school a little more every day. It's not the teachers or the kids. It's the big fat lie of it all. This ridiculous idea that one test cooked up in a lab somewhere can determine our future."

"So why go? Maybe there's another way."

"With Caroline gone, I don't know what else to do."

He sets *Martin in Space* on the table. I still haven't finished it. Acquired taste, I guess. "Do you ever feel like we left Dad in New York, and he's waiting for us?"

"I wish that were true."

"I want to go home. That's where we're supposed to be."

He's right. It will be heartbreaking to be around all those reminders of Fred, but I finally understand it's sadder *not* to be there, to try to avoid the touchstones of our life together. And if Rory wants to go, we go. He earned that.

"I'll start working on it today."

"Do you mean it?"

"Promise."

His face hardens. "But before we go, you have to finish what you started. The people who took Caroline. You have to make them pay."

It feels good to have a plan, a way forward. Having taken care of my dad's personal things, I can hire someone to sort out what remains. I find a service online to handle the donations and haul the rest away. I'll hire a full-service agent to prepare the house for sale and put it on the market. Laura Crowell's business card is around here somewhere. She'll be delighted to beat Harris Ojai out for the listing.

"Throw money at the problem," my more affluent friends back in New York like to say. I never had money to throw at a problem before, but I can put it all on the credit cards for now. Once I sell the house, we'll be fine. Better than fine.

I call Kyle but only get his voicemail. Surfing again? Holly? I use my laptop to do a deep dive on Harris Ojai, but online I find nothing helpful. There are dozens of references to how he is the "#1 Real Estate Agent in America"—mostly from sites that are clearly run by Ojai himself—along with pay-to-play profiles in magazines with names like *Wealth Insider* and *Bay Area Elite*. Other than that, nothing. It's as if he just landed on the planet four years ago with vaults full of money, an orange Bentley, and a plastic surgeon on speed dial.

I send a message to Malia on Confide, asking for additional information. She responds in seconds: Give me a few minutes. BTW, we're set for Iceland. Good news. Red Vine was spotted out front of the establishment on a trip to Warsaw.

Probably meeting Y, I type back.

Yep. A few minutes later a message pings.

Your guy sure has a strange past for a real estate agent. Macau, Malaysia, Canberra, Canadian citizenship in the name Enrique Malone, a Taiwanese passport, connections to the government of Ghana. The usual OC financial connection. Multiple shell accounts in Singapore.

What else?

Here's where it gets interesting. Forty-seven addresses in your little suburban paradise are registered under his shell companies. I'm attaching the report. Also, two hits from our foreign partners. Arrested at Frankfurt Airport two years ago. Apparently he ate his fake visa before they could get it from him. One other possible incident—under a different name. The Saudis deported him, something about slave labor and his housekeeper. If it's him, he got twelve lashes.

Ouch.

Let's connect when we get closer to the RV meeting.

I close out the app and sip my coffee. Part of me wants to pack up the bare essentials, bust Rory out of school, and leave town. Not next week: today. Things are so messed up here. At least New York City is the kind of messed up I understand. I could put together a package on Harris Ojai and Rusty and simply leave it for the San Francisco office to unravel. They have plenty of time to cross their *t*'s and dot their *i*'s, do the whole thing by the book.

Of course, it's more complicated than that. I would need to package it in a way that doesn't bring any heat down on George.

But it's not only about George. The fact is, I don't want to let it go. Not after what Rusty did to Caroline. Kenny is one thing. With the company he keeps, the grow, and the fenced electronics in his Daly City house, he probably doesn't have a shelf life of more than a year or two before he's in prison, or worse.

Rusty is different. He's a predator, a professional. He's unpredictable, smart. *Irredeemable*, as George said. Worst of all, he is only partially motivated by money. He loves the game, the theatrics. He gets a thrill out of wreaking havoc and instilling terror in his victims. He'll never stop being dangerous.

The phone rings. It's the secretary at school, Mrs. Brompton, wanting to know why I haven't called to notify them of Rory's absence.

"What absence?"

"Today."

"No, Rory is at school. I dropped him off this morning."

"Well, Miss Hawthorne and Mr. Young marked him absent."

I can't breathe.

"After the test is over, some kids get wanderlust."

"That's not like him. Could you double check?"

"Ma'am, we are very—"

I interrupt, my panic growing: "Can you check again? Please. He has to be there." There's a long pause, a sigh, chatter in the background. Mrs. Brompton is sending someone to Rory's second-period class. She puts me on hold. My heart is racing, and I'm stuck listening to a Muzak version of "Sweet Child O' Mine," mind spinning.

A minute later, she comes back on the line. "Looks like you may need to have a talk with your son. Since it's his first time to cut, I'll do him a favor and mark it as excused."

"But—" My mind is racing.

I hang up and dial Rory's number. He doesn't answer. I leave a message. I call him four more times just in case the phone is on vibrate in his backpack. Nothing. Please, no. I grab the car keys, my messenger bag with my gun and accessories. As I feel the weight of the bag on my shoulder, the horror strikes me full force. I have done the unthinkable: I put my son in danger. I thought he'd be safe. Kobayashi said they needed him. The kids who disappear are the ones who fail, the ones who bring down the scores, not the ones who succeed.

Why would anyone take Rory? It doesn't make sense. Unless this is personal. Unless it is payback.

I drive around the school in concentric circles, finding only a team of gardeners tending the north field. I show them a picture of Rory on my phone. One of them mentions a white van that was parked in their usual spot around the time of the first bell. A big white dude was sitting in the driver's seat, he says. The other guy thought it might've been one of the painters from the gym, but a third guy disagrees. In a land of black Range Rovers, Audis, and Volvos, a lone white van stands out. The third guy saw the same van near the tennis courts, pulling out a minute after the first bell, driving south on Ralston. Where were the police, I wonder. Where was Officer Kyle? All the mornings he's been assigned traffic circle, and he couldn't be here this morning?

I head south down Chateau, unsure what I'm looking for. I call Kyle's number, but he doesn't answer, and the outgoing message says his voice mailbox is full. I call GPD and ask for him.

"Officer Randall is no longer an employee of the GPD."

"Since when?"

"Since yesterday."

"He quit?"

"No. The department was no longer in need of his services."
The line goes dead.

Shit. They've fired him.

Driving in circles, I find nothing. I dial Rory's cell phone ten
more times. Nothing. I pull over and call George, but he's still on
the plane. I leave another message, explaining the situation. He
might tell me to call the San Francisco office immediately, ask for
help, no matter how far we bent the rules. And I will, just not yet.

I can't call them yet, because I know how it will work. They'll
put dozens of agents on it. They will work it to the exclusion of
almost anything else. We're family, even if I don't know them, and
they'll do this for me, no question. The organization is a freight
train, a powerful force that pushes forward full throttle, shaking
the ground beneath it. But, like a freight train, there's intricate machinery involved, and it takes time to get moving. There's a chain
of command, a protocol, hundreds of moving parts. If I call them
now, instead of going out looking for Rory, I'll be stuck in an office,
being interviewed, filling out forms, retelling this long, strange
story. I've worked this job long enough to know that the next two
hours is exactly the time *not* to be in an office, explaining. I need
to find Rory. I have to do this myself.

I close my eyes for a second, trying to block out the panic,
reconnect with my instincts. Still no call from Kyle. Obviously, I
can't call GPD.

I call Rory's phone again. Please pick up, please.

It goes straight to voicemail.

63

Peter Brook, one of most important stage directors of the twentieth century, describes four categories for theatrical performances: the deadly, the holy, the rough, and the immediate. Which type of performance is the most relevant for this moment in the zeitgeist?

I quickly scroll through my emails and pull up the last few from Malia. I download the Clear report and scan the addresses for Harris Ojai. There are so many fake companies it's difficult to untangle the connections, but the credit report and the cable bills make the place on Rondelay Court the most likely choice for his personal address. The GPS shows it as a cul-de-sac off Skyfarm, somewhere near the top of the hill.

I race up Ralston and back onto Chateau, the Jeep's tires squealing as I make the sharp left turn onto Rondelay. I slow down to approach the address quietly. It's palatial. I pull it up on Zillow, looking for photos: 18,000 square feet, 7 bedrooms, 8.5 bathrooms, guest house, pool, sauna, Jacuzzi, helipad off the south lawn, wine cellar, solar generator room, 10-car garage, movie theater, gym. The house is built on the side of the hill, one floor at street level, with three floors below, hugging the side of the canyon. It looks like there are only two viable entrances, unless I hike up the canyon from below. That would probably be the safest ingress, but I don't have time. With 18,000 square feet, it would take three SWAT teams to clear the place with any measure of security. I park on the street, slip my gun into the small of my back, and take two additional mags from my messenger bag. I also grab the old carbon fiber baton they gave me at Quantico.

The driveway is steep and curved, soaring oak trees on both sides. It's so quiet I can hear the wind whistling through the canyon. The orange Bentley is in the driveway. The garage doors are open to reveal six more luxury cars lined up in a row. Amazon and FedEx boxes litter the front porch. I can hear K-pop music echoing from inside, the bass beat vibrating the windows.

I approach the front door and try the handle. It's unlocked. I slip inside. The house is decorated with fussy white furniture, glass tables, lurid gold accents. The smell of cigar smoke permeates the walls. I move through the foyer, the kitchen, the enormous dining room, and an office suite—all empty.

In the living room, I'm startled by the sight of myself in the huge gilded mirrors. Down a hallway, two bedrooms are side by side, the beds piled high with gold-fringed pillows, price tags still attached. The floors are cluttered with open boxes filled with calendars, mugs, and knickknacks, all bearing Harris Ojai's face and logo. In every room, a thousand small images of Harris Ojai stare back at me.

The beat of the K-pop song stops. I stop cold, listening for movement. Seconds later a new song starts, the vibration from below pounding through my sneakers. I find the stairs and silently make my way down, hand on my gun. On the next level is a second family room, a massive television on the wall tuned to Bloomberg, the ticker scrolling across the screen. Behind a white leather sectional, fitted with recliners and cup holders, is a fully stocked wet bar. Still no one. The music is coming from the floor beneath this one.

I move methodically through hallways and bedrooms. Inside a mahogany-paneled office, dozens of real estate contracts are stacked on a desk. The computer is on, four monitors, the keyboard between them still warm. Outlook is up, all the passwords unlocked. I move around to get a better look. I scan the names in the inbox—Laura Crowell, Chinese investment companies, something in Cyrillic, and the police chief Jepson. I copy and paste the inbox to a folder that I copy to my alias Dropbox account. Over ten thousand emails. I scan the computer's file directory structure and move the entire tree titled "Greenfield" over to my box as well.

Past the office, I find a game room outfitted with a foosball table, billiards, six flat-screen TVs, a row of pinball machines, a layer of dust across everything. Six clocks hung high on the wall show the time in Beijing, Manila, New York, Singapore, Jakarta, and Geneva. At the far end of the room, another staircase.

I descend. At the bottom, I peer around the partition and see a workout room with wooden floors, a ballet bar, lots of mirrors. A massive screen covers the opposite wall. An aerobics instructor on a live feed is leading a workout session. In the middle of the room: Harris Ojai, clad in a green tracksuit, dripping sweat. He's facing the screen, grooving to the workout, step two, three, four, arms pumping. The instructor is yelling at Harris, hurling abuses. "You call this a workout? You're pathetic! Knees up! Core tight! Faster!" She has a headset on, her words booming through the speakers.

I don't know how much of the room she can see, but the mirrors leave me feeling exposed.

I slip my gun into the holster, pull down the hem of my sweater to conceal it, and try to affect the air of an assistant sheepishly interrupting her boss's workout session. Ojai, focused on the screen, doesn't notice me entering the room. I'm six feet behind him when the music stops.

The woman hits a button on her headset, and her angry persona instantly disappears. "Harris, you have company. Let's pick it up tomorrow. Remember to watch your carbs."

As Harris turns around, the screen goes blank.

"Lina! What are you—"

"I let myself in."

Through a forced, nervous grin, "You want to talk about selling your house, I presume?"

"Harris, where is my son?"

Sweat pours down his face and darkens the armpits of his tracksuit. He shakes his head. "What are you talking about?"

I move toward him. "Where. Is. My. Son."

He backs away, his orange neon sneakers squeaking against the floor. "Lina, whatever you're thinking, I assure you—"

My right hand slides into my pocket, feeling for the foam handle of the tactical baton. "Where is my son, Harris?"

"Please, Lina, you are mistaken."

I remove the baton from my pocket. With a single flick the carbon fiber expands, locking into place. Harris's eyes go wide, fixated on the weapon.

"I don't know. I don't know. I don't know."

"Where is my son?" I repeat, inching closer to him, holding the baton aloft, ready to swing.

"Why would I take your son?" he says frantically. "Your son is a superstar. He scored 1,927. No one in the state ever scored 1,927 before! Your son is a gift, a miraculous gift! He makes me money! He makes money for the whole group!"

I step back, processing the information, lowering the baton to my side. "The group?"

"Yes, the group." His eyes go wide. "You didn't think it was just me, did you?"

"What group?"

"There are overseas investors and, of course, a few helpful, involved local citizens."

"Investors in *what*, exactly?"

"Lina, I run the one of the most successful residential real estate funds in the country." He is unable to hide the pride in his voice. "I buy and sell houses, yes, but so much more than that. It's simple math. The test results increase property values by unbelievable margins every year. Didn't you ever wonder why our home prices perform better than anywhere else? Don't you wonder why they go so high, so fast? Don't you wonder why, when interests rise, tech companies fold, and the market hits a downturn, none of it affects this town? What we do isn't only for the investors. Our work is a gift to the homeowners. Even you, Lina!"

I stare at him in silence.

"This year's scores will increase property values by fifteen to twenty percent, easy. Affluent parents don't just want to live in a neighborhood with good schools anymore, they want the *best* schools. The Wonder Test is *the* benchmark. We didn't make the rules, we just seized the opportunity. Our town has 3,302 houses. The average house value is 4.9 million. Take fifteen percent, conservatively, multiply by 3,302 houses. Lina, you understand."

Harris seems giddy, frantic. "Intelligence is genetic," he sputters. "I know you have no problem with math."

He's talking about 1.78 billion dollars. I move closer, feeling the energy of the baton in my hand, lightweight but rock-solid.

"Are you not understanding me? 1.78 billion dollars. Just this year. And that's conservative. And it doesn't even count our related rental project. The fund is flush, 7 billion dollars in equity, and our returns are impressive by any measure. Every year after the scores come in, we sell some of the houses we own and rent out others. We reinvest the profits and pay extraordinary dividends. We are not monsters. We are businesspeople. Billion, Lina, with a *b*."

"Businesspeople don't kidnap children."

Harris is red, dripping sweat. "No, no, you must understand. We prepare every student as well as we can: the best tutors, the best software, even the best nutrition. And, for those who still cannot be relied upon to ace the test, we provide amazing opportunities: luxury vacations, private campus tours of Ivy League schools, all perfectly timed to miss a few days of school."

"What about the Lamey twins, Gray Stafford, Caroline?"

"I can explain." Harris's voice cracks and he takes another step backward. "That was an anomaly. A mistake. Until the twins, it worked like magic. The Stafford boy, that came as a shock to me too. It wasn't supposed to go that way. These were blips on the radar. Were they regrettable? Yes. Terrible? Yes. But they were isolated incidents. I thought we had ironed out the kinks. The Rekowskis enjoyed Dubai, the Kingsley boy was on the set of a Scorsese movie for a week. As hard as we tried, we could *not* find that French girl's parents, and she refused to sit the test out. So *stubborn*. I feel awful about the whole thing."

I'm trying to wrap my head around the scale of it. "The woman who talked to Caroline last Sunday, trying to persuade her not to take the test. *You* sent her. Who was she?"

"An assistant. When someone refuses, we must make adjustments. The investors demand perfection. They demand higher and higher dividends. And it is my job to deliver. No children were supposed to get hurt, though. My instructions were clear." He smiles, feigning sweetness. "And I hear the French girl is safe now, back with you. No harm, no foul."

"No *harm*?" I say, taking two steps forward.

He backs up, sputtering, "It wasn't ideal, but . . ."

"*Who* are your investors?"

"They are wealthy, well-connected men, primarily members of the Communist Party in China. In a volatile market, a nearly risk-free investment like this is priceless. And it provides a perfect way for these overseas investors to move money offshore."

I knew Harris was greedy, but the full extent of his greed is staggering. I inch closer. "Where is my son?"

Harris is now standing with his back to the mirrored wall. "I *do not know* where your son is. I swear on my life."

With a single sweeping motion, I swing my arm, the baton whistling through the air, picking up speed. I barely feel any resistance when the tip of the baton catches Harris's nose.

I step back, surprised to see that he is still standing. For a second, I think I must've missed entirely, but then I notice that Harris's nose is no longer properly aligned. It is bent grotesquely to the left. He stares at me in shock. The perfect symmetry of his face, tens of thousands of dollars and years of plastic surgery, is suddenly undone, his facial features wildly off-kilter. A flood of bright-red blood lets loose, pouring out onto his hands, down his tracksuit, and onto the wood flooring. It is only after he sees the red that he falls to the ground, whimpering.

"Where is my son?"

"I don't know!" he cries. "You have to believe me!" He pulls his bloodstained hands away from his face and reaches out to me. "I'm just a businessman," he whimpers.

I flick the baton. The bone above his wrist breaks quickly and evenly, with little resistance. I look down and notice a wide diagonal stripe of blood across my white shirt. Harris rolls onto his side, cradling his broken wrist.

He screams, a gurgling sound rising up from his throat. He holds his broken wrist high above his writhing body. "Okay, okay, okay," he whimpers. "I hired one guy."

"What guy?"

"Kenny. *He* hired someone else, I never knew his identity, to take the twins and the Stafford boy, and Caroline too. But *not* your son, I swear, your son is gold."

My mind is racing. Harris is telling the truth. He would give up the information if he had it. He is a coward, hiding behind his cars and his mansions, crumpling at the slightest pressure. But if he doesn't know where Rory is, who does?

I hold the baton aloft again. "I want names."

Harris leans back in terror, his head hitting the mirrored wall. He catches a glimpse of his bloodied, misshapen face in the mirror. "What have you done, Lina? What have you done?"

"Who. Is. In. The. Group. Who can tell me where to find my son?"

Harris wipes off his Rolex, squinting through blood and tears to see the time. "My video conference room is at the end of the hallway. The video chat was supposed to start three minutes ago. They'll be wondering where I am. But they will not be able to help you. Go. See for yourself."

I take a jump rope from a peg on the wall and tie his arms behind his back as he whimpers. Using an exercise cord, I secure his ankles. I don't want to waste my handcuffs on him; I might need them later. I back out of the room, keeping my eyes on Harris. He's writhing on the floor, a pool of blood smeared across the hardwood.

I hear voices. I move toward the sound, unholstering my gun. Behind me, I can still see Harris staring in the mirror at the ruined canvas of his face, sobbing.

The door to the conference room is open a crack. I glance in. A six-foot-wide screen is filled with squares. Each box shows a different room and phone number, people staring into webcams. They are all waiting for Ojai. They are mostly conference rooms, PRC country codes, Singapore too, Malaysia, but also a few local numbers. I see Chief Jepson. I see Dave Randall's mother, the head of the school board. I see Laura Crowell. I search for Kobayashi's face, but he isn't here.

On a desk in the middle of the room is a computer monitor with a webcam. I step into the room, hold up my phone, and take a photo of the wall of people. Then I approach the monitor, allow my hand to pass in front of the webcam, using the F keys to take a screenshot.

"Harris, you're late," Laura Crowell says.

I move toward the chair in front of the computer. The inset box on the monitor shows me what they can see: my shoulder, the corner of my white shirt, striped with blood, my chin.

"That's not Harris," Jepson says. Instantly, his screen goes dark. And then another. I sit down in front of the monitor, showing my face. I see confusion in people's eyes. I see fear.

"Where is my son?"

More squares go dark. Slowly at first, one at a time. As the participants realize what's happening, the speed at which they disappear increases. Twenty boxes fill the monitor, then fifteen, then five. It happens in a matter of seconds.

"Where is my son?" I shout as the screens go black.

Finally, only one box remains. An empty chair. The background is familiar. I'm trying to place it, trying to remember, when I see the photograph hanging on the wall—a single swimmer slicing through an expanse of blue, snow in the background, the word "Helsinki" scrawled in red across the bottom of the photograph.

I hear her voice. A familiar face appears. Her eyebrows go up, that universal microexpression of resignation. Brenda, who welcomed me into her home, whose son invited Rory over after school. Brenda, who pretended to be my friend.

"Brenda, where is Rory?"

"Lina, it wasn't us. We didn't take Rory. You have to believe me." Then all is quiet. "I'm sorry," she finally says. Her screen goes black.

64

El Niño or la Niña: too much or too little. Discuss
the importance of perspective.

The screen is black now, but the red record button is still blinking.
I click Save Recording. Harris's minitower server is connected to
the desk by a dozen cables. I pivot and yank until the server comes
free. I tuck the server under my arm and retrace my steps. Harris
remains where I left him, bound and sobbing.

Outside, the temperature has dropped, the eucalyptus bending
and creaking in the wind. I stumble up the driveway, head spinning.
On the street, I see a familiar figure running toward me. Long legs,
great stride. As he flies past, I can hear the Clash blasting from his
headphones. He doesn't seem to register me standing on the street
in a bloodied shirt, gun in one hand, minitower in the other.

He gets thirty yards up the street before he loops back around.
When he reaches me, his eyes take in the entire scene. He reaches
up and takes out his earbuds.

"What the hell?"

Only then do I realize I'm shaking. I think of the sticky note I
found attached to my father's desktop computer monitor. "For Wi-Fi
or other issues, call Mr. Beach," my father had written. "Good guy."

All those afternoons they spent together, watching VHS tapes of old track meets. Glen Park was friends with my father. I know I can trust him.

He notices my hand, my shirt, covered with Harris's blood. "Jesus, do you need help?"

"They've taken Rory." I still can't believe the words as they come out of my mouth.

"What? *Who?*"

"You really don't know?"

"This has to do with the other kids, doesn't it, Stafford and the twins?"

"Yes." I hold out the server toward him. "Take this home with you. Hide it. If you don't hear from me by tomorrow, I need you to take this to the FBI in San Francisco, Golden Gate Avenue. No GPD, you understand?"

He nods. "No GPD."

"When you get through security at the Federal Building, they're going to direct you to the duty agent. Give them my card." I pull my creds out of my bag and pull my FBI business card out. "Tell them it's evidence in a case."

He nods. "Federal Building, Golden Gate Avenue. Evidence."

"Promise me."

"I promise. Is there anything else I can do?"

I point to the computer in his hands. "Guard it with your life. Don't talk to anyone about this. Teachers, parents, school board. Nobody."

"Got it."

I look around nervously. No cars pass. The houses on the street are silent. No one has seen us together. "Thank you."

He gives me a little salute and takes off up the street, the server clutched tightly to his chest, red hair whipping crazily in the wind.

As I'm getting into my car, my cell phone rings, and for a moment my heart lifts with hope. But no, it's not Rory. It's George.

"I got your message. You okay?"

"No. It's bad. Really bad." My voice breaks. "Rory is missing."

"Listen, I ran checks, made a dozen phone calls. Where are you?"

I give him Harris's address and tell him about the wall of screens, the faces. "George, it's bigger than we thought. The police chief is involved, like we suspected, but others from the school board, realtors, major investors in the PRC. They swear they didn't take Rory."

I turn the key in the ignition.

"I ran Rusty's selectors," George says. "He was on the Peninsula this morning. At nine twenty-five, he ghosted."

I feel all of the air sucked out of me. "Where are you?"

"Still at Dulles, but I'm taking the next flight back."

I'm so stupid. Why didn't I deal with Rusty when I had the chance? We could have ended it there, on the compound.

Another call comes in—the school secretary. That frisson of hope, again. "Is Rory there?" I blurt.

"I was wrong about Rory skipping class. He *is* absent, but Ms. Bellina saw him leaving campus at nine fifteen with his father."

"What?"

No. *No.*

The hope vanishes.

"We don't have his father on record, so we'll need to correct the paperwork, but that's not really why I'm calling. I just learned that when his father escorted him off campus, Rory swiped another student's mobile from the phone table."

"His father is dead."

"What? The teacher said he identified himself as Rory's father."

"What did he look like?"

"I didn't see him." Worry edges into her voice. "But Ms. Bellina said he was big, a flashy dresser."

Oh, Rory. How many times did I tell him over the years, if anything happens, always stay where the people are? *Never* let someone isolate you. It's always better to run or fight than to find yourself alone with a predator. But Rory had a reason. Rusty must have had a gun. Rory must have known he was willing to use it.

My mind races. "Whose phone did Rory take?"

"Michael Panico."

Michael Panico? The name doesn't ring a bell.

"If it wasn't his father—" she says. And then, "Oh, God, is Rory in trouble?"

I try to piece it together. As I pull away from the curb, I realize I don't even know where to go. The compound? I think of the stables, the kennel, the dungeon. I shudder. But no, Rusty wouldn't go there. It's too risky, too easy for me to call in SWAT. He wouldn't do that.

The air feels different, charged. Clouds are gathering, a spring storm moving in.

Focus. I need to focus.

I replay our conversation in my head. On the compound that day, in the hot tub, Rusty promised me a third act. But that's not all. "I think we'll need new scenery," he said at the end. "Change up the set a bit."

A new set. Definitely not the compound. But *where?*

Think, I tell myself. *Think.* Then it hits me.

"What kind of phone?" I ask.

"What? Why?"

"What kind of phone does Michael Panico have?"

"Samsung Galaxy. Orange Giants case."

"What's his phone number?"

"I can't—"

"I'm an agent with the FBI. It's in Rory's file, under parent occupation. I need the number. Now."

I hear the click of her computer keyboard. She reads the number to me.

I hang up and call Nicole. She picks up on the first ring.

"I need you to trace a number. It's an emergency."

I imagine Rory passing by the phone table where students are required to leave their devices during morning assembly. I told Rory about the triangulation, about Nicole's Android trick, about how long it takes to follow the proper channels and get a court order to trace a phone. Rory has an iPhone. If he had the presence of mind to swipe a phone, he would have swiped an Android. That's why he took a Samsung. He would have known that if he could keep the phone hidden, it would lead me right to him.

"What do you need?" Nicole asks.

I read out the number. "I need to know where that phone is. Now."

"On it."

I start driving north, toward Daly City, toward Kenny Pao's place. It's all I can think of, because I know they're not in Guerneville. Daly City doesn't feel right either. But where?

377

I'm on I-280, going ninety-five miles per hour, fat raindrops pelting the windshield when Nicole calls back. "The phone is pinging from the same spot as the others, Lina—"

"Guerneville?"

"No, not there. The *other* spot. Right where Ivy and John Murphy's phones were on the day the kid showed up. From the middle of the ocean. The exact same spot."

With horror, it dawns on me. A different stage set. "I need the GPS coordinates."

"They took another kid?"

"They took my son." I screech across three lanes to take the next exit at Skyline.

"Shit. Sending now."

Focus. "Can you send me coordinates every five minutes? I need to know if he moves."

"I think so."

"Make it happen. *Please.*"

"I will."

I press the gas pedal harder, weaving in and out of traffic. I need a boat.

I use voice activation to call a dozen people who might be able to help. I call Timofey, George's Russian friend from the Dolphin Club. I call Kyle's personal phone. Why is no one answering? I head toward Pillar Point Harbor. Maybe I can rent something, a fishing boat, a charter, a dinghy, anything. Finally, my phone rings. Twelve frantic messages I've left on twelve different phones, and it is Timofey who calls me back.

"Lina." The sound of his voice, that distinctive voice— professional, a former Russian intelligence officer, a man who knows how to get things done—gives me hope. "I got your message. Are you ready to copy?"

"Ready."

"I have a friend. Let's call him Ivan. He will meet you at the pier in El Granada. He is waiting now. Slip ninety-three. The boat is named *Odessa Dream*."

"Timofey, thank you."

"It is my pleasure."

The tires of the Jeep squeal as I speed down the backside of the San Bruno Mountain into Pacifica, through the Montara tunnel. Another text comes in from Nicole, another set of coordinates. They're moving out, farther into the ocean. At the pier, I skid into a parking spot and grab my bag. At slip ninety-three, a short man with dyed black hair is standing in the rain beside a fishing boat, the name in cursive across the back, *Odessa Dream*. A small, well-worn, working boat. There are deep-sea rods stacked all along the back rails.

"I'm Lina—"

"Names are not important," he says with a halting accent. Ukrainian, I think. "You are a friend of Timofey." He motions me onto the boat, unties us from the dock.

"Coordinates?" he asks, moving toward the wheelhouse. I read out the second set from Nicole. Ivan steers us out of the harbor. Once we're pointed toward the deep sea, he pushes the throttle to full and consults his charts. It's cold and windy, the boat bouncing wildly on the choppy waves. My stomach lurches, my mind flashing back to a brutal week I spent on a trawler off Long Island, dragging the ocean for airplane parts and worse. All those body parts, bones in the sand being dragged to the surface. All these cases from my past, following me like ghosts.

Focus. I step out of the cabin. A spray of cold, salty water hits me in the face. I move toward the front of the boat and look down the coast, but I can't see anything. All of the other boats have already returned to the harbor, escaping the coming storm.

My phone vibrates. There's a new text from Nicole. The phone is no longer moving. The coordinates are the same as they were ten minutes ago.

Rusty is waiting for me. He baited me, he knows I'm coming, and now he waits.

I go back inside the cabin. "What should I expect when we arrive?" There is no fear in Ivan's voice.

"My son has a phone that pinged to these coordinates. He's been kidnapped."

"Hang on."

I grab the railing to steady myself. Ivan pushes the throttle, and the boat picks up speed, lurching beneath us.

"Who are we dealing with?" Ivan's calm demeanor tells me that this is not his first rodeo either.

"One man, working alone. Big. Mean. Armed and dangerous."

"Okay."

"I need you to get me close to the boat. But not too close."

"Of course." He returns to his charts, his depth finder, and his GPS. "Look in the hold. You will find my daughter's wet suit. It is a little big for you and only a chill factor of five. You will not be comfortable, but you will survive." His eyes skim over the back of my shirt, where the bulk of my holstered weapon is visible. "Freezer bags in the cupboard."

Down below, I find several wet suits, flotation devices, an array of fishing gear and crab netting. On the wall is an old, tiny picture in a wooden frame—Ivan and a girl, his daughter. "Natalia, 1997" is scrawled in black ink across the bottom.

I struggle into the wet suit. I take my gun out and seal it in a freezer bag. Then I place the gun in the small of my back and zip the wet suit over it. I find a pair of flippers and a hoodie and return to the wheelhouse.

Ivan smiles. "No one has worn that in a very long time." When I turn to the side, his eyes rest briefly on the bulge of the gun. "Be careful. I wouldn't want you to get a hole in Natalia's wet suit." He winks.

Nicole texts again. This time, the coordinates have shifted, leading us farther out to sea. The wind whips up. We've been on the water for twenty-six minutes when a shape appears. Ivan slows the boat and picks up his binoculars. In the distance, several hundred yards away, is a recreational fishing vessel. Ivan turns the wheel, cuts the motor, and drops anchor. He hands me the binoculars.

"Your friend is not a fisherman."

"No," I say, scanning the water. "How do you know?"

"The angle, the condition of the boat, his clothes."

I look through the viewfinder, but at first I see nothing. It's far away, the waves are wild. I catch a flash of yellow and adjust the focus.

There.

Rusty is standing on deck, messing with something at the far end of the boat. He isn't looking this way. I judge the distance. Swimming won't be easy. It will take most of my strength just to get there. But I don't want to risk going closer. I need the element of surprise.

Ivan looks at my feet. "Those fins are too small. One moment." He heads downstairs and returns with two long fins. "For speed. They are for abalone diving. The weather will get even worse. You need to be careful. He will not see you go into the water if you do it from the rear starboard."

"Thank you, and I'm sorry. I don't want to make trouble for you." Who knows what it took for him to get to this country, what it takes for him to stay here? I sense that what he's doing for me comes with considerable risk, yet he does it without question.

"Trouble does not concern me."

I struggle to get into the fins and the tight hoodie. The boat rocks up and down with the waves. I brace myself for the cold water, trying not to think about the vastness of the ocean, the sharks, all the unknowns. I focus only on Rory. I take two steps toward starboard, sit on the railing, and tilt backward into the sea. The icy water shocks my skin as it permeates the wet suit. As I put my head down and begin working my way toward the boat, choppy waves rise up, filling my mouth with briny water.

The long fins are difficult to maneuver at first, but after a few floundering strokes I manage a methodical, consistent motion. My speed picks up. I glance behind me to see Ivan is stacking crab pots. If it weren't for the fact that all of the other fishing boats have gone in to escape the weather, he would look perfectly normal.

I keep craning up over the crest of the waves, trying to get a look at Rusty's boat. It's at least twice the size of Ivan's. I don't see Rusty. I don't see Rory.

I pump my arms, my legs. My shoulders burn. When it feels as if my legs will give out, I turn onto my back and begin a steady backstroke. The distance between the two boats shortens. I'm moving fast, but is it fast enough? How much time do I have? Am I already too late?

Rory, please be okay.

About fifty yards out, I slow down and tread water, looking at the boat, looking for Rory. Still nothing. At the rear, a ladder is affixed to the railing.

Something brushes against my legs. Something substantial. I look around, frantically. I think of a story I read on SFGate recently about two surfers who were attacked by sharks not far from here. One survived. I peer beneath the water, looking for the phantom gray thing. The ocean is dark, impenetrable, and the cold, salty water burns my eyes.

65

If a highly infectious disease strikes a ship's captain and officers on the open sea, what percentage of the crew must approve before the diseased officers can be thrown overboard? Discuss the ethical implications of this decision.

At twenty yards, I take one final breath, go deep, and propel myself forward. My fingers touch the boat. Relief, dread, a rush of adrenaline. I stay close to the hull. Rusty can see me only if he comes out on deck. The wind whips the waves, blowing spray into my face. The salt burns my eyes, my lungs ache. Despite the frigid water, I'm warm from the swim, my heart beating fast.

I push myself along the side of the boat toward the ladder. When I come up, I see the name of the boat written in gold cursive from one end to the other, *Rodeo King*, and then underneath, *Bodega Harbor*. I reach down to pull off the fins. I pull off the hood. I fold the ladder down into the water and hook my foot onto the bottom rung. I stay hunched down, out of view.

With my free hand, I find the dangling cord that attaches to the wet suit zipper. I pull it down just enough so that I can reach the plastic bag. Hooking one arm around the ladder, I open the bag and remove the gun. I carefully slide the gun up higher on my back, still concealed, but more easily reachable. I have only one magazine, twelve rounds, and another in the chamber. Service ammo, sealed tight, hollow point.

I pull myself up and peer across the deck. It doesn't look like a working boat. It's more of a yacht than a fishing outfit. The deck is spotless, scrubbed clean and waxed, slick with rain. Black vinyl seating lines both sides. Deep-sea fishing poles are attached to the deck, but they're so pristine they've probably never been used. Netting and perfectly coiled ropes are arranged beside two swivel chairs. A bright yellow kettlebell attached to a metal chain rests incongruously between the chairs. The only thing on deck that looks used is the bar area. A communications antenna and a weather station line the roof. The helm is up two steps, behind a wooden door. Most likely, inside the bridge there are stairs down to one or two cabins below deck.

I climb the ladder and hoist myself up. I stay low, hoping to avoid any mirrors or cameras. I move forward, cringing every time the wet suit squeaks. I approach the door of the bridge in a crouch, grateful for the noise of the wind and the sea, the thump of the ropes, the creaking of the hull. I position myself with my feet spread shoulder width, trying to counteract the sickening, roiling motion. Other than this boat and Ivan's far in the distance, I haven't seen a single vessel on the water.

From the motion, it occurs to me that Rusty has dropped anchor. Across the rising waves, through the rain, I can see the empty beach in the distance. The starboard side is parallel to the beach, making the rise and fall more extreme.

Third act, just like he said. What's the plan? I consider taking my gun out, but the timing isn't right. Not yet. I'm 98 percent sure

Rusty is in there, facing the door, waiting for me, gun drawn. Rory took the phone, but Rusty *let* him take it. He wanted me to follow. He is expecting me.

If this turns into a duel, Rusty owns the advantage. I can't let bullets fly until I know where Rory is. Safety rule number three: know your target and what's behind it. No, Rusty needs to believe I'm unarmed.

I reach out and slowly turn the door handle. I open the door a sliver and peer inside. Rusty is sitting in the captain's chair, facing the door, just as I expected. "Don't be shy, Lina. Come on in. I've been waiting for you."

Behind him, the wheel, controls, and miles of choppy sea. But no Rory.

66

Is it quicker to travel to Africa from Florida or from Maine?
Are our perceptions a tool or an obstacle?

Rusty is wearing bright yellow pants, a tight polo, and brand-new boat shoes. In his right hand, he holds a Ruger SR9. Eleven rounds if he bought it in California. He uses the gun to wave me into the room. The heat in here is a shock after the cold of the ocean, the wind.

"Come in, darling, come in. I love the wet suit. Nice costume, very authentic."

I step through the door and into the cabin and see the source of the heat—two space heaters, one on either side of the chair. Rusty's face is slick with sweat. On a table to his left sits a mug of coffee.

My heart jumps: there is Rory's backpack on the counter next to a maritime chart. Beside the backpack is Rory's iPhone and the Samsung in the orange Giants case.

"Where's my son?"

Rusty gives me a disappointed look, the barrel of his gun trained on me. "Don't rush me. You promised the third act would be the best. I hate to break it to you, honey, but I'm the one directing this production."

"Is he here?" I feel the cold of my gun against my back.

"Yes, the boy is indeed here." A pause, an evil flicker in his eyes, "Oh, he's fine, mama, I'm no *monster*." He thinks for a second. "Or am I?" His hand never leaves the Ruger. "I forgot to mention, last time we met, how absolutely beautiful that girl's skull is. Gave me the shivers when I shaved her head. Strong personality, that one. A fighter. Do you believe in phrenology?"

"No." I feel the rage simmering, but I must remain calm, focused.

The boat drifts, pulling against the anchor. "But I digress. Really, we're here for one reason. I need to teach myself a lesson once and for all. The lesson is this, Lina: If you want something done right, do it yourself. It's hardly rocket science. The more people involved, the more it will get fucked up."

He catches my eyes. "Yes, Lina, I did my homework. L-i-n-a."

I don't respond.

"I'm not saying it was easy. A lesser man might've failed. The internet barely knows your name. You are one off-the-grid retro-chic woman. But I did a deep, deep dive, eventually learned quite a bit about you," Rusty smiles, clearly impressed with himself. "I had to go to the microfiche. I found a 'hometown-girl-makes-good' story about some award you won. Cute little picture of you and W in the Rose Garden. You might be able to clean the interweb, but once something makes the local press it's there for good. And once Rusty finds a little bone, he never lets it go!"

I nod, acknowledging Rusty's professionalism. It seems important to him.

"Anyway," he says. "Where was I? Oh yeah, rule number one: no moving parts. No. Moving. Parts." He shakes his head, droplets of saliva stick to his lips. His calm demeanor has vanished. He's more dangerous this way but also more vulnerable. More likely to make a mistake.

I glance again to the left, where Rory's backpack and the phones lie on the counter. When Rusty notices, he smiles. "I told Rory to bring his Apple *and* an Android. I wanted to cover all my bases, make it easy on you. When you showed up at that spot in Guerneville where I lost my phone, I figured out your trick. Surely you know there were cameras there? Hindsight may be twenty-twenty, but true vision is digital. The miracle of technology, of course, is that *all* of them are watching us. Not the *gub*ment, but the corporations. You may be *my* problem, darling, but you and your set are no longer *the* problem."

"True."

"When I dropped in at the school this morning and persuaded your son to come with me, I was delighted to see those phones, just sitting there for the taking. To be honest, I hadn't worked out precisely how I would lure you out to the boat for act three, but the universe smiled on me."

I'm watching Rusty, waiting for him to look away, waiting for him to take his hand off the Ruger. He doesn't. He's enjoying his moment in the director's chair.

"If you're wondering, Lina, Rory didn't seem too compliant, looked like he was about to cause a fuss, until I showed him my friend here"—he wiggles the Ruger—"and told him I don't have any qualms about shooting up a school."

"I don't think you'd go that far." I'm stalling for time, listening for Rory. "If that's who you were, you wouldn't have sent the other kids back."

"You're right. Not my style. What would *I* get out of that? School shootings are so last Tuesday. And I genuinely wanted to see you again." He raises his eyebrows. "We have unfinished business. I *hate* unfinished business. So, we took the phones and waited. It wouldn't be a party without you."

The boat is drifting sideways. When a swell hits, Rusty has to steady himself with his other hand. "The phones were clever. The rest of it was a bit Nancy Drew. The boy on the beach leads back to that dunce John Murphy, *obviously*. The moment I saw him on the dock, I knew I should've done it myself, like I did with the twins. In our line of work, is it not the golden rule?"

"It is."

"Murphy led back to the tweaker, Travis." Rusty looks at me, almost as if he's trying to see if I'm impressed by his crafty detective work. The fact that he hasn't mentioned Ivy improves my opinion of both Travis and Murphy. They didn't give up her name.

"Which one of them do you think cried the most?" he asks.

I'm scanning the room for clues, for additional weapons, for some sign of Rory, some sign he left for me. But the boat is immaculate, nothing out of place.

"Which one of them cried the most?" Rusty demands again. "Murphy, the tweaker, or Kenny?"

"You tell me."

"Come on, Lina!" Rusty is getting impatient now. "It's act three, snap the fuck out of it. Read your lines, play your fucking part."

In my head, I'm calculating the odds of a hundred different scenarios.

He's getting more impatient. He speaks loudly, one word at a time. "Who. Do. You. Think. Cried. The. Most. Yesterday. When

I killed them. Kenny, Travis, or Murphy?" He slams his free hand down on the table, and his coffee cup crashes to the floor. "I'm going to hold you responsible for that, Lina. You went and made me angry, and now I've soiled my newly mopped floor. I hate messes."

I'm calculating how to answer. Rusty is complicated. He took four kids before today, but he kept them all alive. But now he claims to have killed three people in a single day. Is it possible? Yes. But is it true? Is he bluffing, or has he become increasingly unhinged, increasingly unpredictable?

I look in his eyes, and I know. Yes, he is capable. What does that say about the range of possible endings for our interaction?

I have to get to Rory.

"Lina, it's not a difficult question. I even made it multiple choice."

"Kenny," I respond. "Obviously."

Rusty pauses for a second, a little caught off guard. "Correct. How did you guess?"

"Clearly it wasn't Murphy. He'd been expecting this day for a year. Kenny is a bit of a whiner. With Travis, I suppose it depends on where you found him."

"Santa Cruz," he blurts out. "No lie, Travis was on the shitter in a beautiful little cottage by the sea, didn't hear me coming." Rusty is smiling, totally dialed in, relishing our conversation. It occurs to me that he sees me as an equal. He's a classic narcissist, someone who thinks he's smarter than most everyone he meets, and he's excited to be able to finally have a discussion with an opponent he deems worthy. "Unfortunately, I ruined some lovely tile work."

"Santa Cruz? Really? I thought Travis was smarter than that."

Rusty smiles. "He may have been a little hazy. Does that make my feat less impressive?"

"Little bit."

"Don't be petty. It was a good kill. Efficient too. More importantly, it was the most lucrative."

"Lucrative how?"

"Product, my dear. I couldn't just leave all those nice little white packets there. I had to make five trips to and from the car. Crazy. That kind of good fortune will pay the property taxes on the ranch for years. Now, I can finish the barn conversion, more rooms, more money. Vrbo is a godsend, darling. Do you know how hard it is to make a living?"

"As a matter of fact, I do."

"I suppose you would. Nobody goes into the civil service for the money, am I right? Anyway, I did them all a favor. Pathetic, the three of them. The charm of that Westlake Doelger was completely lost on Kenny. Did you see what he'd done with the kitchen? Ripped out the original counters, covered those gorgeous hardwood floors. And Murphy? He was eating a Hot Pocket when I showed up. I'm not a psychic, Lina, but if a grown man eating a Hot Pocket doesn't scream 'please kill me,' then I don't know what does."

"Where is my son?"

Rusty ignores my question. "I've lived on my compound for many years now," he says, leaning back in his chair, casually retraining the gun on me. "Every time I peek my head out into the world, every time I'm forced to do an unofficial job to keep my little utopia alive, I see a slightly different world. So much ugliness, so much despair. And it's getting worse. Mother, mother, mother, mother, it is definitely getting worse."

"Where is my son?"

"I admit I may not be helping the situation. Some of the things I've done haven't exactly made the world a better place, but I think you will agree with me, Lina. The world will not miss Kenny or Travis or even Murphy. Cleansing the human race one piece of shit at a time."

Rusty shifts in his chair, uncrossing his legs and lifting his arm. Something stops me cold: there are several small dots of blood on the cuff of his otherwise meticulous pants. Another small line of blood spatter runs diagonally along the back of his left sleeve.

Is it Rory's blood? Please, don't let it be Rory's blood.

"Rusty, there's blood on your shirt."

"What?" He seems genuinely surprised, as if emerging from a trance. "Blood?"

I point to his shirtsleeve, his pant cuff.

He looks down. "God dammit."

"Occupational hazard," I say. "Been there. I once ruined a nice Lanvin sweater with the blood of a Latin King."

His hand is still on the Ruger, but his eyes keep looking down to the bloody spots. "You're a smart man, Rusty. And we're not so different, are we? Neither of us is getting past the pearly gates."

Rusty smiles. Maybe I've broken through the top layer.

"You need to give me Rory. Professional courtesy. SWAT is on their way. If you let me get off this boat with Rory right now, you may yet be able to get out of this alive."

Rusty stares straight at me, assessing. He looks, for a moment, as though he likes me. "I don't believe you about the feds," he sighs. "That is not who you are, Lina. I knew the moment you showed up with Near Bear, you like to do things your own way. Nice try, though."

He's staring at me, trying to read my face. I keep my expression blank. He tilts his head, steely eyes focused on me. And then he lets out a whoop. "I am right! Cowgirl Lina came out here all by herself! No backup. She was not interested in going by the books. This one was too personal. Like I said, if you want something done right, do it yourself. My motto too. Boy, I do respect you!"

I remain silent. My skin itches where the gun nestles up to my spine.

"Anyhoo, the boy's downstairs. He's actually fine, scout's honor. He must be terrified, but he didn't even show it. You trained him well." He glances at the spatter of blood on his cuff. "Not his blood, honest to Betsy. Children ain't my thing. Not at all. He's down in the bunk room. He did what he needed to do. He played his part. This isn't really about him, but you know that." Rusty's voice has turned soft, almost childlike.

"You can still save yourself," I say. "Kenny? Travis? Murphy? All lowlifes. I'm not concerned about them, and police around here don't get too worked up about dead drug dealers. What I do know is that all four of those kids you took came home. No reason to get in over your head now. Just let Rory go." I lock eyes with him.

Rusty looks away for a split second, but then his eyes come back to me. I hold his gaze, trying to try to pull him in to my way of thinking. He seems to be momentarily lost, confused. But then he snaps back to himself, shaking his head like a dog coming out of the water. "Darling, were you trying to hypnotize me? Were you," he repeats, his voice getting louder, angrier, "trying to hypnotize me? Hard stop."

I blade my body away from him, making myself a smaller target. "I was just—"

"I know exactly what you were doing. I've read your background. I read the book, *Blue Squared*, not too hard to tie it back to you. I know all about your profiling, all about your bag of tricks, about how *persuasive* they say you are. Personally, I'm not seeing it, but let's not get ahead of ourselves. Anyway, what about Chekhov? You did promise me a complete production, the full three acts. And, honey, the pistol is still on the wall."

I remain silent, muscles tensed.

"Come on, you know the line. A rifle hung on the wall in the first act must go off by the third. And honey child, here we are."

Rusty is more agitated now. His face is red, his chest pushed out.

"You know the next line?" I ask.

Rusty cocks his head. "Pray tell?"

"Don't make any promises you don't intend to keep."

"Oh, I keep my promises, darling. We must give the audience a show." He sweeps his left hand to indicate some imaginary theater. His right hand fidgets with the Ruger. "We have to tell a story, even if we're only telling it to ourselves. It's what separates us from the lower primates."

Rusty's shifting back and forth in his chair, growing more twitchy and agitated, his skin splotchy, his hand shaky. Sweat dapples his forehead and soaks the underarms of his Fred Perry shirt. Every time I move, the neoprene of my wet suit squeaks. Rays of sun poke through the ominous clouds. The boat has drifted into a better position, taking the swells head-on, rather than rolling side to side.

After we crest a swell, for a split second, it is calm. In the quiet, from down below, I hear Rory's voice, calling out. "Mom?"

And that's it. My son. It clarifies everything. He is down there, waiting for me.

"Rory has nothing to do with this," I say. "You don't have to hurt him."

Rusty waves his left hand in the air. "You are correct, Lina. I'm not going to kill him at all." He pauses long enough for hope to unfurl in my brain, a whiff of possibility. But then, in a delighted tone: "No, darling. *You* are! Don't you want to hear my ingenious plan?"

A swell lifts the boat, and the phones slide off of the countertop, clattering onto the floor. As he glances at them, I reach for the zipper cord dangling at my waist, grab the clasp, and pull, bringing the gun within reach.

"So, get this," he says. "I've got this body bag. Bought it online from China, Alibaba, cheap but still decent quality. I'm gonna shoot you, just not badly enough to kill you. Apologies for that, Miss Lina. And then I'm gonna slide your little body into the bag, zip it up, fix the whole thing up with that chain and fifty-pound kettlebell I have out there, attach it to that manly little son of yours, and then push the two of you overboard. Body bag, six-foot chain, and a kettlebell. You would not believe how cheap it all was. Seriously, guess how much?"

Rusty giggles for a second, like a guilty child, and I know he means to carry out his plan. That's when I know for sure that at least one person will die on this boat. It won't be Rory.

"Alibaba is changing the world, Lina. Death has never been so cheap! They even do two-for-ones. Love me a good deal!" Rusty waves his hand around and takes a deep breath. "Where was I? Oh yeah. I don't kill kids, Lina. You know that. You never should've suggested otherwise. You, on the other hand, today, can't say the same. Your body will drag that boy down so fast he won't even be able to enjoy his last breath. And, the beauty of it all is this: It won't even be my fault. It will be *your fault.*"

"You don't want to do it, Rusty." I arch my back and feel the gun slide down my wet suit, closer to my waist.

"I don't *want* to, but you made me."

The boat tilts violently. I think I hear Rory calling for me, but the ocean is too loud to know for sure.

67

One day, water will cover the entire planet. How long after
the inundation will civilization entirely disappear?

Rusty tosses a yellow pad across the cabin. It lands on the counter
to my right. "Loose ends, Lina, loose ends. I need the identifiers for
that Near Bear you so rudely brought by my ranch."

"Why would I tell you that, if you just plan to kill us anyway?"

"Drowning, they say, is a euphoric death. Plan A is drowning, you and your boy go out seeing rainbows. Plan Be won't be so
pleasant."

"Ted Lincoln." It's the name of a kid I hated in grade school.
Long gone. Living in Malaysia now, if you can trust Facebook.

"Write it down. Telephone and address too, darling."

I place my right elbow on the table to write on the yellow pad,
careful not to turn my back to Rusty. "Email?" I ask, stalling.

"I need it all, Miss Lina. I've got to wrap this thing up with a
nice tight bow."

"Rusty, it's not too late." But of course it is. I know it is. I'm still
hunched over the counter, pen in hand. I write Ted's name down,
followed by the address for the Russian embassy in Washington
and a fake phone number.

"Give me the pad, darling. Let me check out your penmanship."

I'm ten feet away from Rusty, a narrow counter between us, maps and depth charts spread across it. The heaters are still going full blast; both of us are sweating. The wind is blowing swells up over the bow and into the window. The ocean is grayish green. The heat in the cabin is unbearable, a scent of Dove soap and peppermint emanating from Rusty's body, just like Caroline said. Adrenaline rips through me.

"The pad, darling," he says, wiping his brow.

With my right hand, I toss the yellow pad in his direction, slow, high, and arcing toward him. As his eyes dart upward, catching the trajectory of the pad in the air, I slide my weapon out of the wet suit, across my body. In a flash the barrel of the gun is pointed at Rusty.

They tell you the training will come back without even a thought. They like to call it muscle memory, though that term makes no sense to me. The memory isn't in your muscles but in your neural cortex, a rapid-fire series of instructions delivered from brain to nerves. I hated all of those hours spent shooting with my left hand, all through the first year at Quantico and four times a year since. Sixteen years, thousands of bullets. Over and over. Five on the left, five on the right, again. It seemed like wasted time. Why shoot with my left hand when my right hand was so much more accurate? "You never know," the firearms instructor used to say. "You never know."

All of the training comes back at once. *At close range, eyes on the target, no need to pick up a sight picture. Eyes. On. The. Target. Up close, high stress, your gun will shoot where your eyes look.*

And in that split second, Rusty looks like a kid, his freshly pressed clothes nearly perfect, his belt notched too tight on his big stomach, mouth open, his eyes focused on the pad floating toward him, anticipating his great catch, like a boy on a playground. And through it all, he doesn't notice the movements of my left hand.

My body bladed, stable stance, hands forward, fluid motion, smooth and fast. *Smooth is fast.* From day one that's what they always said.

Now.

I fire two shots to the body, center mass, and one to the head. Eliminate the threat. Two and one, my eyes focused on him, no hesitation. The Mozambique drill—up close, two to the body, one to the head. The voice in my head, *Mozambique, two to the body, one to the head. Repeat.* My torso is low, my feet spread, leaning against the counter for support, each shot straight and level, careful there is no ricochet to the deck below.

The noise is deafening, *bam-bam-bam.*

And then it is silent. The waves hit the starboard side, the boat rocks.

For a moment a cold terror grips me: Could I have missed?

But Rusty is motionless, a look of surprise on his face. The yellow pad and the Ruger fall to the floor. I cover down on him, both hands on my weapon.

A narrow stream of blood rolls down the side of his face. I caught him high and right, just at the hairline. As his right hand reaches feebly toward the blood, a red circle forms at the center of his shirt, quickly spreading outward.

"Oh, Lina, darling," he mumbles.

He falls forward, the full, massive weight of his body crashing through the counter between us, arms flopping to his side as he collapses onto the floor. The boat shudders with the tremendous crash, all three hundred–plus pounds coming down at once.

With both hands on the weapon, I shuffle around the counter to kick the Ruger across the room and get a better look. His eyes are wide open, but Rusty is gone.

He looks surprised that it ended this way. That was not his plan.

A terrified voice from down below. "Mom?"

68

Nature or nurture? How much of who we are is determined by our upbringing, and how much is simply embedded in our being? Are children destined to repeat the sins of their parents?

I race out of the wheelhouse and climb down to the galley. At the end of the galley is a wooden door. I grab the handle and turn, but it's locked. I look for a key on the table, the counter. Nothing. "Rory!" I call. "It's me. Stand back."

I hunch down and thrust my shoulder against the door with all my strength. The door splinters down the center, the momentum tossing me backward. I kick through the crack, creating a hole. I grab the broken center of the door with both hands, twist the door off the hinge, and step through.

On the bunk, Rory lies on his back, fully clothed, his wrists and feet tied to the bedframe. He is crying, shaking. A handkerchief that had been in his mouth is now free, wound around his neck.

He lifts his head. His eyes find me. "Mom," he sobs. "It's you."

"It's me. You're safe." I sit on the edge of the bunk and hug him tight, kiss his forehead. Tears are streaming down his face and mine. "He can't hurt you."

The ropes are tightly knotted in a complicated configuration. "I have to get a knife to cut you free. I'll be right back."

I run back to the galley, pull out a chef's knife, and return. I scrape at the ropes, slicing through the thick fibers. First the right wrist, then the left. With his hands free, he sits up, staring at me in shock, as I tackle the ropes on his ankles. I help him lift his legs over the edge of the bed. "Can you stand?"

He stands, his face crumpling. He leans into me. "Mom, I'm so sorry. I should've gotten away. He said he'd shoot up the school. I—"

I stand and pull Rory in tight, hugging him hard. "You did everything right, son. *Everything.* I love you so much."

His skin is cold, and he is shaking. I rummage through the cabinets in search of a blanket. Instead, I discover the body bag.

I find life vests, fishing equipment, goggles, fins, a wet suit. "Put this on."

"Where is he?" Rory asks, as if the picture is beginning to take shape for him. "What happened?"

I grab the body bag. "I'll be back in a few minutes. There's something I have to do."

In the wheelhouse, a pool of blood fans out beside Rusty's head. It's still spreading. His shirt is drenched, dark red.

I stand over the body, trying to figure out my next move.

I lay the body bag out beside him. I tug at his enormous arms and legs, struggling to roll him into it. He's so heavy, an awkward weight. It feels like the blood has glued him to the floor. I push with all my strength, trying not to slip. Unable to get him into the bag, I move around to the other side of the body, my feet losing traction, sliding in his copious blood. I brace my legs against the wall for leverage and, with one big shove, roll him in.

I push both of his heavy arms into the bag and zip it up. My hands, feet, and wet suit, are covered in Rusty's warm, sticky blood. Disgusting, yes, but, in its way, comforting. He can't hurt us. He can't hurt anyone.

I grab the two handles of the bag and pull. I need to drag it to the door, to the rear deck, but nothing happens. I push off the wall, trying to slide it in both directions, but it's too heavy. Rusty is an immoveable force.

How do you handle a dead body on a boat? You call the police, obviously. The Coast Guard. The *FBI*, for God's sake. Somewhere, in the MAOP, the bible of all administrative guides, there is probably a procedure, complete with a series of forms, requirements, notifications, and testimony. *FD-209g: Large Body Disposal.* With one simple call you initiate a long, preordained set of protocols. There will be interviews, casual at first, followed by intricate, weeks-long sessions with attorneys and administrators. There will be photographs, reenactments, computer-generated simulations, a shooting review board, and a simple, determined, unavoidable question about the case: "Who else was there?"

Long interviews with Rory, testimony, more questions, "But how did you find him? How did you get there?" Interviews with George, Nicole, Ivy, my old partner, my whole squad, an internal inquiry, a notification to DOJ, an investigation by the Office of Professional Responsibility, internal criticism, public criticism, newspaper articles, talking heads on TV. Rory's picture all over the internet. Investigative journalists vying for the story, calling and calling, showing up at Rory's school, our home. Feds looking into Ivan's boat, Timofey's identity blown—the list goes on. If I were younger and more naïve, each step would come as a new surprise, as I slowly dug myself further into a hole, a crater that would consume Rory, me, Caroline, George, my colleagues, my whole world.

Perhaps, in the end, everything would be "fine" for everyone, but by then it might just be too late. But I'm not younger, and I'm not naïve. I've followed procedure before, and where did it get me?

Rory has one parent left, and I'm it.

Is there anyone out there who gives a shit about Rusty? Rough circles. Dark web. Would anyone be surprised if he disappeared? Would anyone care? Would anyone even notice?

Rusty was right about one thing: sometimes you just have to handle it yourself.

69

If scientists search for truth and philosophers search for morality, what does a criminal trial search for? In what instances, if ever, can moral necessity serve as a logical rejoinder to justice?

I find a can of motor oil in the cabinet. I'm hunched down on my knees, trying to pour the oil beneath the body bag to reduce friction, when I hear the bridge door open. Rory stands before me in the wet suit. It's too short for him, and I almost laugh at the sight of him, the sight of my beautiful, awkward boy. Alive.

But then I realize he's staring at me, staring at the body bag, the blood, a look of horror on his face. So much blood, so much red, warm blood. It's on my hands, my arms, my legs, my cheeks, my hair. His face goes pale. He doubles over and vomits, the stench mingling with the metallic smell of Rusty's blood.

I want to say something comforting, but the words don't come. I want to hug him, but I can't. I'm covered in blood.

After emptying his stomach, Rory stands to his full height, staring. He is pale, eyes wide. He wipes his mouth, squares his shoulders. "I'll help."

"No, Rory. Go back down into the cabin. I'll call you when I'm finished."

"I'm *going* to help."

My genes, for better, for worse. He steps around me, to the other end of the body bag.

"On three," he says resolutely. "One, two, three."

We drag the heavy bag across the oily floor onto the deck. Every few feet we rest, and I pour more oil along our path, the bag sliding along the greased trail. By the time we've maneuvered the body to the end of the boat, we're both exhausted, breathing heavily. Despite the crazy wind and sideways rain, we're sweating.

I unlatch the gate, and we inch the body bag closer.

Rory is about to give it one final shove when I stop him. "Wait."

I walk over to the fishing chairs and return with the chain and kettlebell. I loop the chain through the kettlebell and through the two handles at the bottom of the bag.

"One," I say.

"Two," Rory says.

"Three," we say together.

With one final effort, we push Rusty off the boat and into the cold ocean. The bag floats for a second, a whale-like object with none of a whale's grace, the plastic making a sucking sound as it clings to the form of the body. The chain slides off the deck, the kettlebell drags across the deck and splashes into the water, jerking the body bag down beneath the surface.

Rory and I stand, staring at the water where the bag once was. Rory seems mesmerized by the rocking of the boat, the rhythm of the waves. I put my hands on his shoulders, looking into his eyes. No way to protect him from Rusty's blood now.

"Listen, I need you to go find all of the life vests, two sets of fins."

He returns a minute later, arms full. I set aside the fins and two life vests and make a pile of the other vests. He looks out across the horizon. "Mom, there's a boat watching us!"

"That's the boat that brought me here. My new friend Ivan. That's where we're headed."

He frowns, uncertain. "The water looks rough."

"It's okay. I swam here. We can do this. *You* can do this."

The storm clouds are darkening. The wind has picked up even more, whipping the spray into a frenzy. The swells continue to rise and fall and rise. The rain turns the blood on my shirt into rivulets. Blood runs down my legs, across my feet, flowing onto the deck. I rummage around, find more oil, a can of gas, matches. I grab the two sets of fins, two vests, the goggles, and I meet Rory at the back of the boat. The Odessa Dream is moving toward us.

"Put these on."

Rory pulls on the vest over his wet suit, shoves his feet into the fins, and snaps the goggles over his head. "What now?"

"Now, we swim and we don't look back. Can you do that?"

He looks out across the water, estimating the distance, calm and calculating. He's determined now, sober, awake. "Yes."

"I have one more thing to do. I need you to jump into the water and get at least twenty yards away, and then swim toward Ivan's boat."

"Are there sharks?"

I look Rory in the eye, but I see Fred, and the promise we made that day so long ago: the promise that we would always tell our boy the truth.

"You're going to be okay," I say. "I'll meet you out there in two minutes."

With a look of trust that nearly breaks my heart, he pulls his fins on and drops into the water.

I pick up the gas can and run back into the wheelhouse. I grab the phones, the two guns, the six spent shells. I put on my life jacket, pour the gas all along the path where we dragged the body. At the biggest pool of blood, where Rusty first fell, I empty everything left in the oil cans. I turn on the engine, retract the anchor, and slowly angle the boat east, away from the Odessa Dream, away from the shore, off toward the vast ocean. I look to the back of the boat to see Rory and the orange of his life jacket a safe distance away. I disassemble Rusty's gun, empty the magazine, and scatter the parts in the ocean. I throw Rory's backpack on the pile of life vests and flotation devices. I turn the final gas can upside down, the contents soaking into the pile, splashing across the boat, rivers and puddles forming.

I strike a match.

The flame ignites and quickly spreads, the heat flaring up, the smoke burning my eyes.

I hold onto the wheel and push the throttle hard, sending the boat lurching out to sea. I race through the door, across the deck, grab the fins, and jump into the ocean, propelling myself toward Rory, the sound of the boat in my ears, speeding away from us.

I pull the fins onto my feet. They're too small, the rubber cutting into the skin, but as I move my legs back and forth they push me forward, gaining momentum. The water is freezing, but adrenaline keeps me moving. Rory is on his back, ahead of me, his fins moving fast, methodically, like a motor. I call out to him over the sound of the waves. "Keep going, Rory!"

As each wave crests, the Odessa Dream comes closer into view. It's moving toward us.

Rory picks up speed. I'm grateful for his youth, his strength, his health, grateful that he inherited his father's broad shoulders and strong arms, grateful for the adrenaline pumping through his veins. A big wave comes from out of nowhere, rushing over me, pushing me down. I tumble in the wave, rolling, disoriented. Salt water gushes into my mouth, I feel my energy draining out of me. I feel lost beneath the dark surface as my body spins. The wave passes, and I pump my arms, searching for the surface, trying to pull myself up. My lungs ache, I need air, there is no light to guide me toward the surface. I'm so tired. I have done such terrible things.

I hear my father's voice in my head, the words he used to tell me when I was little, and he was teaching me to swim, and I would panic in the water. "Just float," he would say. "Relax, just float." I stop fighting the water. I stop struggling against the current. I feel my body buoyed upward, and my head lifts above the surface. I gasp, pulling air into my lungs. I gasp again.

I look around, disoriented. Where is Rory? Where is the boat?

A strange calmness overtakes me. It would be so easy to just be carried away with the current. Lost from view, gone, like my father, like Fred. It would be so easy to just let go. But I hear Rory's voice. I see him ahead of me, swimming. He has turned around, and he is calling for me.

I lift my arm in a wave, urging him to keep going.

Propelling myself above the wave, I see the splash of Rory's arms, moving forward. He is thirty yards ahead of me, closing in on the Odessa Dream. I feel a burst of energy. A wave blocks my son from view, then recedes. We are so close now. Minutes later, I feel arms pulling me up, my body slapping against the surface of the boat.

I lie, face up to the sky, panting, my lungs aching, eyes searching for my son. I struggle to catch my breath. Where is Rory? A dark cloud shifts, and a ray of sunlight flashes briefly through the rain, blinding me. I blink, the salt water and sun stinging my eyes.

Then I see him: Rory, standing above me, hands on his knees, still panting. His eyes meet mine. Rory.

"This has been one fucked-up, shitty year," I sputter.

Rory collapses beside me. "'Annus horribilis,' the Queen would say."

My chest heaves—sobs and laughter, gasping for air. Do you see, us Fred? Can you believe it? We are here, and we are alive.

70

Will the world end in lightness or darkness? Approach from both a philosophical and astronomical perspective.

The cold seawater rinsed the blood from my body. My skin feels raw but clean. I wrap myself in the blanket Ivan gave me. Rusty's boat is now a speck on the horizon. The shifting winds dissipated some of the smoke, and the gray clouds and dark swells camouflage the rest. *Burn*, I think. *Burn*.

I step into the wheelhouse where Ivan is standing, peering through binoculars. The radio is turned up loud. "Small craft advisory in effect," a voice announces.

"How does it look?" I ask Ivan.

"It's taking on water. It will disappear in the next ten minutes, give or take. Boat's empty?"

"Yes."

"No radio traffic about it. Everyone's in the harbor."

A minute later, still gazing through the binoculars, he says, "Well, look at that."

"What?"

"Fire weakened it. The swell took her apart, should be below surface momentarily. That was quick." He turns to look at his charts on the counter. "Good timing. The swells are high, and the tide is going out. There is a small chance debris will come ashore to the south." He looks at his charts, his gauges. He takes a pencil, lines up his compass, and draws a line. "Worst-case scenario, you see debris float up south of Pescadero, north of Davenport. We need to get out of the area. I'll head north. We can't go in now."

I wrap my arms around his neck and hug him. "Thank you."

"For what?"

"For staying."

"It is nothing," he says. But it is everything.

Ivan uses the full motor to head north, then west. Soon we are out of the area, the beach no longer visible. Ivan focuses on steering, positioning the boat against the larger swells. The dark rain clouds are moving east.

His eyes still fixed on the seas in front of us, Ivan says. "I'm sorry, but—"

"But what?"

"We probably should not go into the harbor empty-handed. Fish, you know. This is a fishing boat. For the sake of authenticity."

"You're the captain."

"There are more clothes downstairs. Why don't you and the boy get warm, and I'll get a couple of poles set up."

I go down below and put on the clothes I left behind when I changed into Ivan's daughter's wet suit. I rummage around and find some ill-fitting jeans and a Giants warm-up jacket for Rory. He's quiet, and I know he is processing everything he has seen. Everything he has done.

He sits on the bunk, facing me. His hands are trembling. "Did you have to kill him?"

"Yes."

"Don't they teach you to shoot someone in the shoulder or leg or something?"

"No. They teach us to eliminate the threat. He had a gun, and he planned to use it."

For a brief moment I see the boy Rory was at seven, the boy who sat on that Central Park Carousel between me and Fred every Sunday afternoon. The teenage years are a puzzle. Rory is so mature, so tall, so seemingly grown-up in so many ways that I sometimes forget the little boy inside.

"I suppose there is a world in which I could have shot him in the shoulder. Maybe he survives, and maybe he gets a chance to shoot me, and worse, much worse, to hurt you. Or maybe I manage to subdue him. Maybe he lives, he gets his day in court. But I couldn't take that chance."

"If you *could* have shot him in the shoulder, if you could have eliminated the threat without killing him, would you?"

Rory will carry this burden forever. When he is an old man, he will still live with what happened today. I don't want to tell him the truth, but I owe it to him. "No." I can tell there is more he wants to say.

"The other thing, what happened *after* you killed him? What we did. Was it like that time with the pizza guy? Did you just *lose* it?"

I didn't have to push Rusty overboard. I didn't have to burn the boat. How do I explain to my teenage son, who is still developing his moral compass, the crucial inner voice that he will carry with him throughout his life, that the decision to dump the body was not a crime of passion? How to explain to him it was a crime of purpose and intent?

"No, I didn't lose it. After what he did to Caroline, after what he did to you, he didn't deserve a burial. I wanted to *erase* him. I wanted to wipe him off the planet."

The expression on Rory's face isn't anger. It isn't sadness. It isn't fear. It's simply thoughtful, analytical. "I'm glad we did."

I hand Rory a pair of rubber boots. "We have some fishing to do."

He looks at me, puzzled, but he pulls the boots on anyway. Up on deck, Ivan sets us up with two deep-sea rods. When it becomes clear that Rory has no idea what to do, Ivan frowns.

"I've never been fishing," Rory admits.

Ivan throws his hands in the air. "This can't be!"

"Dude, I'm from New York City."

Ivan laughs, gives Rory a quick primer on deep-sea fishing, and returns to the bridge, leaving us alone. We figure the rest out for ourselves. I remember what my dad used to say, on the few occasions when he took me fishing: "Fish where the fish are." We sit back in our chairs, side by side, waiting. The wind picks up, the swells grow higher. It feels so unreal to be sitting here fishing after everything. Every few seconds, a burst of freezing, salty air thrashes us in the face. After what we've been through, it's pure heaven—just sitting here, the two of us, together.

"I wish Dad were here," Rory says.

"Me too."

The rain subsides, the water calms. When Rory reels in a big red rockfish, I use the net to pull it in. As I slide it off of the hook, it slips out of my hands and onto my lap. I jump up shrieking, the fish flopping about on the deck.

Rory throws it into the bucket, looks at me. "Seriously, Mom? *You're* scared of a fish?"

By the time Ivan comes out, we've also caught what looks like a striped sea bass. He peers into the bucket. "Nicely done," he says to Rory. "You learn fast." He turns to me. "Ready to head in?"

Rory looks disappointed. He doesn't want to stop fishing, and I know he also doesn't want to face the world, whatever comes next. "Five more minutes?"

The clouds break, and for several moments, the sun makes a bright circle in the ocean.

Back in the harbor, there are only a few people around, everything locked down. Ivan makes a big show of the fish we've caught, showing them off at the cleaning station. He does a good job of establishing our cover. Just another deep-sea charter trip, we got caught out in a spot where it was safer to stay than to come in. He's a professional. The two fishermen say hello to him. Clearly they know and like him, although they call him Andrey instead of Ivan. The harbormaster walks by. He seems to like Ivan too, though he refers to him as Sergei.

"Would you like me to wrap up your fish?" Ivan asks.

Rory looks at him and whispers, "My mom wouldn't have a clue how to cook a thing like that."

Ivan gives me a mock disapproving look. "Your loss is my gain. Now go, you are a disgrace to this harbor." He flashes me a quick smile and walks away.

71

What is happiness?

On a crisp evening in April, Rory and I walk to a restaurant near our hotel. The air smells clean, a light snow falling over the harbor. As we stroll the streets of Reykjavík, I feel a strange lightness in my step.

We spent the day at our hotel, the Black Pearl, watching *Le Bureau des Légendes*. It's good to see Rory picking up French so quickly. It will come in handy. Because of my new contact, headquarters asked me to do a six-month posting to Strasbourg. If it weren't for Caroline, I would refuse. I would say Rory needs to stay put in his New York City high school, get back to normal life. But what is normal now?

Although he was glad to see his friends, Rory said the streets of the Upper West Side felt different, changed. He had thought a return to New York would make him feel closer to Fred, but it turned out the opposite was true. The city isn't the same; it never will be. Fred left a hole that can't be filled, and we are each, in our own ways, coming to terms with that.

We're waiting for our fish and chips when Rory looks up, his eyes full of questions. "Explain it to me one more time. Harris Ojai was the mastermind?"

I nod.

"And the police chief was involved?"

"Yes, and the head of the school board too. It began with only overseas investors, but Harris realized he needed people on the inside to pull it off. Once he had funding, he got the mayor on board, and then it was simply a matter of time and numbers to convince a few others. Not everybody, obviously, but more than you would think, enough to keep track of which students couldn't perform, enough to smooth over the rough edges."

"And Kobayashi really had nothing to do with it?"

"No. They kept him in the dark. Turns out he was a superstar school administrator from Houston before they hired him. Harris Ojai thought Kobayashi's presence would shield them from scrutiny. Oh, I almost forgot. I got an email from Officer Kyle last night. He quit the police force, moved to Michigan to be with his girlfriend and go to law school. Said to tell you he finished *Martin in Space,* loved it."

Rory looks pleased. "I knew he would."

The plates arrive, crispy fried cod and a side of potatoes to share. A well-dressed young couple takes the table next to us. I glance over, assessing, determine they're just regular people out for dinner, and return my attention to Rory.

"I understand the overseas investors," he says. "They didn't know the kids. It was just business from their perspective. But the others?"

"They got serious money, the kind that pays for Ivy League educations, vacation homes in Hawaii, a major nest egg."

"These people already *had* money. How could they need more?"

"Sometimes, the more people have, the more they want."

"But how could they rationalize what happened to Gray, the Lamey twins, and Caroline?"

I asked Brenda this question after we were back in New York City. I didn't think she'd talk to me, but I had to try. I was astonished and more than a little embarrassed that I had been wrong about her. Had I been blind because she was another mom, because she seemed so *normal?* She told me by text that she would give me five minutes on the phone, friend to friend. I do consider you a friend, she texted, despite everything.

"It started long before the incident with the twins," she told me. "What happened to the kids wasn't in the original plan, but the investors kept pushing for better and better scores. We've all worked so hard to get to where we are. Our kids have worked so hard. Don't we owe it to them to make everything perfect? The world is a competitive place, Lina. It's not enough anymore to be smart, lucky, and hardworking. You need to be exceptional. You need to be a *winner.*"

I tell Rory all of this. He shakes his head, still struggling to understand.

"Want to know the scariest part? She genuinely believed what she was saying."

He frowns. "It wasn't only the investors who profited, though. *Everyone* did, even us."

"Even us."

"So people must have known, right?"

"When the twins went missing, I'm sure it seemed like an accident. But the next year, with Gray, and with others being lured away on trips, people might have suspected something was up. Of course, even if they did, they probably just rationalized it away, convinced themselves it couldn't possibly be true. Still, when you factor in the increases during the years of the Wonder Test, accounting for market fluctuations, discounting for the insane growth of Silicon Valley, the good citizens of Greenfield made more than six billion dollars in equity and home sale profits from this scheme."

"Do you think the district will get rid of the Wonder Test?"

I finish my margarita. "Probably not. They'll chalk it up to a few bad seeds, move on. What did Dad say? 'Everything is far-fetched and impossible until the moment it happens. And then it's just regular life.'"

Walking back to our hotel, we pause to look at the colorful boats in the harbor. The Arctic sun is beginning to set. Standing beside Rory, I still can't get used to how tall he is, towering over me. Has he really grown that much in a few weeks, or is he standing up straighter now?

"There's something else I've been wanting to ask you."

"Okay."

"It's about Caroline. It's about that first day."

I knew this was coming. I've weighed exactly how to explain to him about Caroline's father, about our upcoming trip to Strasbourg and the possible deployment to Paris next year. I've wanted to tell him about that morning at the Royal Donut Shop. More than that, I've wanted to tell him about the struggles I've had these last few months, the nagging fear that I am not an adequate parent, that I can't do this without Fred.

That morning, so badly, I just wanted to pedal away, down Broadway, past the railroad tracks, along the freeway sound wall. I wanted to turn back the clock, return to those days when I still had the paper route, when my family was still intact and the world was new, so many choices ahead of me. But there is no going backward. For better or worse, I can only be the person I am. I can only do the thing I know how to do, the thing that comes most naturally. I can only follow my instincts. And that's what I did.

That afternoon, when Caroline appeared at the curb with Rory, I was surprised by the speed with which he had found her, made contact, and executed the meet. I watched him in the rearview mirror, talking to his new friend, and thought, *Well done, Rory*. Perhaps they would have become friends anyway—two only children, *enfants uniques*, out of place in that strange Northern California suburb. And perhaps in that scenario, they still would have fallen in love.

As for me, I would like to believe I would have gone to such lengths to find the girl if it had been anyone else's daughter. I would like to believe I would have made that trek into the hills above the Russian River for any kid gone missing. But I'm not sure. There is a bond within the business. Whether the nations you represent are friends or enemies or somewhere in between, there is an understanding among individuals who do this kind of work. A mutual respect that often deepens into genuine friendship. A silent acknowledgment that we are not so different. We may be sitting on different sides of the table, but we're all playing the same game.

When I was starting out, all those years ago in New York City, I had no way of knowing how this work would permeate my life. Somehow, the job welcomed me behind a strange curtain, a thin veil, really, that I had never known was there. Since then, little has truly changed in the ways of the world, but now I view everything from an altered perspective, eyes wide open, taking it all in. I see the subtext, the nuance. I see the story within the story.

After Fred died, I thought I could walk away. I dreamed of returning to the person I was before this work transformed my mind and soul. The idea was so alluring: moving back to California, starting over, somehow reclaiming what was lost. Somehow, I believed I had it in me.

But the past months have taught me that there is no starting over. As the narrator of *Martin in Space* says, "I can't unsee what I've seen, I can't unlearn what I know. Each place, each decision, each experience, has become a part of me, no more than my head, no less than my heart."

Life is a series of decisions, forks in the road, this or that, yes or no, left or right. We make our choices, we select our path. When I was young, the options seemed unlimited, so many paths to travel. But here's what I didn't understand: Every path is a one-way street. There is no turning back, no changing your mind, no trying both options. There is only forward motion. With time, your decisions pile up, compounding, interweaving, slowly turning you into the person you are.

Who will Rory become? I find it harder to know what he's thinking these days. A young man doesn't go through what he's been through and come out the same.

"Mom," Rory says, his voice deeper now, like his father's. He's looking at me, waiting for an answer. "Come on, tell me the story."

"Really?"

"Really."

And so I begin. I was out front of the Royal Donut shop, rain on the pavement, a black Peugeot in the parking lot, the man in the red cashmere scarf, the distinctive lapel pin, *trois couleurs*. A pause, a smile, bonjour.

72

Who said "testing is learning, and learning testing"?
Assuming the statement is true, what have you learned
from this test?

I'm standing in front of a design shop in the center of town. It's
the one near the top of the hill, half a block down from Hallgríms-
kirkja, the famous church with the towering organ. I check my
watch—2:51—and step inside to kill a few minutes. The woman
at the counter is the same one who was here last year. She doesn't
recognize me, of course, but I recognize her. Black hair, birthmark
below her right eye, a habit of cracking her knuckles.

When it comes to this business, everyone does the ICP, or
initial contact point, differently. Of course, there are rules: It must
be easy to find, it must be the sort of place that will not go out of
business. There must be clear signage, it can't be a franchise with
multiple locations, and there can't be any factors that might cause
unnecessary confusion. When a source arrives, he must have no
doubt whatsoever that this is the place.

And it has to have business cards. One for me, one for him.
Personally, I like a memorable name or at least a memorable shop,
something we can talk about, something that in an ideal world

might reflect some aspect of our relationship. It has to be a spot where even a year later, even if the business card was burned or shredded or flushed, the location will still resonate in the source's mind. The name of the place never appears on paper, never goes into a file. It remains just a business card in my notebook, waiting until the day I return.

Wandering around the shop, I pick up a sweatshirt. I remember looking at an identical one, maybe this very hoodie, last year. It's hunter green, Fred's favorite color, with a cartoon image of a dancing cookie on the front. What do the Icelanders say? There's no such thing as bad weather, only bad clothes? I considered buying it for him that day but didn't. So many things have happened since then, so many unfathomable things. And yet, here we are. Life goes on. I take the hoodie to the cashier and count out four thousand króna.

Today, I will complete the task I came here to do, close the loop, set a new series of events in motion. A new beginning. It's not atonement but something like it. Not closure exactly, but maybe a step in that direction.

At 2:58, I step outside, glance left, glance right. This is always the most dangerous moment of any sensitive source meet. If the op has been compromised, I am completely vulnerable, a sitting duck. I think of the Chechen on the bike in Germany, two bullets in the back of the head, or the Bulgarian diplomat at the bus stop, an umbrella with a poison tip. And yet, despite the risk, this moment has always been my favorite part of the job—the exquisite quiet, the anticipatory moments just before everything comes together.

Down the street, I see Red Vine's trademark hat, the black leather messenger bag I gave him last year. Inside, there will be documents for me and, if all has gone well, maybe even a memory stick. He has taken considerable risks to be here. Once again, he is putting his life in my hands. As he walks toward me, I carefully scan the surrounding area, the adjoining streets, buildings, and balconies, looking for surveillance, but all is quiet.

He smiles. A subtle nod of the head. And in this moment, for the first time in so long, I feel a sense of calm wash over me. The noise in my head fades, focus returns. I feel at peace. I am exactly where I should be, I know exactly what to do.

Acknowledgments

Thanks to my longtime agent and friend, Valerie Borchardt, for everything. Thanks to Morgan Entrekin at Grove Atlantic for taking me on in the midst of the pandemic and giving this book a good home, to Sara Vitale for her excellent editorial guidance, and to the whole Grove Atlantic team.

Thanks to Jay Phelan for his extensive comments on an early draft. Thanks to Kathie and Jack. Merci to Mary Claypool for help with the French. Thanks once again to Timothy Bracy for the lyrics.

As always, thanks above all to Kevin.